Like David Bowie's Major Tom, "floating in a most peculiar way," Barry Vacker seems to contemplate Planet Earth through the porthole of a spacecraft. Via critiques of the Apollo program and films like *2001* and *Interstellar*, Barry offers us a unique opportunity to step back and think of the contradictions of space exploration and our contemporary society. Barry shows we live in a "post-Apollo" culture torn between a frenetic race towards ever more scientific-technological progress and a just as powerful fall-back into the cultural ideologies of dark tribal ages of the past. For those who can embrace their non-centrality and possible meaninglessness in a majestic universe, yet yearn for a shared destiny in a sane planetary civilization, *Specter of the Monolith* is a wonderful and inspiring work.

— Carine & Elisabeth Krecké
(renowned installation artists and literary authors)

SPECTER OF THE MONOLITH

BARRY VACKER

Morgan
Thanks so much for creating such an awesome video!
Barry
16-Jan 2018

THE CENTER FOR MEDIA AND DESTINY

First published in the United States of America in 2018 by The Center for Media and Destiny, a 501(c)(3) nonprofit organization.

Cover Designed by Haigen G. Pearson.

Printed in the United States of America.

ISBN: 978-0-9798404-7-0 (pbk) / 978-0-9798404-8-7 (ebook)

CONTENTS

INTRODUCTION

PART 1: SPECTER OF THE MONOLITH

PART 2: MOONWALKING INTO THE FUTURE

Dedicated to the 50th anniversary of *2001: A Space Odyssey.*

Greetings on behalf of the people of our planet. We step out of our solar system into the universe seeking only peace and friendship, to teach if we are called upon, to be taught if we are fortunate. We know full well that our planet and all its inhabitants are a small part of this immense universe that surrounds us, and it is with humility and hope that we take this step.

— ***Kurt Waldheim, Secretary General of the United Nations (1977)***

This is the first message on the Golden Record, which is located on the Voyager spacecraft that left the solar system.

INTRODUCTION

THE MONOLITH AND MOONWALKING

> The most terrifying fact about the universe is not that it is hostile but that it is indifferent. If we can come to terms with this indifference and accept the challenges of life within the boundaries of death, our existence as a species can have genuine meaning and fulfillment. However vast the darkness, we must supply our own light.
>
> — ***Stanley Kubrick***

1. *EARTHRISE* AND *2001*

It's 2017. We are almost fifty orbits of the sun since 1968, the year Apollo 8 and Stanley Kubrick gave us the two key existential icons of the 20th-century space age — *Earthrise* and the monolith in *2001: A Space Odyssey*, respectively. Via these two images, we're presented with the ultimate philosophical challenges facing humans in the quest to explore space and find meaning for our existence in a vast and ancient universe.

The Apollo 8 astronauts were the first humans to escape the gravity of Earth. As they orbited the moon, they turned their cameras back toward Earth and took the most beautiful and important selfie ever.[1] By showing Earth against the blackness of the cosmic void, Apollo 8 provided the human species with its first view of its true existential condition, namely that we inhabit a tiny planet floating alone in a massive universe.

Photo 1
Earthrise
Apollo 8, 1968

Across the decades, Apollo 8's journey around the moon has proven more prophetic and influential than Apollo 11's landing on the moon, where Neil Armstrong stepped off the lunar module and stated: "One small step for a man, one giant leap for mankind." Apollo 8's prophetic influence comes from the fact that when confronted with *Earth in the cosmic void* and the specter of human meaninglessness, the astronauts resorted to reading from the Bible's Genesis to a global TV audience approaching one billion people. Five decades later, Genesis and stories of all-powerful Creators still reign as the dominant narratives most humans turn to for explaining humanity's origins and destiny in the universe. In contrast, the overall secular meanings of Apollo 11's moonwalk and Armstrong's phrase have yet to generate any serious challenge to the theologies that inspire most of the people on planet Earth.

Stanley Kubrick's *2001: A Space Odyssey* ranks as the greatest space film and one of the most philosophically profound films of all time. *2001* depicts a past and future in which humans have evolved from apes to astronauts via science and technology along with an assist from a mysterious black monolith. With stunning cinematography and special effects, *2001* taps into the sublime majesty of the cosmos along with the marvels of science and technology. At the same moment in history, NASA and Kubrick both "directed" space odysseys that expressed the highest trajectories of the space age, when humanity first ventured into the cosmos beyond planet Earth. However, neither NASA nor Kubrick provided *the philosophical meaning* for these discoveries and achievements.

The apes see the monolith.
2001: A Space Odyssey, 1968

Though the monolith is famed for inspiring the apes to invent technology and evolve into space farers, the monolith and *2001* also pose the question of what we humans will become as we venture into a magnificent universe in which we are not central, not significant, and maybe not alone. Now that we've touched the monolith, what will we evolve into as artists, thinkers, inventors, and creators of a space-faring civilization? *2001* and the monolith provide starting points for our philosophical evolution, moments when we are challenged to face three key questions about our existence as advanced simians and space voyagers: *(1) Where are we going, (2) what does it mean, and (3) what can we hope for?*

2. "A ROPE OVER AN ABYSS"

In *Thus Spoke Zarathustra* (the book that inspired Richard Strauss to write the symphony *Also Sprach Zarathustra* [1896], which was later used by Kubrick in *2001*), Friedrich Nietzsche speculated that since humans are the superior species that evolved from apes, there might be an equally greater species that would evolve from humans — what he termed the "Ubermensch" or "Superman."[2] Nietzsche wrote how "man is a rope stretched between the animal and the Superman — a rope over an abyss."[3] So what comes next? What will emerge in the next stage of human evolution?

That's the question Kubrick poses at the end of *2001*, with the Star-Child appearing against the blackness of the cosmos, Earth literally rising in his gaze. As a space-faring species, what will humans make of themselves in an awe-inspiring universe with unlimited possibility? That's where the monolith has profound metaphorical meaning. Tall, sleek, and black, the monolith is an icon of awe and the cosmic void, yet it's also a towering blank slate for us to write a new philosophy for the future of the human species.

We are a species with much promise, the very species that touched the black monolith in *2001*. We are simians that emerged from Africa's savannas and evolved into humans, apes who became astronauts, spear throwers who became space farers. In our midst emerged artists and philosophers who wondered about our place in the cosmos, and scientists and technologists who have extended our consciousness into space and across the universe to offer remarkable new perspectives on our origins and destiny. We are a brainy and brave species that looked up to the starry skies with our telescopes and said, "What the hell! Let's go for it!" So we launched Apollo to the moon, orbited the International Space Station around the planet, and pointed the Hubble Space Telescope to the edge of the universe.

The Apollo missions, *2001*, and the original *Star Trek* TV series blasted us into a sublime future with the opportunity to build a unified planetary civilization, but we rejected it because we were unwilling to accept that we are a single species inhabiting a watery rock orbiting a flaming ball of hydrogen in an infinite universe. Apollo and Hubble forced us to confront cosmic nihilism, or the fact that there is no obvious meaning to human existence in a godless universe. Via Apollo, we've walked on the 4.5 billion-year-old moon, and via the Hubble Space Telescope, we've peered across 13.7 billion years of space-time — and there is not a Creator in sight. As Nietzsche famously said long before Apollo and Hubble: "God is dead."[4] But most everyone can't accept it. Apollo's photos of Earth from space and the Hubble Deep Field images have obliterated the rationales supporting the dominant narratives (theology, nationalism, and tribalism) we use to explain our origins, meaning, and destiny. Yet our species remains in utter denial.

We humans apparently can't handle the paradoxical meaning of our greatest scientific achievement and most important philosophical discovery: *The universe is vast and majestic, and our species is insignificant and might be utterly meaningless.* Our species has discovered we inhabit an immense universe in which we are not the center and have existed for only a blip in cosmic time. There may well be no meaning or purpose to our existence in the immensity of the cosmos that spans billions of years in the past and trillions upon trillions of years in the future. Or maybe some cosmic meaning can be found in the notion that *we are one way the universe knows itself.* So far, our species has proven too vain and fearful to move *forward* and develop new philosophies and narratives based on our actual place in the universe, too small-minded to embrace our shared evolutionary origins and create a shared destiny for our long-term future and the health of our planet, the very home that provides the resources for us to live, love, and explore the cosmos. We seem too terrified to embrace the evolutionary and philosophical blank slate symbolized by the monolith.

3. SPECTER OF THE MONOLITH

As a new space age ramps up in the 21st century, future astronauts and the human species itself will inevitably face the specter of the monolith and the challenge of nihilism and meaninglessness. With the phrase "specter of the monolith," I am naming a complex existential moment — the simultaneous experience of the sublime and nihilism. As explained in Chapters 1-3, this powerful concept is evident in the cultural responses to Apollo and in the themes of the greatest space films in history.

The black monolith signifies the complexity of mysteries and meanings, if any, in Stanley Kubrick's "indifferent" universe — the marvelous cosmos that allows us to exist on a tiny planet yet seems eternally unconcerned with the fate of the many species that populate Earth. Like Earth floating in the void in *Earthrise* or the towering star factories in the Hubble images, the monolith is a pillar of beautiful indifference yet also a beacon for wonder and curiosity in a gigantic universe. Simultaneously, the monolith is the void and the hope, the emptiness pregnant with infinite possibility for human reason and understanding. Not unlike how the apes were initially fearful of the monolith and touched it with great trepidation, the Apollo 8 astronauts observed the cosmic void with *Earthrise* and instantly retreated by reading from Genesis. Similarly, when we scan the Hubble's cosmic images and those from the world's many telescopes, our aesthetic sense grasps their beauty while our reason affirms their scale and splendor, yet our minds are blown and we end up dizzy or intellectually paralyzed by what it means for our species, the tiny species with big brains and a yearning for significance. We gaze into the sublime wonders of the cosmos, yet sensing nihilism and meaninglessness we retreat from any new possibilities offered by the cosmic blank slate. Astride the abyss between now and what's possible, we get vertigo and step back into the comfort of the traditional narratives that order life on Earth, even if those narratives are completely false.

In the specter of the monolith are existential conditions and intellectual challenges that haunt the human species. We're the advanced simians who have evolved to be courageous space farers yet still remain cowardly cosmic and Earthly philosophers. Think this is too harsh? Just scan the Google News reader to see the absurd carnival of human events on Earth and those proposed for space (see Chapter 4). Like the apes in *2001*, we have tossed the technological bone in the air, but we have yet to evolve beyond the Star-Child gazing at Earth rising in space. When are we going to launch the philosophical bone into the cosmos?

4. MOONWALKING INTO THE FUTURE

There are no easy exits from our existential condition. If we continue to seek refuge in the pre-Copernican notion of almighty Creators who will rescue us for eternity, and if we insist upon ransacking the natural world and the universe to satisfy our own consumer desires — including strip-mining the moon and terraforming Mars — the human condition will not improve. After all, we have transformed the biosphere of our planet with the global embrace of industrial civilization powered by fossil fuels, from advanced agriculture to electrified cities to consumer society and the 24/7 media spectacle. With the acceleration of industrial civilization possibly triggering the sixth extinction event in Earth's history and our pollution and detritus now generating its own fossil layer, the human species is creating a new geological and ecological epoch on Earth — what scientists call the Anthropocene.[5] In effect, we have "terraformed" Earth and are just beginning to grasp the long-term planetary effects of the Anthropocene. What kind of civilization — if any — will evolve out of the Anthropocene remains to be seen.

It's time to grow up. It's the moment for our collective coming of age. We are *not* the center of the universe; thus we have *no* inherent right to pillage moons and planets for our own entertainment and consumption as we have already done on Earth. What is the meaning for our existence in the universe: conquest, knowledge, survival, flourishing, consumption, entertainment, or something else or nothing at all?

It's as if we're plotting two space trajectories at once: one headed for the cool space hotel in *2001* and the other headed back to the *Planet of the Apes* (1968). Since *2001* and Apollo, we have certainly *accelerated* forward in terms of art, science, and technology. But upon encountering the sublime and cosmic nihilism primarily brought about by the Apollo journeys and the Hubble Space Telescope, humanity has gone into cultural *reversal*, retreating backward into narcissistic, pre-Copernican philosophies that place us at the center of the universe, the center of everything that matters — from theism to tribalism to the 24/7 media spectacle. In some ways we're going forward, but we're going backward at the same time. We're "moonwalking" into the future.

5. ABOUT THIS BOOK

Recent years have seen several books about space exploration that offer multiple perspectives about past and future space exploration.[6] In contrast, this is not a book about the history or science of space exploration, nor is it a book chronicling the many space films. It won't go into heavy scientific detail or examine all the possible "hidden" philosophical messages in various space movies. It's a work of *space philosophy and cultural theory* that considers what space exploration and space films have to say about human destiny and the meaning of human existence in a vast and ancient universe of which we are not the center and seem utterly insignificant. So let's blast off into the cosmos and see what's shaping our future in space.

PART 1

SPECTER OF THE MONOLITH

CHAPTER 1

CONFRONTING NIHILISM AND THE SUBLIME

This arrangement is transitory — lasting a few billion years more or less. Lunar years. Not a long time on a cosmic scale. The sun, our earth and your thought will have been no more than a spasmodic state of energy, an instant of established order, a smile on the surface of matter in a remote corner of the cosmos.

— ***Jean-Francois Lyotard***

1. NASA'S ULTIMATE CHALLENGE

So here we are in the year 2017, almost fifty years since Apollo 8 and Apollo 11 ventured to the moon, almost fifty years since Stanley Kubrick suggested in his groundbreaking film *2001: A Space Odyssey* (1968) that a space-based future would become a reality by the start of the 21st century. Despite the stunning triumphs of the Apollo program and the compelling vision of Kubrick's masterpiece, decades of declining popular interest in space exploration have followed. Many successes came after Apollo, such as the space shuttle program (1981-2011), the Hubble Space Telescope (1990-), and the International Space Station (1998-). But so far, such successes have had little long-term impact on any kind of space philosophy for the human species stuck on Spaceship Earth. That's because NASA's grand achievements — at once astounding and humbling — have collectively destroyed the pre-Copernican narratives humans use to explain their origins and destinies. We're just in denial. As a species, we have ventured into the sublime of the universe and retreated from the nihilism, our minds blown but our philosophy paralyzed in the specter of the monolith.

Space exploration raises the most fundamental questions about human existence, including our *meaning* as a species and our *hopes* for the future. The profound discoveries we've made over the past century about our vast and ancient universe invoke the challenges of nihilism and the sublime, which are almost completely overlooked in discussions of space exploration.[1] That's why NASA's *ultimate challenge* in the 21st century is not the technical issue of getting to Mars or the mission to finally encounter extraterrestrial life — it's to confront the cosmic nihilism and the sublime that were presented to the entire world via the Apollo missions, the Apollo television broadcasts, and the Hubble Space Telescope (particularly the Hubble Deep Field [HDF] images). NASA's challenge is humanity's challenge, too.

Our telescopes and satellites have revealed an epic cosmos, an expanding universe reaching back about 13.7 billion years yet stretching across 100 billion light years, suggesting that the universe is expanding faster than the speed of light. According to the latest discoveries of the Hubble Space Telescope, the observable universe contains an estimated 2 trillion galaxies, most with billions of stars, all attracting and organizing in clusters of galaxies that stretch throughout the observable universe.[2] Evidently, there are dwarf galaxies (containing thousands of stars) orbiting the Milky Way. How strange and unexpected is that?

In the galaxies of the observable universe, there are an estimated three sextillion stars (3,000,000,000,000,000,000,000) along with untold numbers of supernovas and black holes. Orbiting the stars is an innumerable amount of planets, moons, comets, and asteroids. Given the billions of planets orbiting stars within the Milky Way, there is little doubt that humans will discover life on other planets or moons, possibly within our own solar system on moons like Europa. All of these things exist amid the mysterious forces of dark matter and dark energy, which together comprise 96% of the stuff of the universe. Dark matter gives structure to the galaxies, while dark energy emerges from the voids of space to shove the galaxies apart and expand the universe at accelerating rates. Perhaps the observable universe emerged purely from a condensed area of space, as assumed by the big bang theory, or perhaps it emerged from the other side of a mega-supermassive black hole, or perhaps it is the product of colliding universes or a tear in the fabric of an even larger universe. Or maybe our universe is one universe in a vast "multiverse" that exists as part of a larger "existence" that is eternal and always evolving. One thing is certain — as our extensions of human consciousness increase in power, our new knowledge of the cosmos will continue to evolve and expand in tandem with our new questions about the universe.

These technologies and discoveries reflect the best of what is possible among the human species and its consciousness, physically situated on a tiny planet, orbiting a star in only one of the trillions of galaxies. These accomplishments give many people hope for a better tomorrow, for a more enlightened and peaceful planetary civilization. Yet these intellectual triumphs also pose profound challenges for the dominant worldviews of the inhabitants of Earth.

2. PRE-COPERNICAN CENTRALITY AND COSMIC NARCISSISM

Across time, the human species has created numerous *narratives and systems of value, meaning, and purpose* to justify and explain its existence, beliefs, and behaviors. These narratives include loyalty to families, tribes, leaders, nations, conquest, careers, corporations, celebrities, brands, and sports teams, along with "salvation," "love," "freedom," "equality," "happiness," and alleged "truth." There is also loyalty to systems of technology, consumption, and economics, no matter how excessive and wasteful. Above all, there is the belief in and loyalty to an all-powerful Creator who allegedly commands and oversees everything in the universe, including our personal and collective destinies. This Creator is supposed to provide meaning and purpose to human existence in the universe.

These fictions and narratives were created by humans to give purpose to the beliefs and behaviors *within* human society, with the Creator supposedly providing the grounding and purpose *external* to our species. Without these meanings, many people would struggle to find any hope within their daily lives or for their long-term destiny. Without the widespread acceptance of these meanings, the dominant social orders (democracy, theocracy, socialism, capitalism, etc.) and institutions (nations, theologies, military forces, etc.) would lose their validity and purpose. In essence, humans are of a species that psychologically needs a narrative for life with hope, meaning, and a sense of purpose and destiny, even if the narratives are completely false and/or destructive. For most, living a meaningless and purposeless existence is too terrifying a thought. Equally terrifying is a life without hope for a better future, especially if it is eternal — as promised by the Creator in the oral myths and sacred texts. In all of these narratives and meanings, humans have positioned themselves as central to the value of everything on Earth and the universe.

Our presumed cosmic centrality is a pre-Copernican stance, as if Galileo and Edwin Hubble never existed. As a species, our worldviews, narratives, and systems of meaning and purpose are largely narcissistic and inward looking. There is no ideology more cosmically narcissistic than the belief that the Creator — *of the entire universe* — takes time to forgive our sins and answer our prayers and has an eternal destiny for each of us. That our fates are of concern to the creator of everything elevates our importance in the universe, necessarily placing us at a central position. Our cosmic narcissism is also illustrated by our electrified metropolises, the technological carnival where nature and the cosmos are largely erased from our daily consciousness, even as we extract energy from nature and dump pollution back into the natural world. So it is no surprise we might be effecting a sixth mass extinction on our planet and are doing little to prevent it. Such cosmic centrality is assumed in the plans to terraform Mars and strip-mine the moon.

From theology to selfies, narcissism is ultimately the belief that one has some kind of super-specialness and cosmic centrality, another kind of pre-Copernicanism expressed in the underlying existential stance of the iPhone — "I" am the center of the universe. Though cosmic narcissism is partially understandable and defensible, it is also massively delusional. To live a life of purpose and achievement obviously requires that one concentrate on one's self. There's nothing wrong with that. Yet in the endless fixation on our selves and our *particularity* as individual human beings, we overlook the *universality* to our existence as members of the human species.

The focus on particularity leads to a sense of cosmic centrality, while the focus on universality situates one in larger narratives and shared destinies. The counter to narcissism is not altruism but rather a planetary philosophy that connects the needs and desires of individuals, groups, and society to shared narratives within much larger systems of nature, ecology, technology, and cosmology.[3] Unfortunately, cosmic narcissism prevails on planet Earth and offers a shallow counter to the potential universal nihilism faced by the human species.

3. COSMIC NIHILISM AND THE SUBLIME

By contrast, modern science and cosmology show we are the center of *nothing,* with no *self-evident external grounding* for our meaning and purpose. As a species, humans are momentary forms of a long chain of cosmic and biological evolution. Of course, this fact changes everything about our understanding of human existence and our origins and destinies. The pre-Copernican worldviews and our presumed cosmic centrality are false and need to be replaced. Scientific discovery has produced a technological civilization that provides comfort and abundance on scales previously unimaginable, all designed to fulfill our desires and make us feel worthy and super-special. However, scientific discovery and cosmological knowledge — as narratives for grounding human meaning and purpose — have yet to generate any serious challenges to the dominant worldviews and philosophies. Even though science and cosmology have destroyed the grounds for the dominant philosophies and narratives (Creators, nations, etc.), people still desperately cling to pre-Copernican worldviews and narcissistic narratives precisely because science and cosmology have effected a massive intellectual void yet to be filled by art and philosophy. With no Creator in sight and no self-evident cosmic meaning, theism and narcissism proliferate, precisely because theism and narcissism (in their many forms) are the most popular counter to nihilism, the most common ways humans try to overcome the fears of meaninglessness.

Not surprisingly, much has been written about contemporary nihilism in regard to politics, technology, religion, and art.[4] For the critique of space narratives, the issue of nihilism is fairly direct and does not involve politics, economics, or morality. So by nihilism, I am *not* referring to a Nietzschean "will to power" that revels in the sheer destruction of civilization, where political and cultural values have no philosophical foundations outside of power and desire. Similarly, I am not referring to the *Fight Club*-style nihilism in the manly revolt against modernity, consumer society, and the lack of meaning in corporate cubicles and every day life.[5] Rather, I am referring to an existential and *cosmic nihilism* involving the meaning (or meaninglessness) of human existence in the vast universe.

Overcoming such nihilism, if possible, will require us to abandon the dominant narratives, which have technically already been demolished by Copernicus (our cosmic non-centrality), Charles Darwin (our evolution as a species), Edwin Hubble (the expanding universe), and NASA (the views of Earth from space and the views of the vast cosmos). So far, most of the world has countered cosmic nihilism with theism and narcissism, countered the destruction of these narratives with sheer denial and "doublethink" (see Chapter 3). If we are unable to successfully counter cosmic nihilism, then we may well see a global struggle where theism battles Nietzschean nihilism to determine human meaning on planet Earth while narcissists immerse themselves in consumer society, social media, and ever more tattoos. Theism sees itself as the only valid counter to cosmic nihilism.

Lars von Trier's *Melancholia* (2011) confronts the challenge of cosmic nihilism by examining our meaninglessness as a species in regard to the universe at large. In the film, the Earth is obliterated by an ethereal planet whose size, scale, and striking appearance puts humans (and filmgoers) in touch with the cosmic sublime. Yet despite this experience of sublimity, humanity is obliterated anyway. The rogue planet, Melancholia, doesn't care about us — it's on its own nature-based mission. Contrary to what our dominant narratives profess — that we're at the center of the universe — *Melancholia* demonstrates that humanity is *not* at the center, is *not* above being destroyed, is *not* important or valuable enough for the laws of nature to change. For von Trier, weddings, consumer society, and family values are unable to counter the nihilism. In *Melancholia,* with the destruction of the Earth comes the destruction of our dominant narratives and worldviews. Cosmic nihilism and the cosmic sublime meet when we grasp the fact that we are *not* significant to the awe-inspiring universe, a fact that the dominant philosophies and narratives encourage us to ignore and deny.

COSMIC SUBLIME. When we gaze up at the Milky Way or peer through telescopes into deep space and across the universe, the amazement we experience is part of the sublime, a concept that challenged many of the great philosophers, from Immanuel Kant in the 18th century to Jean-Francois Lyotard in the 20th.[6]

In the conclusion to *The Critique of Practical Reason*, Kant offered this famed statement: "Two things fill the mind with ever new and increasing admiration and awe, the oftener and the more steadily we reflect on them: the starry skies above and the moral law within."[7] For Kant, the starry skies above — "worlds upon worlds and systems of systems" — annihilates our importance as individuals and a species, while reducing our planet to a "speck in the universe."[8] In the discoveries of Copernicus and Newton, Kant knew this lawful universe showed no special interest in human affairs, so he stated that the only way humans can preserve their significance and freedom is to postulate the existence of God and immortality as we peer into the starry skies. In effect, Kant conjoined faith with freedom to counter nihilism with theism, a clever philosophical maneuver which has echoed across space and time, right through to Apollo 8 and our contemporary era. Hailed as an achievement for its time, Kant's theistic cosmological system is no longer plausible or tenable in the contemporary era *after* Darwin and Hubble, powered by electron microscopes and space telescopes. Despite Kant's mistaken existential assumptions, his analysis of the many facets of the sublime remain relevant for the 21st century.

The philosopher Jean-Francois Lyotard believed the cosmic sublime is "the sole serious question to face humanity today" and "everything else seems insignificant."[9] In the immensity of the universe, with all its energy and matter, our sun is due to die out in 4.5 billion years and expand to consume Earth, effecting what Lyotard terms the death of human thought. (This will be certainly true unless we migrate to other habitable planets.) Tapping into the sublime in terms of space and time, Lyotard writes:

> This arrangement is transitory — lasting a few billion years more or less. Lunar years. Not a long time on a cosmic scale. The sun, our earth and your thought will have been no more than a spasmodic state of energy, an instant of established order, a smile on the surface of matter in a remote corner of the cosmos.[10]

For Lyotard, these cosmic conditions ultimately *annihilate* and render absurd the passions that consume society, with its wars, politics, economics, and belief that the "smile on the surface of matter" actually matters to the cosmos. Humans are the product of chance and the laws of the universe and have no intrinsic meaning or purpose beyond what we have conjured in our beliefs and thoughts. So far, the cosmos permits us to exist but does not care if we exist.[11]

Borrowing from Kant, Lyotard, and other thinkers, here is what I mean by the cosmic sublime: We encounter the cosmic sublime when there's a tension between our perceptions and our reason, when our senses are *overwhelmed,* yet our minds can still order the percepts into *knowable, pleasurable,* and *terrifying* concepts. The features of the vast universe — immense scales of space and time; dynamic systems of stars, galaxies, supernovas, and black holes; limitless arrangements of energy and matter; sprawling voids and seeming emptinesses; immeasurable realms of cosmic destruction and renewal — confront and stimulate our imaginations in awe-inspiring experiences. In such we grasp the *affirmation* of human rationality and *annihilation* of our centrality, our *exaltation* before the cosmos in tandem with the *extinction* of our species' dominant narratives, and the sense of human *freedom* in conjunction with our *void in meaning.* In our infinitesimalness, we can feel connected to the universe or crushed by its infiniteness. (see Table 1).[12]

The sublime moment is poignant with emotional and cognitive overload; we realize we are no physical match for nature and the cosmos, yet we're confident of our ability to tackle the intellectual challenge of exploring them via science and technology. Because the sublime affirms humanity's right to exist at the same time that it draws attention to the inevitability of our own extinction, it evokes paradoxical emotions in us that coexist, side by side, such as pleasure and pain, attraction and repulsion, and power and fear. Art historian Elizabeth Kessler explains the phenomenon of the cosmic sublime perfectly in her book *Picturing the Cosmos,* describing how the images from the Hubble Space Telescope "invoke the sublime and . . . encourage the viewer to experience the cosmos visually *and* rationally, to see the universe as simultaneously beyond humanity's grasp and within reach of our systems of knowledge."[13]

TABLE 1 **EXPERIENCING THE COSMIC SUBLIME**

The paradoxical feelings and experiences we have when observing the vast universe.

PERCEPTS OF COSMIC VASTNESS, IMMENSITY, LIMITLESSNESS, EMPTINESSES, ETC.		
Ordered via human reason	—	Overwhelmed senses and perceptions
FEELINGS		
Pleasure	—	Pain
Attraction	—	Repulsion
Power	—	Fear
Awe	—	Terror
WHAT HUMAN REASON AND REFLECTION GRASP OR CONFIRM		
Affirmation of human reason	—	Annihilation of our significance
Exaltation before the cosmos	—	Extinction of our previous narratives
The infinite	—	The infinitesimal
Human freedom	—	The void of meaning
Connection to the universe	—	Crushed by the universe

There is nothing mystical or religious about the sublime. Rather, it is a complex *existential and aesthetic experience* that at once emphasizes our connection to the universe while it humbles us, reminding us of our temporal place in the cosmos. The sublime is not a religious experience, yet it can certainly trigger religious beliefs and pre-Copernican worldviews. Those whose feelings and experiences fall more heavily on the right side of the table (overwhelm, pain, repulsion, fear, terror, annihilation, extinction, the infinitesimal, the void of meaning, and being crushed by the universe) may well turn to religion and pre-Copernican worldviews as consolation for the terror and inability to accept their insignificance and infinitesimalness. By contrast, the feelings and experiences on the left side of the table (reason, pleasure, attraction, power, awe, affirmation, exaltation, freedom, the infinite, and connection to the universe) have the potential to inspire a desire for scientific explanation, which then inspires an embrace of our infinitesimalness and the possible void of meaning that requires a new space philosophy. I would not be surprised to discover that the awe inspires more science, while the terror, fear, and denial of infinitesimalness inspire more theology, supernaturalism, and pre-Copernicanism.

Borrowing from Jean-Paul Sartre, it is when confronting the universe and nothingness *simultaneously* that we experience our greatest freedom and our ultimate intellectual challenges. As explained in *Being and Nothingness*, such moments lie at the heart of human existence and our relation to it, such that we may experience what Sartre called "vertigo" and "bad faith" (denial) in knowing that we — and we alone — must project ourselves into the future with a sense of meaning, purpose, and hope.[14] These underlying existential and cosmic conditions are why the great space films, such as *2001: A Space Odyssey*, *Planet of the Apes*, *Gravity*, and *Interstellar*, can be so compelling and inspiring and/or so deflating and terrifying. These vertiginous feelings also explain the world's response to the Apollo program, where the human species faced the specter of the monolith — the simultaneous experience of the sublime and nihilism.

4. THE APOLLO MOMENT

It is difficult for people who were born after Apollo to fully comprehend the global excitement and euphoria the events generated, not to mention the "space race" between the Soviet Union and the United States. (Russian cosmonaut or American astronaut, in the end it does not matter — both nations were pioneers in space exploration.)

On July 20, 1969, Apollo 11 fulfilled President Kennedy's goal of landing a human on the moon (and returning him safely to Earth) by the end of the decade. Before a worldwide television audience, Neil Armstrong stated the following immortal line when he first stepped on the moon: "That's one small step for a man, one giant leap for mankind." People gathered at home with their families to view the moon walk on television. TV monitors and large screens were set up in public spaces — stores, town squares, street corners — and people gathered by the thousands to view the event with friends and complete strangers. The event was rightly viewed as a human accomplishment. Around the world, people saw the Apollo 11 moon walk on their TV screens and exclaimed: "We did it!"

"ONE GIANT LEAP." The Apollo 11 moon walk generated worldwide exhilaration. The astronauts were celebrated on television, on the front pages of newspapers, and on the covers of magazines. The newspaper headlines were typed in all caps and oversized fonts: "Walk on Moon" (*Los Angeles Times*), "Men Walk on Moon" (*New York Times*), "Man on the Moon" (*Daily Mirror*), "Men Land on the Moon: 'Giant Leap for Mankind'" (*Arizona Daily Star*), "Sur la Lune, le Fantastique Danse" (*France Soir*), "To the Moon and Back" (*Life*), and "First Explorers on the Moon" (*National Geographic*). Upon their return, the Apollo 11 astronauts were heroes. There were ticker-tape parades in New York, Chicago, and Los Angeles followed by a forty-five-day "Great Leap" tour of twenty-five nations and visits with prominent dignitaries. In numerous cities, the astronauts were mobbed by cheering and adoring throngs of everyday people who gathered in crowds of epic scale. There has been nothing like it since. Super Bowls and World Cups don't even come close.[15]

Yet the moon landings alone were not the most significant aspect of the Apollo 11 mission. It was when the astronauts turned the television cameras back toward Earth, the home of humanity.[16] There, on the screens, the human species witnessed the specter of cosmic nihilism.

CONTEMPLATING OUR PLACE IN THE COSMOS ON TV. By turning the television cameras back toward Earth, Apollo 8 and Apollo 11 brought about one of the single *most profound moments* in the evolution of our civilization — humans on Earth viewing their home planet from space via television and contemplating their place in the cosmos. While the moon walk itself was indeed a magnificent achievement, the views from space were more meaningful because they illustrated humanity's *universal* cosmic conditions.

Given that we are now well into the 21st century, with the ever more fragmented global consciousness of the internet and readily accessible images of planet Earth, it's too easy to overlook just what was accomplished via television in 1968 and 1969. As part of their missions and flight plans, Apollo 8 and Apollo 11 conducted several global broadcasts while journeying to the moon, orbiting and walking on the moon, and returning from the moon. Though the television cameras of the 1960s had far less technical power than the HD cameras of today, the images they provided still stunned the world. Since Apollo 8 possessed a black-and-white television camera, on TV the Earth resembled a white and grayish orb against a grainy black background. Because the Apollo 8 images generated such acclaim as well as awe among television viewers, NASA later outfitted Apollo 11 with a color television camera that had improved visual power and better long-range focus. Therefore, the Earth could be seen as a blue and white sphere against a blackish background (at least for those with

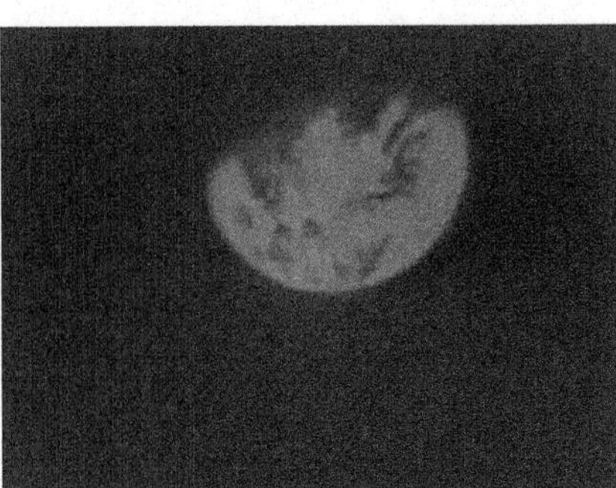

Photo 1
Earth as seen during the Apollo 8 telecast.

color TVs). Yet whether seen in black and white or in color, the views of Earth isolated in space were purely mind-blowing for the era. Earth had never been seen from *the outside*, floating alone in space.

UNITED IN THE CELEBRATION OF HUMAN ACHIEVEMENT. The Apollo 8 and 11 broadcasts reached as many as one billion viewers, or most everyone on Earth within reach of the satellite television signal, which at the time was the largest audience ever assembled for any human event. The global unity was not 100%, which would have been technologically impossible. There were about four billion people on Earth then, and perhaps three billion had no access to television.[17] But the events were experienced in 100 countries around the world as a unifying and glorious moment for the human species.

To this day, the Apollo broadcasts, collectively, are among the most viewed media events in human history, perhaps only surpassed by the funerals for Princess Diana and Michael Jackson and the horrific events of September 11, 2001. In contrast to the tragic fates of Princess Di, Michael Jackson, and the Twin Towers, the Apollo broadcasts (and the subsequent Apollo voyages that drew smaller audiences) represent the only times that the human species has been even remotely *united in the awe and celebration of a great human achievement.*

Though it was only for a fragment in cosmic and human time, NASA and Apollo basically did the impossible: They inspired people to momentarily set aside their daily narcissism, exhibitionism, consumerism, and tribal warfare to look up at the stars in awe and wonder and reflect upon their past origins and future destiny.[18] Pause and think about that moment: Rockets and television empowered our species to (1) collectively celebrate a great human achievement, and (2) simultaneously contemplate its place in the cosmos.

Apollo and the space race between the United States and the Soviet Union provided the answer to the first existential question, *where are we going?* Humans were going to the moon. Despite the fact that it was the United States that defeated the Soviet Union in the race to the moon, most people around the world realized that it was a human accomplishment. Indeed, humans went to the moon and returned back to Earth, televising it for the world to see. Yet the phenomenon of Apollo also posed two *new* existential questions to the 20th-century space age: If we went to the moon and then saw our planet floating alone in space: (1) *What does it mean,* and (2) *What can we hope for*? So far, these two questions have never really been answered, at least not with answers the world has been willing to embrace.

5. THE EARTH "SELFIE"

The first celestial *photo* and the first selfie were taken at the exact same point in human history. In 1839, French painter and physicist Louis Daguerre took the first celestial photos when he combined a camera with a telescope to take photographs of the moon. (Unfortunately, none of these images survived the fire that destroyed Daguerre's studio later that year.[19]) The oldest *surviving* celestial photo was taken in 1840 in New York City, when scientist John William Draper turned his camera upward to the night sky, combining the camera with a telescope to capture an image of the full moon.[20] The first "selfie" was taken in 1839 by American

Photo 2
Earthrise
Apollo 8, 1968

photographer Robert Cornelius when he snapped a picture of himself at the back of the family store, which was located in Philadelphia.

In 1968, over a century later, the Apollo astronauts turned their cameras toward the sky, looked back from almost one-quarter of a million miles away, and took the most beautiful and important selfie ever.[21] The image is known as *Earthrise*, and it's a photo that is much more than what it seems on the surface (see Photo 2).

The Apollo 8 astronauts were the first humans to escape the gravity of Earth. Once Apollo 8 was in orbit around the moon, astronaut Bill Anders used his 35 mm camera to capture the image of Earth floating amid the dark cosmic void beyond the horizon of the moon. In an article on the Apollo 8 voyage entitled "The Triumphant Return from the Void," *Time* celebrated the photo by dedicating an entire page to it with the heading "The Awesome Views from Apollo 8" stamped at the top.[22]

An earlier issue of *Time* stated: "In the closing days of 1968, all mankind could exult in the vision of a new universe . . . a new age, that will inevitably reshape man's view of himself and his destiny."[23] But if the destiny is unbearable, then it may as well be denied. Visible in *Earthrise* are no borders, no nations, no signs of humanity — just the planet's blue waters, white clouds, and brown and green continents, all amid the blackness of space, beyond which are trillions of galaxies with billions of stars. Knowing what we know about the universe, the only conclusion is that humans are a single species, one among many on the planet. The image is exquisite; the feeling it evokes is the cosmic sublime.

Featured in media around the world, *Earthrise* did three things: (1) It provided a "frozen" image of the Copernican Revolution; (2) The image of Earth as a single living system inspired a jump start of the contemporary environmental movement and the annual celebration of Earth Day in April 1970; and (3) The image of Earth floating in the void of space inspired the understanding of our planet as "Spaceship Earth," a term coined by Buckminster Fuller, who viewed Earth as a "vehicle" and humans as "passengers" that were fortunate to have access to the planet's natural resources and magnificent beauty. Yet, as Fuller explains in his 1969 book *Operating Manual for Spaceship Earth*, there is no pilot for this "vehicle" and no instruction manual for guiding us through the cosmos or inhabiting the planet. Without a pilot, we all serve as crew members, with nature, our minds, and our sciences and technologies as the only guides.[24]

THE TWO VERSIONS OF *EARTHRISE*. A very revealing fact about *Earthrise* is that the published version does not represent the true orientation of the original image. Anders's shot featured Earth *next* to the moon, not *above* it (see Photo 3). Had the original photo been widely publicized instead of the altered version, it would have provided us with the first chance to view Earth in the cosmos as it really is: a planet existing amid the vast cosmic void. It is not surprising that everyone, including NASA, preferred the version that was flipped on its side so that the blue and white Earth seemed to be "rising" above the moon's grey horizon.

Thanks to NASA and Apollo 8, we have a groundbreaking photograph of our blue planet against the black void that perfectly demonstrates the cosmic nihilism we face as a species. As symbolized in the original *Earthrise* image, the blackness of deep space suggests there are actually *no* external grounds for our pre-Copernican beliefs, behaviors, and dominant narratives. The obliteration of our Earthbound narratives began with Galileo, but it was NASA and Apollo that eventually made the issue clear for all to see.

THE EARTH "SELFIE" AND COSMIC NIHILISM

THE BLUE PLANET: For millennia, all human values and beliefs were based on a vision of cosmic centrality, with Earth and humanity under the guidance of an all-knowing Creator.

THE BLACK VOID: Surrounding the planet, the blackness of space shows there is no self-evident meaning or purpose to human existence. This poses the greatest intellectual challenge for humanity: to ground human purpose and meaning in something external to our desires, in a vast universe of which we are insignificant and inconsequential.

Photo 3
Apollo 8: Original *Earthrise*, 1968

Against that blackness of space, we have yet to develop a cosmic narrative to counter cosmic nihilism, which is why there was a second version of *Earthrise* to begin with. Earth rising *above* the moon is much more comforting, providing the cognitive warmth of a morning sunrise. By contrast, Earth floating *beside* the moon with nothing above or below it is visually vertiginous, suggesting we could fall off with nothing below us and tumble into the abyss of meaninglessness. The visual vertigo and cosmic nihilism of the original photo were ostensibly unbearable for us — while it generated awe and amazement, it also made us feel insignificant because our systems of meaning were being annihilated. In other words, Anders's original photo rocked the dominant worldviews spanning across previous millennia.

6. CONFRONTING NIHILISM WITH GENESIS

Launched on December 21, 1968, Apollo 8 was recognized as a great human achievement on an epic scale. Upon Apollo 8's return to Earth, the front-page headline for the *Los Angeles Times* trumpeted "Apollo Feat Opens Up New Space Vistas." This has proven to be more than space-age hype, for Apollo 8 paved the way for Apollo 11, the other moon landings, robots on Mars, space probes exploring planets in our solar system, and Voyager exiting the solar system and cruising into the void of deep space. And, of course, Apollo 8's new space vistas led to cosmic nihilism, which still has yet to be countered much less overcome.

THE "EXPANSE OF NOTHING." The sense of cosmic nihilism experienced by the Apollo 8 astronauts was notably apparent during the television broadcast of their orbit around the moon, which happened to take place on Christmas Eve, 1968. Here's what they saw, felt, and said:

> **Frank Borman.** I know my own impression is that it's a vast, lonely, forbidding-type existence, or expanse of nothing. . . .
>
> **Jim Lovell.** The vast loneliness up here at the moon is awe inspiring, and it makes you realize just what you have back there on Earth. The Earth from here is a grand oasis in the big vastness of space. . . .
>
> **Bill Anders.** The sky up here is also a rather forbidding, foreboding expanse of blackness, with no stars visible when we're flying over the moon in daylight.[25]

Along with everyone back on Earth watching the broadcast on television, the astronauts were experiencing cosmic nihilism and the cosmic sublime. Consider the words and phrases Borman, Lovell, and Anders used to describe what they saw — "vast," "lonely," forbidding," "nothing," "foreboding," "expanse of blackness," "no stars visible." Almost all of them convey a certain anxiety about the potential negation of human existence, a fear that there may be no meaning for humans in space other than our belonging to the "grand oasis" of our home planet. With the images of Earth and the moon amid the cosmic void, the astronauts were uniting humanity in the unavoidable task of contemplating our true place in the vast cosmos.

ACCELERATION AND REVERSAL. In the final moments of the broadcast, we witness the simultaneous climax and crash of the space age. At this pinnacle moment of philosophical and scientific modernity, the astronauts concluded the broadcast without any reference to science, technology, art, philosophy, or *anything* suggesting human accomplishment. Instead, in an immense leap backward that spanned the millennia, the astronauts began to recite passages from Genesis:

> **Anders.** We are now approaching lunar sunrise, and for all the people back on Earth, the crew of Apollo 8 has a message that we would like to send to you. "In the beginning, God created the Heaven and the Earth. And the Earth was without form and void, and darkness was upon the face of the deep. And the spirit of God moved upon the face of the waters, and God said, 'Let there be light.' And there was light."[26]

Borman and Lovell continued with subsequent passages from Genesis before Borman concluded with "Merry Christmas and God bless all of you — all of you on the good Earth."

According to mainstream theory and history, Apollo 8 and the Genesis reading "saved" the violent year of 1968, uniting world religions and comforting Americans in a spiritual exaltation for troubled times.[27] Not surprisingly, *Time* magazine designated the astronauts "Men of the Year" for its January 3, 1969 issue, an honor that the Apollo 11 astronauts — those who were the first to walk on the moon and offered the world a more secular message — did not receive. That year, 1970, *Time* gave the honor to "Middle Americans" instead, with the accompanying essay treating Neil Armstrong as little more than a working-class hero. According to the article, "the mysteries of space were nothing" compared to the current disappointments and frustrations of the middle class.[28] How dare the Apollo mission, space exploration, and a new human narrative impinge on the narcissistic worries of middle-class America! It were as if the mission and the views of Earth from space meant *nothing* — particularly nothing new in terms of worldviews or cosmologies.

Decades after the Apollo 8 broadcasts, news media around the world still recall the event as a triumph of technology and *the human spirit*. Why? Because the pre-Copernican theism provided the desperate philosophical *reversal* needed to counter the cosmic nihilism and the cosmic sublime present before the awestruck eyes of the astronauts *and* of the world (via television). Fearing the annihilation of our significance and extinction of our narratives, the existential terror was too much. The dominant worldviews were saved.

Fortunately for the Apollo 11 mission, it was Armstrong's words that prevailed: "That's one small step for a man, one giant leap for mankind." Nothing could be closer to the truth. Yet as beautiful as this secular statement is, it has not remotely generated any challenge to the dominant narratives on Earth, the very theist narratives tapped into by Apollo 8 on global television.

7. APOLLO: WHAT HAPPENED?

As Apollo streaked across the cultural skies, numerous writers, scientists, and philosophers speculated about what the moon landing meant to humanity. One thing was certain: Humans actually left the gravity of Earth to orbit and walk on the moon, and it was damn cool. But what were the forces that made Apollo happen, what were their effects, and what did Apollo mean? Most everyone acknowledged that Apollo achieved something spectacular that should reach far beyond the Cold War and mere technological accomplishment, yet few could agree on what happened in totality. As historian Matthew Tribbe argues, the world's thinkers stumbled when facing "the challenge of integrating this colossal yet largely cryptic event into existing philosophies or, if need be, developing a new philosophy that could accommodate the reality of a space-faring civilization."[29]

NASA was somewhat guilty of dumbing down Apollo's profound significance, allowing the press to portray the astronauts as "average Joes" instead of scientific heroes. *Life* magazine's special issue on Apollo 11 (August 11, 1969) included a glossy photo spread showing Neil Armstrong baking pizza, Buzz Aldrin jogging in the suburbs, and Michael Collins pruning his garden.[30] Space travel was often "domesticated" in articles of this type that seemed to be suggesting there was nothing particularly radical about these three "moon walkers" — sure they were space farers and everything, but now that they were back on planet Earth, they merely returned to the mundane routines and activities of middle-class life. By contrast, author Tom Wolfe paid a more respectful homage to Apollo with his best-selling novel *The Right Stuff*, made into a box-office hit film in 1983. For Wolfe, test pilots and astronauts were still gallant adventurers, and spaceflight and space exploration were a vital aspect of technological society.

But was Apollo a mere triumph of technology and test-pilot bravado? Was the success of Apollo a showcase for large-scale government-corporate planning, leading to technological benefits for everyday citizens on Earth? Despite Apollo's achievements, was the entire program a waste of money better spent on social problems on Earth? Did Apollo symbolize the human drive for exploration and the mastery of nature and the cosmos, for better or worse? Did Apollo point toward a new era for humanity, a transformation of our consciousness, perhaps heralding the end of war and an age of human cooperation?

Weighing in on these questions were intellectual luminaries such as philosopher/anthropologist Loren Eiseley, philosopher/historian Hannah Arendt, the infamous atheist novelist Ayn Rand, scientist/technologist Buckminster Fuller, and two-time Pulitzer Prize-winning author Norman Mailer. All agreed that Apollo was a mind-blowing event, yet each felt it had different meanings and relevance. Eiseley viewed Apollo as symbolizing a species-level survival tactic, an attempt to forge the future survival of humanity by launching men into space like fungus spores so we could eventually exit from our overcrowded and overexploited planet.[31] Arendt argued that the success of Apollo diminished the stature of humanity and undermined our sense of self-worth and cosmic significance.[32] Rand viewed the journey to the moon as the triumph of Apollonian human reason in contrast to the Dionysian world of drugs, hippies, and the managerial disaster of the Woodstock music festival.[33] Fuller saw Apollo as the hopeful signal for the emergence of a planetary society for the "passengers" on "Spaceship Earth."[34] Finally, Mailer saw the event as a nihilist and purposeless endeavor (there was no stated reason to go to the moon), while fearing that Apollo illustrated the triumph of the "squares" over the youthful and rebellious radicals.

Human consciousness was extended to the moon to reveal Earth from space in a moment of the technological and cosmic sublime. As people witnessed the event on their TV screens with excitement and even reverence, they also experienced the terrifying effects of cosmic nihilism, where the dominant worldviews and humanity's cosmic centrality were challenged by a profound comprehension of our physical insignificance. Something had to fall, had to crash — either our worldviews or the Apollo program. For most, it was Apollo.

SPACE SPORES. At the height of the Cold War, the former Soviet Union and the United States launched rockets into space at the same time the human species faced the atomic annihilation of its civilization. Was the Apollo moon program a subconscious survival strategy for a species facing oblivion? In an analysis of Apollo 11, Loren Eiseley suggested this possibility:

> It is a remarkable fact that much of what man has achieved through the use of his intellect, nature had invented before him. *Pilobolus*, [a] fungus which prepares, sights, and fires its spore capsule, constitutes a curious anticipation of human rocketry. The fungus is one that grows upon the dung of cattle. To fulfill its life cycle, its spores must be driven up and outward to land upon vegetation several feet away, where they may be eaten by grazing cattle or horses.
>
> The spore tower that discharges the *Pilobolus* missile is one of the most fascinating objects in nature. A swollen cell beneath the black capsule that contains the spores is a genuinely light-sensitive "eye." This pigmented eye controls the direction of growth of the spore cannon and aims it very carefully at the region of greatest light in order that no intervening obstacle may block the flight of the spore capsule.
>
> When a pressure of several atmospheres has been built up chemically within the cell underlying the spore container, the cell explodes, blasting the capsule several feet into the air. Since the firing takes place in the morning hours, the stalks point to the sun at an angle sure to carry the tiny "rocket" several feet away as well as up. . . .
>
> The tiny black capsule that bears the living spores through space is strangely reminiscent, in miniature, of man's latest adventure. Man, too, is a spore bearer. The labor of millions and the consumption of vast stores of energy are necessary to hurl just a few individuals, perhaps eventually people of both sexes, on the road toward another planet. Similarly, for every spore city that arises in the fungus world, only a few survivors find their way into the future.
>
> It is useless to talk of transporting the excess population of our planet elsewhere, even if a world of sparkling water and green trees were available. In nature it is a law that the spore cities die, but the spores fly on to find their destiny. Perhaps this will prove to be the rule of the newborn planet virus. Somehow in the *mysterium* behind genetics, the tiny pigmented eye and the rocket capsule were evolved together.[35]

In our quest for space exploration, are we war-mongering humans little more than space spores simultaneously avoiding and leaving behind apocalypses? Was Apollo the most successful spore launch in human history, paving the way for future survival efforts in the event of an Earthly apocalypse? (These are, in fact, the very questions *Interstellar* attempts to answer.)

THE MOON LANDINGS WERE NOT FAKED. According to polls and surveys, 7% of Americans and 25% of British citizens believe NASA faked the moon landings.[36] Some people believe that NASA paid Stanley Kubrick to film the fake footage.[37] Given that pseudoscience and antirationalism are widespread in global culture, these results are not surprising. *Interstellar* confronts this issue in the scene where the future educators deny that NASA landed humans on the moon.

Being skeptical of the US government is understandable in general. Like all other political systems throughout history, the US government has lied, currently lies, and will lie again in the future. Governments are always lying about something. But there is zero doubt NASA sent humans to the moon. Though the fake moon-landing claims have been debunked many times, here are some of the most obvious reasons the moon landings could *not* have been faked.

1) The astronauts on the six Apollo missions retrieved 843lbs of moon rocks that were brought to Earth and shared with scientists around the world. If the rocks were not from our planet, the scientists would surely have realized that and called NASA on its trickery.[38]

2) The former Soviet Union could have easily tracked the Apollo spacecraft to the moon with its telecommunications satellites and picked up both the Apollo radio transmissions to Mission Control and all of the television broadcasts. The Soviets possessed such technologies because they too sent spacecraft to the moon in the 1960s (sans cosmonauts). If NASA didn't really send astronauts to the moon, the Soviet Union would have certainly known and taken the opportunity to embarrass the United States on the "world stage" at the height of the Cold War. The possibility of the Soviets going along with such a hoax is far below zero (lower than the winter temperatures in Siberia!)

3) The Apollo 11 and 14 astronauts left behind mirror-like prisms on the moon (the lunar laser-ranging retroreflector array) that are targeted with lasers by scientists at the McDonald Observatory in Texas. The lasers accurately determine the distance from Earth to the moon, which is moving away from the Earth by about 3.8 cm per year.

4) The Lunar Reconnaissance Orbiter has provided images of the Apollo landing sites, including the moon buggies and their tracks and the descent part of the lunar modules.

5) The video and television technologies of 1969 weren't advanced enough to fake the moon landing in any plausible way. We didn't have anything like CGI or Photoshop back then.

6) Approximately 400,000 scientists, engineers, and technicians worked on the Apollo project for over a decade; it is patently absurd to think they all were all somehow tricked or part of a hoax.

7) The United States made six visits to the moon. Let's consider for a moment that they were all staged. If the first "hoax" were successful, the United States would have defeated the Soviets in the race to the moon. Why risk faking five *more* visits and thus increase the chances of slipping up and getting caught by 500%?

In the end, those who deny the moon landings are waging an assault on logic, science, and basic rationality. More importantly, the deniers are attacking and undermining the great human achievement of Apollo, precisely because

TABLE 2 **TEN MEANINGS OF APOLLO**

TRIUMPH FOR OUR SPECIES

1. The Apollo missions were among the most significant scientific and technological accomplishments of the 20th-century.
2. They put us in touch with the cosmic sublime and demonstrated the power of science and human reason.
3. They were also a symbol of the primal human drive for exploration and conquest, for better or worse.

SOCIAL BENEFITS

4. Apollo was an example of successful large-scale government and corporate planning, which had the potential to generate technological and economic benefits for society (taxpayers, citizens, consumers, etc.).
5. It was a waste of money better spent on problems facing humans on Earth.

THE FUTURE

6. Apollo was an attempt to forge the survival of humanity by launching men into space like *Pilobolus* spores.
7. Apollo was a journey into nihilism that revealed the lack of cosmic meaning and purpose of human existence in a vast and indifferent universe.
8. The missions represented the birth of a new planetary cosmology that could unite the "passengers" on Spaceship Earth, thus providing meaning and hope for the future.
9. The missions represented a moment of scientific acceleration and cultural reversal (the simultaneous success of science with the failure of society to develop new cosmic narratives to confront cosmic nihilism).

HISTORY

10. NASA's achievement will rank as the one of most important events of the 20th century, precisely because of the above and the following:

    a) Apollo was the first and only time humans were largely united in celebration of human achievement.

    b) Apollo showed the specter of cosmic nihilism to a worldwide television audience, forcing humans to collectively contemplate their destiny as a species.

    c) Apollo was a potential breakthrough moment for a new space philosophy and cosmic narrative, but when our secular culture looked to the stars, it turned backward to pre-Copernican theism to explain its past origins and future destiny.

the real meaning of Apollo challenges the dominant narratives to which they are desperately clinging to out of sheer existential dread. The hoax was not perpetrated by NASA or Kubrick, but in the minds of the deniers and their pre-Copernican narratives.

MULTIPLE MEANINGS OF APOLLO. The Apollo missions dramatically illustrated the incredible things humans can do when reason, science, creativity, cooperation, ambition, and bravado are applied to the pursuit of genuine achievement and enlightenment and thus tap into the cosmic sublime. From a long-term historical perspective, both Apollo 8 and 11 dwarf the Cold War and its nationalist competition and will certainly go down as two of the most important accomplishments of the 20th century, along with the discoveries of the expanding universe and DNA and the invention of computers and the internet.

Ultimately, Apollo should have initiated the emergence of a more enlightened and unified society, with us humans realizing we are not the center of the universe, that we are part of a much larger cosmic narrative, one that is beautiful and sublime and holds a deeper and more profound meaning for our species. Yet because the cosmic sublime ironically points toward cosmic nihilism and the possibility of a *meaningless* human existence, or at least a species with no significance beyond its own desires and fears, we were overwhelmed by cosmic nihilism, the loss of our cosmic centrality and the external meaninglessness of our existence. This is why the Apollo 8 astronauts read from Genesis and why Apollo 11 astronaut Buzz Aldrin took Communion on the moon, and it's why *Earthrise* was flipped on its side. It's also the reason cosmic doublethink and the "dual system of astronomy" (Chapter 3) prevailed for humanity's artists, thinkers, average citizens, and most every social-political leader. At the same time we leapt *forward* into the future, we jumped *backward* by millennia.

8. VOYAGER AND HUBBLE

When the former Soviet Union launched the Sputnik satellite in 1957, it was hailed a monumental achievement. America soon followed with Vanguard (1958) and Telstar (1962), signaling a new era of global communication and the possibility of greater harmony and understanding among nations. (Of course, the global harmony has yet to arrive, but we managed to survive the Cold War without a nuclear apocalypse.)

Telstar was so remarkable for its era that it was the title of a futuristic instrumental song by the Tornadoes; in 1962, the song reached number one on the pop charts in Britain and the United States. Opening with space sounds followed by drums, lead guitar, and organ, it's a pretty cool song that kind of exemplifies the space-age feeling of *faster, forward, upward* (see Chapter 2).

Humans were not only extending their consciousness around Earth but to the other planets in the solar system. Soon after the launch of the Telstar satellite, NASA launched the Mariner probes (1962-1973) and sent them to Venus, Mars, and Mercury. The success of the Mariner program eventually paved the way for the Voyager (1977) space probe and the Hubble Space Telescope, both of which substantially transformed our understanding of the cosmos.

Launched in 1977, the same year as the release of the first *Star Wars* film, Voyager unfortunately had less cultural impact than George Lucas and his space warriors from the future past. However, its scientific and philosophical feats were considerable. Voyagers 1 and 2 generated the first maps of the outer planets, which led to the ongoing exploration of the planets via the Cassini spacecraft and others. (The missions and discoveries are too numerous to mention here, but the images of Saturn's and Jupiter's moons that were produced have proven remarkable.) In 2012, Voyager 1 exited the solar system and began its trip into the voids of the Milky Way, becoming our first messenger to the stars (other than our torrent of radio and television signals).

PALE BLUE DOT. Voyager has posed great challenges to our cosmic narcissism, especially with the photo known as the *Pale Blue Dot*. By 1990, Voyager 1 had more than fulfilled its many mission objectives, so scientist Carl Sagan persuaded NASA engineers to program the space probe to snap a photo of Earth, by then a distant object receding ever farther in the space probe's journey. Sagan hoped the photo would become an iconic image like *Earthrise*. As programmed from

3.7 billion miles away, Voyager beamed an image of the Earth back home — an image comprised of 640,000 pixels, the planet itself only a single pixel, a tiny speck of light, a *Pale Blue Dot* against the cosmic void. Similar to *Earthrise*, the *Pale Blue Dot* shows Earth as the center of nothing.

In the book *Pale Blue Dot*, Sagan writes that the aim of the photograph was to help humanity better understand its place in the cosmos in hopes we might overcome millennia of warfare and cosmic conceit, better care for our planet, and grasp the fact that Earth was our only home. As Sagan states:

> The Earth is a very small stage in a vast cosmic arena. Think of the rivers of blood spilled by all those generals and emperors so that, in glory and triumph, they could become the momentary masters of a fraction of a dot. Think of the endless cruelties visited by the inhabitants of one corner of this pixel on the scarcely distinguishable inhabitants of some other corner, how frequent their misunderstandings, how eager they are to kill one another, how fervent their hatreds.
>
> Our posturings, our imagined self-importance, the delusion that we have some privileged position in the Universe, are challenged by this point of pale light. Our planet is a lonely speck in the great enveloping cosmic dark. In our obscurity, in all this vastness, there is no hint that help will come from elsewhere to save us from ourselves.
>
> . . . Like it or not, for the moment the Earth is where we make our stand.[39]

For the inhabitants of that planetary pixel, the *Pale Blue Dot* reveals a deep and profound reality. In effect, Earth is disappearing into the vanishing point in Voyager's "rearview mirror," the space probe abandoning its human creators as it hurtles into the cosmic nothingness beyond the solar system. Gliding through interstellar space, Voyager 1 is the most distant circuit in *cyber*space, signaling the convergence of two realms of space-time, two universes — one cosmic and one virtual. Yet as illustrated by the gradual proliferation of the internet and the recent rise of social media, it's clear that most people prefer the virtual realm of cyberspace, as it positions each user at the center of everything.

How the hell can *Earthrise* or the *Pale Blue Dot* compete with that?

MESSAGE OF HOPE. Eight years after the optimistic triumph of Apollo, humanity sent a dire message into the cosmic void. Mounted on Voyager is the famous Golden Record, a gold-plated copper disk with an electronic compilation of life on Earth, encoded with 117 photographs, greetings in 54 languages, 90 minutes of music from around the world, and a selection of sounds from nature and culture, such as animals, symphonies, and a rocket launch. Included was a needle to play the record, with instructions on the record cover and the playing speed of 16 rpm listed in the binary code of ones and zeros. There was also a statement from US president Jimmy Carter:

> We cast this message into the cosmos. It is likely to survive a billion years into our future, when our civilization is profoundly altered and the surface of the Earth may be vastly changed. Of the 200 billion stars in the Milky Way galaxy, some — perhaps many — may have

> inhabited planets and space-faring civilizations. If one such civilization intercepts Voyager and can understand these recorded contents, here is our message:
>
> This is a present from a small distant world, a token of our sounds, our science, our images, our music, our thoughts, and our feelings. We are attempting to survive our time so we may live into yours. We hope someday, having solved the problems we face, to join a community of galactic civilizations. This record represents our hope and our determination and our goodwill in a vast and awesome universe.[40]

President Carter's message illustrated the utopian intellectual spirit of the space age, an enlightened secular view that was characteristic of modernity and the best of humanity, even during the dark moments of the Cold War. Fortunately, the Cold War was ending precisely as Voyager was capturing the *Pale Blue Dot* image. But, like Apollo, Voyager and the *Pale Blue Dot* haven't gotten us any closer to connecting with any "galactic civilizations." Science, technology, and human consciousness are accelerating into the cosmos, but philosophy on Earth is in denial, reversal, or simply not up the task.

VOYAGER, HOLLYWOOD, AND THE MEANING OF LIFE. Voyager has played a symbolic, "supporting" role in two films, seemingly as a means of eliciting questions about the meaning of humanity and self-aware existence. In *Star Trek: The Motion Picture* (1979), a fictitious Voyager 6 is discovered by a giant cloud-like technological machine called V'Ger, which is self-aware and seeking to overcome its meaningless existence in a vast universe. Spock interacts with the machine and reports to Captain Kirk that V'Ger "has no meaning, no hope . . . no answers. It's asking questions: 'Is this all that I am? Is there nothing more?'" Logic and knowledge are not enough to provide meaning for V'Ger. V'Ger is seeking its "Creator" and, in so doing, may destroy the Earth, transforming all "carbon life forms" into "data patterns" (perhaps anticipating Google and Facebook). Disaster is averted through some lame plot maneuvers, particularly when one crew member is uploaded to the cloud system to join V'Ger's data systems. Kirk eventually approaches the spacecraft inside V'Ger, and after rubbing some of the tarnish off the nameplate, the word "VOYAGER 6" is revealed. In the end, Spock and Kirk declare V'Ger to be a new life form.

Voyager plays a rather influential role in *Men, Women, and Children* (2014), a film about humanity's desperate quest for personal meaning and connection within an emotionally vacant society. We're introduced to a group of suburban teens and their parents, whose dysfunctional lives are dominated and shaped by online culture — social media and internet porn in particular. The film explicitly argues that while social media have enhanced our ability to communicate, they have also diminished our proficiency to connect with each other on a genuine level, leaving us rather empty and lonely. The film focuses primarily on a distraught high school teen named Tim, a talented football player who finds himself deeply impacted by a YouTube video about Sagan's *Pale Blue Dot*. Coming to the conclusion that not only is football meaningless but so is life in the grand scheme of things, Tim quits the high school team and sets off on a contemplative inner journey. Scenes of Voyager floating through space with voiceover narration of excerpts from *Pale Blue Dot* bookend the film and are interwoven within the narrative. The Voyager scenes are meant to yank us out of our prevailing narcissism and provide us with a "reality check," reminding us of our actual cosmic non-centrality in the universe yet providing no meaning for the sublime imagery.

THE HUBBLE DEEP FIELD IMAGES. The Hubble Space Telescope has produced some of the most extraordinary cosmic images in history.[41] This includes the Hubble Deep Field (HDF) (1995, 2004, 2012) images, which show us what's in the tiny voids in the night sky of the Milky Way.[42] Since the Hubble orbits in space, it generates much clearer images than terrestrial telescopes.

The first Hubble Deep Field image was taken in 1995. The Hubble was aimed at a single spot in the sky — a speck of darkness, an area about one-hundredth the size of the moon. Located near the Big Dipper, the spot was selected because it was unremarkable and seemingly empty. Over 10 consecutive days, the Hubble took 342 separate images that were compiled into one. Cosmologists and astronomers were stunned to discover at least 1,500 galaxies in various shapes, sizes, and stages of development — some as old as 10 billion years. For the Hubble Deep Field image, the vision capacity of the human eye was amplified by a factor of 4 billion.

In 2005, NASA decided to go even farther across space and time with the Hubble Ultra Deep Field (HUDF). Aimed at a dark and empty spot near Orion, the Hubble used a new camera to capture a single image based on a continuous exposure that lasted over 11 consecutive days. In this spot, which was about one-tenth of the moon's diameter, the telescope revealed at least 10,000 galaxies.[43] In 2009, the Hubble Ultra Deep Field Infrared (HUDF-IR) enabled astronomers to make infrared observations in space and locate several candidates for the most distant galaxy ever spotted. Finally, in 2012, NASA published the Hubble eXtreme Deep Field (XDF) image, which is a compilation of all the previous Deep Field images. The XDF reveals galaxies that existed 13.2 billion years ago and developed a mere 500 million years after the emergence of the observable universe. In effect, the Hubble Deep Fields are like core samples of the cosmos, boring deep into the universe's past. This makes the Hubble much like a time machine, looking back across the cosmos to map its ancient and abundant galaxies. As a result of these and other discoveries, the Hubble has revealed that the galaxies in the universe number in the trillions.

Who knows what will be revealed by Hubble's successors? Scheduled for launch in 2018, NASA's James Webb Space Telescope (JWST) will be located 900,000 miles from Earth and have 100 times the viewing power of the Hubble.[44] Expected to launch in the 2020s, China's first space telescope will orbit Earth next to the Tiangong space station and have a field of view 300 times that of the Hubble.[45] Combined, the two space telescopes will allow humans to peer far deeper into space and map much wider areas of the cosmos.

TABLE 3 **TEN MEANINGS OF VOYAGER AND THE HUBBLE SPACE TELESCOPE**

TRIUMPH FOR OUR SPECIES

1. Voyager and Hubble represent two of the greatest scientific accomplishments of the human species while triggering the cosmic sublime.
2. Through Voyager and Hubble, humans have extended their consciousness and media technologies outside the solar system and across 13.7 billion years of space-time.
3. Voyager and Hubble illustrate the power of science and human reason — furthering 21st-century cosmology and paving the way for the ongoing exploration of the outer planets (Cassini, et al.) and the Kepler telescope's search for exoplanets.

THE FUTURE

4. Voyager is a "space spore" hurtling through the cosmos in our quest to ensure human survival in the future.
5. Like the "eye" of the *Pilobolus* that aims for fertile ground for its spores, the Hubble (and the Kepler) might eventually "see" exoplanets that we can potentially colonize.

PHILOSOPHY

6. Voyager is on a journey beyond our solar system, assisting us in our quest for cosmic meaning.
7. The Hubble's discoveries have made the utter insignificance and non-centrality of human existence blatantly apparent, amplifying the challenge of cosmic nihilism.
8. In the future, Voyager will likely be representative of our extinction, our irrelevance, or a new beginning for humanity.
9. Voyager and Hubble present the opportunity for artists, filmmakers, and philosophers to come up with new space philosophies and narratives that tap into the cosmic sublime.

HISTORY

10. If civilization collapses, theocracies prevail, or humans become extinct, then the Voyager may be one of the last legacies of human existence, along with Apollo's artifacts on the moon and the robots on Mars.

LOOKING AND LAUNCHING INTO THE COSMOS. Understanding our starry origins and cosmic non-centrality might not only help us avert our narcissistic planetary destruction and possible extinction, but it could also justify our existence to the cosmos as well as any future extraterrestrial species we encounter. And that will happen, sooner or later — if we don't destroy ourselves or our living systems first. On the other hand, perhaps more catastrophic events and species extinctions are inevitable, representing the continual challenges that face life and human evolution in the universe, not unlike the challenges posed by nihilism and the quest for meaning.

Could our quest to send humans into space represent an effort to avoid extinction and evade the ecological-planetary destruction we've caused on Earth, as theorized by Eiseley and dramatized in *Interstellar*? Cooper and Brand are less an Adam and Eve of the future than "space spores" fired from atop the NASA pyramid, with the *Endurance* serving as the "capsule" that houses the spores in their journey through the wormhole.

Might the Hubble and Kepler space telescopes represent advanced versions of the *Pilobolus* "eye," which controls the direction of that fungus's spore launches? As *Interstellar* demonstrates, telescopes and space probes will eventually determine where in space humans will be sent next. Similar to the *Pilobolus* "eye" that reacts to the light of the sun, the Kepler telescope and others peer into the universe, "reacting" to dimming starlight that could potentially suggest a habitable planet in orbit around a particular star. The Voyager serves as our first interstellar "spore," having left the solar system and entered the voids of the Milky Way, carrying diagrams for how to find our planet, etchings of what humans look like, and a message of hope from President Carter.

Of course humans should be smarter and wiser than the *Pilobolus* (yet, with all due respect, the fungus does possess nature's wisdom in millions of years of evolution and adaptation). Far exceeding the *Pilobolus* "eyes" are our brain's 100 billion neurons that possess the power to extend our consciousness deep into the universe. The "eyes" of the Hubble and Kepler telescopes are much more powerful than the eye of the *Pilobolus*, and the journeys of the Apollo spacecraft and the Voyager far exceed any distance made by a *Pilobolus* spore launch. So why can't we reprogram our "space spores" to extend enlightenment into the cosmos while uniting as a species and protecting the planet on which we depend for life? After all, it is quite likely that our origins are contained in a space spore that once hitched a ride to Earth on a comet or meteor.

9. JFK'S "MOON SPEECH": HUMANITY'S "NEW KNOWLEDGE OF OUR UNIVERSE"

When writers, historians, philosophers, and space enthusiasts discuss the space age and the Apollo program of the 1960s, they almost always reference the famed passage in President Kennedy's 1962 "moon speech," in which he declared:

> We choose to go to the moon in this decade and do the other things, not because they are easy, but because they are hard, because that goal will serve to organize and measure the best of our energies and skills, because that challenge is one that we are willing to accept, one we are unwilling to postpone, and one which we intend to win, and the others, too.[46]

But they always overlook or ignore a passage that comes later:

> We set sail on this new sea because there is *new knowledge* to be gained, and new rights to be won, and they must be won and used for *the progress of all people*. . . . The growth of our science and education will be enriched by *new knowledge of our universe* and environment, by new techniques of learning and mapping and observation, by new tools and computers for industry, medicine, the home as well as the school. [Italics mine.]

Why ignore this passage? Here's why: We achieved President Kennedy's goal of sending humans to the moon and back, surely an incredible accomplishment. Since President Kennedy's speech, our knowledge of the cosmos has grown exponentially. But we have *failed spectacularly* in using this "new knowledge of our universe" to develop, embrace, and put a new cosmic narrative for the human species into practice. It's been an epic fail in an epic cosmos. It's as if we are terrified of the monolith and the new beginning it offers.

TIME FOR A STATUS UPDATE. A mere glance at the Google News reader suggests that cosmic centrality and cosmic narcissism are prevailing on Earth. Consider this: Do we really, honestly believe that hydrogen atoms evolved for billions of years so that a single species on a tiny planet in a remote part of the cosmos could pretend it was the center of the universe — the center of all that was worth *seeing, doing, and knowing* — when in fact that species was the center of nothing and nothingness? We are surely the center of all worth seeing, doing, and knowing — *or so we think* — when it comes to our own consciousness and the 24/7 electronic media spectacle extending from that consciousness. This delusional cosmic centrality is evidenced by what dominates the news and all social/political/cultural events: war and greed, theism and tribalism, celebrity worship and unbridled consumerism, deities who promise us a special and personal cosmic destiny, and the overall exhibitionist and narcissistic antics of a self-aware species in denial of its true place in the cosmos. The marvels of Apollo, of the Hubble, and of space exploration haven't reduced the increasing madness on Earth. How long will the universe permit our hubris? How long before the universe provides a surprise "status update" for our pre-Copernican worldviews? Perhaps it will be in the form of a very large comet or meteor, one too big to be blown up by Bruce Willis and Ben Affleck à la *Armageddon* (1998).

THE PSYCHOLOGICAL EFFECTS OF AWE. As President Kennedy suggested in his "moon speech," our "new knowledge" of the vast universe might have *enriching* social and psychological effects. Rather than denying or ignoring our insignificance in the vast universe, perhaps we should be finding ways to experience the sublime more often. Recent psychological studies suggest that experiencing awe can inspire people to situate themselves in larger narratives and engage in what some researchers call "pro-social behavior."[47] By experiencing things that are vast or infinite, humans develop a sense of what researchers term the "small self" (the infinitesimal). Awe and vastness also make people feel more connected to a universal narrative for their species. As explained by the authors of one study:

> Awe involves positively valenced feelings of wonder and amazement. Awe arises via appraisals of stimuli that are vast, that transcend current frames of reference, and require new schema to accommodate what is being perceived. Although many stimuli can inspire awe, from beautiful buildings to elegant equations, the prototypical awe experience, at least in Western cultures, involves encounters with natural phenomena that are immense in size, scope, or complexity, e.g. the night sky, the ocean. However elicited, experiences of awe are unified by a core theme: perceptions of vastness that dramatically expand the observer's usual frame of reference in some dimension or domain. . . . Taken together, these studies suggest that awe directs attention to entities vaster than the self and more collective

> dimensions of personal identity, and reduces the significance the individual attaches to personal concerns and goals.[48]

Similarly, when astronauts view Earth from space, they experience a transcendent moment in which they feel connected to humanity and the planet as a whole. In their article entitled "The Overview Effect: Awe and Self-Transcendent Experience in Space Flight," Yaden et al. (2016) state:

> The *overview effect*, as the experience is called, refers to a profound reaction to viewing the Earth from outside its atmosphere. A number of astronauts have attributed deep feelings of awe and even self-transcendence to this experience. Astronaut Edgar Mitchell described it as an "explosion of awareness."[49]

The authors explain there are several features that contribute to the astronauts' experience of awe: (1) the experience of cosmic vastness, (2) the totality of seeing Earth as a complete system, and (3) the juxtaposition of Earth's features against the black voids of space. In other words, the overview effect and the experience of awe combine vastness, totality, and the voids of space, resulting in a transcendent experience that connects astronauts to much larger narratives of cosmic unity.

These astronauts and cosmonauts come to the realization that human narratives on Earth are deeply flawed. Altered perceptions of Earth's existential value are among the most important psychological effects of space flight, which "seems to be one of the few endeavors that can be a true source of collective inspiration."[50] In conclusion, Yaden et al. (2016) state:

> Awe and self-transcendence are among the deepest and most powerful aspects of the human experience: it should come as no surprise that they emerge as we gaze upon our home planet and our whole world comes into view.[51]

Though largely stated in terms of psychological research, these "awe studies" support my explication of the sublime, particularly the simultaneous experience of the infinite (immensity, totality) and infinitesimal ("small self"), the exaltation before the cosmos, and the extinction of our narratives (the need for new schema and a new frame of reference). It is the sublime moment that inspires humans to "transcend current frames of reference" and have "altered perceptions of Earth's existential value." I should point out that I came across these studies quite by chance near the completion of this book. I was very pleased to find research that provides empirical support for a central hypothesis presented here: The sublime can be a unifying experience that *connects humans to the cosmos and larger narratives for our species*. That's why the sublime is key to developing a cosmic narrative and space philosophy for the human species.

WE ARE THE CENTER OF NOTHING. Yaden et al. (2016) are exactly right: Apollo's first images of Earth from the moon did indeed generate a sublime moment and a powerful experience that was shared by the human species. Perhaps for a moment, the human species felt connected to the universe via Apollo. On the other hand, the image of Earth against the black void also triggered our fears of cosmic nihilism and human meaninglessness. Embedded in the sublimity of space is the challenge of nihilism for our species, which has been on full display since Apollo and the Hubble Space Telescope. We know we are not the center of anything, so we must confront our existence at the center of nothing.

Reason, science, and technology have yanked us off the universe's center stage, showing no evidence of us having a central position in the universe. For cosmologists Brian Cox and Andrew Cohen, our scientific discovery of the expanding universe represents "our ascent into insignificance."[52] In my view, our discovery of the cosmic vastness and humanity's non-centrality simultaneously ranks as our greatest intellectual achievement and poses our greatest philosophical challenge — we face the paradox of having discovered an immense and majestic universe, and yet we might be insignificant and our existence might be meaningless.

Here's a status update for humanity: We are indeed the center of nothing, and, as Sartre explained, embracing this nothingness is the starting point for grasping our existential conditions as a species. Nothingness amid the sublime, the infinitesimal connected to the infinite, the freedom to confront the philosophical void — that's the opportunity symbolized by the monolith.

10. WHEN ARE WE GOING TO GROW UP?

If the pre-Copernican cosmic narcissism and ecological destruction continue, it seems certain we can forget the space-faring vision of *Star Trek* because the human species will instead face the scenario presented in *Interstellar*, where we will need to launch a few humans into deep space just to save our species. From space farers to space survivalists, that's the dominant trajectory of our civilization right now. Yet humans are capable of great things and have the ability to alter this trajectory.

The challenge is for us to envision a space philosophy and cosmic cultural narrative that posits our non-centrality as a starting point, the condition that we are the center of nothing and nothingness, the source of all new possibility in the future. We need a narrative that embraces the awe and wonder of the sublime by connecting the infinitesimal (us) to the infinite (cosmos) — made possible by linking our shared origins and destiny to nature and the universe from which we evolved. Perhaps then we can begin transcending our current ideologies and creating a vision for a space-faring civilization that is sane and humane, ecological and technological, optimistic and inspiring, meaningful and beautiful, respectful of other planets and life forms, and grounded in the art and science of the cosmos as best we know it. Any such space philosophy must begin with our "new knowledge" of the universe.

If there is any cosmic justification for our existence as self-aware stardust, as one way the universe knows itself, then we should start acting like wise and knowledgeable beings. As Ann Druyan says, "What is coming of age but realizing that you are not the center of the universe?"[53] Let's think of it another way: In a universe of 2 trillion galaxies, when the hell is the human species going to grow up? That's the question implicit in the specter of the monolith.

CHAPTER 2

SPACE FILMS AND HUMAN DESTINY

Jonathan Nolan: Because *Interstellar* is not about an antagonist. The universe is the antagonist.

Christopher Nolan: Exactly.

Jonathan Nolan: The antagonist is the void of the vacuum that we live in.

Christopher Nolan: Yeah.

1. A PHILOSOPHICAL LAUNCH?

In the wake of Apollo and Hubble, the human species seems trapped in the specter of the monolith. Norman Mailer anticipated these conditions in 1969. In Part I of his epic book about Apollo 11 entitled *Of a Fire on the Moon*, Mailer poses this challenge: "Are we poised for a philosophical launch? There may be no way to do anything less. We will be trying after all to comprehend the astronauts." Part III, the concluding section of Mailer's book, opens with this passage: "There was melancholy to the end of a century . . . a general sense that the century was done — it had ended in the summer of 1969."[1]

In seeking the meaning and significance of Apollo, Mailer's analysis ranged from the minutiae of NASA's technological documents to the personalities of the astronauts to an analysis that featured NASA's "Wasps" and "squares" trumping the hippies and rebels on the planetary stage. Eventually, Mailer was forced to confront the existential and philosophical challenges posed by Apollo:

> It was somehow superior to see the astronauts and the flight of Apollo 11 as the instrument of such celestial or satanic endeavors, than as a species of sublimation for the profoundly unmanageable violence of man, a meaningless journey to a dead arena in order that men could engage in the irrational activity of designing machines which would give birth to more machines which would travel to meaningless places. . . . Heroes or monsters, the Wasps had put their nihilism into the laser and the computer, they were out to savage or save the rest of the world, and were they God's intended?[2]

For Mailer, the race to the moon was a *nihilist endeavor* because it seemed to have no purpose or meaning other than just going because we could. Absent any celestial and cosmic narrative that offers a hopeful and meaningful future, all that's left is satanic, theist, and narcissist narratives to counter Apollo's apparent nihilism. Explicitly and implicitly, Mailer confronted two of the existential questions posed by Apollo — *what does it mean* and *what can we hope for?*

Mailer's thoughts about the "philosophical launch" and the "end of the century" remain profound and prophetic almost fifty years after the melancholic demise of the 20th century in 1969. So far, we've had our *spore launches* via the Apollo and Voyager spacecraft, yet there has been no *philosophical launch* of a new cosmic narrative that gives us meaning and hope in vast universe where we are insignificant. Perhaps we can find meaning and hope in the greatest and most philosophically important space films.

2. THE FINAL FRONTIER

> Space: the final frontier. These are the voyages of the starship *Enterprise*. Its five-year mission: to explore strange new worlds, to seek new life and new civilizations, to boldly go where no man has gone before.

In the famous coda for the original *Star Trek* series, William Shatner's voiceover references President Kennedy's "New Frontier" of Apollo and space exploration, but the visuals say even more. As Shatner says "Space: the final frontier," we see an image of the black vastness of space scattered with stars. The *Enterprise* emerges from a vanishing point in the darkness, accelerating toward us and past us, left to right, then quickly disappearing into another vanishing point. This is the trajectory of humanity in space, an evolutionary path emerging from the voids of the past and disappearing into the voids of the future, in but a few seconds. We are accelerating into the universe that is itself accelerating in all directions.

The design aesthetic central to the space age features curvilinear forms, giving the impression of both *acceleration and elevation*. Speed and uplift are needed for attaining the necessary altitude and escape velocity not only to reach the moon, planets, and rest of the cosmos, but to zoom into the future. That's why the *Enterprise* always looks like it is taking off even when it is stationary. Even the logo on the *Star Trek* crew members' shirts — an arrowhead pointing upward — gives a sense of acceleration and elevation. The *Star Trek* worldview professed that not only would art, science, and technology evolve onward and upward, but so would human consciousness and philosophy via a more enlightened view of humanity and the cosmos. That's why the overall technology, design, and architecture evident throughout the series suggest movement into the future — *faster, forward, upward.*

From the beginning, *Star Trek* launches us into a new cosmology, a new cosmic narrative for the human species, one that some expected to emerge with Apollo. To me, the spirit of that cosmology is expressed in Alexander Courage's confident and hopeful music that accompanies this opening sequence. The imagery and Shatner's voiceover clearly suggest there is no cosmic centrality for humans, though we still have our human reason and desire for exploration. Not only does the cosmic sublime seem less terrifying in the opening sequence — the coda and the music make the cosmic sublime seem open to human possibility.

Yet space still represents the "final frontier" precisely because that's where we confront nihilism and the cosmic sublime. In addition to the original *Star Trek* series and films, five of the greatest space films also directly present and/or confront these issues: *Planet of the Apes* and *2001: A Space Odyssey*, hailing from the 20th century, and *Gravity*, *Interstellar*, and *The Martian*, hailing from the 21st. This is not to say there are no other great space films, only that these are the most philosophically important regarding nihilism and the sublime, plus they have received widespread critical and popular acclaim. For better or for worse, these films have been associated with real-world space narratives and the quest for human meaning and purpose in space.

3. *STAR TREK*

"The future begins"— so claims the tagline for the new *Star Trek*, the 2009 blockbuster that rebooted the film franchise. Though most space films are set in "the future," they are usually commenting on current society and the imagined future as understood during the era in which the films were produced. This is no less true with *Planet of the Apes*, *2001*, *Gravity*, *Interstellar*, *The Martian*, and a host of other space films from the 20th and 21st centuries.

Much has been written about the meaning of the original *Star Trek* TV series and the space-age optimism it represented during the Apollo era — a confident vision of the human world of tomorrow, both culturally and technologically.[3] The series also reflects the highly secular worldview of Gene Roddenberry, an atheist who apparently held religion in low regard.[4] For Roddenberry and many fans, *Star Trek* represents an *enlightened* future, where the ethnically diverse crew of the *Enterprise* serves as an example of humans having put aside centuries of tribal, religious, and nationalist warfare to unite as a secular and democratized civilization on planet Earth. In the original *Star Trek*, humans were recognized as *one species* with common origins and destinies, not the competitive tribes that have dominated human society. Further, technology had eliminated economic scarcity such that equality trumped inequity, while money, greed, and conspicuous consumption were not dominating passions.

In effect, the original *Star Trek* presents a hopeful vision of the future, an idealistic space age where reason and science prevail over ignorance and superstition. *Star Trek* does not present a utopian world of perfected humans, but rather a *utopian worldview* that expresses hope for progress and the transformation of human consciousness. In reviews of the 2009 *Star Trek* film, reviewers Stephanie Zacharek and Manohla Dargis cleverly summarized this worldview. Writing in *Salon*, Zacharek said:

> For kids of the '60s and '70s, "Star Trek" offered a vision of the future that suggested we had something to look forward to, not just in terms of groovy space travel, but in the sense that citizens of the coming centuries would share the same civic values. . . . Initially appearing in 1966, the original "Star Trek" is a utopian fantasy of the first order, a vision of the enlightened future in which whites, blacks, Asians and one poker-faced Vulcan are united by their exploratory mission ("to boldly go"), a prime directive (no intervention) and the occasional dust-up.[5]

Writing in the *New York Times*, Dargis said:

> A bright, shiny blast from a newly imagined past, "Star Trek," the latest spinoff from the influential television show, isn't just a pleasurable rethink of your geek uncle's favorite science fiction series. It's also a testament to television's power as mythmaker, as a source for some of the fundamental stories we tell about ourselves, who we are and where we came from. The famous captain (William Shatner, bless his loony lights) and creator (Gene Roddenberry, rest in peace) may no longer be on board, but the spirit of adventure and embrace of rationality that define the show are in full swing, as are the chicks in minis and kicky boots.[6]

In effect, the original *Star Trek* universe embraces the core ideas of Enlightenment philosophy and intellectual progress, meaning that the evolution of art, science, technology, and human reason *can serve to improve human lives now and into the future.*

Star Trek assumes that not only would art, science, and technology evolve, but so would human consciousness via the development of a more enlightened view of humanity, other life forms, and the cosmos. Such progress is represented by the Prime Directive (which forbids interference in the affairs of other planets) and the stated goal of exploring the universe in a search for cosmic understanding. This vision is expressed in the famed *Star Trek* coda. The coda is an expression of a confident, committed, yet open-minded and rational epistemology that has proven best for gaining new knowledge, for building a better world, and for understanding ourselves and the universe around us. Is this worldview overly optimistic? Sure. But if this worldview does not make a better world and more hopeful future, then whose fault is that?

***STAR TREK* SIMULACRA.** Sadly, the subsequent *Star Trek* series and films have not proven immune to post-Apollo culture (see Chapter 3). While the original series reflected Apollo-era optimism and Roddenberry's secular worldview, the cracks in this contemporary outlook first appeared in *Star Trek: The Motion Picture*. As discussed in Chapter 1, a fictitious Voyager 6 is returned to Earth by V'Ger, a giant cloud-like machine consciousness filled with knowledge yet devoid of meaning for its existence. V'Ger is in search of its "Creator" in whom it hopes to find its origins and destiny. The theological and new age overtones are obvious, especially with the film's use of subtly religious-themed special effects in key scenes. *Star Trek: The Motion Picture* had less in common with NASA's new space shuttle than with America's increased investment in religion and neoconservatism, both of which characterized the Reagan era and have been playing a more considerable role in American society ever since.

In comparison to the *Star Wars* mania of the era, *Star Trek: The Motion Picture* was a not a critical success or commercial blockbuster, thus giving Paramount Studios the clout to diminish the creative control held by Roddenberry. Eventually *Star Trek* morphed into another version of *Star Wars*, with theism inserted to attract more new age and neoconservative ticket buyers. As detailed by authors Michele Barrett and Duncan Barrett in *Star Trek: The Human Frontier*, the original *Star Trek* series focused on space exploration and humanity's existential conditions, themes co-opted by old narratives that extended humanity's religious mania into space. Following *Star Trek: The Motion Picture*, there was the "genesis" concept in *Star Trek II: The Wrath of Khan* (1982), the mystic "Vulcan religion" in *Star Trek III: The Search for Spock* (1984), and a film about "God" in *Star Trek V: The Final Frontier* (1989).[7] In the same era, *Star Trek: The Next Generation* (1987-1994) — the sequel series to the original — generally maintained the scientific humanism.[8] However, the remainder of the *Star Trek* films featuring the crews of Captain Kirk or Captain Picard (Patrick Stewart) were neither great nor philosophically interesting.

Once Roddenberry passed away in 1991, the new television producers were no longer beholden to his secular vision. In fact, they explicitly rejected his hope that "money" and "religion" would not dominate human purpose in the future.[9] Thus, the acceptance and practice of theism and mysticism continued in *Star Trek: Voyager* (1995-2001) and ramped up significantly in *Star Trek: Deep Space Nine* (1993-1999), where reason and science routinely give way to religious faith and superstition.[10] This practice becomes normalized in the latter series and films, such that religious scholars Ross Kraemer, William Cassidy, and Susan Schwartz profess:

> . . . the extrusion of deeply religious themes into *Deep Space Nine* can be partly understood as a reflection of an increasing public discourse regarding religion. . . . After Roddenberry's death in 1991, the producers and writers began to offer richer and more complex representations of religious practices, beliefs, and worldviews, most extensively in the cosmic religious drama that *Deep Space Nine* became.[11]

Religious scholar Anne Mackenzie Pearson concludes:

> Present day North Americans' interest in, if not acceptance of, diverse expressions of spirituality is reflected in the *Star Trek* episodes of the 1990s and it seems that God/god no longer needs to be exposed and dethroned. There is a place for mystery.[12]

As explained in Chapter 3, all of this is nothing more than *cosmic double-think* in the entertainment industry and academia. Additionally, Barrett and Barrett explain that the latter *Star Trek* series embraces many facets of late 20th-century "postmodernism."[13] This is truer than they realize, for the subsequent *Star Trek* films and series have evolved into *Star Trek* simulacra, the copies reigning supreme while the original has largely disappeared.

The insertion of ancient theology into the initial futurism of *Star Trek* cosmology began a decade after Apollo, as *Star Trek: The Motion Picture* roughly coincided with NASA's launch of Voyager (1977) and the space shuttle program (1981-2011). Theological intrusions ramped up after the launch of the Hubble Space Telescope, supposedly reflecting "increasing public discourse about religion," which itself suggests an American public terrified of the discoveries of its cosmic media technologies. As our telescopes extend ever deeper into space, we look backward to superstitions for guidance, showing how the emergence and devolution of *Star Trek* reflects the acceleration-reversal of post-Apollo culture. *Star Trek* gazed into the cosmic sublime with courage, at least for a few years in the 1960s before Voyager and V'Ger's nihilism triggered a journey into mythologies of the past. The more *Star Trek* movies and series we get, the less we see human consciousness transformed.

Given the intellectual devolution of the *Star Trek* narrative, what would extraterrestrials conclude as they'd watch the reruns on their screens? How could they not conclude that humans were prepared to extend their religious warfare into space? Surely, a Klaatu-like extraterrestrial would issue a warning, as dramatized in *The Day the Earth Stood Still* (1951).

STARSHIP NSA. *Star Trek* may provide little in the way of secular narratives for Earthlings who are not Trekkies, but it surely seems to have influenced the National Security Agency (NSA), the top government surveillance force in the United States. In 2013, General Keith Alexander (the former NSA chief) had taxpayers fund a *Star Trek*-style control room for his "Information Dominance Center." According to PBS News Hour:

> It had been designed by a Hollywood set designer to mimic the bridge of the starship Enterprise from Star Trek, complete with chrome panels, computer stations, a huge TV monitor on the forward wall, and doors that made a 'whoosh' sound when they slid open and closed. Lawmakers and other important officials took turns sitting in a leather 'captain's chair' in the center of the room and watched as Alexander, a lover of science-fiction movies, showed off his data tools on the big screen. "Everybody wanted to sit in the chair at least once to pretend he was Jean-Luc Picard," says a retired officer in charge of VIP visits.[14]

The set designers and architects were so proud of their work they produced an informational brochure for the *Star Trek* control room. According to Glen Greenwald:

> The brochure touts how "The prominently positioned chair provides the commanding officer an uninterrupted field of vision to a 22'-0" wide projection screen". . . Its "primary function is to enable 24-hour worldwide visualization, planning, and execution of coordinated information operations for the US Army and other federal agencies." It gushes: "The futuristic, yet distinctly military, setting is further reinforced by the Commander's console, which gives the illusion that one has boarded a star ship."[15]

In effect, the NSA control room is a *Star Trek* set serving as the centerpiece of a planetary panopticon. Some fanboys and Trekkies might think this is all very cool: General Alexander digs Captain Picard, and the NSA represents the Federation of the future. But in reality, this is a sci-fi mask for self-aggrandizing arrogance, far from the original meanings of the "United Federation of Planets" in the *Star Trek* narrative.

So where is the NSA boldly going? What are the strange new worlds and new civilizations? Apparently they include 24/7 surveillance, more drones and waterboards, minimal privacy, and fewer civil liberties. Welcome to another *Star Trek* simulacrum, where the meanings of the original series have been replaced by the empty symbols of *Star Trek*.

TOP GUN FOR TOMORROW. In the new *Star Trek,* director J. J. Abrams partially repackages an optimistic worldview that combines space-age futurism, advanced technologies, and some apparent global pop-culture progress, all symbolized by the *Enterprise* and the space-age skyscrapers of San Francisco. (I say "partially repackages" because it is less than obvious in the film.) Progress and human flourishing seem to be happening on Earth, otherwise you wouldn't have the skyscrapers or Starfleet and the gigantic space station. Global and interplanetary diversity is suggested throughout Starfleet and the *Enterprise* crew. So those are hopeful signs for the future, although nothing is shown about the conditions of the ecosystems on Earth.

Yet in many ways, the new *Star Trek* is little more than a *Top Gun* for tomorrow, with the kick-ass individualists of Starfleet defeating Nero's tribe of identical warriors. Chris Pine's James Kirk is not unlike Tom Cruise's Maverick, the risk-taking pilot in *Top Gun* (1986). Since Kirk and Maverick both lost their "heroic" fathers in military battles, they are forced to cop badass attitudes to prove their manliness and deal with their daddy issues. Since *Top Gun* was a two-hour propaganda film for President Reagan's military and nuclear arms buildup, what is *Star Trek* an advertisement for? Personally, I see it as warrior propaganda promoting the weaponization and militarization of space.

Individualist messages are fine when they are *truly* individualist messages and not mere simulacra of people copping the stance, absent any original thoughts or actions of their own. Plus, any individualist messages must be complemented by other humanist messages and philosophical meanings. But what does it say when the Starfleet security thugs beat a young James Kirk to a pulp because he is flirting with Uhura in a bar near a Starfleet base? Given the number of brutal blows Kirk suffers to the face and head in this scene, he would surely have several facial fractures and a severe concussion. Yeah, I get it: they're showing that Kirk is a tough guy, a player who can hit the bars and hit on brainy babes. Yet isn't it also a clear example of police brutality passing as space-faring entertainment for contemporary society, which accepts such brutality as a normal, everyday event? Later in the film, these same security thugs are seen onboard the *Enterprise,* so, technically speaking, police brutality exists and is rewarded in the new *Star Trek* future.

How can this represent social progress? If police brutality exists, then what other injustices might exist? The new *Star Trek* is loaded with fisticuffs, where even Spock must prove his toughness with his fists and his near-death choke hold on Kirk. Humans may be space farers, but impulsive violence as a quick solution seems to remain, a sure sign that the cultural attitudes of the new *Star Trek* are far less developed than Roddenberry had hoped for. In this regard, the overall worldview of the new *Star Trek* seems to have regressed.

The science and intellectual skills evident in *Star Trek* serve only militarized purposes or are sexually trivialized, such as the notion that Uhura's expertise as an interplanetary xenolinguist has sexual implications. Why can't the space future be sexy without fanboy sexism? The casting of Captain Kirk (Chris Pine), Mr. Spock (Zachary Quinto), and Uhura (Zoe Saldana) is darn good. If all that sexiness is part of the future of space travel, then I'm betting we can count many people in, not just the Trekkies.

THE TERROR OF THE COSMIC SUBLIME. When the new *Enterprise* crew actually ventures to the stars, it crashes into the cosmic sublime. Every time we see amazing cosmic phenomena or vast planetary scenery in the film, something evil or apocalyptic immediately follows. Nero and his massive medieval ship emerge from the black hole, the ship bearing a design style that suggests ISIS will pilot spacecraft in the future. After all, Nero and his warriors use stolen "red matter" to create a black hole to destroy the entire planet of Vulcan, which is home to an intellectually advanced species that practices reason, logic, and science. When Vulcan begins imploding, giant stone statues collapse, not unlike the destruction of ancient art and architecture by ISIS and other related terrorist groups. The spectacular natural scenery on Vulcan is violently extinguished as well. Later, we learn that in the future, a supernova destroyed Nero's planet, an event Spock tried and failed to prevent. Nero holds the grudge and travels back in time (via the black hole) to make the young Spock see the destruction of Vulcan as a payback. Nero even captures and tortures Admiral Pike. Obviously the film is an "origin story" for *Star Trek*, and it seems to say that the war with medievalism will continue.

All in all, the cosmos as portrayed by the new *Star Trek* seems fairly horrifying and meaningless for human existence. Two planets are completely annihilated, causing the deaths of billions of Vulcans and Romulans. Although *Star Trek* celebrates technological marvels via the *Enterprise*, the film has little to say about the cosmic sublime or human existence in space other than presenting the crew as hipster warrior-peacekeepers who thrive in what seems like a highly regimented Starfleet bureaucracy. No meaning is presented for the existence of Starfleet other than as a "peacekeeping and humanitarian armada," which is seemingly necessary, as the interplanetary bloodbaths continue. There are no philosophical questions or challenges, only another time-travel dilemma, which has become the most tiresome and overused plot trick in space films since *Planet of the Apes*. Sure it's fun to think about time travel. But big deal if our destination is still war, sexism, fisticuffs, police brutality, and planetary destruction.

***STAR TREK*: WHAT CAN WE HOPE FOR?** Though the famed *Star Trek* coda is tacked on at the end, its claims are inaccurate, as there has been no real exploration, there are no new civilizations, and there are no new worlds. There are only worlds destroyed. There is nothing new, not one new idea, which is why the new *Star Trek* is more or less another *Star Wars*. Despite the film's partial critique of post-9/11 terror and torture, not much changes in *Star Trek Into Darkness* (2012) — it's just another example of post-Apollo culture.

Directed by Justin Lin, *Star Trek Beyond* (2016) begins with Captain Kirk questioning the purpose of his existence in an "endless universe." The film suggests that the purpose of human existence in space is to send out sexy Earthlings to wear cool uniforms on giant space stations, battle pissed-off reptile people, and fight for the cosmic human right to party and get it on in space. Apparently, the Beastie Boys were supposed to be artist-prophets from a previous millennium, and their music plays a key role in the film. As with *Star Trek* and *Star Trek Into Darkness*, *Star Trek Beyond* shows very little scientific or intellectual discovery, provides no explanation of what the thousands of humans are doing on the space station, and present no meaning for humans in space, other than to battle off the evil entities of the universe and look good while doing it. Maybe that's all there is to human existence: looking good and getting it on in the never-ending Darwinian struggle to survive.

4. *PLANET OF THE APES*

Planet of the Apes and *2001: A Space Odyssey* perfectly illustrate the simultaneous cultural acceleration and reversal amidst the cosmic sublime. But the simultaneity is even more dramatic in terms of film release dates. Though *Planet of the Apes* was released in New York City on February 2, 1968 and *2001* was released in Washington, DC, on April 2, both were released nationwide on the very same day, April 3. The most important space film of all time, one that truly accelerated humans into the future, is instantly countered by the second most important space film of the 20th century, which sent humans into the greatest reversal in film history.

2001 begins with a tribe of apes and ends with humans in outer space, while *Planet of the Apes* begins with humans in outer space and ends with a tribe of apes. Confronting the cosmic sublime with evolution and devolution, respectively, both films end with a single astronaut in a strange place facing an even stranger destiny. In the context of the human species in space, both films can be mapped across several trajectories (see Tables 2 and 3).

SPACE AGE TO STONE AGE. Famed for its clever depiction of apes ruling humans, *Planet of the Apes* offers insights into the existential conditions of seeking meaning and destiny in a vast universe of which we are not the center. Directed by Franklin Shaffner and coauthored by Michael Wilson and Rod Serling, *Planet of the Apes* portrays the story of an astronaut propelled centuries into the future only to discover a post-apocalyptic world in which atomic warfare leads to civilizational destruction and human devolution. The astronaut is hurtled into the technological future and discovers that humans have reverted to the barbarian past — the human species went from the space age to the Stone Age.

THE EMPTINESS OF THE COSMIC SUBLIME. Like the original *Star Trek*, *Planet of the Apes* opens with images of starry skies amid expanses of darkness. Yet these stars are strangely different from typical twinkling stars. With some stars moving, expanding, bending, twisting, and glowing with prism-like colors, these skies suggest the warping of space-time or the spectroscopy used to estimate the movement and distance of stars in the expanding universe. The star scenes are accompanied by Jerry Goldsmith's haunting discordant score, which is perhaps the greatest soundtrack of any science-fiction film.

As the stars move across the screen, the captain of the mission, George Taylor (Charlton Heston), opens the film with the following words: "And that completes my final report until we reach touchdown. We're now on full automatic, in the hands of the computers." Taylor and crew are on *autopilot into the future*.

The remainder of the monologue is accompanied by cuts between two sets of images — Taylor seated at the control panels inside the spacecraft and his view of the warping stars outside the window. His monologue continues:

> I've tucked my crew in for the long sleep, and I will be joining them soon. In less than an hour we'll finish our sixth month out of Cape Kennedy. Six months in deep space — by our time, that is.

The onboard clocks show the following. SHIP TIME: 7 / 14 / 1972. EARTH TIME: 3 / 23 / 2673. Taylor continues:

> According to Dr. Hesslein's theory of time in a vehicle traveling nearly the speed of light, the Earth has aged nearly 700 years since we left it, while we've aged hardly at all. Maybe so. This much is probably true; the men who sent us on this journey are long since dead and gone. You who are reading me now are a different breed. I hope a better one. I leave the 20th century with no regrets. But one more thing (if anybody is listening that is): nothing scientific, it's purely personal. Seen from out here, everything seems different.

At this point, Taylor leans forward toward the window as he pensively gazes out at the warping stars and philosophizes about humanity and individuality:

> Time bends, space is boundless. It squashes a man's ego. I feel lonely.

This expression of the sublime, nihilism, and insignificance is followed by a long pause, and then Taylor completes the monologue:

> That's about it. Tell me though: does man — that marvel of the universe, that glorious paradox who sent me to the stars — still make war against his brothers, keep his neighbor's children starving?

As Taylor talks, he stares through the windshield of the spaceship; the sky is black and nearly devoid of stars. Perhaps Taylor's journey anticipates the future of the cosmos, with the galaxies all moving apart such that skies are dark from any perspective outside one's own galaxy. Or maybe the empty sky suggests a future devoid of meaning. What meaning can humanity's inhumanity have in this future?

Taylor then injects himself with a sleeping potion, seals himself in the vacuum-tight hibernation chamber, and enters deep sleep. Throughout the opening credits, various stars pass by, appearing even more bent and warped by a spacecraft traveling near the speed of light. The final star covers almost the entire screen, followed by smoke, cloud-like vapors, and the sound of a massive explosion, symbolizing an atomic bomb or the big bang. Like much of our contemporary society, the astronauts and humans are *asleep at the wheel — accelerating forward and devolving backward*. In this opening scene, the sublime represents more terror than awe. We are in awe of the scale of time travel, yet the stars and the mood of the accompanying music suggest serious trouble awaits in our journey into deep space.

The spacecraft makes a dizzying descent toward the planet below, eventually crash-landing in a lake in the desert. (This scene was filmed amid the alien planet-like landscapes of Lake Powell, Utah.) Like Plato's Atlantis, the spacecraft meets its destiny, disappearing beneath the waters, a metaphor for the fate of the modern world, seemingly destined to disappear in the atomic apocalypse of the Cold War. Before climbing out of the spacecraft, Taylor checks the clocks and sees that they are now 2,000 years in the future: EARTH TIME: 11 / 23 / 3978.

A SCIENTIST, A PATRIOT, AND AN EXISTENTIALIST. The three surviving astronauts represent three separate archetypes. There is Dodge (Jeff Burton), the *scientist* who seeks to discover truth about the physical world. There is Landon (Robert Gunner), the *patriot* who seeks to be a hero for his nation back on Earth. Finally, there is Taylor, the *existentialist* who seeks philosophical meaning amid the cosmos. Wandering amid the desert, the three astronauts are also metaphors for passengers on Spaceship Earth, which is hurtling through the cosmic expanses of the starry skies, with humans as the species burdened with the task of making meaning in an indifferent universe. Patriotism and nationalism are meaningless in this universe, only providing encouragement to those warriors unwilling or unable to acknowledge humanity's actual existential conditions. As Landon plants a tiny American flag on the planet's surface, Taylor bursts out laughing at the absurd gesture.

The very next scene shows the three astronauts as tiny figures along a distant desert horizon, trudging toward the vanishing points in space and time. This is followed by numerous images of the astronauts trudging along the desert landscapes, often dwarfed by the vastness and seeming emptiness. The desert is what it is, completely full in its existence. We humans are the ones who supply the sense of emptiness. Having hiked numerous desert trails in the American Southwest myself, it's clear to me that the desert — rather than being empty and desolate — is full of cosmic meaning and thus reveals our true existential conditions. Like the three astronauts, humans are a single species inhabiting a thin web of life on a rocky and watery planet that orbits a flaming ball of hydrogen in a vast universe.

COSMIC NIHILISM. Though astronauts and cosmonauts were celebrated as heroes and symbols of human achievement in the 1960s, the astronauts in *Planet of the Apes* are entering the vanishing points of the space age. Outside the machine of the spaceship — the realm of technological control and power — the astronauts are without a purpose, without a clear mission other than to survive, discover any life on the planet, and seek meaning in the universe. These conditions and challenges are chiefly illustrated in several dialogues between Taylor and Landon. Shortly after washing ashore from the lake where they crash-land, the dialogue begins:

> **Taylor.** You've gone gray. Apart from that, you look pretty chipper for a man who is 2,031 years old. I read the clocks. They bear our Hesslein's hypothesis. We've been away from Earth for 2,000 years, give or take a decade. Still can't accept it? Time's wiped out everything you ever knew. It's all dust.
>
> **Landon.** Prove it. If we can't get back, it's still just a theory.
>
> **Taylor.** It's a fact, Landon. Buy it. You'll sleep better.

Fearing possible nihilism and meaninglessness, Landon remains in denial, even though the science and technology have propelled him into space somewhere.

Later, as the astronauts walk amid the sprawling desert, Landon thinks they will have a better chance for survival if they know their location on the planet:

LANDON. If we could just get a fix.

TAYLOR. What would that tell you? I've told you where you are and when you are.

LANDON. All right, all right.

TAYLOR. You're 300 light years from your precious planet. Your loved ones are dead and forgotten for twenty centuries. Twenty centuries! . . . There is just one reality left. We are here and it is now. You get a hold of that and hang on to it, or you might as well be dead.

LANDON. I'm prepared to die.

TAYLOR. He's prepared to die. Doesn't that make you misty! Chalk up another victory for the human spirit!

Taylor laughs loudly as he says these words, ridiculing the naïve and warrior-like virtues too often enshrined as heroic by humans in their quest for purpose and meaning in life. Landon thinks he has to die for his country so his existence will have meaning. Taylor calls him out on his blind patriotism and nationalism. The dialogue continues as the astronauts hike amid sand dunes:

LANDON. You're no seeker. You're negative.

TAYLOR. And I'm not prepared to die.

LANDON. I'd like to know why not. You thought life on Earth was meaningless. You despise people. So what'd you do? You ran out.

TAYLOR. No, no, it's not like that Landon. I'm a seeker too. But my dreams aren't like yours. I can't help thinking somewhere in the universe there has to be something better than man. Has to be.

For Taylor, "life is meaningless" in the sense of life as a patriot or serving a nationalistic destiny, yet life can have meaning and purpose for the seeker in search of something better in the cosmos. Tragically, Taylor is going to discover that "something better than man" is what man evolved from — apes.

HUMAN DEVOLUTION. Eventually, Dodge discovers plant life: a solitary weed. The astronauts soon find other weeds and grasslands that lead them to a waterfall cascading into a pond surrounded by numerous trees and plants — a veritable Garden of Eden. However, this garden is also a jungle. Populating this jungle is an old (but new) species of humans, a tribe of hunter-gatherers, now mute and largely ignorant, apparently not having recently bitten into the apple from the Tree of Knowledge. This old species of future humans is ruled by apes, suggesting a cultural and intellectual devolution, sort of like Darwinism in reverse. How can this not be a metaphor for a contemporary species that's dedicated to waging war while keeping its collective head in the sand with regard to its place in the cosmos?

Like today's creationists and fundamentalists, the ruling apes have their own antiscientific mythologies of origins and destiny in which the scientific future must conform to the superstitious past. In a stroke of Hollywood genius, the buildings in the ape village reflect the curvilinear style of space-age architecture.

Rather than steel, glass, and poured concrete, the ape village is made of stone and resembles cave-like dwellings. (Given the existentialist and apocalyptic themes in *The Twilight Zone* series [1959-1964], it is not surprising that Rod Serling had a major hand in shaping the overall aesthetic and existential vision of *Planet of the Apes*.[16])

By the end of the film, Taylor and his mate, Nova (Linda Hamilton), are freed by the apes. Wearing only caveman-like clothes, Taylor and Nova will try to survive and perhaps breed, becoming the next Adam and Eve. More importantly, Dr. Zaius (Maurice Evans), the head scientist and evolution denier, ominously declares that Taylor will discover his "destiny." Taylor soon learns the fate of humanity on an ocean shoreline, coming across something that is utterly horrifying. After Taylor and Nova dismount their horse, Taylor falls to his knees in the waves crashing on the shore. Looking up at a scorched Statue of Liberty half-buried in the sand, Taylor stutters and then shouts:

> Oh my God. I'm back. I'm home. All the time. You finally really did it. You maniacs! You blew it up! Damn you! Goddamn you all to hell!

In this famed final scene of the film, Taylor learns humans had unleashed an atomic apocalypse. It then becomes clear where the astronauts are and when they are. Where they were? On Earth. When they were? In the future that is the past. "Ground Zero" happened, blasting humans back to the Stone Age.

"SOMETHING BETTER THAN MAN." In his journey into the vast universe, Taylor is inspired by the belief that there has to be a species superior to humans. This quest echoes Friedrich Nietzsche's yearning for the "Ubermensch" to supercede humankind on Earth. In *Thus Spoke Zarathustra*, Nietzsche explores the death of God, the eternal recurrence (the endless recycling of world events), and the possible rise of the Ubermensch (the "Overman" or "Superman"). While I am referencing Nietzsche, this does not mean I agree with him on everything or anything; here I am only interested in his concept of the Ubermensch because it poses a great philosophical question that is implicit in *Planet of the Apes, 2001*, and *Interstellar*, among other space films.

Since humans are the superior species that evolved from apes, Nietzsche theorized that something better might evolve from humans, especially in a modern world where God is dead, having been slayed by Copernicus, Darwin, and industrialization. As discussed in the Introduction, Nietzsche believed that new being might be the Ubermensch or Superman, a far superior version of the human species:

> What is the ape to man? A laughing-stock, a thing of shame. And just the same shall man be to the Superman: a laughing-stock, a thing of shame.[17]

Nietzsche suggested the next stage of human evolution could occur if we accepted our place on Earth — in the material world — rather than looking to otherworldly Gods for meaning and purpose. If space exploration represents the next phase of human evolution and destiny, then what might evolve or emerge from humanity on its quest? What might we become, at least philosophically and symbolically? *Planet of the Apes* offers one scenario, while *2001* and *Interstellar* offer other possibilities.

Though there has been much debate about what forms the Ubermensch might take, it need not be a master race, dominating conquerors, or mere cartoon superheroes inspired by Nietzsche's concept (Superman, Batman, etc.). In my view, the highly evolved Ubermensch could simply be a *much more intellectually advanced human species* that embraces its place on Earth and in the cosmos and develops an advanced space philosophy for the human species. In effect, the human species has produced a *technological Ubermensch* — the massively evolved techno-civilization far beyond anything conceivable at the time Nietzsche was writing. This new form of technological civilization is best seen in space exploration and the great triumphs of Apollo, Voyager, and the Hubble and Kepler telescopes (among many others). Yet humanity has nowhere near produced a *philosophical Ubermensch* — an intellectually advanced and enlightened species that might represent the next stage in human evolution in terms of the art, philosophy, science, and cultural values needed for a united planetary civilization. That's why we are nowhere near the original *Star Trek*. We are missing the cultural philosophy to complement the science and the mind-bending technological discoveries.

In the same passage as his quote above, Nietzsche also provided a subtle warning that prefigures the ending of *Planet of the Apes*: "Once were ye apes, and even yet man is more of an ape than any of the apes."[18] Shortly before Taylor discovers the annihilation of civilization, Cornelius (the chimpanzee archaeologist) reads aloud from an ancient scroll with a similar warning about humankind: "Beware the beast man. . . . Alone among God's primates, he kills for sport, for lust, for greed. Yea, he will murder his brother to possess his brother's land. Let him not breed in great numbers, for he will make a desert of his home and yours. Shun him, drive him back into his jungle lair, for he is the harbinger of death."

Though the product of a now-dead civilization, Taylor and the fellow astronauts are technological Ubermensches — Superman space farers traversing vast stretches of space and time into the future. Near the peak of Apollo culture, astronauts were presented as the next stage of evolution in space exploration. Yet at the height of the Cold War, the astronauts left behind a civilization armed with thousands of nuclear weapons that could destroy global society in a single day. In the film, the ape and beast within humanity prevail and destroy civilization, leaving the apes to reign over the planet (perhaps an example of Nietzsche's eternal recurrence). Alone with Nova to discover his destiny, Taylor is a variation of "the last man" on Earth.[19] Taylor is the terminal human who exists at the moment when either: 1) humanity destroys itself or dies off, leaving the apes with a new reign on Earth; or 2) humanity enters a higher stage, the stage that Nietzsche hoped might herald the Ubermensch.

Since Taylor is the existentialist for whom God is dead, it is not surprising that he is seeking something in the universe "better than man." So far, that species has yet to appear on Earth or in our part of the cosmos. Given the vastness of the universe, I think that species is out there — or, in the words of Taylor: "has to be."

***PLANET OF THE APES*: WHAT CAN WE HOPE FOR?** *Planet of the Apes* offers the hope of major scientific and technological breakthroughs in space travel, such that the human species may be able to traverse massive distances across the universe. The film suggests we will be able to time travel into the future, like "superman" space farers. However, we may not like what we learn about our destiny. It's here that *Planet of the Apes* offers three warnings:

> 1) Our sciences and technologies are on autopilot, accelerating us across the universe while many of our ideologies are in reverse. Antiscientific ideologies and pre-Copernican mythologies (theism, creationism, etc.) pose a direct threat to progress and an enlightened human civilization in the future.
>
> 2) Tribal and territorial warfare will be our eventual undoing, with nuclear weapons destroying civilization and leaving the remaining society for the creationists who will return humans to the Stone Age. Landon is not a hero — he is a deluded madman. He just doesn't know it. The Dodges and the Taylors had better learn to reign in the patriots, warriors, and pre-Copernicans, or it will mean the demise of humanity.
>
> 3) Given that tribal warfare and theism (in all its forms) persist in the 21st century, the film has one direct and obvious meaning: Spaceship Earth is still home to the "planet of the apes" — the same beasts who spent $20 trillion waging war since 2001 and still have 22,000 nuclear weapons (see Chapter 4).

As for the cosmic sublime, it remains empty and meaningless. After Taylor's monologue, the journey moves from the quest for meaning to the discovery of the destruction of human civilization. In the future, the humans struggle to merely survive and exist — it is the only meaning they have.

5. *2001: A SPACE ODYSSEY*

Directed by Stanley Kubrick and coauthored with Arthur C. Clarke, *2001* was one of the largest cinematic blockbusters of the 1960s and early 1970s. It is probably hard for contemporary readers to grasp that the year 2000 once stood for "the future," a world of tomorrow filled with optimism for art, science, technology, planetary ecology, social equality, and universal progress. With the 2 replacing the 1, followed by three 0s, the future beyond 2000 just had to be better, wiser, cooler, and overall more awesome. This hope for a better future after 2000 is why Kubrick and Clarke set their space-age odyssey in 2001 — a future for the human species that has hardly been realized. By "space-age" future, I am not referring to jetpacks, hover boards, and flying cars, which are little more than techno-fetishes for those boys and girls who want to get "back to the future" somewhere in Tomorrowland. Of course, we have the Hubble Space Telescope and the International Space Station, but they have had zero impact on human narratives down on Earth. By space-age future, I mean a space-faring species peacefully exploring the universe, perhaps visiting space hotels and space stations orbiting Mars and the moon, representing an enlightened and cosmic civilization.

2001 depicts a past and future in which humans have evolved from apes to astronauts through art, science, and technology, along with an assist from a mysterious black monolith. Importantly, *2001* taps into the awe and wonder of the cosmos along with the marvels of science and technology. At the same moment in human history, Kubrick and NASA directed space odysseys that expressed the highest trajectories of the space age, when humanity first ventured into the vast universe beyond planet Earth — yet neither Kubrick nor NASA provided *the philosophical meaning* for these discoveries and achievements. Kubrick wanted *2001* to *show* a human space narrative but not explain it or detail it. He believed too much language would reduce the universality of the narrative in the film. Thus, it is not surprising scores of books and essays have explored and interpreted the meaning of *2001*.[20] The goal here is not to challenge any particular interpretation of *2001* but rather to present possible existential meanings by concentrating on how *2001* confronts issues involving our cosmic centrality and the cosmic sublime.

Kubrick organized *2001* into three parts — "The Dawn of Man," "Jupiter Mission: 18 Months Later," and "Jupiter and Beyond the Infinite." "The Dawn of Man" deals with our prehistory up to the year 2001, while "Jupiter Mission" is set entirely in 2001. "Beyond the Infinite" seems to accelerate us across space and time, only to arrive at the year 2001 and a space-faring species seeking its meaning and destiny.

STONE AGE TO SPACE AGE ("THE DAWN OF MAN"). Part 1 begins in the emptiness of a vast desert landscape, perhaps symbolizing the African savannas, where humans first evolved. Kubrick taps into the natural sublime with numerous shots of immense vistas and landscapes that dwarf the apes and other species. Technology does not yet exist, so the slate is clean and the possibilities are open-ended.

Amid the technological nothingness, a tall black monolith appears in the middle of the night. Tribes of apes gaze upon the monolith, at first in terror and then seemingly with wonder and reverence. After shrieking wildly for a few moments, the apes gather around the monolith, touching it gingerly and eventually caressing it with affection. Later, we see an ape digging amidst a pile of bones. The ape pauses momentarily, and then we see a quick flashback to the monolith against the sun, followed by the ape figuring out that a bone can be used as a tool. Soon the bone is used to kill for food and even kill a rival ape, anticipating the paradoxical human use of technology: as tool and weapon. As for the ape inventor, it was *thinking of the monolith* when it made its discovery.

In the greatest jump cut in cinematic history, the ape hurls the bone high in the air, and just after the bone peaks in its ascent, the scene cuts to a spacecraft orbiting Earth against the black void of space. The cut from the bone to the spacecraft brilliantly captures in a single moment and in a single thought the entire trajectory of human technological evolution, from the Stone Age to the space age.

FROM SIMIANS TO SPACE VOYAGERS. After the jump cut we see four different spacecraft, whose function or purpose is never explained as they orbit the Earth. The fifth craft we see is the gigantic circular space station, spinning on its axis to generate gravity inside the structure. In a scene accompanied by Johan Strauss's *Blue Danube*, a space plane is shown arriving and docking at the space station, giving the impression of a technological ballet in space. The overall feel is that we are witnessing the natural and inevitable trajectory of modernity and human civilization — *faster, forward, upward.* *2001*'s space technologies stimulate the technological sublime, at once generating awe and wonder while displaying the vision of an artistic, rational, competent, and curious human species. The computers and space pilots have everything under control; the pilots just push a few buttons to dock the spacecraft at the space station or on the moon base. To paraphrase Taylor in *Planet of Apes*, everything seems under control, and we're on full automatic — *on autopilot into the future.*

The sleek space plane is far more beautiful and elegant than the recently retired NASA space shuttles. The only aerial technology to approach the elegance of the *2001* space plane is the *Concorde* jetliner, with its classic space-age design. Produced by France's Aerospatiale and the British Aircraft Corporation, the *Concorde* first flew in 1969 (the year of Apollo 11) and then regularly from 1976 to 2003, after which it was retired due to the aviation downturn following the September 11 terrorist attacks and the decision by Airbus to discontinue maintenance support.

The interior of *2001*'s space plane consists of computers, electronic screens, windows for stargazing, leather-clad seating and detailing, and an overall minimalist elegance, with little to no ornamentation. The minimalism is also evident in the wardrobes of the pilots and flight attendants created by British designer Hardy Amies. The flight-attendant uniforms reflect some of the "moon girl" fashions of French designer Andre Courreges, who was famous for merging the space age with Paris runways in the mid-1960s. I can only speak for myself, but it would be damn cool to fly in that space plane. It beats the heck out of anything flying in 2017, with the sheer banality of the airplane interiors, not to mention the uniforms of the pilots and flight attendants.

The space station is a timeless merger of modernism, minimalism, and space-age sensibilities, though the all-white interiors and floors seem highly impractical. It's likely the white interior architecture is meant to convey a purity of vision for the future and human enlightenment, symbolized by the ambient glowing light inside the space station, which contrasts with the starry dark void outside the windows. Space-age furniture is present throughout the space station, including Herman Miller's "Action Office" desks (1964), Eero Saarinen's pedestal tables (1956), and Olivier Mourgue's red "Djinn chairs" (1965).[21] Inside the space station, there is a phone booth where passengers can make videophone calls to Earth, an idea borrowed from the AT&T "Picturephone" from the 1964 New York World's Fair. (Of course, videophone calls are now commonplace with Skype and FaceTime.)

In summary, the spectacular scenes of the space plane, space station, and moon base make *2001* one of the best advertisements ever produced for space tourism. Imagine seeing Earth from the space as shown in *2001*:

- Leaving Earth behind while aboard the space plane on the way to the space station

- Viewing Earth from the space station as it orbits our planet
- Viewing Earth from the lunar hotel and the moon base

How great would that be? Every day would feature an *Earthrise*. We would experience the awe and wonder of the entire scene, seeing our planet floating amid the blackness dotted with radiant stars. This would permit us to revel in our cosmic non-centrality, experiencing exaltation at the majesty before our eyes.

Kubrick's vision also permits us to fly over the lunar surfaces and even walk among the craters near the Clavius moon base. The Apollo 8 astronauts saw a terrifying desolation and turned to the Bible, but future humans might see the moon as a celestial work of art, an aesthetic object produced by the laws of the universe, the forces of gravity and energy, and eons of time. Seeing Earth from space in such settings — how could that not inspire us and force us to see our planet as home to the human species, a *single species* living among millions of other species on a rock orbiting a star? To know that we are the simians who became space voyagers is an affirmation of the power of our reason and existence — that is, as long as we do not trample asunder the moon's landscapes and strip-mine its resources for our consumption.

WHAT OF PAN AMERICAN, HILTON HOTEL, AND HOWARD JOHNSON'S? Though the space plane and space station remain design classics, Kubrick did seem to miss out on the Pan American space airline, along with Howard Johnson's restaurant and the Hilton Hotel inside the space station. But it's less Kubrick's fault than the result of radically changing economic conditions since the 1960s. Once the most glamorous airline in the world, Pan American went bankrupt in 1991 after a series of unwise business decisions and a spike in jet fuel prices caused by the Persian Gulf War (a mere prelude to September 11 and the Terror War). Howard Johnson's was a successful chain of 1,000 restaurants that were mostly found along America's post-WWII highways, but by 2015, the chain was down to only 2 restaurants.[22]

Hilton Hotels used to be a symbol of modern tourist cosmopolitanism, but now they're just another one of the banal corporate hotels that blight the highways and skylines of the world. Kubrick's inclusion of the Hilton Hotel reflected a moment in the popular zeitgeist of the 1960s. According to the BBC, Barron Hilton (son of Conrad Hilton, the founder of Hilton Hotels) launched a promotional effort to imagine a Lunar Hilton on the moon:

> Barron, who was then president of Hilton, told the *Wall Street Journal* that he was planning to cut the ribbon at an opening ceremony for a Lunar Hilton hotel within his lifetime. He described the Lunar Hilton as a 100-room hotel that would be built below the surface. Guests would gather around a piano bar in an observation dome that allowed them to gaze back at earth.
>
> Barron's desire to build a Hilton on the Moon — whether it was merely clever PR or something more sincere — struck a chord with people all over the world. The hotel group even printed promotional "reservations cards" for customers to reserve a hotel room on the

> Moon. . . . [P]eople really wanted to know that sometime in [their] lifetime we'll have hotels on the Moon.[23]

The space-age dreams of civilians going to the moon were not limited to a hotel chain or *The Jetsons*. During Apollo 11's journey to the moon, Pan American actually took reservations for flights to the moon, which was reported by ABC News during its coverage of the Apollo 11 moonwalk on July 20, 1969. News anchor Frank Reynolds reported that over 17,000 people made reservations. There were several people interviewed about why they would want to go to the moon, including a young boy and young girl around the age of 11 or 12 and not identified by name in the broadcast. In the interview, the boy calmly says he expects to see "craters" on the moon. The young girl — attired in a shiny silver space-age dress and hat perfect for *2001*'s moon base — cheerfully and prophetically states, "If I ever go to the moon, I think it would be very fun. I just hope to go very, very soon and I hope I'm not really that old."

Sadly, that cheerful little girl never got her wish. So what do we make of this vision of civilians and optimistic children hoping to visit the moon in sleek space planes?

Did Kubrick present an impossibly idealistic scenario? Were Hilton and Pan Am merely cynical exploiters of the transient enthusiasm generated by the Apollo program? Does the fact that we have no journeys to the moon in the 21st century reveal the laughable folly of youthful space-age delusions? Or are the lack of moon journeys and sleek space stations an indictment of our current society? (You know — the world run by the adults, the allegedly serious and mature folks with their fixation on endless consumption, nationalism, and tribal and religious warfare . . . In my view, it's the adults running this madhouse who are fucked up and delusional, not Kubrick's vision or the kids who want to visit the moon in shiny clothes!)

DISCOVERY ONE ("JUPITER MISSION: 18 MONTHS LATER"). Part 2 presents a decidedly less optimistic view of our technological evolution. *2001* is still tapping into the technological sublime but also stressing the terror of unchecked technological power. *Discovery One* is a colossal spacecraft, resembling a linear molecule built on a massive scale. Soaring through the solar system, the spacecraft contains a labyrinth of circular interiors, almost all white and always illuminated, representing a fully mediated environment. In *Discovery One*, we see a metaphor for the cradle-to-grave womb of technological existence.

As in *Planet of the Apes*, *Discovery One* is seemingly on autopilot, with everything under the control of computers. The astronauts have little to do but conduct routine maintenance checks, glance at some computer screens now and again, play chess, draw portraits, exercise, and do the occasional television interview. *Discovery One* features the most influential vision of a computer in human history, precisely because it is the conceptual prototype for the 24/7 computer, surveillance, and artificial intelligence networks toward which our global media environments are rapidly evolving. Of course, that computer is the famed HAL 9000, the computer that controls the spacecraft and oversees the humans. Also known as "HAL," the computer mimics, copies, or simulates human intelligence and seems to have a certain agency and self-awareness.

Though humans have made the leap from apes via technology, Kubrick and Clarke suggest we have given birth to another sentient species, a technological and sentient being that may endanger us.

In *2001*, the astronauts aren't depicted as brave test pilots with "the right stuff" the way Armstrong and Aldrin were; they are more like brainy scientists with "the right PhDs" whose main function is to take care of the spacecraft — under HAL's supervision — until it arrives at its destination for the mission. Thus, the technological utopia has its flip side — the digital dystopia, where the circular spacecraft illustrates panoptic surveillance, with HAL starring as the digital Big Brother, albeit with feelings, chess-playing skills, and artistic sensibilities. *2001* provides a clear warning about submitting to total surveillance and technological control, dramatized when HAL makes a mistake and then tries to cover it up by murdering several astronauts.

THE COSMIC SUBLIME ("JUPITER AND BEYOND THE INFINITE"). Part 3 begins with astronaut Dave Bowman (Keir Dullea) journeying into the cosmic sublime. (Perhaps the surname "Bow-man" is suggestive of the human arrow shot into the universe?) After exiting the *Discovery One* in the space pod, Bowman zooms right toward us, seemingly headed toward a black monolith floating beyond Jupiter. As viewers, we see much of this journey from Bowman's visual perspective.

Known as the Star-Gate sequence, this ten-minute scene features an array of cosmic and technological patterns along with massive acceleration. The sequence is accompanied by music from avant-garde composer Gyorgy Ligeti, including his *Requiem* (1965) — its mysterious and otherworldly sounds rising toward an uncertain crescendo — and *Atmospheres* (1961), which features monotonal ambience and sound textures. Via the visuals and music, Kubrick and his team have constructed an artificial infinity, a stand-in symbolizing the sheer immensity of *space* and *time* — the infinities that dwarf our senses but thrill our reason, all in the experience of the sublime.[24] Designed by special-effects titan Douglas Trumball, the journey begins against the blackness of deep space. Soon dots and lines of multicolored light slowly approach us, emerging from both sides of a vertical horizon in space, suggesting — at least to me — design by an intelligent species somewhere in the universe. Splitting the movie screen symmetrically, the dots and lines of lights increase in frequency and intensity, clearly resembling the grids and patterns of computer circuitry as well as electronic waves and spirals and various other forms. Is Bowman traversing outer space, cyberspace, or both?

The colors and patterns are spectacular as this cosmic imagery accelerates. For a moment, Bowman's face conveys surprise as his helmet begins shaking wildly. He squints and then shuts his eyes, unable to handle what he is seeing. The lights are shown reflecting off Bowman's space helmet visor, at one point covering his eyes with bright white light. This is followed by several close-ups of Bowman's face, distorted, mouth agape, suggesting that he is experiencing sheer terror. Bowman's journey passes through numerous psychedelic light patterns and then through a series of cosmic forms suggesting galaxies, stars, supernovae, star clusters, and the warping of space and time, along with bio-cosmic images suggesting sperm, emergence, evolution, energy, and life. We then zoom rapidly over various desert and mountain terrains, filmed in a multicolored X-ray style. Amazingly, we zoom over Monument Valley and the same desert landscapes where Taylor crashed in *Planet of the Apes*.

Given the sperm imagery and other bio-cosmic forms, Bowman seems to represent yet another version of Loren Eiseley's space spores — fired into the cosmos not to save the human species but to signify our launch as a space-faring species. Does Bowman's frightened gaze signal that the acceleration is too much, that we are speeding toward an escape velocity whose existential meaning is beyond our grasp? Does his horror merely symbolize humanity's inability to handle the experience of the cosmic sublime? Later, there are several close-ups of one of Bowman's eyes, its color constantly changing, from hues of purple and green to blue and orange. The eye seems to be focusing and adjusting, suggesting a new awareness and a new "vision" of the future. Has Bowman accepted this new vision of the universe? Or maybe his journey is just a cosmic LSD trip for Kubrick and his crew? Unlike *Planet of the Apes*, there was to be no crash from this trip, only a strange landing site and a new destiny.

NO EXIT. Perhaps Bowman's multicolored eye signals an awareness of his cosmic destiny in the new universe. After the Star-Gate journey, the space pod lands in a strange suite of rooms reminiscent of those in an exclusive luxury hotel. Bowman emerges from the pod. Glowing in ambient light, the suite is white with a few accents of pale green, and neoclassical paintings and sculptures adorn the room. The décor of the various rooms is highly ornate, with abundant molding and symmetry. Since the suite is largely white and pale green, it is impossible to classify the décor with perfect precision, but the styles are surely from the periods near the time of the Second Empire in France or represent some of those styles copied during that time (c. 1850-1870). Here we see what appears to be a simulacrum, a copy, a cloned reality of a past future. Is this suite merely an extraterrestrial zoo or theme park, where humans are fed and comforted in a copy of their native surroundings while gazed upon by the aliens?

Does Bowman being alone in this mysterious suite signify cosmic loneliness? After turning off HAL and exiting *Discovery One*, Bowman becomes the most "alone" person in the history of the human species, the individual most separated from its tribe. At Jupiter, he is at least 350 million miles from Earth and the moon, sites for the nearest living humans. So far in actual life, those farthest removed from humanity to date have been the six command module pilots for Apollo. These were the astronauts who did not walk on the moon but orbited around the moon alone, including being on the dark side and out of radio contact.

Kubrick's cosmic suite could indeed be a clever reference to *No Exit*, Jean-Paul Sartre's famous and influential play. After all, Sartre won the Nobel Prize for Literature in 1964 and was at the peak of his influence as a writer and philosopher. In the suite, there are no windows, no doors, no exits, and no switches to turn off the lights. Though Bowman blinks a few times, his eyes are mostly wide open. The parallels between this suite and the hotel-like suite in Sartre's play seem unmistakable. In *No Exit*, the décor is also of the Second

Empire and the suite is always illuminated with electric lights that can never be turned off. In addition, there are no windows or door handles. This is the hotel "hell" where people can never shut their eyes, never sleep, and must confront the lives they lived, the destinies they made, the meanings they have for their identity and existence. In Sartre's play and overall philosophy, there are no excuses and no exits.[25]

In *2001*, the cosmic hotel suite seems to be of two realms. The ornate walls and furniture rest on a floor organized in a large grid pattern, with light glowing through translucent panels. Overall, the floor is not unlike the ceiling of the all-white space station. It is as if two eras have merged, or two realms of space-time, the rational grid of pure information and the simulated forms of past tradition. Bowman slowly walks through the rooms, his bright red spacesuit of the future contrasting with décor from the past. This scene offers a future-past combined in a sci-fi synthesis of Sartre's *No Exit*.

Eventually exchanging the spacesuit for an elegant robe and pants, Bowman seems to have accepted his new home, his new position in the universe. Bowman sees himself having dinner at a table, having aged significantly. The pod is no longer in the suite. As with the characters in *No Exit*, Bowman will not leave the suite alive. Seemingly serene, the older Bowman then sees himself in the ornate bed, now extremely old and obviously near death, perhaps to be transformed into the infant Star-Child in the womb-like glowing orb. But perhaps the Star-Child symbolizes that the space spore was successful in its fertilization; it is the first child of a truly space-faring species in search of its meaning and purpose in the vast and ancient universe. Is Bowman's journey now humanity's destiny in an expanding universe of matter and voids from which there is *no exit*?

MEANINGS OF THE MONOLITH. To further determine the contemporary relevance of *2001*, we should explore the possible meanings of the mysterious black monolith. One of the most memorable icons in film history, the black monolith appears in four key scenes, each suggesting a possible meaning (see Table 1).

Meaning 1: In a moment of the sublime, the "desert" monolith inspired pre-human simians to discover technology and look to the stars. The monolith first appears in the desert scene with the apes, as small tribes battle over scarce resources. During one scene, we see the close-up of an ape's face as the ape glances right, then left, then skyward. We see a sunset of deep orange with a dark sky above. The next morning the monolith appears, standing perfectly upright in the desert as if it had been planted there with intent. There is no explanation for its origins. As the apes gather around, we hear Ligeti's *Requiem*, the music rising in a crescendo. The monolith is then shown against the morning sky, with the sun eclipsed as it rises above the top edge. A crescent moon is positioned above the sun. This linear and symmetrical arrangement suggests the monolith is pointing toward the sun and moon and thus directing the apes to look toward the stars. This observation is confirmed in the famed jump cut from the bone to the spacecraft. The technological apes are motivated by *the sublime*.

When the apes first see the monolith, they are experiencing an all-too-human moment of the sublime — the simultaneous feeling of awe, wonder, and terror when gazing upon something majestic and mysterious that seems to overwhelm their reason and sensory perceptions (detailed in Chapter 1). We can see the awe and terror of the apes as they approach the monolith, first staring at it and then quickly touching it and removing their hands in fear. Their reason overwhelmed, the apes remain curious. Eventually the sleek monolith seduces their reason and senses, leading them to caress it as an object of mystery and desire, even if they have no idea where it came from or what it means. Inspired by the monolith, the apes are soon using bones as technology and evolve to become the space farers we now are.

The scene where the ape transforms the bone into technology is accompanied by Richard Strauss's *Also Sprach Zarathustra* (1896), as kettledrums and symphonic sounds rise to a triumphant crescendo. (*Also Sprach Zarathustra* is also heard in later appearances of the monolith.) Strauss's composition was inspired by Nietzsche's *Thus Spoke Zarathustra.* Surely Kubrick and Clarke knew the inspiration for the music, suggesting that the extraterrestrials in *2001* are the space-faring gods who inspired the apes to become humans, not the human-created anthropomorphic God who is dead to Nietzsche. In fact, this is the idea Kubrick intended, as he states in his 1968 *Playboy* interview:

> I don't believe in any of Earth's monotheistic religions, but I do believe that one can construct an intriguing scientific definition of God, once you accept the fact that there are approximately 100 billion stars in our galaxy alone, that each star is a life-giving sun and that there are approximately 100 billion galaxies in just the visible universe. Given a planet in a stable orbit, not too hot and not too cold, and given a few billion years of chance chemical reactions created by the interaction of a sun's energy on the planet's chemicals, it's fairly certain that life in one form or another will eventually emerge. It's reasonable to assume that there must be, in fact, countless billions of such planets where biological life has arisen, and the odds of some proportion of such life developing intelligence are high. Now, the sun is by no means an old star, and its planets are mere children in cosmic age, so it seems likely that there are billions of planets in the universe not only where intelligent life is on a lower scale than man but other billions where it is approximately equal and others still where it is hundreds of thousands of millions of years in advance of us. When you think of the giant technological strides that man has made in a few millennia—less than a microsecond in the chronology of the universe—can you imagine the evolutionary development that much older life forms have taken?[26]

Kubrick is clearly offering a cosmic, secular, extraterrestrial notion of a "God." This is not a God of our creation and narcissistic insecurities, but the idea that a sufficiently evolved and advanced extraterrestrial species — with the science and technologies to traverse the light years — would be like gods to us or any less-advanced species. Would these extraterrestrials be like Nietzschean supermen or more like Hollywood superheroes? Or more like scientists and philosophers contemplating microbes in a petri dish? Perhaps that explains the monolith left behind for the apes on the petri dish of planet Earth. Since the extraterrestrials would likely have no need to conquer our planet for its resources, why would they want to destroy us? Kubrick thinks it's possible (though not certain) they would be benevolent, as suggested by the desert monolith in the film.[27] In the spirit of Nietzsche's Ubermensch, perhaps the monolith-bearing extraterrestrials have evolved beyond their early evolutionary stages, becoming peaceful and benevolent space farers on a quest for discovery, beauty, and cosmic meaning. Perhaps they have already developed and embraced a space philosophy that unites their species as they explore the universe.

Meaning 2: In the same interview, Kubrick points toward the second meaning of the monolith:

> But at a time [1968] when man is preparing to set foot on the Moon, I think it's necessary to open up our Earthbound minds to such speculation. No one knows what's waiting for us in the universe. I think it was a prominent astronomer who wrote recently, "Sometimes I think we are alone, sometimes I think we're not. In either case, the idea is quite staggering."[28]

The "moon" monolith proves to the simians-turned-humans that they are not alone in the vast universe, no longer are they cosmically central, nor are they the top species in the cosmos. Discovered by scientists on the moon in the year 2001, the second monolith was buried four million years previous. Like the desert monolith, the moon monolith stands perfectly vertical. The difference is the moon monolith is beaming a radio frequency toward Jupiter. The scientists realize this is a monumental discovery, and it prompts the visit to the Clavius moon base by Dr. Heywood Floyd (William Sylvester). However, the humans on Earth have not yet been told of the discovery. As Floyd says to a gathering of scientists at Clavius:

> Congratulations on your discovery, which may well prove to be amongst the most significant in the history of science. . . . Now I'm sure you're all aware of the extremely grave potential for cultural shock and social disorientation contained in this present situation if the facts were prematurely and suddenly made public without adequate preparation and conditioning.

After making this statement, Floyd informs the scientists that "security oaths" will be required of them until it is decided when and how to inform the public. With this plotline, Kubrick and Clarke also provide artistic motivation for the world's space conspiracy theorists. Among the most popular conspiracies are that NASA faked the moon landings, NASA or the military has found extraterrestrial life but refuse to tell us (Steven Spielberg's *Close Encounters of the Third Kind* [1977]), and mainstream scientists and archaeologists have conspired to deny evidence that proves "ancient astronauts" have visited Earth (*Ancient Aliens* [2010-]).

Meaning 3: The "Jupiter" monolith is a symbol of the cosmic sublime and the infiniteness and mysteriousness of the universe. The monolith provides the apes with an experience of the sublime, thus inspiring them to develop technologies that eventually send them into the stars when they become humans. Such vastness and mystery will seduce the ever-curious human species into leaving Earth and exploring space. On the *Discovery One* spacecraft, Bowman accidentally uncovers the existence of the moon monolith when he comes across a video announcement in the spacecraft's computer system (as he is turning off the HAL 9000 computer). An unnamed spokesman states:

> Eighteen months ago, the first evidence of intelligent life off the Earth was discovered. It was buried 40 feet below the lunar surface, near the crater Tycho. Except for a single, very powerful, radio emission aimed at Jupiter, the four-million-year-old black monolith has remained completely inert. *Its origin and purpose still a total mystery.* [Italics mine.]

The idea of the monolith as a symbol for the sublime and cosmic mystery is confirmed in the next scene, when we see the Jupiter monolith (black with a cobalt blue tint) floating and slowly tumbling against the blackness of the starry skies surrounding Jupiter and its moons. *Discovery One* is shown stationary near Jupiter. Soon, Bowman exits *Discovery One* in the space pod, flies toward us in space, and then enters the Star-Gate sequence. Seduced by the monolith, Bowman ventures untold numbers of light years through the immensity of the universe and its array of cosmic and intergalactic forms.

Meaning 4: The "hotel suite" monolith symbolizes the void in human meaning, yet in pursuit of that meaning or meaninglessness lies human destiny, a fate from which there is no exit. Of course, the other monoliths symbolize this indirectly. The monolith makes a final appearance in the hotel-like suite where Bowman has arrived upon conclusion of his journey through the Star-Gate. After rapidly aging to become a very old man lying in bed, Bowman's last act is to point toward the monolith standing at the foot of his bed. Bowman dies or is transformed while *thinking of the monolith*.

Kubrick zooms into the blackness of the monolith, which envelopes the screen. As *Also Sprach Zarathustra* rises to a final crescendo, we are instantly returned to our area of the universe. We see the moon, followed by Earth and then the Star-Child, who is either Bowman reborn, the infant heir to his space-faring

TABLE 1 MEANINGS OF THE BLACK MONOLITH IN *2001: A SPACE ODYSSEY*

1. **DESERT MONOLITH**: Inspires the apes to discover technology and look to the stars, thus becoming simians-turned-humans (or apes who became astronauts) with no origins in a Creator or Adam and Eve
2. **MOON MONOLITH**: Proves to humanity that we are not alone, no longer cosmically central, and are not the most advanced species in the universe
3. **JUPITER MONOLITH**: Symbolizes the cosmic sublime and the infiniteness and mysteriousness of the cosmos, which will seduce humans into leaving their planet and exploring space
4. **HOTEL SUITE MONOLITH**: Symbolizes the void in human meaning and purpose, while in pursuit of that meaning and purpose (or meaninglessness and purposelessness) lies human destiny, from which there is no exit
5. **SPECTER OF THE MONOLITH**: Symbolizes our simultaneous experience of the sublime and nihilism, which blows our mind yet paralyzes our ability to develop a universal narrative.

TABLE 2 **TRAJECTORIES OF THE HUMAN SPECIES: *PLANET OF THE APES* AND *2001: A SPACE ODYSSEY***

	PLANET OF THE APES	*2001: A SPACE ODYSSEY*
COSMIC IMAGES	**Reversals** • Starry skies to desert	**Acceleration** • Desert to starry skies, Star-Gate
SPECIES	• Humans to apes	• Apes to humans
TECHNOLOGY	• Spacecraft and spacesuits to animal-skin clothing	• Bones to spacecraft, space stations, moon bases, HAL, etc.
HUMAN ERA	• Space age to Stone Age	• Stone Age to space age
TRAJECTORY IN TIME	• To a future that is the past • From the current era, we are propelled 2,000 years forward into the future (the year 3978).	• From the past to the future • From our simian past, we are propelled millions of years forward into the future, to the year 2001. — via the jump cut from ape with bone to space station • From 2001, we are propelled to some time in the future. — via Bowman's journey into the Star-Gate and the cosmic horizons
ACCELERATION	• The spacecraft is hurled 2,000 years into the future, confirming Hesslein's hypothesis. • We assume the space-age rockets also carried the nuclear missiles that accelerated human annihilation.	• Upon the arrival of the desert monolith, the evolution of humans is accelerated into the space age. • Upon the arrival of the Jupiter monolith, Bowman is accelerated into the cosmic sublime.
HUMAN DESTINY	• **Reversal:** Acceleration leads to knowing that a future human destiny is in the past.	• Acceleration leads to a new human destiny in space and on Spaceship Earth (in the final images of the film).
THE NEXT HUMANS (UBERMENSCH OR NOT?)	• **Reversal:** Taylor and Nova are the next "Adam and Eve," hunter-gatherers of the new species with a new destiny.	• The Star-Child symbolizes the next human: the cosmic Ubermensch, the space farer with a new destiny.
SPACE FARERS OR SPORE BEARERS	**Spore Bearers/Reversal** • The astronauts are "spores" that are launched to seed the next human civilization. • Taylor represents the "spore," as he "breeds" with Nova.	**Space Farers** • Bowman and the Star-Child are spore bearers for a future of space farers.

legacy, or the first of a new cosmic Ubermensch that evolved from current space-faring humans. Perhaps Bowman's rebirth as a Star-Child symbolizes the Nietzschean recurrence, though now the Star-Child represents the superhumans who explore the universe with a new space philosophy. The Star-Child gazes down at Earth and then straight at us, eyes wide open as the film ends. With the Star-Child, the trajectory seems complete, from ape to astronaut to astral species. Through Bowman the space spore, we have returned to "The Dawn of

Man" — Star-Child, stargazer, space voyager, and seeker of beauty, meaning, and purpose.

Meaning 5: As discussed in the Introduction, humans are still facing the specter of the monolith, with the 21st century space age simultaneously confronting a sublime universe and the void of cosmic nihilism and human meaninglessness. We have yet to embrace the sublime as a potential counter to nihilism in developing a universal human narrative for a space-faring species and a peaceful planetary civilization.

***2001*: WHAT CAN WE HOPE FOR?** The very opening of *2001* begins with three minutes of a completely black screen, accompanied by Ligeti's *Atmospheres*. The monotonal sound textures suggest a monochromatic existential void, the beginning of the intellectual journey for the human species. The origins and purpose of the monoliths are never explained, though they trigger and inspire events. Bowman's journey and the hotel suite are never explained. In the end, the black monolith that seduced the apes seems to have given birth to a Star-Child and space-faring species in search of its cosmic meaning and existential purpose.

2001 has several meanings that indicate what we can hope for now and in a future space philosophy:

> 1) We are an evolutionary species capable of great things. We evolved from apes to artists to astronauts, from simians to scientists to space voyagers. Inspired and seduced by the monolith, we created a technological civilization capable of exploring the stars and seeking to understand its origins and destiny via art, science, and philosophy. This is an incredible achievement for our species of which we should be proud.
>
> 2) We are not alone. The existence of the monolith with the apes is a hopeful message, in that the extraterrestrials were benevolent and sought to inspire the most advanced species on Earth at the time.
>
> 3) We need to be careful with our advancing digital technologies. Via the flawed artificial intelligence of the HAL 9000, *2001* provides a warning to humans about the seductive power of our technology. We might find ourselves serving the technology rather than the technology serving us. More radically, perhaps HAL symbolizes the next leap in evolution, the technological Ubermensch to succeed humans.
>
> 4) We face the challenge of cosmic nihilism. As symbolized by the final two monoliths, we face a philosophical void, for there is no intrinsic or self-evident meaning for human existence in a vast and wondrous universe.
>
> 5) There is no exit from the cosmic sublime. Though our art, science, and technology are accelerating into the universe as if on autopilot, *2001* suggests our discoveries will disrupt our traditional narratives and that our journey into space is the next step in the continuing

TABLE 3 **THE COSMIC SUBLIME: *PLANET OF THE APES* AND *2001: A SPACE ODYSSEY***

	PLANET OF THE APES	*2001: A SPACE ODYSSEY*
SPACE: INTO THE STARRY SKIES	• Opening scene: The stars are warped, distorted, and asymmetrical.	• Opening scene: The sun and moon move in a linear, symmetrical manner, suggesting a direct path to the stars for humanity.
VOIDS: INTO THE VASTNESS	• Against the black void: The stars are warped, and the spacecraft hurtles into the void of the future.	• Amid the black void of the cosmos: We see stars, planets, the *Discovery One* spacecraft, and the dead astronaut floating into the void.
AWE	• We're awed that the astronauts journeyed so far into future; as Taylor says, "the clocks bear out Hesslein's hypothesis."	• We're awed by planetary movements, spacecraft moving through the cosmos, the images and phenomena in Bowman's journey through the Star-Gate.
AFFIRMATION	• The journey affirms the power of science and reason, but terror and annihilation lie ahead as a result of tribal ideologies.	• The jump cut from the ape with the bone to the space station affirms our species in its magnificent evolution.
EXALTATION		• The movement of the sun and moon with Strauss's *Also Sprach Zarathustra* • The poetic motion of the spacecraft accompanied by Strauss's *Blue Danube* • The film's ending, featuring the Star-Child
TERROR	• Taylor is not horrified by the stars, just in facing the possibility of a meaningless fate.	• On his journey through the Star-Gate, Bowman's face expresses his terror.
INSIGNIFICANCE	• Taylor: "From out here, space squishes a man's ego. I feel lonely."	• We might feel we're insignificant in the cosmic voyage of *Discovery One* or during Bowman's journey though the Star-Gate.
ANNIHILATION/ EXTINCTION	• Taylor feels the sense of annihilation upon seeing the scorched Statue of Liberty, knowing civilization was destroyed centuries before. The surviving humans have devolved toward near extinction.	• In the end, Bowman seems to have come to terms with his destiny as a space spore launching humans on their quest for meaning and purpose in the cosmos.

existential quest. In the search lies our destiny, a species seeking meaning and purpose amid the awe-inspiring galaxies and voids.

6) Our first space spores have been launched. As symbolized in *2001* (and by technologies such as Apollo and Voyager), we are launching our first spores into the cosmos. In effect, *2001* is one of those spores, though it is artistic and philosophical. With our knowledge

of the cosmos, we have the opportunity to become Star-Children and philosophical Ubermensches, to be the artists, scientists, philosophers, voyagers, and tourists of the cosmos — seeking not merely to survive but peacefully pursue our existential quest in a beautiful and sublime universe.

6. *GRAVITY*

So far, *Gravity* and *Interstellar* rank as the two most important space films of the 21st century, precisely because they both involve cosmic nihilism and the cosmic sublime. This is not to say there are no other excellent or thought-provoking space films in the new century. *The Wild Blue Yonder*, *WALL-E*, *Melancholia*, and *The Martian* come to mind for me. What I am saying is that *Gravity* and *Interstellar* point toward key issues facing space exploration and human destiny.

At the 2014 Academy Awards ceremony, Alfonso Cuarón won the Oscar for Best Director, thus becoming the first director to win for a science-fiction film. Lost amid all the discussion of its 3-D special effects and Sandra Bullock's Oscar-nominated performance were the existential meanings suggested by the plot and title of the film. It is as if the spectacle of special effects and space locale overwhelmed the apocalyptic and vertiginous meanings of the film.

REPAIRING AND UPGRADING THE HUBBLE. *Gravity* begins with a team of scientists and astronauts upgrading the Hubble Space Telescope as it orbits Earth. This is not mere science fiction, for space shuttle missions to repair or upgrade the Hubble have indeed happened. As an extension of human consciousness, the Hubble represents humanity's most powerful "eyes." But there was a major problem when the Hubble was first launched into space in 1990 — the original mirror was slightly defective by 2.2 thousandths of a millimeter. Thus the images of the universe were blurry and ruined. Lacking the precision needed for accurate astronomical observations, the Hubble was technically "blind." Designed to be the most perfect mirror ever constructed, the original could not be replaced; its vision could only be corrected. This required NASA to launch the most complex repair job in human history in 1993. The space shuttle *Endeavor* carried astronauts to the Hubble with the task of refitting the telescope with new corrective equipment.[29] In effect, the Hubble was given a "pair of glasses." Over the past 23 years, space shuttle astronauts have performed several upgrades to the Hubble, such that it has far exceeded NASA's original expectations.

The character of Dr. Ryan Stone (Sandra Bullock) in *Gravity* is partially a composite of real NASA astronauts, including Story Musgrave, leader of the team that corrected the Hubble. According to Brian Cox and Andrew Cohen, this is how Musgrave described the significance of his experience with the Hubble:

> Majesty and magnificence of Hubble as a starship, a spaceship. To work on something so beautiful, to give it life again, to restore it to its heritage, to its conceived power. The work was worth it — significant. The passion was in the work, the passion was in the potentiality of Hubble Space Telescope.[30]

Here, Musgrave is expressing the technological sublime, the amazement felt toward the marvel and power of space technologies. It's inspiring to think of the Hubble as a spaceship, a starship dedicated not to war and conquest but to scientific discovery and the sublime beauty of the universe.

SPACE JUNK AND ZOMBIE SATELLITES. Since the industrial age polluted the planet and atmosphere, it should be no surprise that the space age has polluted the space immediately *beyond* the planet and atmosphere. Since the Soviets launched Sputnik, there have been over 4,000 launches into space, with increasing amounts of debris left behind. NASA defines orbital debris as "man-made objects in orbit about the Earth which no longer serve a useful purpose."[31] Examples of space junk include the following:

> Derelict spacecraft and upper stages of launch vehicles, carriers for multiple payloads, debris intentionally released during spacecraft separation from its launch vehicle or during mission operations, debris created as a result of spacecraft or upper stage explosions or collisions, solid rocket motor effluents, and tiny flecks of paint released by thermal stress or small particle impacts.[32]

NASA's estimates of the size and quantities of space junk are staggering:

> More than 21,000 orbital debris larger than 10 cm are known to exist. The estimated population of particles between 1 and 10 cm in diameter is approximately 500,000. The number of particles smaller than 1 cm exceeds 100 million.[33]

The large objects are tracked and monitored by the United States Space Surveillance Network, while objects as small as 3 millimeters can be detected by ground-based radar. These objects are orbiting Earth at speeds reaching 4 to 7 miles per second, creating significant hazards for satellites and space vehicles carrying humans.

Prior to 2007, the largest pieces of space junk were upper-stage launch vehicles that remained in orbit after their usage. More recently, new sources of space junk include "derelict spacecraft," such as defunct satellites that remain in orbit long after their demise. No longer able to communicate but still in orbit around the Earth and posing a serious risk of collision with other satellites and spacecraft, these derelict satellites are also known as "zombie satellites." For example, the famous Telstar telecommunications satellite launched in 1962 is now a zombie satellite and destined to orbit the Earth for many years to come.

In 2007, China launched a missile that destroyed its defunct Fengyun 1-C weather satellite. The destruction left a 3,300-piece debris field that now circles the planet in the previous orbit of the satellite; the orbital debris trail will last for centuries. In 2009, the first collision of two satellites occurred when the 2,000-lb Russian Cosmos 2251 satellite (a defunct zombie satellite) accidentally smashed into the 1,200-lb American-made Iridium commercial satellite. Since the satellites collided at an estimated speed of 7.3 miles per second (or about 26,000 miles per hour), it is no surprise that they shattered into over 2,000 pieces of orbital debris, some of which have drifted into different altitudes that may threaten the International Space Station. As dramatically shown in *Gravity*, space junk can effect a chain reaction, with the debris from one collision causing other collisions.

"LIFE IN SPACE IS IMPOSSIBLE." Cuarón stated that *Gravity* is not a "tale that takes place in the future," but rather an expression of "how we see contemporary space exploration."[34] Cuarón's vision of space exploration seems rather bleak, with implications that reach into the foreseeable future. *Gravity* opens with ominous warnings about the human future in space. Against a black background, the following message appears (in all caps, in a relatively small font):

AT 600KM ABOVE PLANET EARTH THE TEMPERATURE

FLUCUATES BETWEEN +258 AND -148 DEGREES FAHRENHEIT

After this text fades from the screen, this message appears:

THERE IS NOTHING TO CARRY SOUND

NO AIR PRESSURE

NO OXYGEN

After this text fades, filmgoers are treated to this message:

LIFE IN SPACE IS IMPOSSIBLE

Of course, life is impossible in space, absent the technologies of space exploration — spacesuits, spacecraft, and space stations. But then human life is impossible in contemporary society without the technologies of modern civilization. Absent our technologies, humans would be reduced to barbarism in the struggle to survive, with billions dying off in weeks. Nuclear warfare and ecological destruction may threaten our existence, but absent technology, we would soon be back with the warring apes of *2001*. In *Gravity*, the astronauts do fine until *life on Earth* impinges upon their *life in space*.

The space apocalypse begins when Russia destroys one of its satellites, leaving an orbital debris field that hurtles around the planet and sets off a deadly chain reaction. The debris soon crashes into satellites, generating more debris. Soon, large and small chunks of the debris crash into the space shuttle and Hubble Space Telescope, destroying both. Stone and Matt Kowalski (George Clooney) are the sole surviving astronauts, but Kowalski eventually floats to his frozen death in deep space.

The telecommunication satellite systems have been largely destroyed, thus wreaking havoc with media on Earth. Mission Control in Houston reports that many satellites "are down and they keep on falling." Satellites that communicate at the speed of light but are falling down to Earth — yet another illustration of the acceleration-reversals of post-Apollo culture.

Informed of the impending communications blackout, Kowalski gets the only witty line of the film, remarking that "half of North America just lost its Facebook." As Stone chaotically tumbles through empty space, Earth, as seen behind her and from her perspective, is at once beautiful and seeming to orbit out of control. Under the force of gravity, Stone comes crashing down to Earth — just like a *rock* falls to the ground when dropped from our hand. By the end of the film, the International Space Station and Russia's Soyuz spacecraft have been destroyed along with NASA's *Explorer* shuttle and the Hubble.[35]

Gravity makes it seem as if the Cold War never ended. After all, the reasons Russia would blow up its satellite are twofold: 1) to destroy a defunct spy satellite; and 2) to demonstrate to China and the United States that it also has weapons for use in space. In *Gravity* and in the 21st century at large, it seems little has changed in terms of the tribal-nationalist ideologies of these powerful nations. Shooting down satellites and militarizing space — it's all madness.

THE VOID OF THE COSMIC SUBLIME. Cuarón and his son, Jonas, coauthored the screenplay for *Gravity*, creating a story that directly confronted the cosmic sublime. According to Jonas, the thematic idea of the film began with an "astronaut just floating into the void . . . a character drifting into nothingness."[36] Given the lack of cosmic narrative for confronting the void, it is not surprising that the film is a scary and vertiginous journey that ends by crashing back to Earth.

As if picking up where *2001* concluded, *Gravity* opens with a shot of a beautiful Earth floating in space. Instead of a Star-Child looking at us, we see the space shuttle *Explorer* coming toward us, manned by the apes who have become astronauts, thus fulfilling a small part of the promise of *2001*. Like the *Enterprise* in the opening to the original *Star Trek*, the *Explorer* emerges from a vanishing point. There are numerous scenes with wondrous views of Earth surrounded by the black voids of space, each offering a high-definition version of the *Earthrise* image. "Spaceship Earth" is seen as a beautiful and complex planetary system, including scenes looking down upon oceans, continents, cloud systems, and the Aurora Borealis. The majesty of Earth is juxtaposed with the physical insignificance of the astronauts, who are often seen as tiny specks floating amid the black voids of space. After the chain-reaction catastrophe, Stone is shown tumbling away from Earth and toward the center of the Milky Way, facing certain doom until she is retrieved by Kowalski in his jetpack. All in all, space travel and exploration is presented as awe inspiring and terrifying at the same time.

Jonas Cuarón says the space apocalypse and Stone's journey are metaphors for confronting "inertia" and overcoming "adversity" in life, along with being "reborn" and reconnecting with Earth. All of that may indeed be true, but *Gravity* is saying something far more profound and disturbing — at least for the future of human narratives. This is illustrated in Sandra Bullock's summary of the meaning of the film's ending:

> We've gone from seeing how small we are in this massive universe to all of the sudden taking your baby steps. And the vantage point it gives you is [as] though you're a giant. . . . [Cuarón is] giving you both sides of humanity, who we are in this great universe of space and Earth. And he ends it with giving you all the power as a reborn human being.[37]

Bullock echoes one of the main themes of post-Apollo culture, in that we counter the cosmic sublime with delusions of grandeur. Of course, the word *reborn* is loaded with new age and theological implications in *Gravity*, especially considering Stone splashes down in water and is symbolically cleansed of her past "sins," which necessarily include exploring space.

To its credit, *Gravity* borrows ideas from real missions of shuttle astronauts, for the purpose of the *Explorer* mission in *Gravity* is to install a "new scanning system" on the Hubble Space Telescope. However, the most troubling meanings of the film involve the Hubble. This can be seen in a brief conversation between

Kowalski and a third astronaut, Shariff (Phaldut Sharma), during the upgrade. While the two astronauts are spacewalking, the following exchange occurs:

> **Kowalski.** So what is this scanning system?
>
> **Shariff.** Oh, nothing man. It's just a new set of eyes to scan the edge of the universe.

For non-astronomers and *most* humans on Earth, the Hubble is indeed "nothing," offering nothing to seriously think about, nothing to reflect upon, nothing to make life better on Earth. What is scanning the edge of the universe when you can scan every instant of your life with the full array of social media? Seriously, of the billions of humans on Earth, how many really care about Hubble images and what they truly mean? For 99.9%, the Hubble images are nothing compared to gazing upon selfies, celebrities, and footballers.

Not long after the above dialogue, the Hubble and *Explorer* are destroyed by the orbital debris, and all but Stone and Kowalski are immediately killed. When Stone and Kowalski retrieve Shariff's corpse, which is in floating space, we see that Shariff's helmet and face feature *a brick-sized hole* that has gone all the way through his frozen head. His brains are completely blown out! Kowalski's very next words are: "Jesus Christ. Here's hoping you have a helluva insurance policy, Houston. The damages to *Explorer* are catastrophic. Commence search for survivors."

So what can be made of this horrific imagery? Shortly after Shariff explains the purpose of the mission — to enable the Hubble "to scan the edge of the universe" — he is utterly lobotomized by orbital debris caused by tribalism and nationalism on Earth. Through the hole in his head, we can see the cloudy surface of the Earth below him. How can this space lobotomy not signal the void in meaning on Earth for peering to the edge of the universe? What's next — Jesus Christ as a back-up plan in the search for meaning?

GRAVITY: WHAT CAN WE HOPE FOR? Not very much. Beginning with the opening line, the goal of the film is to terrify moviegoers about space exploration. "Life in space is impossible" and we have deadly space junk orbiting all around our planet, destroying our best space technologies and most powerful "eyes." Here's what *Gravity* offers:

> 1) Each of us can overcome the odds and survive our personal challenges. The Cuaróns tell us that Stone's survival is supposed to symbolize triumph over adversity, the battle against inertia. Like the latest self-help book or made-for-TV docudrama, perhaps this will motivate a few individuals to overcome adversity in their personal lives.
>
> 2) Much like Kubrick's *2001*, Cuarón's *Gravity* shows the human species as rational, competent, and incredibly creative and skilled in launching such amazing technologies into space — the shuttle, the Soyuz, the Hubble, and the International Space Station. In the opening of the film, the shuttle seems to be on autopilot, cruising around Earth at 5 miles per second, 18,000 miles per hour, all while the astronauts spacewalk to upgrade the Hubble. That we can make

such accomplishments is a testimony to the power of the human species and its curiosity about what's "out there."

3) Despite our space achievements, a nationalist-caused apocalypse awaits just off the Earth. Here's what Marsha Ivins (astronaut on five space shuttle missions) said about *Gravity*:

> The views of Earth and the sunrise, the lighting on Sandra Bullock's face (light in space is so different from light in the atmosphere) — perfect. Her body positions inside the spacecraft, the astronauts' tether protocol during the space walks, the breathing in the helmet, even the excruciatingly slow movement of the Soyuz undocking from the space station — spot on. These things made me happy.
>
> The massive, fatal, horrific, total destruction of *every single spacecraft*? Not so much. I guess I take spacecraft destruction personally, movie or not. For me, it's just too hard to watch. The scene in which debris is falling through the atmosphere, breaking up into streaking balls of white finality brought slamming back to mind the real-life image burned there forever of the last moments of the *Columbia* shuttle. And I had to look away. I wanted to ask, *who is going to like this movie, and why?* If it's because of all the destruction, that just makes me so sad I couldn't face it. So I didn't ask. . . .
>
> The trailers are misleading in a way. They string together 40 seconds of the most destructive, flash-framed, violent, and — did I mention — destructive moments from the film, coupled with heart-pounding, insistent crescendos of music, leaving you gasping for breath and blindly reaching for something to hold on to. But they downplayed what I felt was a significant thread in the film. George Clooney's character, in a rare and fleeting quiet moment, says to Sandra's character, "Beautiful, don't you think?" And the scene is the sunrise in space. Hold on to *that*.[38]

Ivins is absolutely correct. *Gravity* portrays a horrific view of space exploration. The film makes me sad, too. Despite the beautiful views of Earth from space, *Gravity* portrays a ballet of space destruction caused by nationalism in the face of cosmic nihilism.

4) There is no real meaning or destiny for humans in space. The awe-inspiring beauty of Earth from space is displayed in the film, yet it's presented as a mere backdrop for human events, as if the *views of Earth from space* have absolutely zero relevance or meaning for *life on Earth*. Symbolized by the fate of Shariff, the Cuaróns offer a cosmological lobotomy. The winner of seven Academy Awards, *Gravity* illustrates the fears of cosmic nihilism.

5) *Gravity* shows we are still living amid the acceleration-reversal of post-Apollo culture. In my view, the *real adversity* has been denied in *Gravity*. For all their spectacular use of CGI in the film, the Cuaróns

> have absolutely no answer for the cosmic sublime. All that's left is the 3-D celebration of nihilism and the intellectual reversal implicit in Shariff's lobotomy along with the complete destruction of space shuttles, space telescopes, and space stations. Nationalist militarism of the new Cold War has destroyed our space habitat and eliminated our ability to see the edge of the universe. Scared, we reverse course and crash back to Earth.

After Stone passes through the atmosphere on her descent to Earth, it becomes clear she is going to splash down in a lake that snakes though a canyon landscape. What lake is this? It is Lake Powell in the southwestern United States, the very same lake where Taylor and the astronauts splash down in *Planet of the Apes*. In explaining the site of the *Gravity*'s ending, Cuarón excitedly stated: "I kept on referencing *Planet of the Apes*."[39] After filming in Lake Powell, Cuarón and his team used CGI to make the desert landscapes look like a "garden paradise."[40] Of course, that's the CGI cover for the fact that the film has the same meaning as the 1968 film. In the 21st century, *Gravity* shows we are still living on the *Planet of the Apes*.

7. *INTERSTELLAR*

Released in 2014, Christopher Nolan's *Interstellar* became the next *2001: A Space Odyssey* and hence the greatest philosophical space film of the 21st century. Like *2001*, *Interstellar* is not dumbed down to placate the masses, the faithful, or the studio execs worried about the bottom line. The film is filled with big ideas and big challenges for science and the human species. As summarized by film critic MaryAnn Johanson:

> *Interstellar* is so thrilling, intellectually and viscerally. It is full of stirring visions of what humanity might be capable of, and follows through with the breathtaking adventure that necessarily follows. Or, well, the adventure that necessarily follows if we chase those possibilities instead of ignoring them. It is full of enormous risk-taking in the quest for something bigger and better for all of us. It is full of hope for humanity. And that is a refreshing thing right now. . . . It isn't at all unfair to see shades of *2001* in *Interstellar*, not when it concerns itself with both the most intimate of human emotions and desires — love and survival, loneliness and despair — and the biggest of ideas: the boldness of humans as a species, the future to which we might aspire, the daring it will take to make that future happen.[41]

Johanson is correct in seeing the influence of *2001* in *Interstellar*. However, *2001* and *Interstellar* present different futures with differing existential reasons for exploring space. In contrast to the evolving civilizations in *2001* and *Star Trek*, civilization is devolving in *Interstellar*, with space exploration being necessary to keep the human species alive amid an ecological apocalypse.

Since *Interstellar* is an extremely complex film, especially regarding plot and science, this discussion will *not* attempt to discuss every plotline or scientific concept. Such efforts would require at least a book or magazine. Indeed, *Wired* devoted an entire issue to *Interstellar*, and famed astrophysicist Kip Thorne authored a book explaining the science of the film, including everything from the apocalyptic blight to Gargantua to the Tesseract.[42] Thorne consulted with Christopher Nolan on the scientific and cosmological concepts in the film and was given an executive producer title. In what follows, I will reference Thorne as needed on scientific concepts, but the critique will focus on the sublime and space narrative within the film along with its vision of meaning and hope.

CONTRASTING CIVILIZATIONS: *2001*, *STAR TREK*, AND *INTERSTELLAR*. *2001*, *Star Trek*, and *Interstellar* inhabit the same epic universe revealed by science and our cosmic media technologies. In these films, humans must overcome the vast distances via some kind of technological power or cosmic force they have mastered in order to *accelerate* through the cosmos. Otherwise, these films would have little purpose or meaning. In *2001*, how can the astronauts get to Jupiter without faster spacecraft? How can Dave get through the Star-Gate without massive acceleration? How can one boldly seek out "new civilizations" if all humans can do is send a few astronauts to the moon and maybe Mars? How could the human species survive in *Interstellar* if Mars is the only planetary option? That's why *Star Trek* needs warp drive (which is faster than the speed of light) to propel the *Enterprise* across vast distances. That's why *Interstellar* needs a wormhole and black hole — to accelerate the astronauts into the cosmos so they can explore the habitability of planets in a distant galaxy.

While traversing the universe, *2001*, *Star Trek*, and *Interstellar* offer contrasting assumptions about space narratives and the future of human civilization (Table 4). This difference is poetically expressed in the coda of *Star Trek* and the *raison d'etre* of *Interstellar*. In *Interstellar*, Professor John Brand (Michael Caine) borrows key lines from Dylan Thomas's untitled poem known as "Do not go gentle into that good night," first published in 1952. Professor Brand utters these lines to provide the astronauts with motivation and remind them of their purpose: to do whatever it takes to reach other habitable planets and stave off human extinction:

> Do not go gentle into that good night,
> Old age should burn and rave at close of day;
> Rage, rage against the dying of the light.

For *2001* and *Star Trek*, the future promises cultural evolution and space exploration. For *Interstellar*, the future promises cultural devolution and possible species extinction, followed by the emergence of a space-faring civilization. Compare the sleek spacecraft in *2001* and the futuristic skyline of San Francisco in *Star Trek* with the dusty and decaying farmhouses in *Interstellar*. In *2001* and *Star Trek*, the overall society seems to be largely cosmopolitan, while *Interstellar* shows a society that is regressive and going backward technologically and intellectually, with supposedly knowledgeable "educators" denying that NASA landed humans on the moon. Here, *Interstellar* shares a similar concern that appears in *Planet of the Apes*, namely the rise of antiscientific worldviews. In fact, *Interstellar* shares several plot similarities with *Planet of the Apes* and *2001* (Table 5).

In *2001*, humans have managed to avoid the nuclear apocalypse of the Cold War, though the film offers a warning about surrendering our autonomy to

TABLE 4 **COMPARATIVE SPACE/CULTURAL NARRATIVES: *2001*, *STAR TREK*, AND *INTERSTELLAR***

	2001: A SPACE ODYSSEY	*STAR TREK*	*INTERSTELLAR*
COSMIC SUBLIME	• Awe, wonder, and hope	• Awe and wonder in the original series; some awe and mostly terror in the 2009 2012, and 2016 films.	• Awe, wonder, terror, and hope
FUTURE CIVILIZATION	• Flourishing	• Flourishing	• Facing extinction
SOCIETY	• Cosmic, cosmopolitan (From what is seen in the space station and space plane)	• Cosmic, cosmopolitan (From what is seen in the original series and in the new *Star Trek* films)	• Small-town decay (Based on what is seen in the American Midwest)
CULTURAL TRAJECTORY	• Evolving, moving forward	• Evolving, moving forward	• Devolving, in reversal, then evolving after the "quantum gravity" problem is solved
APOCALYPSE	• Apocalypse avoided in the past, but the film offers a warning about future technology (HAL)	• Apocalypse avoided in the past but is possible in future battles	• Ecological apocalypse coming in the future, but humans manage to survive in space
MEANING AND PURPOSE FOR HUMAN EXISTENCE	• None provided, but film implies it may be found in space	• Meaning and purpose sought via exploration and knowledge (the coda)	• Survival is initial purpose, made possible by awe-inspiring black hole • At end of film, humans move toward goal of flourishing
SPACECRAFT AND ITS SYMBOLISM	• *Discovery One*: Science, knowledge, enlightenment, and an open future	• *Enterprise*: Prosperity, freedom, creativity, and exploration	• *Endurance*: Grit, perseverance, hardship, and suffering
SPACECRAFT CREW	• Brainy, intellectual, and perhaps boring	• Hip, confident, sexy, and brainy and brawny	• Grim and reluctant but still sexy and very brainy
SPACE FUTURE	• Humans as spore-bearing species that becomes space faring — An uncertain yet glorious future filled with awe-inspiring possibilities	• Humans as space-faring species — A somewhat glorious future, yet war is still waged in space	• Spore-bearing species that becomes a space-faring species — A strange future where astronauts are glorified fungi and heroic explorers

technology. In *Star Trek,* the civilizational apocalypse did not happen, for the humans united as a species to set aside war and explore space. In *Interstellar,* the civilizational apocalypse is nearing completion, as nature and the ecological support systems have turned against humanity, thus requiring that humans venture into space to survive. Even the names of the key spacecraft are revealing: *Discovery One, Enterprise,* and *Endurance,* respectively. The *Discovery One* implies science, knowledge, enlightenment, beginnings, and open possibilities for the future. The *Enterprise* implies prosperity, freedom, creativity, exploration, and a future with unlimited possibilities. The *Endurance* implies grit, perseverance, hardship, suffering, stamina, holding up, and trudging toward a future of survival after abandoning Earth for space stations and other habitable planets. In contrast to the hipster astronauts commanding the starship *Enterprise* in the new *Star Trek,* the survivor astronauts piloting the *Endurance* in *Interstellar* are mostly a grim bunch. Courageous, to be sure, but, grim and solemn. After all, how much "fun" can be had when you might die trying to prevent human extinction? Then again, there are probably many moviegoers who would enjoy spending some space time next to the sexy astronauts played by Matthew McConaughey and Anne Hathaway, the latest interplanetary Adam and Eve.

Finally, *2001, Star Trek, Interstellar,* and other space films point toward another question, the answer of which is important to our survival: Is there any meaning to our existence or our destiny as a species in the cosmos? In *2001,* the human species is capable of great things, and in the quest for meaning lies our destiny. The original *Star Trek* suggests human meaning may be found in exploration and in the quest for knowledge and understanding, while *Interstellar* suggests human meaning and purpose are largely found in survival, though it points toward a quest for meaning in the sublime. While *2001* and *Star Trek* show a largely glorious future, *Interstellar* shows humans as glorified fungi, capable of launching spores into wormholes and black holes to overcome extinction. *2001, Star Trek,* and *Interstellar* show different types of human destiny in space — evolution, exploration, and flourishing versus reversal, survival, and extinction. In the real future to come, will humans be enlightened space farers or near-extinct spore bearers?

CULTURAL REVERSAL AND CIVILIZATIONAL COLLAPSE. In *Interstellar,* humans face an ecological apocalypse. A similar doomsday scenario is depicted in *WALL-E,* the Disney space film featuring lovable robots and the detestable humans glued to their hover chairs and holographic screens as they gulp down junk food in a spacecraft cruise ship, as pollution has rendered Earth uninhabitable. Given the robots' discovery of a solitary plant back on Earth, the humans somehow muster the willpower to pull away from the 24/7 spectacle to return to Earth in hopes of bringing plant life and agriculture back to Earth.

According to Thorne, Nolan's vision for Cooper's world included the unexplained and/or unstated assumptions that "some combination of catastrophes has reduced the population of North America tenfold or more, and similarly on all other continents."[43] To determine if this were plausible, Thorne invited several scientific experts at the California Institute of Technology to join him in discussing *Interstellar* over wine and hors d'oevres. (Thorne reported that there was "great food" and "superb wine," so let's hope the science was equally supreme.) In sum, the scientists suggested Nolan's doomsday scenario in *Interstellar* was unlikely but could result from some combination of blight, climate change, exhaustion of resources, and "anti-intellectual ideologies" that deny evolution and turn away from science and technology to prevent future disasters.[44] Perhaps the blight (microbial disease) and pathogens were spread across numerous crops and plant food sources, thus endangering the food chain and cycle of photosynthesis upon which human life depends. Overall, Thorne and the scientists believed this nightmare scenario was "highly improbable" but still conceivable.[45] To me, the apocalyptic scenario in *Interstellar* is a metaphor and a warning for our planetary pollution and over-exploitation of the world's ecosystems.

Given these conditions, *Interstellar* presents a future with a massive cultural reversal, with humanity retreating backward into an agrarian and hunter-gatherer society. Since *Interstellar* shows only scenes from the American Midwest and does not show scenes from urban metropolises anywhere in the world, we can only surmise that the cities are in decay and largely empty or abandoned (given the tenfold population decline). As *Interstellar* makes clear, anti-intellectual and antiscientific forces reign. NASA is defunded and driven underground, civilization is collapsing, and humanity faces likely extinction.

Though the eco-extinction event might be highly improbable, the anti-intellectualism and dumbed-down society is all too real, and it dominates much of mediated society in the United States today.[46] For a recent example, consider the 2016 presidential candidacies of New Yorker Donald Trump (anti-intellectual power seeker) and Texan Ted Cruz (anti-evolution fundamentalist power seeker), chair of the Senate Subcommittee on Space, Science, and Competitiveness that oversees NASA. Only a cultural reversal and the widespread acceptance of cosmic doublethink can make it possible for a reality-TV star to become president of the United States and a fundamentalist politician to oversee NASA, perhaps the most important scientific organization in world history. (For more on cosmic doublethink and President Trump, see Chapter 3). Not surprisingly, Cruz's view is that that NASA should not be studying Earth sciences or climate change, the very antiscience and head-in-sand ecological scenario implied in *Interstellar*.[47]

SPACE SPORES. The choice in *Interstellar* is this: Either humans extend human life *off* Earth or they face extinction *on* Earth. This story resembles the plot of *When Worlds Collide*, the 1951 classic that shows humans rocketing to another planet to save the species. In the film, astronomers discover a rogue star (Bellus) moving through space on a trajectory that will cause the star to smash into Earth and obliterate our planetary home. Fortunately, there is a potentially habitable planet (Zyrus) orbiting Bellus, not unlike the planets orbiting Gargantua. Scientists calculate that Zyrus will get caught in the sun's gravity, thus leaving Zyrus to orbit the sun and become a new planet in the solar system. Since Zyrus could be our replacement for Earth, a team of scientists and engineers build a rocket in hopes of flying to the new planet. The plan works — a few dozen human spores are launched into space to save humanity.

TABLE 5 ***INTERSTELLAR*'S SIMILAR NARRATIVES TO *PLANET OF THE APES* AND *2001***

PLANET OF THE APES (1968)

Massive acceleration: The astronauts confirm Hesslein's theory of time travel at near light speed in *Planet of the Apes*, not unlike how solving the "gravity" problem and journeying through the wormhole accelerates humans into a distant galaxy in *Interstellar*.

Anti-intellectual concerns: Much like the ruling apes in *Planet of the Apes* deny evolution, the educators in *Interstellar* deny NASA landed on the moon.

"Prepared to die": As Dr. Mann tries to kill Cooper, he explains: "When I left Earth, I thought I was prepared to die." This echoes Landon's assertion that he's "prepared to die" for his country.

American flags on planets: Wolf Edmunds and Dr. Mann plant American flags on their planets in *Interstellar*, not unlike Landon planting a flag in *Planet of the Apes*.

The next Adam and Eve: Cooper and Dr. Brand are the next Adam and Eve; they populate a desert-like planet in *Interstellar*, much like Taylor and Nova in *Planet of the Apes*.

2001: A SPACE ODYSSEY (1968)

Mysterious assistance: In *2001*, extraterrestrials provide the black monolith to inspire apes and humans on their journey into space. In *Interstellar*, "they" provide the wormhole and Tesseract. By the end of the film, we learn "they" are "bulk beings" and probably highly evolved humans of the distant future, perhaps even representing Nietzsche's Ubermensch.

Surviving scarce resources with technology: In *2001*, the apes survive wars over scarce resources by creating bone technology that leads to space technology. In *Interstellar*, humans survive scarce resources by launching into space via space technology.

Circular space station: Though not as cleanly elegant as the circular space station in *2001*, the *Endurance* is also a circular spacecraft, its cluttered interiors resembling those of the International Space Station.

AI-powered computer-robots: TARS is the action-figure version of HAL.

Surprise murderer: In hopes of staying alive, HAL and Dr. Mann murder astronauts.

Jupiter and Saturn as starting point for cosmic voyages: In *2001*, the moon monolith beams a radio signal to Jupiter, near where Dave enters the Star-Gate. In *Interstellar*, the wormhole sends the *Endurance* crew to another galaxy. The wormhole is just floating in space near Saturn like the monolith near Jupiter.

Massive acceleration: Dave is propelled through the Star-Gate, not unlike the *Endurance* in the wormhole and Cooper in the black hole.

Parallel horizons: In *2001*'s Star-Gate, there are parallel horizons. In *Interstellar*, there parallel horizons in the wormhole. On the ice planet, there are parallel horizons on landscapes above and below the spacecraft.

Strange voyages for solitary astronaut: Cooper's journey into Gargantua is a scientifically ramped-up version of Dave's journey into the Star-Gate. A few times we even see Cooper's face distorted, echoing Dave's distorted face in the Star-Gate journey.

Astronaut ends up in strange place: At the end of his journey through Gargantua, Cooper ends up in the Tesseract, not unlike Dave ending up in the hotel suite after the Star-Gate.

Into the blackness: Much like viewers being propelled through the blackness of the monolith at the end of *2001*, Cooper must venture through the blackness of Gargantua in *Interstellar*.

Human floating in space: In *2001*, the Star-Child floats in space, signaling the birth of a space-faring species. After exiting the singularity, Cooper floats in space and soon departs for Brand's planet, symbolizing a spore-bearing and space-faring species in *Interstellar*.

When Cooper (Matthew McConaughey) asks Professor Brand about his "plan to save the world," Brand replies, "We're not meant to save the world. We're meant to leave it." Thus, NASA and Professor Brand conceive the "Lazarus Mission," which includes sending twelve astronauts through a wormhole in search of planets suitable for human migration and survival of the species. *Lazarus* is a biblical name that means "raised from the dead," but the mission reflects something less theological and much more biological and Darwinian.

NASA and Professor Brand could have given the survival plan a more fitting name — the "Pilobolus Mission." As discussed in Chapter 1, the human motivation to survive by blasting into space is very similar to the spore launches of the tiny *Pilobolus* fungus. *Interstellar* presents humans as a spore-bearing civilization, with NASA blasting twelve "spores" — incredibly courageous astronauts, scientists, and explorers — into the vast cosmos in hopes of finding habitable planets. Four other astronauts soon follow: Cooper, Dr. Brand (Anne Hathaway), Romilly (David Gyasi), and Doyle (Wes Bentley). The astronauts are joined by TARS, the robot computer with a sense of humor. The cosmic journey in *Interstellar* focuses on the fate of this crew as they traverse the solar system and pass through a wormhole to reach a distant galaxy.

To avert complete despair and hopelessness, Professor Brand concocts "Plan A" and "Plan B" to motivate the NASA workers to launch its spores. Plan A falsely promises the NASA workers their possible survival in space, which is necessary so they will keep working on the spacecraft to carry out Plan B and the genetic repopulation of habitable planets. Scientifically, Plan B is the only workable plan, *unless* Professor Brand or Murph (Jessica Chastain) solve the complex equations for the "quantum gravity" problem so Plan A becomes viable and NASA can vault colonies of human spores into space, not just a handful of astronauts.

THE QUANTUM DATA. Though much of the science in *Interstellar* is valid, some of it is also highly speculative. For example, *Interstellar* embraces the scientific concept that our four-dimensional universe is a membrane (a "brane") *within* a higher-dimensional "hyperspace," which physicists call the "bulk."[48] As explained by Thorne:

> When physicists carry Einstein's relativistic laws into this bulk, as Professor Brand does on the blackboard in his office, they discover the possibility of gravitational anomalies — anomalies triggered by physical fields in the bulk.[49]

Physicists are far from certain the bulk exists and whether gravitational anomalies can be harnessed, yet it is a scientific speculation that Thorne and many physicists are happy to entertain — "at least late at night over a beer."[50] This does not mean Brand's quest for the "quantum data" is bogus, just extremely speculative at this time. According to Thorne:

> *If Professor Brand could discover the quantum gravity laws for the bulk as well as our brane . . . he could deduce the precise form of the equation.* And that precise form would tell him the origin of the gravitational anomalies and how to control the anomalies — how to employ them (he hopes) to lift colonies off Earth. In my extrapolation

> of the movie, the Professor knows this. And he also knows a place where the quantum gravity laws can be learned: inside *singularities*.[51]

Professor Brand has solved half of the equations but would need the "quantum data" available beyond the event horizon of Gargantua, the massive black hole. As suggested by Romilly, there might be a "gentle singularity" inside Gargantua, a plausible singularity that could be survivable according to Thorne. Hence the journey of Cooper and TARS into Gargantua and the Tesseract, to the singularity where they hope to retrieve the quantum data.

GARGANTUA. The climax of *Interstellar* occurs inside Gargantua and the Tesseract, in one of the most spellbinding cosmic scenes ever filmed, rivaling the trippy Star-Gate sequence and hotel suite in *2001*. According to Thorne, the rendering of Gargantua is a scientifically valid depiction of a possible black hole, which Thorne spends several chapters explaining in his book.[52] After working with Nolan's team on the development of Gargantua, Thorne claims the computer models taught him new insights into the behavior of black holes, which physicists will be exploring in future scientific papers.[53] About *Interstellar*'s representation of Gargantua and its accretion disk, Thorne exclaims:

> What a joy it was when I first saw these images! For the first time ever, in a Hollywood movie, a black hole and its disk depicted as we humans will really see them when we've mastered interstellar travel. And for the first time for me as a physicist, a realistic disk, gravitationally lensed, so it wraps over the top and bottom of the hole instead of being hidden behind the hole's shadow.[54]

As it passes over it the accretion disk and heads toward the event horizon, the *Endurance* is a spinning speck against the vastness. Very riveting are the scenes where the *Endurance* uses the gravity of Gargantua to sling shot Dr. Brand to Edmunds's planet, while TARS and Cooper detach in the *Ranger* shuttle to enter Gargantua. By venturing into Gargantua, Cooper is going back in space but not back in time. Inside Gargantua, he will be heading toward the singularity and through the wormhole and gravitational anomaly near Saturn. But first he must pass through the famed Tesseract.

THE TESSERACT. Like Dave after the Star-Gate journey lands him in the strange hotel suite in *2001*, Cooper finds himself in the strange Tesseract inside Gargantua. A basic "tesseract" is a cube within a larger cube, but Nolan has created a much more complex tesseract in *Interstellar*.[55] Ascending from the singularity in Gargantua, the Tesseract is a three-dimensional representation of our four-dimensional reality (three physical dimensions plus time) inside the five-dimensional (four dimensions plus time) hyperspace inhabited by the "bulk beings." Most likely, the bulk beings are humans from a more advanced civilization in the future, perhaps examples of the Ubermensch theorized by Nietzsche. As Cooper explains to TARS: "Don't you get it yet, TARS? They're not beings. They're us! What I've been doing for Murph, I've been doing for me. For all of us."

Not unlike how the extraterrestrials inspired the apes to evolve and become humans in *2001*, the advanced humans are helping Cooper, TARS, and Murph "save the world" because it will make possible the existence of human beings in the future. Recall that Murph is Cooper's science-oriented daughter whom he left behind on Earth, an event that left Murph feeling Cooper may well have abandoned her in the effort to save himself in space. While Cooper is traversing wormholes and black holes, Murph becomes a genius physicist working with Professor Brand to solve the quantum gravity problem.

Functioning like a labyrinth across time, the Tesseract contains a physical representation of all possible times in Murph's bedroom, from childhood to when she is a physicist. By navigating through the Tesseract, Cooper is able to view Murph as a child and adult. The walls of the Tesseract are like event horizons inside Gargantua. Light can pass from Murph's room to Cooper, but not from Cooper to Murph's room, precisely because no light can escape from a black hole. That's why Cooper can only contact Murph via gravity through space-time. As TARS says: "You've seen that time is represented here as a physical dimension. You've worked out that you can exert a force across space-time." Thus, by slamming his fist against the walls of the Tesseract, Cooper sends gravitational waves into Murph's room and causes the books to fall on the floor (back when she was a child).

Showing how art and science can sometimes be in sync historically, scientists recently discovered the existence of gravitational waves. As explained by Dennis Overbye:

> A team of scientists . . . recorded the sound of two black holes colliding a billion light-years away, a fleeting chirp that fulfilled the last prediction of Einstein's general theory of relativity. That faint rising tone, physicists say, is the first direct evidence of gravitational waves, the ripples in the fabric of space-time that Einstein predicted a century ago. It completes his vision of a universe in which space and time are interwoven and dynamic, able to stretch, shrink and jiggle. And it is a ringing confirmation of the nature of black holes, the bottomless gravitational pits from which not even light can escape, which were the most foreboding (and unwelcome) part of his theory.[56]

This discovery is a testament to the amazing power of human reason, science, sophisticated technologies, and a century of hard work by physicists. That Nolan and his team can poetically dramatize the gravitational waves shows the power of art in a science-fiction film. Of course, the scientists did not discover evidence of the Tesseract, too. That's because inside Gargantua is where the *science* of black holes meets the *science fiction* of the Tesseract and the singularity that permits to Cooper and TARS to exit the black hole.

Once inside the Tesseract, TARS is able to extract the quantum data from the singularity. In another improbable sci-fi leap, TARS translates the quantum data into Morse code and Cooper sends it to Murph as tiny gravitational waves that alter the movement of the second hand on her Hamilton watch, which Cooper gave to Murph as a child and which is sitting on a dusty bookshelf next to a lunar module from Apollo's heyday. TARS is skeptical that she will get the data, since Murph is in the process of abandoning the house because of the impending eco-apocalypse. Motivated by Dr. Brand's belief that love is something perceptible that "transcends dimensions of time and space," Cooper believes the quantum data will get to Murph via the watch she kept as a symbol of their love.

Just before leaving the house for good, Murph retrieves the watch and notices the second hand moving backward and forward in irregular movements. She soon figures out that Cooper is sending her the quantum data, which she then uses to solve the gravity problem. Murph rushes to NASA to deliver the good news. Soon "interstellar" space travel will happen. With colonies of people set to launch into space, humanity will be saved by science, creativity, and bravado. In a beautiful sequence, the Tesseract quickly closes in a vanishing point near Cooper's eye, perhaps suggesting the Tesseract is a product or discovery made by humanity's vision in the future. After the Tesseract closes, Cooper is floating in space near Saturn, the location of the wormhole and the gravitational anomalies. Cooper then wakes up in a hospital room on a space station and learns that he and TARS — along with Murph, Professor Brand, Dr. Brand, and NASA — succeeded in preventing the extinction of the human species.

DESTINY IN THE VOIDS. Like the black monolith in *2001*, the black hole in *Interstellar* symbolizes the philosophical void into which humans must hurl themselves in the quest for cosmic meaning and destiny. Upon entering Gargantua, Cooper exclaims, "Heading toward blackness. It's all black. It's all blackness!" Rather than turn away from the void in fear, Cooper hurtles himself into directly into it, not unlike Dave following the monolith toward the Star-Gate. In fact, the final scene of *2001* occurs after we pass through the blackness of the monolith and into our destiny as a space-faring species.

Two of the key existential observations in *Interstellar* are offered by Romilly and Dr. Brand. Pondering the vastness outside the *Endurance*, Romilly remarks to Cooper, "This gets to me, Cooper. This [gesturing toward the exterior skin of the *Endurance*]. Millimeters of aluminum. That's it. And nothing out there for millions of miles that won't kill us in seconds." The cosmic nothingness may "get to" Romilly, but he and the *Endurance* crew have the courage to venture into the voids. Of course, human survival is at stake, but it still takes massive amounts of courage to hurtle one's self into the cosmic and existential voids.

After discussing the loneliness of the astronauts' journeys into the wormhole, Dr. Brand and Cooper have the following exchange:

> **Brand.** Scientists, explorers, that's what I love. You know, out there, we face great odds. Death, but not evil.
>
> **Cooper.** You don't think nature can be evil.
>
> **Brand.** No. Formidable, frightening, but not evil.

Dr. Brand's comments counter just about every science-fiction space film since *2001*, wherein the future in space is scary, filled with monsters (*Alien*), evil empires (*Star Wars*), and mass destruction (*Gravity*). In *Interstellar*, there are no monsters or evil empires, only humans struggling to survive in a vast cosmos via science, technology, and the courage to take risks. According to Jonathan Nolan (coauthor of *Interstellar*'s screenplay), cosmic nihilism is central to meaning of the film: "The antagonist is the void of the vacuum that we live in."[57] As explained earlier, this sounds very much like the "astronaut just floating into the void" in *Gravity*. That's why *Gravity* and *Interstellar* are not mere survival tales, for both films also imply a quest for meaning amid the cosmos. Indeed, the universe is formidable and frightening and perhaps renders us meaningless, but it is also knowable and understandable via reason, art, science, technology, and — yes — even "love."

LOVE AND EVOLUTION. As personified by Dr. Mann (Matt Damon), evolution is often portrayed and understood in simplistic notions of "survival of the fittest," meaning that humans will kill to survive into the future. While he is trying to kill Cooper on the ice planet, Dr. Mann (surely symbolizing "mankind") explains how the fear of death in the evolutionary instinct drives individual survival and thus the perpetuation of the human species. This is fear-driven evolution. It works for individuals and species collectively: Adapt and evolve, or die and become extinct. Of course, this is true. The apes in *2001* show this, as does the history of human warfare and extinction events on Earth. But *2001* also shows that evolution operates on multiple levels for our species, including our consciousness and the human cooperation necessary to build a technological civilization — the monolith inspires the bone technology that leads to space technology and human exploration of the cosmos. In addition to fear, love also drives human evolution. After all, the apes were soon caressing the monolith, as if *in love* with the mysterious sleek object and what it might represent.

Dr. Brand is correct when she says, "Love isn't something we invented. It's observable, powerful. It has to mean something. . . . Love is the one thing we're capable of perceiving that transcends dimensions of time and space. Maybe we should trust that even if we can't understand it yet." I think we trust love in our evolutionary process more than we realize, for it is our love of ideas and things of value — like art, beauty, science, discovery, wonder, nature, architecture, hope for the future, and so on — that propel us forward, individually and as a species.[58] It is love — love of life, love of existence, love of people special to us — that also fuels the evolutionary extinct and the quest to overcome the annihilation of our significance. Of course, there is craving for pure sex, sheer greed, utter gluttony, and total narcissism, too. But we must love things other than mere survival and sheer hedonism, otherwise most of the artifacts of technological civilization would not exist. Fear and love reside deep in the human psyche, side by side, especially when confronting the sublime and the annihilation of our significance and narratives.

VOYAGE INTO THE COSMIC SUBLIME. The single most important meaning and hope in *Interstellar* involves the voyage into the cosmic sublime. In her review of *Interstellar*, Johanson is moved by the magnificent imagery in the film:

> Nolan takes plenty of time for a deep-space grandeur that was surely inspired by *2001: A Space Odyssey*. The image of the tiny, tiny ship Coop and his small crew leave Earth in passing in front of the immensity of Saturn brought tears to my eyes with its juxtaposition of the might of nature and audacity of humanity in the face of it.[59]

In sum, the *Endurance* and crew must venture through the vastness of the universe, first to Saturn, then through the wormhole to another galaxy, then finally to the water and ice planets orbiting Gargantua. Next, Dr. Brand and Cooper slingshot around Gargantua, with Dr. Brand speeding toward the desert planet while Cooper and TARS hurtle into the black hole and Tesseract and then back to a space station near Saturn. On the voyage, there are numerous scenes that trigger the sublime:

1) Viewing Earth from Space: After blasting off via the *Ranger*, the astronauts are treated to several stunning views of a blue-and-white Earth from space. These views are met with no comment from the astronauts, who are just happy to make it to the *Endurance*. Once the astronauts are onboard the *Endurance*, Earth can be seen through the windows as the *Endurance* spins on its axis to generate gravity, echoing scenes from *2001*.

2) Passing by Saturn: On the journey to the wormhole, the *Endurance* is shown passing by the massive planet Saturn and its spectacular rings. As Johanson noted, the *Endurance* is but a speck gliding below the rings of Saturn, spinning in Saturn's shadow cast upon the planet's rings. We also see Saturn's rings and the sun passing by the windows as the *Endurance* spins.

3) In the Wormhole: Spinning as it enters the wormhole, *Endurance* is a tiny craft moving into the elegant, spherical wormhole, the inside of which is spinning. While moving through the wormhole, the *Endurance* passes several galaxies and all kinds of star formations and cosmic phenomena on the surface of the sphere, not unlike the Star-Gate sequence in *2001*. After passing through the wormhole, the *Endurance* is shown spinning as it travels through space amid galaxies and vast voids.

4) Gargantua: What can I say? Gargantua is truly spectacular, with its orange-tinted accretion disk providing a Saturn-like elegance. Every image of Gargantua is spectacular, easily the coolest and most beautiful cosmic phenomena in sci-fi film history. In Disney's *The Black Hole*, Dr. Reinhardt journeys into a black hole only to find hell and the biblical endpoint for humanity — the cosmic sublime is presented as apocalyptic and theological. By contrast, Cooper finds the Tesseract, the singularity, and a new starting point for the human species — the cosmic sublime is presented as wondrous yet crucial to human survival, destiny, and meaning in the universe.

The journey into the sublime yields the quantum data, which is necessary for human survival. Further, the ending of *Interstellar* may imply that Murph's solution to the quantum gravity problem is the key to unifying relativity (the universe at the intergalactic level) and quantum mechanics (the universe at the subatomic level) into what Stephen Hawking refers to as "the theory of everything."[60] Perhaps that unity in physics will lead to confirmation of the existence of hyperspace, which empowered the advanced humans or bulk beings. Perhaps it will ultimately lead to a better species, the Ubermensches who evolve new space philosophies and discard the old superstitions. Of course, we're not there. We're progressing in some ways, regressing in others. Near the end of their journey in the Tesseract, TARS tells Cooper there is no way humans could build the Tesseract, to which Cooper replies, "No, not yet. But one day. Not you and me. But a people, a civilization that has evolved past the four dimensions we know. What happens now?"

INTERSTELLAR: WHAT CAN WE HOPE FOR? In an early scene in *Interstellar*, Cooper laments: "We used to look up in the sky and wonder at our place in the stars. Now we just look down and worry about our place in the dirt." This world-weary observation follows a long tradition of humanity looking up at the starry skies in awe and wonder but also feeling fear and terror, triggering one to look away from the stars, down into the dirt of Earth. Thus another key existential theme of *Interstellar* centers on the contrast between stars and dirt as guideposts and endpoints for human destiny. In the film, we experience the awe of wormholes and black holes (central to human survival) yet face the terror of our possible annihilation in an ecological apocalypse that renders us extinct beneath piles of blowing dirt. Here's what we can hope for:

1) In the short term, our ecological and intellectual futures are very bleak. There is no better expression of this dystopian and apocalyptic vision than Professor John Brand's declaration, "We're not meant to save the world. We're meant to leave it." This suggests there is no hope for protecting the planet's ecosystems, no hope for cleaning up the oceans and environments, and no hope for a sustainable civilization. As symbolized by educators denying that Apollo missions landed on the moon, the future for science and life on planet Earth looks hopeless.

2) We face our possible extinction. Due to the blight-caused apocalypse and to anti-intellectualism, billions of humans have died off and the human species faces its possible extinction event. Given that human narcissism and consumer society may be causing a sixth extinction, it seems fitting that we might perish, too.[61] The trash and remnants of our civilization will become fossils studied by a future species.

3) We can make the impossible possible. Humans can be audacious risk-takers capable of achieving great things with art, science, and technology. Without doubt, *Interstellar* presents a vision of heroic scientists and astronauts who risk everything to save the human species, made possible by love, vision, courage, creativity, technology, and an overall rationality and commitment to science and evidence. NASA's plan to go through the wormhole is audacious, as is Cooper's seemingly impossible quest to retrieve the quantum data in the black hole. Both examples serve as powerful metaphors. *Interstellar* seems to be retrieving the vision of Apollo, where the impossible was made possible for the world to see via reason, science, technology, and a risk-taking spirit.

4) We have a lonely journey into the vastness of space. In one conversation during their journey to Saturn, Dr. Brand explains to Cooper that the twelve previous astronauts had embarked on "the loneliest journey in human history." Given that there is no sign of intelligent life in our tiny part of the Milky Way, our initial journeys

into space will require the astronauts to be more alone than any other humans have been.

5) There is no exit from existence, no exit from the future. Throughout *Interstellar*, it is clear: To save the human species, we had to follow the laws of the universe. There is no exit from this responsibility, or there would be no escaping the extinction event. To save us, there is only us and our brains, with no Creators, no prayers, no miracles, and no raptures. As symbolized by Cooper inside Gargantua and the Tesseract, there is no escaping the universe, no escaping the future. But it is a future of our making. While on the space station and recovering from his journey, Cooper muses: "I don't care much for this pretending we're back where we started. I want to know where we are, where we're going." Later, Murph advises Cooper where to go: "Brand, she's out there. Setting up camp. Alone, in a strange galaxy. Maybe, right now, she's settling in for the long nap. By the light of our new sun. In our new home."

6) We have the courage to venture into cosmic nihilism and the cosmic sublime. The *Endurance* as a tiny speck next to Saturn and Gargantua signifies our physical insignificance, yet it is a testament to the power and sheer bravado of the human species — to use the laws of the universe to venture that far into the cosmos. In the quest for survival and meaning, we will find our destiny. We need a philosophical launch to accompany the spore launch.

8. *THE MARTIAN*

Mars has long fascinated humans and Hollywood. First published in 1898, H. G. Wells's *The War of the Worlds* jump-started a century of wonder about the red planet. In Wells's novel, Martians land in England and soon start killing humans with a death ray. The human species is saved when the Martians die off because the immune systems of the invaders have no resistance to microbes on Earth (perhaps Wells's tip-of-the-hat to Charles Darwin). Orson Welles adapted the sci-fi novel for the famous CBS radio drama that was presented as a real-time news story on the night before Halloween in 1938. So realistic and dramatic was the broadcast that some listeners actually believed Martians were invading New Jersey. Hollywood jumped onboard with the film version of *The War of the Worlds* (1953) followed by *The Angry Red Planet* (1959) and *Robinson Crusoe on Mars* (1964). Arnold Schwarzenegger and Sharon Stone starred in *Total Recall* (1990), which depicts Mars as a corporate controlled strip-mining site, Wild West party planet, and virtual-reality tourism fantasy.

The end of the millennium gave us the completely forgettable *Red Planet* (2000) and *Mission to Mars* (2000), Brian De Palma's pathetic attempt at making a *2001*-esque film. *Mission to Mars* ends with Gary Sinese exploring the stars in search of the ancient astronauts who left a crystalline chamber buried on the desert planet. *Red Planet* and *Mission to Mars* both hoped to stimulate popular interest in venturing to Mars in the new millennium, but the public yawned and logged in to internet chat rooms instead. After September 11, 2001, few were interested in going to Mars except those wanting to flee the Terror War breaking out on Earth. By 2005, Steven Spielberg offered a dreary remake of *The War of the Worlds* (starring Tom Cruise) that supposedly aimed to reflect the terrorist anxieties of post-9/11 society.

HUMANS CAN BE CREATIVE, COMPETENT, AND COOPERATIVE. Based on Andy Weir's best-selling science-fiction novel, Ridley Scott's *The Martian* celebrates science, human creativity, and the inventive and benevolent side of hacker culture. It is refreshing to see a film in which the human species is portrayed as rational, competent, and cooperative, unlike the greedy, violent, war-mongering people that dominate science-fiction films. It's good to see China and the United States collaborating to save the stranded astronaut and later venturing together to Mars, a symbol of the human species collectively creating a space-faring civilization in the future. Additionally, there are no space monsters to kill (*Alien*), no evil empires to conquer (*Star Wars*), and no Martian invasions to resist (*The War of the Worlds*). Such optimism toward humanity and the future makes *The Martian* an unusual film. On the other hand, the film is philosophically bankrupt when it encounters the cosmic sublime.

"FUCK YOU, MARS." Presented in a quasi-documentary style, *The Martian* tells the story of an astronaut stranded on Mars after a massive dust storm forces the other astronauts to blast off in a shuttle and retreat to the orbital spacecraft that will return them to Earth. The stranded astronaut, Mark Watney (Matt Damon), is knocked unconscious by flying debris and presumed dead by the other astronauts, who barely make it off the planet alive. While NASA officials scramble for a way to save the stranded astronaut, he must figure out a way to survive for four years on Mars with less than a year's worth of food supplies. Fortunately, Watney is a botanist and knows how to use science to grow food in very creative ways. Of course, he manages to survive until NASA and China's National Space Administration (CSNA) collaborate to save Watney as the world watches on from Earth.

To give himself hope while living alone for years, Watney declares, "Mars will fear my botany power." Later he exclaims, "Fuck you, Mars." Given the worldview of *The Martian*, these are understandable lines. That's because Mars itself is presented as the adversary as opposed to monsters or alien Martians. Mars is just another planet to conquer in our image, with no explanation why. *The Martian* never explains why the scientist-astronauts are exploring Mars in the first place other than to collect soil samples. Are they looking for ancient fossils, microbial life forms beneath the red sand, or evidence of how Mars lost its seas? If microbial life forms were found in the Martian soil, that would be the one of most important discoveries in the history of human existence.

There is no attempt to approach or even mention these topics, unusual given that Watney — a scientist, no less — has plenty of time to reflect on them. How could anyone not think about those ideas as they wander around the planet? Watney creates a small crop of potatoes using Martian soil, but there is no mention of possible life forms in the dirt. The film is much more invested in playing 1970s disco as a soundtrack for exploring Mars. All we see on Mars is a clever scientist seeking to survive, not a scientist wondering about fossils or life on

TABLE 6 **TRAJECTORIES OF THE HUMAN SPECIES: *GRAVITY*, *INTERSTELLAR*, AND *THE MARTIAN***

	GRAVITY	*INTERSTELLAR*	*THE MARTIAN*
COSMIC IMAGES	• Earth and humans amid the black void	• Saturn, the wormhole, the black hole, the tiny spacecraft — all amid the black void	• A few shots of starry skies, a rescue mission in space
TECHNOLOGY	• Spacecraft: the *Explorer* shuttle, the Soyuz, the International Space Station • The Hubble Space Telescope	• Spacecraft: The *Endurance* and the Ranger • Laptops, genetics, and cryosleep	• Spacecraft: The *Hermes* • The Martian biosphere, vehicles, and satellites
HUMAN ERA	• 21st-century space age	• Mid-to-late 21st century	• 21st-century space age
TRAJECTORY IN TIME	• Reversal: From the present to the past, with no Hubble or ISS in space	• Acceleration: Several decades into the future and then a century into the future (after Cooper returns from Gargantua)	• Set entirely in the near-future, although it represents a reversal if the crucifix implies divine intervention
ACCELERATION	• Though the Hubble and the shuttle *Explorer* are orbiting Earth at almost 20,000 mph, we see them as if they are moving gracefully in space. • The only objects accelerating are orbital debris and the chain reaction of destruction.	• The wormhole accelerates the *Endurance* crew into another galaxy where there are potentially habitable planets. • Humans also propelled through Gargantua to save the future of the human species.	• Humans accelerate to Mars.
HUMAN DESTINY	• **Reversal:** Under the power of gravity, Dr. Stone hurtles back to Earth.	• **Reversal:** Cooper enters into the black hole and Tesseract to go back in space to send the quantum data back to Murphy.	• **Reversal:** Did the crucifix save Watney and suggest divine intervention on Mars?
THE NEXT HUMANS (UBERMENSCH OR NOT?)	• **Reversal:** Tribal warfare triggers the destruction of our best cosmic-space technologies. • **Reversal:** With the Hubble destroyed, we have blinded our most powerful "eyes." • **Reversal:** We go from astronauts to devolved humans learning to walk again.	• After Murphy solves the "gravity" problem, humans are propelled into space, thus saving the human species from extinction. • Cooper and Dr. Brand repopulate a desert planet.	• Humans begin the colonization and terraforming of Mars. • Humans will become Martians.
SPACE FARERS OR SPORE BEARERS	**Space Farers No More** • The surviving space farer crashes back to Earth.	**Spore Bearers** • Cooper and Dr. Brand are the Adam and Eve of the future. **Space Farers** • Murphy solves the quantum gravity problem, and humans become space farers.	**Space Farers** • The United States and China join to begin colonizing Mars.

Mars. Meanwhile, moviegoers are entertained with disco, and their worldviews are utterly unchallenged.

The discovery of Martian fossils or life forms would further destroy the pre-Copernican narratives by offering more evidence of our cosmic non-centrality and showing Earth is not the only home to life in the vast universe. Discovering why Mars lost its seas might improve our understanding of climate change or global warming, but *The Martian* steers clear of any controversial ideological stances. Why? Most likely, it was to not offend theist or anti-global warming moviegoers. I seriously doubt that Ridley Scott and Matt Damon are oblivious to these issues.

CRUCIFIX ON MARS. The appeasement of pre-Copernican worldviews begins soon after Watney is stranded. Looking for items that might help him survive, Watney rummages through the belongings of the other astronauts, all of whom were forced to immediately abandon their stuff to avoid perishing in the dust storm. Watney comes across a crucifix — with Jesus nailed to the cross — carried aboard by Martinez (Michael Pena), one of the other astronauts. About the size of a human hand, the crucifix is made of wood and violates NASA's policy of packing only nonflammable materials (according to Watney), but no one seems to care when the crucifix announces the arrival of Jesus on Mars. Later, Watney whittles some wood shavings off the bottom of the crucifix. The shavings are used for a fire that heats his mini-biosphere for growing potatoes in the Martian soil (fertilized with his feces). As Watney lights the fire, the crucifix is lying on the tray next to where the flame starts.

Scott steers clear of any commentary, leaving it up to the moviegoer to make a judgment. Does the burning of the cross signify that religion is meaningless for surviving on Mars? After all, Watney declares that to survive, he is going to have to "science the shit out of this." So he uses whatever is at his disposal, including the crucifix. Yet does the scene showing the crucifix lying next to the flame suggest that a Creator and his dead son are providing some divine intervention on Mars? Of course, moviegoers are going to judge that scene through the lens of their own cosmology. In one sense, *The Martian* is part-*Robinson Crusoe on Mars* and part-"Astronaut Saved by a Crucifix on Mars."

The appearance of the crucifix still begs the following question: Why bring pre-Copernican cosmologies and myths to Mars? As with Apollo 8's Genesis reading, it is cosmic doublethink that enables such practices. *The Martian* is the latest example of how humans will extend their pre-Copernican ideologies off Earth and to other planets. In so doing, we will eventually extend our tribal and religious warfare into space, thus showing we have no business colonizing or terraforming any planet. While *The Martian* was playing in theaters around the world, ISIS terrorists killed at least 130 people in an assault on civil and secular society in Paris, while a Christian terrorist killed 3 in an attack on women's reproductive rights at a Planned Parenthood clinic in Colorado Springs. For all the worthy science and human rationality on display in *The Martian*, the film's cosmic doublethink and the ongoing Terror War suggest that, in 2017, we are living on the *Planet of the Apes* and far from attaining anything like *2001: A Space Odyssey*.

THE DESERT VOIDS. In *The Martian*, there are numerous shots of the magnificent Martian landscapes, which are depicted as having *absolutely no meaning whatsoever*. Only once are they mentioned in the film, when astronaut Mark Watney writes to a friend back on Earth, "Every day I go out and look at the vast horizons, just because I can." Later, while walking on a rock formation, he remarks to himself that Mars is "4.5 billion years old" and he is the first person to be alone on a planet. Rather than saying, "Fuck you, Mars," why not imagine saying, "I love you Mars" or "Mars, you're blowing my mind today"? The makers of *The Martian* seem *utterly oblivious* to the possibility that the sublime Martian landscapes have anything to say about human narratives on Earth or our destiny in the universe.

Above the desert landscapes, the Milky Way would have been radiantly visible at night. How could Watney *the scientist* not marvel and wonder about the stars above? How can the film completely ignore the significance of the Milky Way shining above a

TABLE 7 **THE COSMIC SUBLIME: *GRAVITY, INTERSTELLAR,* AND *THE MARTIAN***

	GRAVITY
SPACE: INTO THE STARRY SKIES	• Orbiting a beautiful Earth, the astronauts upgrade the Hubble Space Telescope.
VOIDS: INTO THE VASTNESS	• There are numerous shots of Earth amid the black voids of space, along with numerous shots of astronauts as specks amid the voids. • Dr. Stone is shown tumbling toward the center of the Milky Way.
AWE	• There are numerous views of Earth represented as a beautiful and complex planetary system.
AFFIRMATION	• The views of Earth from space and the astronauts repairing the Hubble affirm human reason and our right to exist.
EXALTATION	• We see the views of Earth from space and the Milky Way.
TERROR	• The opening warning is "Life is impossible in space." • The entire sequence of the destruction is presented against the backdrop of Earth and the blackness of space. • There's the vertiginous imagery and the descent of Dr. Stone.
INSIGNIFICANCE	• We see numerous shots of the astronauts as specks floating amid the blackness of space.
ANNIHILATION/ EXTINCTION	• Although our best space technologies and cosmic media technologies are utterly destroyed, humans are still alive.

	INTERSTELLAR	*THE MARTIAN*
SPACE: INTO THE STARRY SKIES	• The astronauts are on a voyage through a wormhole to reach potentially habitable planets in another galaxy.	• Humans are in the early stages of colonizing Mars.
VOIDS: INTO THE VASTNESS	• There are numerous shots of cosmic vastness and emptiness; we see the vortex of the wormhole and the void-like blackness of Gargantua.	• Watney launches directly into the stars with no top on the spacecraft.
AWE	• There are numerous scenes of galaxies, cosmic vastness, Saturn, Gargantua, and the wormhole.	• There are numerous scenes of the vast Martian landscapes, which have existed for 4.5 billion years.
AFFIRMATION	• The voyage of the *Endurance* is an affirmation of our right to coexist with the sublime forces of the cosmos.	• Watney's inventive survival strategies and human cooperation on Earth affirm human reason and our existence as an advanced species.
EXALTATION	• How can one not feel exaltation toward Saturn, Gargantua, and the cosmic phenomena in the wormhole?	• There are the views of Martian landscapes, and we see successful humans doing incredible things.
TERROR	• Human extinction is very possible. • The terror of dying on the voyage of the *Endurance* is sublimated, countered by the astronauts' reason, courage, creativity, and scientific discoveries. • Cooper briefly experiences terror in the Tesseract.	• There's a massive dust storm on Mars. • Watney is alone on Mars and facing death by starvation. • Watney tumbles through space to reach the *Hermes*.
INSIGNIFICANCE	• The *Endurance* is a tiny speck next to Saturn and Gargantua.	• We see numerous shots of Watney and the NASA camp as tiny specks on Mars.
ANNIHILATION/ EXTINCTION	• Humanity's near extinction shows the annihilation of our meaning, but our survival is a symbol of our non-annihilation. • Cooper and Dr. Brand survive to extend human life to other planets, thus reducing our chances for extinction. • Survival seems to be our ultimate meaning in space, with the evolutionary instinct fueling love, science, and risk-taking.	• Watney's survival and rescue are symbols of our non-annihilation. • No meaning for humanity is provided beyond our survival in space.

single astronaut alone on Mars? Perhaps the filmmakers never considered the question because the film is oriented toward human centrality, survival, and conquest. From Apollo 8 to *The Martian*, almost fifty years have passed and humans are still blindly stuck in the same existential starting points — confronting nihilism and the sublime by packing a Bible and crucifix for cosmic comfort.

***THE MARTIAN*: WHAT CAN WE HOPE FOR?** With *The Martian*, Ridley Scott offers a largely optimistic view of the human future in space, which is a welcome relief from all the doom, destruction, and monsters. Though Watney is forced to survive a one-night dust storm on Mars, the film is a hopeful depiction of humans exploring Mars, especially if you buy into the dominant space narratives. Here's what we can hope for in *The Martian*:

1) Nations will cooperate in space. The key vision of hope in *The Martian* is the prospect of long-term cooperation between China and the United States. One of the first steps toward peaceful space exploration is developing long-term cooperation among the space-faring nations, which should include China, Russia, the United States, India, Japan, and the European Space Agency all setting aside their nationalism and cooperating as a single species in space exploration.

2) Humans can be rational and competent in space. That astronauts were able to reach Mars assumes that the successful exploration of planets by humans is possible in the future. No reasons are presented for why humans are on Mars, but Watney's creative deployment of science should encourage geeks, hackers, and scientists everywhere.

3) Humans will extend their myths and superstitions into space. Why else bring a crucifix?

4) *The Martian* is an advertisement for terraforming and colonizing Mars, with the United States and China leading the way. Why? Because we can, it seems. There is no explanation of why we are on Mars, what we might discover, or what it means.

5) *The Martian* seems utterly oblivious to the cosmic sublime and the beauty of the Martian deserts and the Milky Way above. In this sense, *The Martian* offers no answers to the most challenging and meaningful issues facing human destiny in space. Aside from the hopeful vision of US-China cooperation, the dominant space narratives remain, absent any cosmic meaning.

9. SPACE FILMS: WHAT CAN WE HOPE FOR?

In the cosmic sense, it is amazing that we exist and create films like *2001* and *Interstellar*. It is perfectly causal and scientific yet still incredible that the universe produced the human species, that hydrogen atoms evolved for 13.7 billion years to produce advanced simians aware of their own existence and the universe beyond themselves, capable of experiencing cosmic beauty and contemplating its place in this vast and ancient cosmos. Yet we are burdened with the quest for meaning and purpose, never more so than now, when our greatest intellectual accomplishment — discovering the epic universe with 2 trillion galaxies stretching across 100 billion light years — has destroyed all our previous narratives that explain human origins and destiny. Cosmologists Brian Cox and Andrew Cohen call it "our ascent into insignificance."[62] But we're in denial.

Our struggles with nihilism and lack of a new cosmic narrative in our greatest space films are summarized in Table 8. Is human civilization ultimately doomed in the face of perpetual tribal warfare, where creationist monkeys prevail over science and secularism — the massive cultural reversal symbolized in *Planet of the Apes*? Will our space weaponry and space debris render us no longer a space-faring species, as suggested in *Gravity*? In *Planet of the Apes*, the humans are mute and ignorant, while in *Gravity* we are left cosmically blinded, with our most powerful "eyes" destroyed. Will we continue on the path of ecological destruction and intellectual devolution suggested in *Interstellar*?

Philosophically motivated by *2001* and *Interstellar*, will we *not* wait until our extinction is imminent to confront the cosmic sublime and explore new meanings within the awe and annihilation? Will we cooperate as a scientific species to colonize to Mars, as symbolized in *The Martian*? Most idealistically, could be we become the civilization of peaceful space farers and space tourists portrayed in *2001*, a human species unafraid to venture ever deeper into the cosmic sublime in the uncertain quest for our meaning and destiny? As suggested in *2001*, will our explorations into nihilism and the vast cosmos produce an Ubermensch, a much more intellectually evolved species that explores in peace, protects the ecosystems of the planets it encounters, and journeys through the cosmos in the quest for beauty, sublimity, and the experience of the infinite? Or will we merely be a species capable of producing technological Ubermensches in space while still behaving like warrior apes far removed from a philosophical Ubermensch and truly advanced species?

Hope, meaning, enlightenment and a new space philosophy for our species and future are possible, but far from certain. Overcoming nihilism and Creators will take a lot of hard work by a lot of artists, filmmakers, scientists, theorists, and philosophers, motivated by hope for a human species connected to the cosmos from which it emerged. If we collectively fail in this task, then we will surely extend into the universe all our worst features — hyperconsumption and ecological destruction, tribal and religious warfare, and all the pre-Copernican and narcissistic ideologies that let us pretend we are the center of the universe and everything of value. If the human species is to ever become a worthy space-faring civilization, like something approximating the best philosophical ideals of *2001* and *Interstellar*, then it will need a new, shared cosmic narrative for its origins, purpose, and destiny. Otherwise we will remain a "planet of apes" needing an interstellar spore to survive.

TABLE 8 **SUMMARY OF SPACE/CULTURAL NARRATIVES IN THE GREATEST SPACE FILMS**

	PLANET OF THE APES	*2001: A SPACE ODYSSEY*	*GRAVITY*
ON AUTOPILOT Space technology moving smoothly forward	• Taylor's spacecraft	• Space planes, the space station, *Discovery One*	• The space shuttle, the Hubble telescope
ACCELERATION	• Into the future that became the past	• Into the future, arriving at the year 2001	• Crashing back down to Earth
REVERSAL	• Space age to Stone Age; humans devolve to mute hunter-gatherers	—	• Into the pre-shuttle, pre-Hubble, and pre-space station era
APOCALYPSE	• War: atomic	• Technology: HAL running amok and killing astronauts	• War: weaponization of space
NIETZSCHE'S UBERMENSCH	• Propelled into the future, the astronauts are like technological Ubermensches, the next stage in the evolution of space exploration. • What superceded mankind is not an advanced species but an ape civilization that rules the planet, while humanity has devolved.	• The HAL 9000 might signal the technological Ubermensch that could one day supercede humanity. • The Star-Child signals a new space-faring civilization and perhaps the birth of an advanced species, a cosmic or planetary Ubermensch to supercede current humanity and its outmoded narratives. • The peaceful space-faring civilization signals an improving and evolving human species.	• None — but the beauty in the opening scenes of the film, with the world's space farers peacefully working on the Hubble Space Telescope, show that a better species is possible. They are like technological Ubermensches. • Tribalism and nationalist philosophy send space farers crashing down on the *Planet of the Apes*.
CONFRONTING NIHILISM	• Survival as our meaning and purpose	• Our destiny located in the discovery of our meaning and purpose	• Survival as our meaning and purpose
CONFRONTING THE SUBLIME	• The astronauts display ambivalence and cosmic loneliness amid the vast universe and desert landscapes.	• Dave experiences awe, wonder, terror, and mystery in the Star-Gate and hotel suite, suggesting we can survive the sublime as the first step in our cosmic journey.	• Dr. Stone's terrifying crash back to Earth suggests a retreat from the sublime.
WHAT CAN WE HOPE FOR?	**Absolutely nothing** • Unless you are a member of ISIS, the Dominionists, or other creationist-fundamentalist group • Unless you are a fan of Tyler Durden or the Unabomber or are a total Luddite or primitivist	**An enlightened future with abundant hope** • Humans as a rational, competent, creative, and curious species • Scientific exploration coexisting with space tourism • Humans embracing their cosmic non-centrality by abandoning outdated creation myths	**Not much** • Stone's survival: a symbol of personal triumph over adversity • War on Earth extending into space • Our rational and curious side destroyed in space • Human species is cosmically blinded

	INTERSTELLAR	*THE MARTIAN*
ON AUTOPILOT Space technology moving smoothly forward	• None: NASA is underground with a tiny budget and minimal staff	• Colonization of Mars for no reason other than that the technology is there to make it possible
ACCELERATION	• Into the future *and* into the past (to save the human future)	• Into the future of Mars colonization
REVERSAL	• Going backward toward an agrarian hunter-gatherer society	• From space age to primitive agrarian age
APOCALYPSE	• Ecology: collapse of ecosystems	• Nature: massive dust storm on Mars
NIETZSCHE'S UBERMENSCH	• The "bulk beings" might be the philosophical Uber-mensches that evolved from humanity. • The scientists and astronauts are like technological Ubermensches as they propel themselves through the wormhole and black hole to save humanity and allow it to continue evolving.	• None — but the astronauts on Mars might be seen as technological Ubermen-sches, signaling the next phase of human space exploration.
CONFRONTING NIHILISM	• Survival as our meaning and purpose	• Survival and conquest of Mars as our meaning and purpose
CONFRONTING THE SUBLIME	• Cooper and the astronauts experience awe, wonder, terror, and mystery of the wormhole and Gargantua; our opportunity for survival is in the sublime.	• Watney is lonely, but there is no human meaning presented other than colonization.
WHAT CAN WE HOPE FOR?	**The possible survival of our species** • Ecological apocalypse; most life and humans die off • Human species saved by rationality and bravery of NASA • Human species exits Earth, becoming a space-faring (unified?) civilization	**Cooperation among nations as humans colonize Mars** • Humans taking the first step toward colonization • US and China collaborating to save Watney and later teaming up to venture to Mars

10. "MOMENTARY MICROBES" AND "SPASMODIC SMILES."

Stanley Kubrick and Arthur C. Clarke visualized a philosophical launch in *2001: A Space Odyssey* but provided few details. About humanity's quest for philosophical and existential meaning in an epic universe, Stanley Kubrick said:

> The most terrifying fact about the universe is not that it is hostile but that it is indifferent. If we can come to terms with this indifference and accept the challenges of life within the boundaries of death, our existence as a species can have genuine meaning and fulfillment. However vast the darkness, we must supply our own light. . . . If man merely sat back and thought about his impending termination, and his terrifying insignificance and aloneness in the cosmos, he would surely go mad, or succumb to a numbing sense of futility. Why, he might ask himself, should he bother to write a great symphony, or strive to make a living, or even to love another, when he is no more than a momentary microbe on a dust mote whirling through the unimaginable immensity of space?[63]

The black monolith is a symbol for the challenges described by Kubrick. Like it or not, these are our cosmic existential conditions, as revealed by space exploration and the scientific cosmology that ranks as our species greatest intellectual accomplishment. In my view, there is no turning back, no delete button, no exit from confronting these conditions and embracing the challenges. If we cannot meet the challenge, then, as Jean-Francois Lyotard wrote, we will remain little more than "a spasmodic state of energy, an instant of established order, a smile on the surface of matter in a remote corner of the cosmos."[64]

If human existence is to mean we are more than momentary microbes and spasmodic smiles, then we must confront the specter of the monolith. Like a *Pilobolus* spore launch, we need a philosophical launch directly into nihilism and the sublime. Creating a cosmic narrative and space philosophy with universal meaning for the passengers on Spaceship Earth in this *epic cosmos* — that's the single greatest challenge facing art and philosophy. An epic cosmos needs an epic narrative for the stardust that has become self-aware. Thirteen billion years of hydrogen atoms deserve no less.

PART 2

MOONWALKING INTO THE FUTURE

CHAPTER 3

POST-APOLLO CULTURE

This is Major Tom to Ground Control
I'm stepping through the door
And I'm floating in the most peculiar way
And the stars look very different today
For here am I sitting in a tin can
Far above the world
Planet Earth is blue
And there's nothing I can do.

— *David Bowie ("Space Oddity")*

1. FROM *2001* TO THE *PLANET OF THE APES*

The Apollo moon landings were perhaps the single greatest technological achievement of the human species. Neil Armstrong's moonwalk might be the most important event of the 20th century. Most of the world celebrated in awe and wonder, exclaiming, "We did it!" Then we suddenly pulled the plug on the Apollo program and canceled future landings after Apollo 17. Why? What the hell happened after the Apollo voyages?

Some people say *Vietnam, Watergate, the 1970s recession, tight government budgets, or the thaw of the Cold War* or present the latest theory about the moon landings being faked. These are all just excuses for lazy thinking.

The truth is that we could have *easily* afforded to continue the voyages to the moon and beyond *if humanity had really wanted the voyages.* But we would much rather wage wars — cold wars, hot wars, and the terror wars of the 21st century. Rather than bringing us the future as depicted in *2001: A Space Odyssey*, 2001 brought us a battle for the past. Instead of Kubrick's awesome space hotel, that very year we got annihilated skyscrapers and a war where Christian and Islamic fundamentalists were fighting over creation myths and against the modern world, while secular society submitted to total planetary surveillance and a massive erosion of privacy and civil liberties.[1] Meanwhile, the advanced simians running planet Earth were busy with their narcissistic world of status updates and endless consumption while largely in denial of climate change and the possibility of causing a sixth extinction. The American simians even elected a sexist and racist reality TV star as president. It's no wonder we had no odyssey by 2001: We have yet to escape from the *Planet of the Apes*.

In the wake of Apollo and the cosmic nihilism it televised, we found ourselves facing two potential paths into the future:

1. We could deny the cosmic nihilism and continue seeking meaning in our pre-Copernican narratives (Creators, tribes, careers, corporations, nations, wars, etc.), while maintaining the illusion of cosmic centrality with theism, consumerism, and social media technologies.

2. We could develop a new cosmic cultural narrative and space philosophy that overcame the nihilism by integrating our planet and species into the cosmology of the expanding universe.

Since Apollo, most everyone selected some combination of path 1. While our arts and sciences have continued to accelerate into the future and into ever-deeper space, most of our cultural ideologies have reversed inward toward pre-Copernican cosmic centrality, symbolized by the narcissistic fixation on Creators, consumption, and selfies. So in some ways we are going forward, but in many ways we are going backward.

Welcome to post-Apollo culture. We are moonwalking into the future.

2. TWO "MOONWALKERS": NEIL ARMSTRONG AND MICHAEL JACKSON

Although images of the Apollo 11 moon walk resurfaced on MTV in the early 1980s (as part of the network's hourly station identification), introducing a new generation of youth to NASA's iconic photos, the images were devoid of much meaning. While Armstrong's moon walk was still culturally noteworthy enough for MTV to utilize it as a marketing tool, another "moonwalk" would soon surpass it in significance, first on American television and ultimately worldwide. It was the moonwalk dance step devised by Michael Jackson.

This is nothing against Jackson, who was one of the most electrifying pop performers of the past fifty years. Like millions of people in the 1980s, I too hit the dance floor to move to Michael's songs. At Jackson's memorial service in July 2009, Berry Gordy, founder of Motown Records, eloquently expressed the cosmic cultural trajectories of Jackson: "From the first beat of 'Billie Jean' and the toss of that hat, I was mesmerized. But when he did his iconic moonwalk, I was shocked. It was magic. Michael Jackson went into orbit and never came down."[2]

In our exploration of post-Apollo culture, it is useful to compare the two "moon walks." Armstrong's moon walk occurred at the pinnacle of the space age and represented the culmination of a decade-long race to the moon. Apollo 11 signified scientific understanding and technological accomplishment for the human species, along with the symbolic Cold War triumph for the United States. Though the broadcast of Armstrong's moon walk was an inevitable media spectacle, it took place *on the moon*. The event itself was a demonstration of human progress and advancement. As a result, astronauts became the most revered heroes of that era's generation.

Jackson's "moonwalk" occurred amid the explosion of the nonstop information age. When Jackson debuted the dance move in 1983 on an NBC program celebrating Motown's 25th anniversary, cable TV and personal computers were just beginning to shape the 24/7 electronic media spectacle we all now inhabit. Jackson's moonwalk became a lasting media image like Armstrong's, but it took place *on a stage*. At this point in time, stars of the media spectacle — rock stars, movie stars, TV personalities, and gladiator footballers — became the most revered heroes of that era's generation.

Among Jackson's countless musical appearances was his role as a spaceman in Francis Ford Coppola's 17-minute 3-D short, *Captain EO* (1986). The film, which ran for nearly a decade at the Disney theme parks and cost a whopping $30 million, qualified then as the priciest flick per minute in history. Soon after, Jackson wrote, starred in, and served as executive producer for the film *Moonwalker* (1988), which was immediately followed up by the *Michael Jackson's Moonwalker* video games.

Jackson's memorial, held on July 9, 2009, was broadcast on 18 networks in America, reached approximately 200 nations, and streamed throughout cyberspace. By comparison, the 40th anniversary of Neil's moon walk 11 days later on July 20 was practically ignored.

In the end, Armstrong's moon walk was about going forward, while Jackson's "moonwalk" only *appeared* as if it were going forward when it was actually going *backward*. And that's exactly what we're doing in the 21st century — moonwalking into the future, as our arts, sciences, and technologies advance and accelerate while most of our ideologies and narratives regress and reverse.

3. ELVIS: ALOHA FROM SPACE

Within months of the Apollo 11 moon walk, the worldwide excitement and euphoria dissipated. The topic of space exploration all but vanished from the front pages of newspapers and prime-time telecasts, and the space age entered a stage of global entropy from which it has yet to fully recover, despite the developing space projects of the 21st century. Hardly anything really changed, as if *Earthrise* and the moon walk meant *nothing* to the human species that made it possible.

On January 14, 1973, less than one month after the early shutdown of Apollo, Elvis Presley performed a live concert in Honolulu called *Elvis: Aloha from Hawaii* that was broadcast via satellite to Japan, Australia, New Zealand, the Philippine Islands, and other countries in the Far East, with possible viewers in Communist China.[3] The next day, the concert was rebroadcast to 28 countries in Europe. (Since the Super Bowl was airing on the same day of the concert, NBC waited until April 4 to broadcast it in America.) According to Susan Doll, writer and pop-culture historian, "When it finished airing around the world, *Elvis: Aloha From Hawaii* was seen in 40 countries by at least 1 billion people."[4]

Five hundred million or 1 billion, it doesn't really matter. What matters is the symbolism of the moment. It was the first global telecast since the end of the Apollo program. The Elvis concert signified our return to life as usual, our denial of the cosmic nihilism evoked by Apollo and our desperate need to fill the emptiness it left behind.

Such conditions were quite evident within the opening scenes of the broadcast as well as in the cover art for the top-selling album. The show begins with an image of Earth receding into the blackness of space. Suddenly, the recession is halted with an animation sequence of a satellite in space that's beaming the word "Elvis" down to Earth in various languages. Following the opening credits (consisting of just the show's title), we're confronted with the bare belly of a female hula dancer in a grass skirt. Next up is Elvis's arrival in a helicopter and shots of him greeting throngs of fans, intermittently intercut with a montage of scenes suggesting leisure and luxury: American tourists, yachts, modern high-rise condos, exotic mixed drinks, and more scantily clad Hawaiian women. It took less than a month to counter cosmic nihilism with the Earthly distractions of entertainment, spectacle, and recreational eroticism, restoring our sense of cosmic centrality and putting us back at the center of everything.

The *Elvis: Aloha from Hawaii* album cover replicates the outer-space view of the satellite and the Earth, but this time the satellite is "beaming" Elvis himself to Earth. We see a concert image of Elvis adorned in his famous "American Eagle" jumpsuit, with the rock star enclosed in a large circle that covers almost a quarter of the Earth; it's almost like some sort of space capsule. It's Elvis who is consoling the humans back on Earth in their newfound isolation; it's Elvis who's left to confront the cosmic nihilism and the fact of our meaninglessness. (No wonder he was dead a mere four years later.)

Less than one month after Apollo 17, larger-than-life astronauts are replaced by larger-than-life entertainers, NASA spacesuits by Elvis's famed jumpsuits, and the cosmic void filled with global entertainment.

4. THE PREMATURE ARRIVAL OF THE FUTURE

Alvin Toffler's sweeping work of social theory entitled *Future Shock* was published in July 1970. It offered deep insight into humanity's philosophical plight at the climax of the space age. For Toffler, our fast-paced, "super-industrialized" society had disrupted the traditional social order so dramatically that we had become traumatized. Entering a future that was hurtling toward us at ever-increasing speed with ever-increasing patterns of change, we were finding ourselves overwhelmed by the *cultural* transformations of the industrialized and electrified world. As Toffler explains:

> Future shock is the dizzying disorientation brought on by the premature arrival of the future. It may well be the most important disease of tomorrow.
>
> Future shock will not be found in *Index Medicus* or in any listing of psychological abnormalities. Yet, unless intelligent steps are taken to combat it, millions of human beings will find themselves increasingly disoriented, progressively incompetent to deal rationally with their environments. The malaise, mass neurosis, irrationality, and free-floating violence already apparent in contemporary life are merely a foretaste of what may lie ahead unless we come to understand and treat this disease.
>
> Future shock is a time phenomenon, a product of the greatly accelerated rate of change in society. It arises from the superimposition of a new culture on an old one. It is culture shock in one's own society.[5]

For Toffler, technology has launched society so far into the future that traditional values and conventional notions of family, work, education, community, and the like have been drastically altered. It's as if we don't recognize our own culture and destiny, plunging us into uncertainty and doubt. In addition, Toffler asserts, the more technology develops, the less stable our culture will be, preventing us from ever feeling fully settled or sure of where we are going:

> In the coming decades, advances in [sciences and technologies] will fire off like a series of rockets carrying us out of the past, plunging us deeper into the new society. Nor will this new society quickly settle into a steady state. It, too, will quiver and crack and roar as it suffers jolt after jolt of high-energy change. For the individual who wishes to live in his time, to be a part of the future, the super-industrial revolution offers no surcease from change. It offers no return to the familiar past.[6]

Toffler provides an exhaustive number of plausible examples to back up his thesis, although one does not have to agree with all of them to grasp the essential truth of his insights. Future shock is the emotional anxiety and existential dread felt toward a future that challenges all previous cultural narratives. As science and technology advance, humanity too will accelerate into this future — but upon encountering cosmic nihilism and non-centrality, we will become culturally paralyzed and retreat into the security of tribes and the past.

"SPACE ODDITY." Space, future shock, and cosmic vertigo played starring roles in the pop songs of 1969. David Bowie's "Space Oddity," supposedly inspired by the artist's multiple viewings of *2001: A Space Odyssey,* was released on July 11, just prior to the Apollo 11 launch. The BBC used the song as the "soundtrack" for its television coverage of the moon walk (strangely oblivious to the idea that the astronaut in the song had a communications malfunction and was stranded in space).

The song concludes with these lines:

> Ground control to Major Tom,
> Your circuit's dead, there's something wrong
> Can you hear me, Major Tom?
> Can you hear me, Major Tom?
> Can you hear me, Major Tom?
> Can you . . .
> Here I am floating 'round my tin can
> Far above the moon
> Planet Earth is blue
> And there's nothing I can do

The astronaut, Major Tom, is us, stranded on Spaceship Earth, feeling lost amid the cosmos and knowing "there's nothing [we] can do." That's the philosophical effect of nihilism in the wake of Apollo 8 and *Earthrise,* that blue Planet Earth far above the moon.

"IN THE YEAR 2525." For six weeks during the summer of 1969, the song "In the Year 2525" by one-hit wonder Zager & Evans was at number one, including the very week the Apollo 11 astronauts walked on the moon. It's an apocalyptic tune that forecasts humanity's spiritual, ecological, and technological doom and even incorporates some theist elements in its mention of Judgment Day:

In the year 7510
If God's a-comin' he ought to make it by then
Maybe he'll look around himself and say
Guess it's time for the Judgment Day

In the year 8510
God is gonna shake his mighty head
He'll either say "I'm pleased where man has been"
Or tear it down and start again

The song concludes with these lines and the hints of cosmic nihilism:

Now it's been 10,000 years
Man has cried a billion tears
For what he never knew
Now man's reign is through
But through the eternal night
The twinkling of starlight
So very far away
Maybe it's only yesterday

THE LATE, GREAT PLANET EARTH. Our culture's current fascination with apocalyptic religious prophecies has roots in a rather strange book from this era that's entitled *The Late, Great Planet Earth*. Published in 1970, the book not only provided readers with plenty of vapid entertainment to fill the cosmic void left by *Earthrise* and Apollo 11 — it also served to amplify our fear of comic nihilism. Hal Lindsey, the book's "author" (the book was actually ghostwritten by Carole C. Carlson), was a fundamentalist preacher in late 1960s Southern California. *The Late, Great Planet Earth*, or *LGPE* for short, was comprised of lectures Lindsey had been delivering for a few years at UCLA. Lindsey's main prophetic "theory" was that past, present, and future catastrophic events had been predicted in specific Bible passages, from Communism and nuclear warfare to economic calamity and technology-based disasters. Using casual language and slang to make the book personable, Lindsey assumed the role of a modern-day prophet possessing privileged, divine knowledge, guiding humanity safely through a tumultuous era. The "inspirational" book market was booming as a result of the rampant renewed interest in religion; as a result, Lindsey's book sold several million copies by 1975.[7] In 1979, *LGPE* was made into a documentary film narrated by Orson Welles.

Lindsey was a Creationist and was vehemently antiscience and anti-technology. Like other conservative fundamentalists, Lindsey believed that our industrial-secular society was in service of the Antichrist. He scoffed at space exploration, claiming it had nothing on the Rapture ("the ultimate trip"), which would eventually put humanity in touch with divinity, not merely land us on the moon: "Without the benefit of science, space suits, or interplanetary rockets, there will be those who will be transported into a glorious place more beautiful, more awesome, than we can comprehend . . . It will be the living end."[8]

In an interview with PBS, University of Wisconsin history professor Paul Boyer credits Lindsey with having initiated the cultural fascination with apocalyptic religious prophecy that continues into the present day: "He represents another one of those moments of breakthrough, when interest in Bible prophecy spills out beyond just the ranks of the true believers and becomes a broader cultural phenomenon."[9] It's no coincidence that this "moment of breakthrough" occurred immediately after Apollo 11. Several of the covers of *LGPE's* early editions as well as the original film poster convey this clearly — the Earth is shown arcing on a trajectory through the black cosmic void, the top portion of the planet fully aflame. There is no mistaking these images as clear references to *Earthrise*. In fact, the film poster seems to have used an Apollo photo of Earth from space that's arranged to look like *Earthrise*, upside down and on fire.

Returning back to Bowie's "Space Oddity," the line "And there's nothing I can do" captures the essence of how minimally *Earthrise* and Apollo 11 impacted the world, for it seemed that, despite their landmark scientific achievements, nothing had changed. Absent a universal meaning for the cosmic sublime, our space-age destiny was too unbearable for much of humankind, so most of us went in reverse, looking backward for answers. As historian Matthew Tribbe posits in *No Requiem For the Space Age,* the 1970s were filled to the brim with complex reactions to Apollo that relied on age-old superstitions and new age mysticisms.[10] When the Apollo era came to a close, Tribbe explains that "America [was] taking its *first steps to nowhere,* as its Space Age visions of progress and mastery of the universe succumbed to cultural forces that even the earth-shaking rockets of the Apollo era could not overcome."[11] [Italics mine.]

At the heart of these "cultural forces" was a perpetual allegiance to theologically based narratives and literature from pre-scientific eras; hence an allegiance to a "dual system of astronomy." We were existentially driven to arrest the acceleration, to reverse the cosmic trajectories, to explain and justify our existence by remaining at the center of the cosmic stage. When we took our "first steps to nowhere," we began to moonwalk into the future.

5. SPIRITS IN THE SKY

For its April 8, 1966 issue, *Time* featured a cover story entitled "Is God Dead?," a reasonable and provocative question for an era of unprecedented scientific and technological discovery.[12] Yet after Apollo forced us to confront cosmic nihilism, we once again sought refuge in the notion of an all-powerful God, denying the new knowledge Apollo had presented us regarding our place in the universe. Emblazoned on the cover of *Time*'s final issue of the decade (December 26, 1969) was the question "Is God Coming Back to Life?"[13] The answer was ostensibly yes. With a rebound back to religion, the "dual system of astronomy" was still alive and well.

Pop music in particular reflected this sudden resurgence in faith and yearning for the spirit in the sky. Andrew Lloyd Webber's rock opera *Jesus Christ Superstar* debuted in 1970 and became a Broadway hit in 1971, and Norman Greenbaum's "Spirit in the Sky" sold two million copies before the end of the decade:

> Goin' up to the spirit in the sky
> That's where I'm gonna go when I die
> When I die and they lay me to rest
> Gonna go to the place that's the best
>
> Prepare yourself, you know it's a must
> Gotta have a friend in Jesus
> So you know that when you die
> He's gonna recommend you
> To the spirit in the sky

In November 1970, ex-Beatle guitarist George Harrison released "My Sweet Lord," the lyrics of which reflect an integration of Eastern and Western religious terms:

> I really want to see you
> Really want to see you
> Really want to see you, Lord
> Really want to see you, Lord
> But it takes so long, my Lord (hallelujah)
> ....
> Hmm (hallelujah)
> My sweet Lord (hallelujah)
> My, my, Lord (hallelujah)
> ....
> Now, I really want to see you (hare rama)
> Really want to be with you (hare rama)
> Really want to see you Lord (aaah)
> But it takes so long, my Lord (hallelujah)

It's no surprise that Harrison and most of humanity wanted *to see* the Lord, as He was notably absent from *Earthrise* and all the Apollo images. The song immediately topped the charts worldwide. In 1971, it went on to become the top-selling single.

Well into the 21st century, the spirit is still "in the sky" somewhere for many of the "passengers" on Spaceship Earth who hold fast to a belief in their own cosmic centrality. A Pew study conducted by the Pew Forum on Religion and Public Life found that, as of 2010, 84% of Earth's "passengers" identified with a religion:

> The demographic study — based on [an] analysis of more than 2,500 censuses, surveys and population registers — finds 2.2 billion Christians (32% of the world's population), 1.6 billion Muslims (23%), 1 billion Hindus (15%), nearly 500 million Buddhists (7%) and 14 million Jews (0.2%) around the world as of 2010. In addition, more than 400 million people (6%) practice various folk or traditional religions, including African traditional religions, Chinese folk religions, Native American religions and Australian aboriginal religions. An estimated 58 million people — slightly less than 1% of the global population — belong to other religions, including the

> Baha'i faith, Jainism, Sikhism, Shintoism, Taoism, Tenrikyo, Wicca and Zoroastrianism, to mention just a few.[14]

About 16% had no religious affiliation, but they still might have had "belief in God or a universal spirit even though they [did] not identify with a particular faith."[15]

6. FROM *2001* TO *MOONRAKER*

Stanley Kubrick's *2001: A Space Odyssey* was released in 1968. Although it initially garnered mixed reviews, *2001* became one of the biggest box-office hits of the decade and generated much discussion about its meaning (see Chapter 2 for an in-depth analysis of the film). For example, what the hell *was* the black monolith anyway, and where did it come from? Where *did* astronaut Dave Bowman end up in his cosmic journey? The 35 mm and 70 mm versions of the film played in theaters well into the early 1970s, but because the thrill of Apollo had worn off by that point, *2001* faded from popular consciousness, even as its prestige eventually skyrocketed.

"ROCKET MAN." By 1972, Dave Bowman was dead somewhere out in the cosmos, and Bowie's Major Tom and Elton John's Rocket Man were space castaways — both alone amid the voids in meaning. As Elton sang:

> She packed my bags last night pre-flight
> Zero hour, nine a.m.
> And I'm gonna be high
> As a kite by then
> I miss the Earth so much
> I miss my wife
> It's lonely out in space
> On such a timeless flight
>
> And I think it's gonna be a long long time
> Till touchdown brings me round again to find
> I'm not the man they think I am at home
> Oh no, no, no, I'm a rocket man
> Rocket man
> Burning out his fuse up here alone

"Zero hour," "lonely out in space," "not the man they think I am," "burning out his fuse" — can there be any more poetic description of the demise of Apollo and the entropy of the space age?

ZIGGY STARDUST. Given that 1972 was the year of the final Apollo flight, it is no surprise David Bowie's Ziggy Stardust arrived on the pop-culture scene with his pioneering glam rock band, the Spiders from Mars. The youth of the world had been enthralled with Apollo and were promised a space-age future that was utterly unrealized by the adults running the show on Spaceship Earth. These youth were ready for the next best thing — Ziggy Stardust, the strange earthling who served as the emissary for an extraterrestrial with a message of hope. Ranking as one of the most influential rock albums of all time, *Ziggy Stardust and the Spiders from Mars* (1972) appeared against the backdrop of future shock, the terror of the Cold War, the emerging diversity of consumer society, and the meaningless planetary oblivion suggested by Apollo. The *Ziggy Stardust* album featured "Starman," Bowie's first popular hit since "Major Tom" in 1969. In "Starman," Ziggy advised us not to "blow it" because "it's all worthwhile":

> There's a starman waiting in the sky
> He'd like to come and meet us
> But he thinks he'd blow our minds
> There's a starman waiting in the sky
> He's told us not to blow it
> 'Cause he knows it's all worthwhile
> He told me
> Let the children lose it
> Let the children use it
> Let all the children boogie

Sadly, the humans did blow it, at least in regard to creating any unifying cosmic and secular narrative for the human species. The real meaning of Apollo blew their minds. All that was left was a desperate quest for meaning, identity, and individuality on Earth, often expressed through our iconic artists and musicians. Not only was Bowie one of the truly great musicians — he was way ahead of the curve on cultural changes and fluid identities, well before Madonna, Michael Jackson, Lady Gaga, Cindy Sherman, and a wide range of lesser artists and performers. Beginning with "Major Tom" and Ziggy Stardust, Bowie's sampling of *cosmic* and *personal* identities clearly anticipated much of contemporary culture's focus on constructing an identity in the attempt to stand out and express one's self yet also feel connected to something tribal and meaningful within what seemed like a meaningless universe.

"STEVE AUSTIN, ASTRONAUT. A MAN BARELY ALIVE." The pilot episode of the hit 1970s television series *The Six Million Dollar Man* aired in March 1973, three months after the cancellation of the remaining Apollo moon flights. If there is any doubt the space age crashed amid acceleration-reversal and future shock, consider the fate of Colonel Steve Austin, the NASA astronaut played by Lee Majors (one of the "sexy man" archetypes of the 1970s). The very first words of the narration for the series' opening credit sequence spell it out: "Steve Austin, astronaut. A man barely alive . . . "

At the beginning of the original broadcast episode, entitled "The Moon and the Desert," Austin is sent to the moon, where he is shown stepping down from the lunar module and then walking on the moon. (The scene is obviously making a clear reference to Neil Armstrong's first steps.) When Austin returns to Earth, he's affable and carefree, an individualist and a dreamer. He's at one with the cosmos. When he returns to test piloting, he crashes while landing a futuristic jet, and his body is horribly mutilated. He loses one eye, one arm, and both legs, and advanced computers keep him alive while his body is fitted with a cybernetic eye — complete with zoom lens and infrared capabilities — and new limbs that will give him superhuman strength and speed. As payback for being revived, Austin is forced to become a secret agent for a shadowy US government agency. His space-age dreams have crashed. The astronaut, once the world's hero, is now a cyborg 007, a sexy six-million-dollar man with nowhere to go in 1973 but backward.

Austin's first assignment is to rescue an Arab leader held by "terrorists" in the Middle East. The astronaut-turned-cyborg is now dashing across the desert instead of walking on the moon, kicking up waves of sand and battling terrorists armed with tanks and planes. Austin is initially captured, but he easily breaks the chains. He finally rescues the leader while hurling grenades at the terrorists. (The astronaut is obviously no longer "coming in peace.") At the end of the episode, Austin returns to America, the last line of the episode stating that he will now "serve mankind," a blatant bastardization of Neil Armstrong's humanist phrase.

Less than one year after the demise of Apollo, the Terror War was anticipated in a 1973 television show about a cyborg astronaut. Steve Austin's technologies propelled his body into the future, but Earthly ideologies reversed his trajectory back *down* to Earth and into the *past* to confront a religious war. It's the same in 2017. Science and technology are advancing (although NASA's manned program is dead, at least for now). Meanwhile, America's soldiers are armed with night-vision goggles, surveillance technologies, and drones and smart bombs, all advanced versions of Steve Austin's cyborg eyes. Also like Steve, our soldiers have cutting-edge medical technologies, powerful computers, and global communication networks, the very electronic components that emerged during the space age and the Apollo program.

As Steve Austin said to the scientist who rebuilt him: "When I was up there on the moon, doc, about a quarter of a million miles away from the real world, I felt a lot closer to it then than I do now."

At the same time Steve Austin was crash-landing on TV, NASA launched Skylab, the United States' first space station. Though Skylab was damaged during takeoff, it did not require a cyborg for repairs. It was eventually repaired by astronauts and became home to rotating crews of three at a time. Numerous scientific experiments were conducted, the most significant of which involved using the Apollo Telescope Mount to create a solar observatory in space. We were able to gain new knowledge about both the Earth and the sun from the photographs that were taken, plus the experiment inspired the development of many other space probes and telescopes. By 1979, Skylab's orbit had decayed, disintegrating as it reentered the Earth's atmosphere, with portions crashing down in western Australia.

The Skylab crashed just like Steve Austin . . . just like the space age.

SPACE-AGE CONSPIRACY ATOP THE SPACE NEEDLE. Given what happened to Steve Austin, it's not surprising that space-age trajectories were warped and distorted in 1970s Hollywood (see Table 1). In *The Parallax View* (1974), the space age collides with conspiracy theory when a presidential candidate is assassinated in the restaurant atop the Space Needle in Seattle. Warren Beatty plays a journalist who manages to uncover a Kennedy-like assassination conspiracy.

So, let's get this space plot straight: A presidential candidate is gunned down atop the Space Needle, which was built for the space age and celebrated at the

1962 Seattle World's Fair, the same year that President Kennedy ramped up the space age with his "moon speech" before he was assassinated in 1963.

THE SPECIES THAT FELL TO EARTH. In *The Man Who Fell to Earth* (1976), Nicolas Roeg's strange and surrealist sci-fi film, David Bowie plays a humanoid extraterrestrial reminiscent of Ziggy Stardust but with a different hairstyle. Arriving on Earth from a drought-stricken planet, Bowie assumes the name of Thomas Newton and aims to retrieve some of our planet's water for his species — water that this species had seen via our television broadcasts echoing out through space. Since his civilization is more advanced, Bowie produces patents on several innovative technologies involving energy, electronics, and photography, thus enabling him to create a global media and energy empire known as World Enterprises. Newton hopes the wealth his empire generates will enable the construction of spacecraft and technology that will allow him to return to his planet with water. At times, *The Man Who Fell to Earth* seems to anticipate the rise of the selfie and the 24/7 media spectacle, with its instant photo technologies and Newton's ability to comprehend the programming on twelve televisions at once. Newton yearns to return to his planet but remains trapped on Earth because of greedy corporations and the paranoid government. In the end, Newton spends his time drinking and watching television.

A metaphor for the crash of space-age dreams — where all of the human species has fallen back to Earth — *The Man Who Fell to Earth* suggests that space exploration has little meaning and is a waste of money. All that's left is to get rich, get wasted, and get it on, all while leaving the television turned on. As far as I know, this is the only film in which some of the sex scenes are intercut with shots of microscopes and telescopes, microbes and solar flares — apparently suggesting that interspecies sex is one way to unite the infinitesimally small and the infinitely large. As Newton and his lover, Mary-Lou (Candy Clark), are happy and joyful as they look through the telescope and then have sex, the film might be suggesting that stargazing is also a good way to get turned on.[16]

FAKING A MISSION TO MARS. *The Parallax View* meets Disneyland in *Capricorn One* (1978). It's a mediocre action film for sure, but the depiction of the fake Mars landing is brilliant, so brilliant that it's likely responsible for spawning additional conspiracy theories and pseudo-documentaries about NASA faking the moon landing. As explained in Chapter 1, the moon landings were not faked.

SPACESUITS TO LEISURE SUITS. By the time disco and leisure suits arrived in the 1970s, the new cosmic narratives Apollo and *2001* had offered us were mostly MIA. After all, how can the miniscule number of stars visible in the skies *above* the electrified metropolis compete with the strobe-illuminated dance floors *below* our feet? There's no need to seek a destiny amid the starry skies when you can "get high" on cocaine instead and dance the night away on a glowing dancing floor. The mirrored disco balls reflected "stars" throughout the darkened clubs, thus providing a sense of human centrality in a meaningless universe. Let's not forget that the name of the dance club in *Saturday Night Fever* (1977) is "2001 Oddyssey."

HOUSTON: FROM ASTRONAUTS TO URBAN COWBOYS. In 1978, *Esquire* magazine sent writer Aaron Latham to Gilley's Saloon in the Houston, Texas suburb of Pasadena to cover the thriving cowboy subculture that had recently appeared. Latham's piece, "The Ballad of the Urban Cowboy: America's Search for True Grit," put Gilley's and its Wild West wannabes in the spotlight. Latham and James Bridges wrote the script for *Urban Cowboy* (1980), which became a major box-office hit.

In his article, Latham asserts that this cowboy subculture, preeminent among the town's blue-collar refinery workers, had developed as a way of coping with what Toffler refers to as "the acceleration of change" — because society had launched so far and so quickly into the future, it generated anxiety, which in turn caused people to revert to the old and familiar to get their bearings. "As the country grows more and more complex, it seems to need simpler and simpler values," Latham declares. As a result, the residents of Pasadena sought refuge in a conventional, all-American icon of the region's legendary past: the cowboy, which Latham classified as America's "most durable myth."[17]

Latham's claim is largely true, as NASA and the 1977 Voyager launch ostensibly proved too cosmic and cerebral for "true grit" in late 1970s America. By upholding cowboys as America's true heroes and subsequently displacing astronauts and other space farers from bearing the title, both Houston (home to Mission Control) and Hollywood had engaged in a major cultural reversal. Heroes commanding lunar modules were replaced by macho men conquering mechanical bulls. The Apollo astronauts all but disappeared behind media culture's horizon, wholly eclipsed by the various other types of simulacra representing so-called masculine heroism.

With the publication of the *Esquire* article, Gilley's temporarily became the pop-culture "center of the universe," as stated in the documentary *Urban Cowboy: The Rise and Fall of Gilley's* (2015), produced by the CMT (Country Music Television) network. Moving from the Hustle to the Two-Step and Cotton-Eyed Joe, the Gilley's cowboys were figuratively moonwalking in Pasadena, Texas before Michael Jackson showcased the step for the first time onstage in Pasadena, California. Almost all of these cowboys were simulacra of the original cowboys that were no longer needed in a shrinking frontier dominated by corporate agriculture. These were theme-park cowboys, men traumatized by feminism and future shock, acting out a desperate quest for masculinity and authenticity, now reduced to driving their pickup trucks across the concrete frontiers of the sprawling cities.

MAX ROCKATANSKY. Even the low-budget *Mad Max* (1979) illustrated the entropy of the space age. Set in a dystopian and apocalyptic future, the antihero is a highway cop who battles motorcycle gangs and a corrupt legal system. What's the antihero's name? Max Rockatansky (or perhaps Max Rocket and Sky). Surviving the attacks of tribal road warriors is the most one can hope for in a future with no trips into the starry skies.

MONSTERS AND SPACE APOCALYPSES. Hollywood closed out the future-shocked 1970s with three films about space travel and human destiny — *Alien*, *The Black Hole*, and the James Bond film *Moonraker,* all released in 1979. The

TABLE 1 **THE DECADE AFTER APOLLO: STRANGE TRAJECTORIES OF 1970S SPACE FILMS**

1971 — *DIAMONDS ARE FOREVER*: Sean Connery's 007 ventures to Las Vegas to prevent Blofeld from using the global satellite system to either destroy or trigger the world's nuclear arsenal. There's a silly chase scene featuring 007 in a NASA moon buggy; since no one is going to the moon soon, why not a joyride in the Nevada desert?

1971 — *THE ANDROMEDA STRAIN*: A satellite crashes to Earth, carrying a virus that kills everyone in a small town except a baby and an old man. Space exploration brings the biological apocalypse.

1972 — *SILENT RUNNING*: Fleeing an over-industrialized Earth, an astronaut traverses through space in a spacecraft-biosphere filled with plants and trees.

1974 — *THE PARALLAX VIEW*: A presidential candidate is assassinated atop the Space Needle, the iconic skyscraper built for the 1962 Seattle World's Fair and dedicated to the launch of the space age. (This is basically a conspiracy film, although the space age is clearly implicated.)

1976 — *THE MAN WHO FELL TO EARTH*: David Bowie portrays an extraterrestrial who comes to Earth seeking water to save his dying planet. While on Earth, he becomes a capitalist media mogul.

1977 — *STAR WARS*: Science and technology have accelerated into the future, while the cultural tropes have reverted to the past.

1978 — *CAPRICORN ONE*: Congressional budget cuts and a faulty life-support system inspire NASA to fake a manned Mars mission in hopes of overcoming public apathy and cynicism. The walk on Mars is faked in a movie set in the Texas desert and televised to the world, with the audience none the wiser.

1979 — *ALIEN*: Our space-faring civilization is met by a spore-bearing monster in Ridley Scott's horror masterpiece.

1979 — *THE BLACK HOLE*: What's inside a black hole? According to this big-budget Disney film, it's apparently a biblical version of flaming hell.

1979 — *MOONRAKER*: Roger Moore's 007 ventures on a space shuttle to thwart an evil industrialist hell-bent on using satellites to deploy a deadly virus to wipe out a flawed humanity.

extraterrestrial creature in *Alien* scared the hell out of most moviegoers, giving outer space a bad rap. *The Black Hole*, the most expensive Disney movie at that time, offered some cool images of black holes along with a decent soundtrack, but the laughable ending was little more than a rehash of Revelation. Finally, in *Moonraker*, 007 has to defeat an evil industrialist who's plotting to use space technology (satellites, space shuttles, and a space station) to deploy bioweapons in order to kill off a flawed humanity to make way for a utopian future on Earth and in space. What will replace humanity and repopulate the Earth in *Moonraker*? Women who look like 1970s supermodels, of course, with a few guys who aspire to look like Steve Austin.

7. *STAR WARS*, SPACE SHUTTLES, AND SPACE STATIONS

The Voyager space probe and the *Star Wars* film franchise were both launched in 1977, with Voyager leaving for the outer planets and *Star Wars* arriving in the multiplexes. Voyager and its scientific discoveries would end up largely ignored by society, while *Star Wars* and its spectacle of apocalyptic warfare and hero journeys would be revered throughout popular culture. *Star Wars* features a complexity of other themes, too — the importance of friendships, our relationship with machines, the control of one's destiny, the battle between good and evil, and the resurrection of religion for our post-Apollo culture. There is perhaps no better pop-culture example of how we're moonwalking into the future.

MAY THE FAITH BE WITH YOU. The *Star Wars* saga hurtled filmgoers into the technological future while retreating into the cultural past, celebrating all the tropes of medieval yesteryear — beautiful princesses (Leia), reluctant heroes (Luke Skywalker), virtuous knights (the Jedi), evil rulers (Darth Vader), civil wars (the Rebel Alliance versus the Galactic Empire), and wise old wizards (Obi-Wan Kenobi). In the wildly popular reboot, *Star Wars: The Force Awakens* (2015), Leia is no longer a princess but a "general." Within the patriarchal military narrative of society, that's surely cultural and feminist progress. But within the larger cosmic narrative for the human species, "General Leia" represents a *simulation* of progress — she's merely showing that feminist babes can kick ass and wage war like their macho-men counterparts. Both General Leia and Katniss Everdeen from *The Hunger Games* series (2012-2015) represent the same basic notion — feminist progress is possible amid a regressive and militaristic vision of the future.

Star Wars perfectly illustrates the acceleration-reversal triggered by the space age with its fast spaceships, lasers firing throughout the skies, and the ultra-cool light saber, all of which are countered by the religious wars and bloody narratives of the human past. As many movie fans know, George Lucas was heavily influenced by the work of mythology expert Joseph Campbell, who wrote extensively about myths and the journey of the hero. It's true that every culture needs stories of heroines and heroes. Yet why must we consistently explore the cosmic sublime via ancient myths and age-old war? Do we really need more stories that celebrate militarized conflict? Can't we imagine space heroes *beyond* war and religion?

Apparently not, according to Lucas. In a 1999 interview with Bill Moyers on PBS, Lucas explains that the first *Star Wars* film aimed to reboot faith and religion for the youth of the world, celebrating a belief in God around the planet at the end of millennium (see Table 2). Lucas was certainly responding to future shock and post-Apollo culture when he chose to modify the film's original title, adding the subtitle, "*A New Hope*." For Lucas, religion and faith are the hope and glue that holds society together, enabling us to remain "stable" and "balanced" and to "hang on" to whatever we're hanging on to. For Lucas, faith counters Toffler's future shock. In the interview, Lucas himself engages in doublethink when he initially claims he does not see *Star Wars* as profoundly religious yet moments later states (yes, in the same interview!) that justifying religious narratives was the "whole point" of *Star Wars*. If we take Lucas at his word, then *Star Wars* is a masterpiece of religious propaganda, with God wars masquerading as "star wars." Embraced by religions around the world, *Star Wars* has proven prophetic. The Terror War is largely a religious battle for the past, with two tribes of theists claiming "the Force" is on their side.

A mere eight years after Apollo 11 and Neil Armstrong's secular poetics, Lucas used *Star Wars* to transform and expand Apollo 8's Genesis reading into a coda for the youth of the world. Given the global popularity of *Stars Wars*, can we doubt that humans will extend their religious warfare into space? Meanwhile, Voyager hurtles through the cosmic void with Lucas's God nowhere in sight.

That *Star Trek* of the 1960s was eclipsed by *Star Wars* of the 1970s and 1980s is very telling. The mere titles — *Star Trek* and *Star Wars* — say it all: a "trek" for discovery, a "war" for death. "Live long and prosper" was replaced by "May the force be with you." The science of *Star Trek* was replaced by the religion of *Star Wars*. Just before the final installment of Lucas's original film trilogy, *Return of the Jedi,* was released in 1983, President Ronald Reagan ramped up the Cold War with the Strategic Defense Initiative (SDI) — otherwise

TABLE 2 **THE ROLE OF RELIGION IN *STAR WARS***

Excerpts from an interview with George Lucas by Bill Moyers.[18]

BILL MOYERS: What do you make of the fact that so many people have interpreted *Star Wars* as being profoundly religious?
GEORGE LUCAS: I don't see *Star Wars* as profoundly religious. I see *Star Wars* as taking all of the issues that religion represents and trying to distill them down into a more modern and more easily accessible construct that people can grab onto to accept the fact that there is a greater mystery out there. When I was 10 years old, I asked my mother — I said, 'Well, if there's only one God, why are there so many religions?' And over the years I've been pondering that question ever since. And it would seem to me that the conclusion that I've come to is that all the religions are true, they just see a different part of the elephant. A religion is basically a container for faith. Faith is the glue that holds us together as a society. Faith in our culture, our world, our — you know, whatever it is that we're trying to hang on to is a very important part of, I think, allowing us to remain stable.
MOYERS: And where does God fit in this concept of the universe? In this cosmos that you've created? Is the Force God?
LUCAS: I put the Force into the movies in order to try to awaken a certain kind of spirituality in young people. More a belief in God than a belief in any particular, you know, religious system. I mean, the real question is to ask the question, because if you [have] enough interest in the mysteries of life to ask the questions, is there a God or is there not a God?, that's for me the worst thing that can happen. You know, if you asked a young person, 'Is there a God?' and they say, 'I don't know.' You know? I think you should have an opinion about that.
MOYERS: Do you have an opinion, or are you looking?
LUCAS: Well, I think there is a God. No question. What that God is, or what we know about that God I'm not sure. . . .
MOYERS: One reason . . . critics said that *Star Wars* has been so popular with young people [is that it's] religion without strings attached, that it becomes a very thin base for theology.
LUCAS: Well, it is a thin base for theology, that's why I would hesitate to call the Force God. When the film came out, almost every single religion took *Star Wars* and used it as an example of their religion and were able to relate it to young people and . . . relate the stories specifically to the Bible and relate stories to the Koran and, you know, the Torah and things. And so it's like, you know — if it's a tool that can be used to make old stories be new and relate to younger people, *that's what the whole point was. . . .* [Italics mine.] I didn't want to invent a religion. I wanted to try to explain in a different way the religions that have already existed.
MOYERS: You're creating a new myth.
LUCAS: Well, and I — I'm telling an old myth in a new way. I'm just taking the core myth and I'm localizing it. As it turns out, I'm localizing it for the planet. But I guess I'm localizing it for the end of the millennium more than I am for any particular place.

TABLE 3 **EVOLVING SCENARIOS IN SPACE FILMS: 1980-2000**

Ten examples *not* involving the *Star Wars, Star Trek,* or *Alien* film franchises.

1980 — *SATURN 3*: Living in a space station far from an overcrowded Earth, Kirk Douglas and Farrah Fawcett make love and do hydroponic research until the arrival of a psychotic Harvey Keitel and his killer robot.
1981 — *OUTLAND*: Sean Connery provides law and order on a space station.
1984 — *2010*: A tepid sequel to Kubrick's *2001,* this film proved that if we go into space, we'll need a great director.
1984 — *BUCKAROO BANZAI*: This was one of the few films that made science and space faring seem fun, featuring Peter Weller as the cool Buckaroo with the "right stuff" for the post-Apollo youth of MTV — he's a test pilot, physicist, neurosurgeon, and the lead guitarist for a new wave band.
1995 — *APOLLO 13*: Directed by Ron Howard, this is Hollywood's *only* film about an actual Apollo mission. If not for the incredible ingenuity of the scientists and technicians at Houston's Mission Control, the astronauts would have been doomed to cruise through space for an eternity.
1997 — *THE FIFTH ELEMENT*: Along with *Buckaroo Banzai,* Luc Besson's film makes space travel entertaining for the space tourists lookin' fab on a space station. For all-time future fashion coolness, the wardrobe from Paris designer Jean-Paul Gaultier rivals that of Ridley Scott's *Blade Runner.*
1997 — *CONTACT*: Based on Carl Sagan's best-selling novel, Jodie Foster uses the Very Large Array (radio telescopes) to search for evidence of extraterrestrial civilizations. Though the film collapses intellectually at the end, it remains among the most thoughtful "extraterrestrial" space films since *2001.*
1997 — *GATTACA*: This futuristic flick directed by Andrew Niccol suggests that it will be mostly the genetically elite (as opposed to test pilots and space cowboys) who'll venture into deep space, the men attired in black double-breasted suits and the women in dapper, black suit-like dresses. Nevertheless, the film offers a thought-provoking meditation on genetic determinism and free will and provides sound reasons for exploring outer space.
2000 — *SPACE COWBOYS*: Clint Eastwood and the gang prove that the old guys still have the "right stuff." (Too bad it's the new century that's in need of something other than another tired Cold War narrative.)
2000 — *MISSION TO MARS*: Apollo meets *Ancient Aliens,* as imagined by Brian De Palma. In one word: lame.

known as "Star Wars" — and made veiled threats against the "evil empire" of the Soviet Union.

Due to their multiple smash sequels, *Star Wars* and *Alien* would dominate the space film genre for the rest of the 20th century. Hollywood did reboot *Star Trek* between the 1970s and 1990s, but most of the films were largely insignificant. (Sorry Trekkies, but it's a fact, despite the directors' noble intent.)

On television, tribal and religious warfare squeezed its way into the episodes of *Star Trek: Deep Space Nine* (1993-1999) as well as the *Battlestar Galactica* TV series (2004-2009). Overall, space films between 1980-2000 were a bit less apocalyptic than those of the 1970s, probably because filmmakers were absorbed by post-Apollo culture, obviously struggling to imagine a new human destiny in a vast universe (see Table 3).

ORBITS OF HOPE. Although Hollywood was invested in depicting space as a war zone during this period, NASA was at least attempting to introduce manned spaceflight with the space shuttle program. Launched with much fanfare in

1981, the phenomenon of the space shuttle quickly bored most folks, generating big news only when they exploded (on takeoff with the *Challenger* in 1986 and on reentry with the *Columbia* in 2003). However, the space shuttle performed countless experiments in space and in 1993 conducted the most complicated repair effort on any machine in human history in its adjustment of the flawed mirror on the Hubble Space Telescope. Without the space shuttle, the Hubble would have been a complete failure. The space shuttle also provided us with spectacular views of Earth from space, reminding us of the borderless planet we share and enabling us to experience the cosmic sublime.

Though the former Soviet Union would soon collapse, it managed to launch the space station Mir in 1986, which stayed in orbit until 2001. Mir's most significant contribution was in revealing that humans could inhabit space for long periods of time, hence demonstrating the possibility of permanent human space habitation. Then in 1998, the International Space Station (ISS) was launched and its first modular components sent into orbit around Earth. Operated primarily by the United States, Russia, Europe, Japan, and Canada, the ISS is the largest artificial object orbiting the planet and can be seen with the naked eye on clear nights away from city lights. According to NASA, the ISS is "the most politically complex space exploration program ever undertaken . . . bring[ing] together international flight crews; multiple launch vehicles; globally distributed launch, operations, training, engineering, and development facilities; communications networks; and the international scientific research community."[19] The ISS motto is "Off the Earth, for the Earth."

The space shuttles and space stations have been quiet reminders that there is still a future that is *not* in shock, that humans are still a potential civilization of space farers. The ISS is a model of what is possible for the human species — peaceful cooperation and the expansion of knowledge via the exploration of the cosmos. With the ISS, one sees a glimmer of hope for the human species.

8. AFTER THE YEAR 2000

It might be hard to believe in 2017, but during the second half of the 20th century, the year 2000 was a symbol of "the future," a world of tomorrow filled with optimistic prospects for art, science, technology, and general human progress toward a new and better era for humanity. After all, this hope for a better tomorrow is why Stanley Kubrick set his space odyssey in 2001. Thanks to higher education, cultural wealth, and new production technologies, our quality of life has certainly improved in many respects. Major developments in science and medicine have helped us to live longer and healthier (if we choose to exercise, eat right, and drink in moderation). We have increased access to arts and culture, and our major cities are teeming with a plethora of restaurants, museums, and theaters. There's been significant progress in civil rights, best personified by the 2008 election of President Barack Obama in the United States and the increasing number of women and minorities playing ever more important, visible roles in cities and nations around the world. The increased ethnic and sexual diversity in society reflects the natural order of the human species, and such evolutionary diversity should be protected and celebrated.

Similarly, we need to continue the progress toward universal human rights for all peoples and individuals.

The bad news is that attacks on civil liberties and human rights have increased, and human rights are being abused — particularly through terrorism, torture, and repeated police brutality incidents. Though secularism is the chief reason for the emergence of equal rights in many parts of the world and cultural diversity flourishes in urban areas, it still hasn't initiated any widely accepted, long-term "grand narrative" outside of the global continuation of consumer society, celebrity culture, and our self-absorption via the internet and social media. Meanwhile, overconsumption is producing tons of waste and trash that's polluting the planet while destroying the ecosystems drastically enough that a sixth extinction may well be underway.[20] Just think: an extinction event in the wake of post-Apollo culture! (That's the very ecological future *Interstellar* portrays.)

THE BETTER ANGELS OF OUR NATURE? The famed Harvard psychologist Steven Pinker has marshaled a massive array of statistics (from a wide array of sources) that suggests that human society has become less violent, more peaceful, and more civilized over the centuries, especially post-WWII.[21] If Pinker is indeed correct, his findings correlate with the secular, democratizing forces that developed over the past hundreds of years. Science writer Michael Shermer posits that such developments were possible as a result of our enhanced scientific understanding of humanity and the universe.[22]

Though uneven in their development and application, the idea of universal human rights flows from the Enlightenment and democratizing ideologies. Obviously there is still much work to be done in the area of civil rights. Yes, minorities are subjected to less discrimination and have access to more career and job opportunities; there are more laws in place to protect women, people of color, the gay and transgender community, the aging population, and other disadvantaged groups. In addition, some believe certain "animal rights" should be extended to other species who share our planet. Such trends are great and need to spread around the world to help build a peaceful and sustainable global civilization, which acknowledges we are one species sharing a planet with millions of other species. Yet if we continue to abuse the planet's ecosystems, and if the underlying secular ideologies are supplanted by theist and antirational cultural worldviews, Pinker's and Shermer's optimistic forecast on societal evolution will be in serious peril. After all, what else does the election of President Donald Trump symbolize other than a massive cultural reversal into irrationalism (denying the science of climate change) and naked tribalism (racism, sexism, and religious warfare)?

In keeping with Pinker's optimism, the three newest *Star Trek* films provide visions of a notably better tomorrow, at least in terms of science and technology. This is in distinct contrast to the parade of post-2000 space films that depict a future filled with doomsdays and apocalypses *for humanity on Earth or in space* (see Table 4). Desperate for anything optimistic that shows human progress and survival in the future, science-fiction fans have largely embraced the new *Star Trek* visions. Directed by J. J. Abrams and Justin Lin, the *Star Trek* films do

TABLE 4 **21ST-CENTURY SPACE FILMS: FUTURE APOCALYPSES AND REVERSALS**

2005 — *WAR OF THE WORLDS*: In this remake of the 1953 classic, space aliens wage war on humans for unclear reasons, wiping out human civilization and rendering our species almost extinct. Steven Spielberg offers some vague allusions to the Terror War and post-9/11 society.
2005 — *THE WILD BLUE YONDER*: Werner Herzog's ironic take on a future planetary apocalypse and the cosmic meaninglessness of human existence.
2008 — *WALL-E*: After humanity's pollution destroys Earth's ecosystems, the remainder of the human species inhabit a space cruise ship, living as bloated humanoids glued to hover chairs and electronic screens.
2009 — *AVATAR*: James Cameron's space fable offers a critique of colonization and ecological destruction, with stunning special effects mixed with a ridiculous Pocahontas story.
2009 — *STAR TREK*: Two planets are annihilated and billions perish, but human civilization seems to be thriving, the *Enterprise* looks fairly cool, and the crew is a sexy bunch.
2011 — *MELANCHOLIA*: Earth is completely obliterated by a beautiful giant planet in Lars von Trier's ode to humanity's fear of cosmic nihilism.
2013 — *GRAVITY*: Russia blasts one of its satellites, and the remaining space debris destroys the space shuttle, the Hubble Space Telescope, and the International Space Station. George Clooney is killed, but Sandra Bullock defies the most astronomical odds in film history to make it safely down to Earth.
2013 — *OBLIVION*: Human civilization is annihilated during a war with extraterrestrial invaders seeking our planet's resources. Tom Cruise lives a cool space-age pad and has been cloned, which alone suggests a scary future. Tom defeats his clone and retreats to the natural world with a supermodel space farer.
2013 — *ELYSIUM*: While the 99% struggles to survive on an ecologically ravaged Earth, the 1% live on a space station above our planet. The space station seems to be a hybrid of theme parks, Las Vegas hotels, and the space station from *2001*.
2014 — *INTERSTELLAR*: Echoing *WALL-E*, a few humans manage to abandon our ecologically ravaged planet. The space-faring, spore-bearing survivors are led by Matthew McConaughey and Anne Hathaway, the Adam and Eve of the future.

indeed offer a glimmer of hope for some human progress, however shallow the overall vision. But in general, the films are more or less space-age simulacra, copies with an original barely in sight (see Chapter 2).

That Abrams directed *Star Wars: The Force Awakens* shows that both film franchises are utterly interchangeable and indistinguishable in terms of meaning and vision. As of this writing, *Star Wars: The Force Awakens* is the all-time box-office champ in America and seems destined to surpass *Avatar* as the top film of all time (in terms of ticket sales). It looks like George Lucas's space-based faith remains popular around the world.

COSMOS ON TV: 1980 AND 2014. Despite the popularity of science-fiction films, real science and cosmology are of little interest to most people. Many scientists have written numerous books and articles to explain the new cosmology to readers and popular audiences. Some have even produced widely viewed documentaries on the subject. Carl Sagan's *Cosmos* was one of the best-selling science books of all time; Sagan also starred in *Cosmos: A Personal Voyage* (1980), the brilliant 13-part science documentary series that has been viewed by 500 million people around the world.[23] Yet as best I can tell, Sagan's heroic efforts couldn't halt the increasing spread of creationism, fundamentalism, superstition, and paranormalism in America or elsewhere. More recently, astrophysicist Brian Cox provided an elegant and thoughtful perspective on human origins and destiny in the cosmos in the three-part series *Wonders of the Universe* (2011), produced by the BBC and aired on the Science Channel in the United States.

Then in 2014, Neil deGrasse Tyson, Ann Druyan (Sagan's widow), and writer/producer Seth MacFarlane rebooted *Cosmos* with the new documentary series *Cosmos: A Spacetime Odyssey* (2014). Hosted by Tyson, this series was the most expensive and most promoted science programming in television history. On the IMDb's "Top 250" TV shows chart, which features a list of 250 TV series and TV miniseries shows rated by IMDb users, Tyson's *Cosmos* ranks at number 6 and Sagan's *Cosmos* ranks at number 7. It inspires hope to see these scientific TV series receive an extremely strong rating by approximately 80,000 people, even in an informal poll. Yet unfortunately, the number of actual viewers of Tyson's *Cosmos* in 2014 reflected the general intellectual wasteland of American television and pop culture. The opening episode attracted 10.8 million viewers on several Fox-owned networks and then plummeted to a mere 3 million for the 13th and final episode.[24] That means only 2.9% of all Americans tuned into the first episode and less than 1% of them bothered to tune in to the season finale.[25]

Why such low ratings? Perhaps it was because the series presented a godless cosmos in which humans found that they possessed great *intellectual* power but were *physically* insignificant and not located at the center of the universe like they'd thought. In the *Cosmos* series, Sagan and Tyson present the triumphs of science and reason that most of human culture has, ironically, yet to recover from. If you want a snapshot of the low intellectual standards in present-day America, just consider that 97-99% of all Americans did not bother to tune into the most promoted science documentary in television history. And the scientifically literate has become just another niche audience in the 24/7 media spectacle.

TOP TV MOMENTS: FROM APOLLO 11 TO SEPTEMBER 11. In 2012, Sony commissioned Nielsen to rate America's most memorable TV "moments" from the past 50 years.[26] The results are provided in Table 5.

Note that 17 of the top 20 moments feature death and destruction, while 2 involve presidential elections and 1 involves a celebrity wedding. September 11 secured the number-one spot. At one time, the Apollo 11 broadcasts would have ranked as the number-one moment. Yet not surprisingly, Apollo is quietly disappearing from popular consciousness, retreating into the memory banks of the internet and YouTube — the digital eternity where Neil Armstrong can compete with Michael Jackson for Most Popular "Moonwalker."

How can Apollo 11 being overtaken by September 11 not signal a massive cultural reversal?

COUNTDOWN AT GROUND ZERO. The origin and demise of the Twin Towers are situated in key moments of the space age. Designed by architect Minoru Yamasaki, the World Trade Center debuted in scale-model form at the 1964 New

TABLE 5 **TOP TV MOMENTS: APOLLO NOWHERE TO BE FOUND**

1. September 11 attacks (2001)
2. Hurricane Katrina (2005)
3. O. J. Simpson murder verdict (1995)
4. *Challenger* space shuttle disaster (1986)
5. Death of Osama bin Laden (2011)
6. O. J. Simpson car chase (1994)
7. Earthquake and tsunami in Japan (2011)
8. Columbine school shooting (1999)
9. BP oil spill in the Gulf of Mexico (2010)
10. Funeral of Princess Diana (1997)
11. Death of Whitney Houston (2012)
12. Capture and execution of Saddam Hussein (2006)
13. Barack Obama acceptance speech (2008)
14. Prince William and Kate Middleton wedding (2011)
15. Assassination of John F. Kennedy (1963)
16. Oklahoma City bombing (1995)
17. Bush-Gore election results (2000)
18. Los Angeles riots/Rodney King beating (1992)
19. Casey Anthony murder trial verdict (2011)
20. Funeral of John F. Kennedy (1963)

Source: Sony/Nielsen, 2012

York World's Fair, the utopian event that celebrated the international "future" of the space and information ages. Construction on the towers began in 1966 and was not fully completed until 1973, the year after the Apollo program was cancelled. The buildings were destroyed in 2001, the year of Stanley Kubrick's space odyssey. All of these parallels are rather indicative of the profound reversal signified by the buildings' horrific annihilation. We can be certain that the Islamist terrorist attacks on September 11 were in-part responses to rampant American and Western imperialism in the Middle East, but the destruction of the World Trade Center symbolized much more in the context of modernity, global civilization, and the entropy of secular narratives now being countered by the world's fundamentalisms (Islamist, Christian, and all the others).[27]

The World Trade Center was imbued with multiple meanings across the cultural landscapes of the world. In terms of design, it was the ultimate in modernist abstraction and monolithic architecture — form and function unified in symmetry of epic scale. In the eyes of many Americans, the Twin Towers represented progress and achievement, while for many developing countries they were the epitome of the very modernity and industrialization that threatened their traditions, values, and way of life. For the Right, they symbolized economic freedom and American capitalism, and for the conventional Left, corporate empire and monolithic globalization.

The very design of the World Trade Center seems to have foreshadowed the rise of digital technology and the information economy, for the Twin Towers were like two binary digits — 1s turned on (as opposed to 0s turned off) — towering above the Wall Street district and the Lower Manhattan skyline. They were mirrors of each other, both simulacra with no original, 110-story Xeroxes, icons of binary code — 1s waiting to become 0s at Ground Zero.

Instead of being treated to Kubrick's space odyssey in 2001, the world encountered jetliners crashing into buildings, people jumping off skyscrapers, civil liberties in retreat, and a global Terror War. Sadly, September 11 and its aftermath are currently regarded as the first and foremost "events" of the 21st century and the new millennium. (I would argue that the discoveries made by the Hubble and Kepler telescopes are the most important.) Furthermore, September 11 certainly signaled a reversal in the trajectories of secularism, modernity, and civilization's political systems. The actual 2001 we experienced was far more regressive than the fictional 2001 Kubrick envisioned.

BACK TO THE *PLANET OF THE APES*. Somehow civilization survived the Cold War and the fanatical battle between tribes of socialist-communist-atheists and tribes of democratic-capitalist-theists collectively armed with 60,000 nuclear bombs. Civilization could have been destroyed in a single afternoon. The Cold War was sheer madness, as shown by Stanley Kubrick in his Cold War masterpiece, *Dr. Strangelove: Or How I Learned to Stop Worrying and Love the Bomb* (1964), which he made prior to *2001*. So far, we have avoided the total nuclear apocalypse, and that's a damn good thing!

During and after the Cold War, the narratives of enlightenment, secular hope, and human rights evolved into a global consumer society and 24/7 media spectacle, precisely as science revealed a vast universe and apparent meaninglessness for human existence.

Humanity's hopes for meaning and cosmic purpose are again being monopolized by the world's theologies, with cosmic nihilism countered by cosmic narcissism, especially the narratives of evangelicalism and fundamentalism. The Terror War involves a complexity of regressive ideologies that span the planet in the context of globalization and nihilism — a toxic mix of bigotry, racism, fanaticism, fundamentalism, aggressive tribalism, hypermasculine and patriarchal culture, the desire to kill or convert sinners and infidels, the utopian fantasy of returning to the mythical purity of the past, and the delusion of believing one is at the center of a cosmic plan ordained by the Creator of everything. These beliefs and dogmas are united in the pre-Copernican cosmologies of evangelicals and fundamentalists of all stripes — all of whom are cosmic narcissists claiming an imaginary Creator dropped off a cosmic behavioral plan 2,000 years ago and ordained said narcissists rulers of a tiny planet in the Milky Way. It's pre-Copernican ideologies haunting post-Apollo culture.

Like the Cold War, the Terror War is sheer madness, and it is dragging civilization back toward the *Planet of the Apes*.[28] Civilization might not be destroyed in an afternoon, but it could radically devolve over a century, especially in the wake of an act of nuclear terrorism. Ultimately, the Terror War is a holy war that reaches back 2,000 years and seems certain to continue well into the future. Given the widespread decay of secular narratives, it is quite likely that the forces of faith and cosmic centrality will be waging wars deep into the 21st century. As British philosopher John Gray concludes:

> The danger that goes with the death of secular hope is the rebirth of something like the faith-based wars of an older past. A renewal of apocalyptic belief is underway, which is unlikely to be confined to familiar sorts of fundamentalism. . . . Interacting with the struggle for natural resources, the violence of faith looks set to shape the coming century.[29]

It would be naïve to think space exploration is immune to these issues. The very fact of space weaponization makes it frighteningly easy to imagine the Terror War and future Holy Wars being fought somewhere other than planet Earth. If not checked by a new cosmic secular philosophy, pre-Copernican cosmologies will not only wreak havoc on the modern world but on future worlds in space, where cosmic crusades, interplanetary jihads, and war criminals on secret space stations will torture the sinners, infidels, and other types of non-believing earthlings or extraterrestrials.

"IT'S A MADHOUSE!" The Terror War and its accompanying ideologies alone are proof that much of humanity has yet to advance into the new millennium. Antiscientific cosmologies, cultural reversals, and delusions of cosmic-centrality are causing us to arc back toward *Planet of the Apes*. In the words of astronaut George Taylor (Charlton Heston): "It's a madhouse!"

To any youthful and idealistic readers: Don't let the faithful, the experts, the educators, the celebrities, the talking heads, or the power brokers running and defending these houses of horrors tell you otherwise. It *is* a madhouse.

You can change this, but not just from within Facebook, Instagram, and Twitter or in the embrace of blind tolerance absent any critical philosophy. "Tolerance" and "freedom of belief" are important and worth preserving, but it does not follow that we abandon critical philosophy or that all faiths and beliefs are free from critique. We must face our greatest philosophical challenges and not remain wedded to pre-Copernican delusions, still pretending to be the center of the universe via theology, technology, and consumerism.

9. COSMIC CENTRALITY 1: THE "DUAL SYSTEM OF ASTRONOMY"

In Chapter 4, I discuss Brother Guy Consolmagno, the Vatican astronomer who claims the Bible's doctrines apply to any extraterrestrials we might encounter in space. Not surprisingly, Brother Consolmagno thinks that if humans and extraterrestrials believe in God, such belief automatically places them at "the center of the universe."[30] He's right about such believers and their yearning for cosmic centrality. After all, if any humans or extraterrestrials believe the Creator — the entity who created and oversees the entire universe — has answered their prayer, cured their disease, guided their life, enabled their touchdown, made them famous, approved of their wealth, and planned their space mission, then they *must have been cosmically central* to the Creator's universe, if but for a moment in time. For the fortunate beings, this imaginary cosmic centrality is reinforced by the fact that the Creator *does not bother* to do any of the following for others — answer all prayers, cure all diseases, make all people famous, approve of great wealth for all, enable all players to score touchdowns, and plan for all space missions to be successful. After all, the *Challenger* and *Columbia* shuttles exploded in space on TV for all to see.

Given the cosmic nihilism inherent in NASA's triumphs, it is not surprising that post-Apollo culture has seen the proliferation of theism and Creators. Since 1970, old and new religions have exploded around the world (numbering 2,000 in America, up from 350 in 1900).[31] According to Kevin Kelly, former editor of *Wired*, this development was an unexpected one for the 21st century:

> One of the biggest surprises in the last century has been that new religions continue to emerge in modern societies. This was not supposed to happen. By the year 2000 everything was supposed to be rational and logical. And yet religions continue to emerge all around the world. . . . In places like China where there is currently a vacuum of meaning — no scriptures, no constitution, just the little red book of Mao and rampant Darwinian pressure to make money — it should be no surprise that vehicles of something larger to believe in will appear. In Russia, a belief in science mixes with a resident mysticism, producing new religions. In Africa, the dire lack of health care summons all kinds of new faith-healing churches. And in the West, the need to make sense of technology and our own mutating human identity will breed new religions.[32]

Of course, the rise of religions is a complex process, with reasons not entirely uniform. As Kelly points out, we have an inherent compulsion to make sense of the world around us. We also have an emotional need to be connected to a larger cosmic narrative. But in reality, most people are narcissists and want to feel cosmically special and live for eternity. The idea of insignificance and meaninglessness is too terrifying. Having a Creator with a plan is much more comforting.

A 2012 Gallup Poll found that 46% of all Americans believe in creationism, or the idea that the universe is 10,000 years old and humankind was created by God.[33] The total was up from 40% in 2010 but still close to the 44% reported back in 1982. These percentages are significantly higher than in the 24 other nations polled, where creationists amounted to 28% — still high, given the scientific knowledge we now possess about the universe.[34] The poll states that 32% of all Americans believe in God-guided evolution (down from 38% in 1982), and only 15% embrace the view that evolution took place without God (up from 9% in 1982). The 15% roughly matches the 16% in the Pew study who did not identify with any religious group. According to a National Science Foundation survey, not only are beliefs in pseudoscience, astrology, and the paranormal widespread, but many people also swear by the scientific veracity of astrology.[35] I guess, looking at it with a larger perspective, you could say these percentages signify an improvement since the Dark Ages, but still.

COSMIC DOUBLETHINK. Apollo 8's Genesis reading and humanity's fantasies of cosmic centrality are made possible by a certain style of thinking automatically deployed to counter the cosmic sublime and cosmic nihilism. That method of thinking is what I call *cosmic doublethink,* and it makes possible a "dual system of astronomy" to support delusions of cosmic centrality.[36]

As illustrated by the Apollo 8 astronauts reading Genesis from the moon, most of humanity will choose to ignore or remain oblivious to the flaws, hypocrisies, irrationalities, or irreconcilabilities of the pre-Copernican cosmologies, worldviews, and narratives they embrace. Such willful contradictions and false cosmological systems are made possible by what George Orwell ingeniously termed "doublethink" — a type of "thinking" in which people accept and believe that two opposite and antithetical propositions *are both true at the same time*. This is the exact cognitive process that took place among the Apollo 8 astronauts during the Genesis reading. As Orwell explains in *1984*:

> *Doublethink* means the power of holding two contradictory beliefs in one's mind simultaneously, and accepting both of them. The Party intellectual knows in which direction his memories must be altered; he therefore knows that he is playing tricks with reality; but by the exercise of *doublethink* he also satisfies himself that reality is not violated. The process has to be conscious, or it would not be carried out with sufficient precision, but it also has to be unconscious, or it would bring with it a feeling of falsity and hence of guilt. . . . To tell deliberate lies while genuinely believing in them, to forget any fact that has become inconvenient, and then, when it becomes necessary again, to draw it back from oblivion for just so long as it is needed, to deny the existence of objective reality and all the while to take account of the reality which one denies — all this is indisputably necessary. . . . [B]y a fresh act of *doublethink* one erases this knowledge; and so on indefinitely, with the lie always one leap ahead of the truth.[37]

Not only must the believer accept two opposite propositions as being true — he or she must also *feel good* about it, even take a certain *pride* in standing beside such cognitive contradictions. Orwell argues that doublethink would be impossible without this contentment. Doublethink and the avoidance of critical introspection lead to a justification of all wars and religions, all exploitation, all oppression, and all propaganda. All nations and their leaders practice doublethink to rationalize their worldviews, whatever they may be. Apollo 8's reading of Genesis helped the world stay "one leap ahead of the truth" (and feel good about it, too). If this seems implausible, then consider the minimal impact Apollo and Neil's Armstrong's words — "one giant leap for mankind" — have had on global cosmologies and cultural narratives.

To maintain dominant ideologies and worldviews, Orwell posits that doublethink *must extend to the cosmos* in keeping humans and their beliefs at the center of an imaginary universe. The following dialogue between O'Brien (the state torturer for the nation of Oceania) and Winston (the resistor being tortured) from *1984* illustrates this concept:

> "Oceania is the world."
>
> "But the world itself is only a speck of dust. And man is tiny — helpless! How long has he been in existence? For millions of years the earth was uninhabited."
>
> "Nonsense. The earth is as old as we are, no older. How could it be older? Nothing exists except through human consciousness."
>
> "But the rocks are full of the bones of extinct animals — mammoths and mastodons and enormous reptiles which lived here long before man was ever heard of."
>
> "Have you ever seen those bones, Winston? Of course not. Nineteenth-century biologists invented them. Before man there was

> nothing. After man, if he could come to an end, there would be nothing. Outside man there is nothing."
>
> "But the whole universe is outside us. Look at the stars! Some of them are a million light-years away. They are out of our reach forever."
>
> "What are the stars?" said O'Brien indifferently. "They are bits of fire a few kilometers away. We could reach them if we wanted to. Or we could blot them out. The earth is the center of the universe. The sun and stars go round it."
>
> . . . O'Brien continued as though answering a spoken objection: "For certain purposes, of course, that is not true. When we navigate the ocean, or when we predict an eclipse, we often find it convenient to assume that the earth goes round the sun and that the stars are millions upon millions of kilometers away. But what of it? Do you suppose it is beyond us to produce *a dual system of astronomy*? The stars can be near or distant, according as we need them. Do you suppose our mathematicians are unequal to that? Have you forgotten doublethink?"[38] [Italics mine.]

For the state and dominant ideologies to attain total power over the minds of the populace, doublethink must be *applied to the entire cosmos*. Existential truths must be destroyed at all levels, especially on a grand scale with regard to our place in the universe. That's why tribes, nations, and holy warriors are so efficient at producing endless wars and totalitarian societies, with the prophets, populace, and political leaders pretending to be channeling deities and securing destinies at the center of the universe.

Cosmic doublethink is the longstanding yet mistaken belief that science and theology — the "dual system[s] of astronomy" — *both* offer valid explanations of the universe, that the reality of the cosmos and the notion of an almighty "Creator" are intellectually compatible. It's like believing astronomy and astrology are equally valid ways of knowing the cosmos. Scientific cosmology and theology are *not* reconcilable — they are based in entirely different epistemologies. Scientists and theorists who claim otherwise — however well intended — are wholly mistaken and trapped in doublethink. It's cosmic doublethink that allows people to pretend their personal destiny is in the hands of a Creator instead of acknowledging the fact that they're a mere random arrangement of stardust in a vast and ancient universe spanning 100 billion light years. It's this "dual system of astronomy" that permits members of a society to shut down their minds, ridicule dissent, and attack the very notion of cosmic "reality." No doubt many people will rely on cosmic doublethink and the "dual system of astronomy" to dismiss this critique. And they will *feel damn good* about it, too.

We're repeatedly told this Creator spelled out a cosmic behavioral plan 2,000 years ago to a few super-special dudes living on a tiny, rocky, watery planet orbiting a flaming ball of hydrogen. Are we really supposed to believe that a Creator is responsible for the entirety of the observable cosmos — 2 trillion galaxies, 3 sextillion stars, countless numbers of planets, moons, comets, meteors, black holes, supernovas, gamma ray bursts, and other life forms, all existing in galaxy clusters that stretch across 100 billion light years in an expanding universe — and is simultaneously concerned about the happenings and achievements of one person, one tribe, or one species, which inhabits the surface of one infinitesimal planet it shares with millions of other species and individual creatures, all of which are the product of 4.5 billion years of cosmic evolution? Seriously, folks! This is an extraordinary claim requiring equally extraordinary proof that's completely absent. Either the Creator does not exist or it is just too busy to provide us with any empirical evidence of its cosmic existence. Apparently its hands are already full with the world's presidential elections and military outcomes and ensuring that people of the "proper" sexes, races, and religions copulate together, all while calibrating the ratios of dark matter and dark energy to accelerate the expanding universe and mystify contemporary cosmologists peering through the Hubble Space Telescope!

WHY DOESN'T THE CREATOR PHOTO-BOMB THE HUBBLE IMAGES? Why doesn't the Creator confirm the dual system of astronomy and end the nihilism and skepticism? Yet, no Creator or deity has bothered to make an appearance on Spaceship Earth or in space — not even on the moon when the Apollo 8 astronauts read Genesis. So why not in a Hubble image? If there is a Creator out there, what better way to impress humans than by photo-bombing the images captured by the Hubble Space Telescope? A Hubble image would be the perfect photo op. But as of yet, there is no sign of a Creator in the 1.2 million Hubble images or 45 terabytes of Hubble data. If this Creator exists, then what better way to make a splash and refute all atheists and skeptics by showing up in a Hubble Deep Field 3-D image or video? It would reach 1 billion viewers on Facebook and receive endless billions of "Likes" in a matter of minutes. It would be the most epic viral video on YouTube of all time, easily eclipsing PSY, Beyonce, and Lady Gaga.

THE CREATOR AND THE HUBBLE CANNOT HAVE EXISTED BEFORE THE UNIVERSE. Ultimately, the dual system of astronomy rests on a fatal flaw. When the Apollo 8 astronauts read from Genesis, they began with the first verse: "In the beginning, God created the Heaven and the Earth." This line contains a deeply mistaken assumption — that a Creator existed prior to the universe it consciously and purposely created. Theists believe that this assumption cannot be *logically* disproven, a position that prominent atheists like Richard Dawkins mistakenly accept.

Imagining that there was a Creator prior to existence is like imagining that there was a Hubble Space Telescope prior to the universe. Both are forms of consciousness — the Creator supposedly consisting of pure consciousness (or spirit) and the other being a technological device (the property of matter and energy) that extends human consciousness into space. The problem is that *any* form of consciousness existing outside of or prior to existence is an impossibility. The Hubble could not have existed before the universe or existence, nor could it have existed before humans created technologies like the Hubble to explore the universe. If existence did not exist, then what could the Hubble see? The same is true for a Creator. If there *is* no such thing as "existence" yet, what would the Creator/consciousness be aware of? Itself? Impossible. Consciousness can only *identify* itself as being conscious when it is aware of something *external to itself*. Let's return to the Hubble pre-existence. Imagining a Hubble before the universe or before humans begs the following questions: Where did the Hubble come from? How or why does it exist? Who or what created it? If a consciousness of any kind exists, such as the electronic "consciousness" of the Hubble, then it must be part of the existence of which it is aware.

If one posits a Creator prior to existence, the same questions arise: How or why does it exist? Who or what created it? A chain of infinite regression begins. If one wants to assert that the Creator always existed, it is merely a blind assertion. One can counter with the notion that existence always existed, which *is* logically defensible as the grounds for all the forms of the universe. As demonstrated by Jean-Paul Sartre, existence precedes all essences. This means existence — all that is, was, or will ever be — must have always existed and is the starting point for everything, including the universe (or multiverse and whatever existed prior to the big bang), all consciousness, the human species, and any meaning we can discover.[39] Existence can only have come *first*, from which consciousness later emerged and evolved on our planet (and perhaps others). Like the Hubble telescope, the Creator could only come *later* after being invented by humans so we could feel meaningful and special in the cosmos.

10. COSMIC CENTRALITY 2: THE DUAL SYSTEM OF TECHNOLOGY

Using the available media and technologies of any particular time period, humans have mapped and modeled their place in the cosmos throughout history, from Stonehenge to the Sun Dagger to the Paranal Observatory to the Hubble Space Telescope.[40] Across time, we have extended our media technologies ever higher and outward toward the skies. Stonehenge is ground level in England, the Sun Dagger is high atop a butte in Chaco Canyon (New Mexico), the Paranal Observatory is atop the desert mountains in Chile, and the Hubble Space Telescope is in outer space. Have the Paranal and Hubble been countered by Facebook, Twitter, and selfies?

The "dual system of astronomy" has been complemented by the dual system of technology, where the evolution of *cosmic media technologies* has been countered by developments in *social media technologies*. Cosmic doublethink has been complemented by a kind of techno-doublethink so that we can still pretend to be the center of the universe.

COSMIC MEDIA VS. SOCIAL MEDIA. Spike Jonze's science-fiction film *Her* (2013) centers on the social fate of Theodore Twombley (Joaquin Phoenix), a bored and lonely guy who purchases and downloads an artificial intelligence operating system named OS-1. Twombley chooses a female version of OS-1, which names herself "Samantha" (voiced by Scarlett Johansson). More than a mere operating system of the future, Samantha is where Siri meets Google meets Tinder and social media. In fact, OS-1 and Samantha are pretty much the perfect social media apps for lonely people. Twombley falls in love with Samantha, and she apparently evolves to love him, too. Over the course of the film, they develop a funny, touching, and seemingly meaningful relationship. At the climax of the film, Twombley is at home reading a book entitled *Knowing the Known and Unknown Universe* when he realizes he has lost his wireless connection with Samantha. After freaking out, he runs wildly through the streets and eventually collapses in a chaotic tumble. Once Twombley reconnects with Samantha, they have a conversation in which he learns he is *not unique or special* to her and she is not lonely. For Samantha, Twombley is merely one of thousands of customers, real and virtual, with whom she has a loving and meaningful relationship.

Of course, there are multiple meanings to *Her,* for which Jonze won the Academy Award for Best Screenplay. The most relevant meaning here involves the climactic scene described above, where Twombley is reading about the *vastness of the cosmos* and immediately freaks out when he loses his connection to Samantha. The scene shows how social media provide consolation for existential loneliness in a vast universe of which we are not the center and seemingly meaningless and insignificant. In fact, this scene perfectly illustrates what Genevieve Gillespie and I theorized in a publication prior to the film's release — social media are our consolation for the discoveries of cosmic media.[41] In contrast to the accelerating universe of cosmic media, social media reverse inward to us, giving us the illusory sense of being at the center of the universe and never being lonely.

Telescopes, satellites, space telescopes and the like are marvels that I collectively refer to as "cosmic media" technologies, which look away from humans and into the cosmos. (Cosmic media can also peer deep into our cells and atoms via microscopes.) This is in contrast to petroglyphs, television, and Facebook and such, otherwise known as "social media" technologies, which focus exclusively inward, socially and narcissistically, *at* humans and what humans are *doing*. Cosmic media technologies reveal an expanding and *accelerating universe* in which humans are the center of *nothing*. Social media technologies are invested almost exclusively in human behavior and make humans the center of *everything*.[42]

Since the Apollo program, a massive human "launch" has occurred, but it's been more of a virtual journey so far than actual. Rather than journeying into and inhabiting outer space, we've migrated into *cyber*space and inhabit the 24/7 electronic spectacle. When Apollo went to the moon in 1969, there were three television networks in the United States, and the internet consisted of a few nodes in UCLA's computer science building. The final Apollo mission was in 1972, the same year that Magnavox introduced the first mass-produced video-game system, the Odyssey. The Odyssey logo was in computer-style font, and the brand name accurately suggested the next "odyssey" would not be in outer space, as shown in *2001: A Space Odyssey*. The game's name was prophetic, for humans now spend more than 150 billion hours per year playing video games.[43]

TECHNOLOGICAL EXTENSIONS AND REVERSALS. It's important to remember that media technologies are *never neutral* in their effects, for each medium has its message, or an unintended effect on human consciousness.[44] As explained by Marshall and Eric McLuhan in *Laws of Media*, each medium and technology extends our senses while it simultaneously retrieves something previously lost. In addition, each medium contains the genetic code of its own *reversal*, the point where it's pushed to its limit, becoming overextended or "overheated," causing users to lose enthusiasm for its original functions and benefits.[45]

Here are a few examples:

The Car: The car is an extension of our feet, enabling a more mobile society, but its overuse resulted in environmental degradation and traffic congestion, effecting a return to bicycle riding and pedestrian culture. The development of the car engine and the phenomenon of mechanical acceleration resulted in cultural byproducts such as "fast" food and increased waste, which eventually reversed into the "slow" food and city movements.[46]

Television: Television is an extension of our eyes, ears, and consciousness around the planet, while the light *shining through* the screen retrieves cave paintings and campfire tales (television programming). By retrieving images and information from around the planet and the cosmos, TV's glowing screen (the light shining through toward us) effects a reversal of the vanishing point in mirroring the world — thus placing human consciousness at the center of everything. This reversal makes possible the implosion of social media. That's why Facebook is television by other means.

The Telescope: The telescope is an extension of our eyes and consciousness, enabling us to increase our knowledge of the universe as well as further understand our own planet. By gaining this knowledge, we've encountered both the cosmic sublime and cosmic nihilism. This terrified us, causing us to reverse and seek refuge in anything that would return us to the center of the universe, such as theism, television, or social media technologies.

The co-evolution of cosmic and social media technologies that has taken place over the last century demonstrates several revealing parallels and reversals: Each cosmic media technology has been countered by a social media technology (see Table 6).

THE 24/7 MEDIA SPECTACLE. Since Apollo 11, electronic media technologies — social media in particular — have proliferated on a global scale. Here are just a *few* stats about our 24/7 media spectacle, circa 2012-2016:

- In the United States, there are 50+ broadcast channels and 900+ cable channels.
- Americans spent 33 billion hours watching sports programming in 2013.
- Netflix has 75 million subscribers and attracts 3.7 billion viewing hours per month and 45 billion hours per year.
- YouTube has over 1 billion users spending 6 billion hours per month on the site; about 100 hours of video are uploaded per minute.
- There were 2.6 billion smartphone users in 2015. (Six billion users are anticipated by 2020.)

TABLE 6 **PARALLELS AND REVERSALS IN COSMIC AND SOCIAL MEDIA TECHNOLOGIES: HIGHLIGHTS[47]**

	COSMIC MEDIA We are **not** the center of the universe. We are the center of **nothing**. We look outward toward the stars.	SOCIAL MEDIA We **are** the center of the universe. We are the center of **everything**. We look inward toward ourselves and our species.
	EXTENSION OF MEDIA TECHNOLOGIES	REVERSAL OF MEDIA TECHNOLOGIES
1925-1929	**Expanding Universe** • 1925: Edwin Hubble uses the Hooker Telescope to discover galaxies outside the Milky Way. — The universe is much larger than previously imagined. • 1929: Hubble discovers the galaxies are moving away from the Milky Way. — The universe is expanding in all directions in what is now known as the 'big bang.' • 1926: Robert Goddard begins launching his rockets.	**Electronic Screen** • 1925-1926: John Logie Baird transmits the first moving image on a television screen (a human face). • 1927-1929: Philo Farnsworth transmits the first *all-electronic* images (a straight line, a dollar bill, and a human face) on a television screen. — Humans are the center of the electronic screen, an expanding media universe of power and profit.
1968-1969	***Earthrise*** • 1968: Apollo 8 orbits the moon and captures the *Earthrise* image in December. — Television audiences see the Earth floating in the cosmic void. **Apollo 11** • 1969: Neil Armstrong and Buzz Aldrin become the first humans to walk on the moon.	**Hypertext** • 1968: Douglas Engelbart first introduces hypertext in December. — No longer a passive viewer, each human is a central navigator of his or her place on the screen. **ARPANET** • 1969: The first nodes of ARPANET are hooked up at UCLA, thus creating the first node of the internet. — Screens and computers begin linking together to create the internet.
1973	**Very Large Array** • 1973: Construction begins on the Very Large Array, the world's largest radio telescope (or the largest cell phone).	**Personal Computers and Cell Phones** • 1973: Dr. Martin Cooper demonstrates the first "cell phone" call in NYC, thus ushering in the age of mobile phones and mobile media. • 1973: Xerox-PARC invents the world's first personal computer to feature Engelbart's "graphical user interface" (GUI).

	COSMIC MEDIA We are **not** the center of the universe. We are the center of **nothing.** We look outward toward the stars.	SOCIAL MEDIA We **are** the center of the universe. We are the center of **everything.** We look inward toward ourselves and our species.
1990	***Pale Blue Dot* and Hubble Space Telescope** • 1990: The Voyager space probe captures the *Pale Blue Dot* in February. • 1990: NASA launches the Hubble in April; the universe is soon revealed as much larger and older than expected.	**World Wide Web** • 1990: Tim Berners-Lee introduces the World Wide Web in December. — Humans and hypertext are placed at the center of the global information network represented on the electronic screens.
2004	**Hubble Ultra Deep Field (HUDF)** • 2004: The Hubble Ultra Deep Field is completed in January. — Thousands of galaxies are discovered, revealing a universe of mind-boggling size and scale.	**Facebook** • 2004: Facebook is launched in February. — Humans are nudged even further toward the center via a social media universe created for them, starring them.
2012-2013	**Hubble eXtreme Deep Field (XDF)** • 2012: The Hubble XDF is released in September. — Ten years' worth of Hubble images are assembled into a single portrait of humanity's deepest view into the universe, revealing 5,500 galaxies in a tiny spot of the sky.	**Google Glass** • 2013: Google introduces Glass in February. — The optical user interface reaffirms cosmic centrality in the banality of daily existence while pointing toward live video streaming of everyday life. — Though Glass was not a success, it set the precedent for products to come.
2014-2015	**MUSE Images** • 2014-2015: The European Space Agency produces the MUSE (Multi-Unit Spectroscopic Explorer) images. — The MUSE images peer deeper into the Hubble Deep Fields to reveal galaxies that are even farther away than assumed and were undetected by the Hubble.	**Periscope and Facebook Live** • 2015: Periscope is launched in March. — This live video-streaming app lets anyone transmit what they are currently viewing through their own camera over the internet. • 2016: Facebook Live is launched in April. — This live video-streaming feature lets anyone stream video through their Facebook timeline.
2018+	**James Webb Space Telescope** • 2018 is the expected launch of the successor to the Hubble. — It will have 100 times the viewing power of the Hubble.	**To Be Determined in the Future** • History suggests that a new social media technology will be introduced, one that will certainly reaffirm our pre-Copernican delusions.

- Facebook has 1.5 billion users spending an average of 20 minutes per day on the site, the equivalent of almost 500,000,000 hours or *56,000 years per day*.
- Per day, Facebook has 4.75 billion contents shares/updates, 4.5 billion "Likes," 10 billion sent messages, 500 million video views, and 350 million photos. So far, 250 billion photos have been uploaded to Facebook
- Instagram has 400 million active users, 40 billion photos, and 3.5 billion "Likes" per day. Collectively, Instagram and Facebook have 2.9 trillion "Likes" per year.
- Twitter has 310 million active users creating 500 million tweets per day.
- At least 1.8 billion photos are uploaded to the internet per day and at least 100 million are selfies.
- There are over 3.6 billion social networking accounts and over 4.3 billion email addresses; over 200 billion emails are sent per day.
- Google indexes 30 trillion web pages; it processed over 1.2 trillion searches in 2015.
- US adults average over 11 hours per day with electronic/digital media and a mere 32 minutes with print media.[48]
- By 2020, the expanding electronic media universe may reach 44 zettabytes (44 trillion gigabytes).[49]

Depending on the source or survey, these statistics may vary, but they all convey the fact that the 24/7 media spectacle is augmenting at warp speed. The electronic universe is having an immense effect on our cosmic priorities and how we see our importance, as individuals and as a species (conditions that are represented in *WALL-E*, one of the most beloved space films of all time).

It's a great privilege to have the internet — a global library and real-time memory bank that's accessible anywhere in the world and that provides us with abundant information, knowledge, and entertainment. The internet is one of the greatest of human accomplishments. And yet with such technology, we're practically merging with our computer and smartphone screens, becoming lost in them and lost *to* them. The space around us and our planet disappears as we become ever more enthralled by the glittering spectacle that our society and culture have become.

THE SPACE AGE MEETS THE FACE AGE. The push-button society of the space age became the point-and-click society of the information age. Liftoffs have been countered by uploads, splashdowns by downloads, Mission Control by the trackpad, and Hubble's Ultra Deep Field image by the selfie. Apple's latest iteration of products all illustrate this technological reversal toward cosmic centrality — the iPod, the iPhone, and the iPad, as in "I am the center of the universe."

Rather than extending our camera out to the skies, we're extending our *selfie sticks* to the sky and turning the camera around toward *ourselves*. Trillions of galaxies have been countered by billions of selfies. The space age has been countered by the face age.

SELFIES AS ELECTRONIC SPORES. Like the *Pilobolus* fungus spores, perhaps tweets, selfies, and status updates act as society's "electronic" spores, launched by individuals seeking to survive in a Darwinian digital universe, the central location for all secular human meaning. The selfie: a glorified spore launch. Evolve or die (by living a meaningless life).

TRUMP'S FUTURE-SHOCKED TRIBES. Donald Trump was elected president of the United States after this manuscript had been completed and gone through the final edits. Trump's election must be briefly discussed because it perfectly illustrates two key elements of post-Apollo culture: 1) The massive cultural reversal into naked tribalism and ignorance; and 2) The dark side of the deep and profound effects of electronic media technology — the shaping of tribal consciousnesses.

President Trump is not a cultural anomaly. His rise to power has been foreshadowed in Hollywood films stretching back six decades, including *Ace in the Hole* (1951), *A Face in the Crowd* (1957), *Privilege* (1967), *Rollerball* (1975), *Network* (1976), and *Idiocracy* (2006). With the exception of *Idiocracy,* all of these films show a world where electronic media are central to the creation of a celebrity persona that taps into the emotions and tribalisms of the democratic masses. The films anticipate the role that "reality TV" will eventually play in channeling and shaping viewer emotions and tribal reactions. That being said, none of the films could have anticipated how profoundly television would extend itself to the internet and social media.

Trump's tribal world is tailor-made for a society preoccupied and obsessed with visual media. On television and on the internet, we can watch Trump's TV show, his beauty pageants, his talk-show visits, and his appearances at wrestling events; we can also observe his overtly wealthy and sexist playboy lifestyle and listen to his racist trash talk. We can watch him play the numerous tribal roles he's known for: gangsta tough guy, supposed investor genius, former football team owner in the defunct USFL, and so on. Everything his "empire" produces is ideal for consciousnesses that are wedded to screen-based realities. The only place these roles can make sense and seem coherent is the world of reality TV and social media (reality TV by other means). Trump himself is walking-talking reality TV. He's a human Twitter feed. And just like TV and Twitter, he can be at once horrifying and hilarious.

As Marshall McLuhan explained 50 years ago in *Understanding Media* and *The Medium Is the Massage,* electronic media favor tribal behavior precisely because they collapse space/time into instant communication to and from anywhere in the world—a.k.a., the "global village."[50] We have instant global communication as if face-to-face in a tribe or village. But rather than *reflectively* embrace the global (and its full implications, which require the new modes of human species-level thinking outlined in Chapter 4), most people *reactively* embrace the tribal and local instead.

Thus we have tribal villages prevailing in our local and national cultures. Connected by screens and links, electronic tribal villages replicate and proliferate throughout social media, from Twitter to Facebook to Instagram. With their instantaneity, TV screens, computer screens, and pocket screens favor reaction, not reflection; the mediated, not the actual; the tribal instead of the global or universal. The people who favor Trump are the most delusional (the deniers of evolution and climate change) and reactionary (the "alt-right" tribes).

With people gazing at screens 10 to 14 hours a day, capital and media technology have been able to produce a pre-shrunk consciousness for a world of endless consumption and nonstop entertainment, leaving little room for enlightenment. It's an instant consciousness conditioned for mediated realities, artificial worlds that favor the personal and tribal, not the universal and global; the viral, not the philosophical; consumption, not consideration; emotion, not reason; fear, not wonder; now, not long-term. In the electronic spectacle, what counts as true and real are "Likes," slogans, sound bites, factoids, clichés, fallacies, non-sequiturs, instant analyses, shallow profundities, insults posing as insights, TV channels chock full of thousands of images, the echo chambers of Twitter feeds, antics displayed on Facebook, and the crimes and carnival of human events detailed on the Google News reader.

Celebrated on our TV and computer screens is a culture populated with a virulent mix of tribes (racists, patriots, nationalists, theists, fans, celebrity worshippers, etc.) and bigots (sexists, homophobes, xenophobes, etc.). Our screens also feature talking heads, movie heroes/heroines, sports heroes/heroines, rich people, trash talkers, warrior cops, doomsday preppers, evolution deniers, ancient alien theorists, ghost hunters, paranormal believers, the paranoid and conspiratorial, the delusional and delirious, the evil this and evil that, and the unchallenged species-level narcissistic belief that humans are at the center of the universe, even as they wreak ecological havoc all over their only planet. All of this nonsense is the basis for the existential ground of President Trump's mediated world. Add on Mike Pence, the creationist and evolution-denying vice president, and we have a simultaneous intellectual collapse and winning presidential ticket. That is not a contradiction. It demonstrates the combined effects of TV, social media, and theism, all of which embrace various forms of tribal and cosmic narcissism.

As with the voters who elected Ronald Reagan (the movie star president) and George W. Bush (the tough-talking poseur Texan), it's clear most of Donald Trump's voters are future shocked, terrified of a tomorrow accelerating toward increasing complexity and diversity on a planetary scale, a future different from the pure and simple world they were supposed to rule — an industrial America ordered under God, consumption, and entertainment. Now they are desperately clinging to the past, to a "great" America now found only at Disneyland, Sunday school, the shopping mall, and football stadiums. US political culture is showing the full effect of pop culture's and theism's continued attacks on reason, science, and general enlightenment. Trump's successful election represents an intellectual collapse of epic proportions as well as widespread failure of the educational systems — any other conclusion is delusional and involves doublethink.

Just think: Tribes of advanced simians thumped their chests in the Twitterverse because a reality-TV star was elected as their president on the *Pale Blue Dot*. And it happened in the most scientifically advanced tribal nation *on* that dot. That's because Trump's fraction of that dot is heavily populated by tribes of mediated, future-shocked voters. McLuhan and Toffler saw it coming 50 years ago. It's the *Planet of the Apes* — a madhouse!

SOCIAL MEDIA: TV BY OTHER MEANS. With Trump's election, Silicon Valley and the tech cheerleaders must finally accept that social media do not inherently represent a technology of progress, revolution, and cultural enlightenment. Social media are networked echo chambers operationalized for government and corporate surveillance and targeted advertising while also providing delusions of narcissistic self-importance, emotional assurances, tribal identity, and cosmic centrality. It's TV by other means; it's the tribal village on a global scale. Any enlightenment that evolves from social media is mostly accidental, merely quantum particles that randomly organized into a chance moment of fleeting wisdom and then instant oblivion.

11. COSMIC CENTRALITY 3: THE DUAL SYSTEM OF EXISTENCE

Many space enthusiasts seem to believe that sending humans to Mars will somehow galvanize support for space exploration, unite the world, and create a better future. I wish this were true. But such space-bound excursions cannot possibly unite us because of the ways in which secular narratives have evolved (or devolved) since Apollo. As much as Apollo signifies the beginning of space exploration, it clearly marks the end of an era for media events with universal meanings for unified global audiences. In my view, a mission to Mars (with humans) would only be a transient enthusiasm, another media event consumed on electronic screens, thus serving the needs of another niche in the consumerist global entertainment industry.

The dominant secular and space narratives of the 21st century cannot be understood outside the trajectories of technology during the 20th century. Simply put, we've built a technological civilization in which nature and the cosmos have been almost completely removed from daily existence. Though we are part of the universe, we have divorced ourselves from the stars and the natural world on Earth. To power our civilization, we extract energy and resources from the natural world and then pump the waste back into it, polluting the planet's air, land, and oceans. Our separation from nature and the cosmos is made complete at night, with our electric lights and screens erasing the starry skies from human consciousness. We know nature and stars are "out there," but they have little meaning or relevance in our daily lives. In effect, we live in a dual system of existence, where civilization and the cosmos are different realms.

That's part of the irony of post-Apollo culture. We discovered a majestic and mind-blowing universe, erased it from our consciousness, and then still pretended to be the center of it all. It's cognitive acceleration and reversal happening at the same time.

GLITTERING METROPOLISES POPULATED WITH TRIBAL CONSUMERS. Around the world, our civilization is based in the *electrified* and *mechanized* metropolises, towering with skyscrapers and sports stadiums; sprawling with suburbs, highways, and communication networks. We drive, fly, and take trains from one city to another. Glittering by day, glowing by night, our cities and their technologies are impressive by any measure. But this wondrous electrified civilization we've constructed is so far removed from nature and the universe that we rarely witness our impact on the Earth's ecosystems and forget that we live in an ancient and complex biosphere that is part of the cosmos. We've made some fractional progress toward living more sustainably, passing environmental laws and recycling a small percentage of our waste products. But the fact is we're a technological society that cannot run without its machinery — our civilization is organized *within* technology.

Our everyday existence is more or less akin to a human carnival inside a technological shell, where most everyone is scurrying about in a desperate search for meaning and relevance, supposedly satisfied by our tribal identities, consumption, and super-specialness. The very cultural narratives we need right now require the integration of cosmology, ecology, and technology. Such cosmic cultural narratives have the potential to unite human society over the long term — that is, if we can find them and embrace them. But how can we when our civilization is divorced from the universe?

With no connection to nature or the universe, today's dominant secular narratives are devoid of any sense of universal meaning or shared cosmic destiny, seemingly bent upon celebrating consumerism, entertainment, and all forms of diversity, tribal differentiation, and cosmic centrality. These narratives have been reduced to the following: 1) Find and adopt an identity within a tribe; 2) Endlessly consume products and services to reflect this tribal identity and differentiate yourself from the other tribes; 3) Remember that you are unique and super-special; life is all about you enjoying yourself, being entertained, getting it on, expressing your feelings, and praying as needed. (Don't get me wrong; I like pleasure as much as anyone. But sheer hedonism and emotionalism cannot overcome cosmic nihilism.)

Screens, selfies, and sex, with some guilt for the sinners . . . I rock, you rock, we rock, and some are going to heaven. What kind of universal relevance can NASA, Mars, and a new space philosophy *possibly* have in a culture dominated by hedonism, narcissism and cosmic centrality — where everything is oriented toward *us* being at the center of the universe?

PRODUCTION AND DESIRES. With no new secular grand narratives since Apollo, we have been left to follow the trajectories in technology, production, and consumption, which have been evolving toward ever more entertainment, customization, and cosmic centrality. In effect, the economics of *scarcity* have dramatically evolved with the introduction of new technologies and changing demographics — from *goods* to *desires* to *attention*.

Critics of capitalism assume these desires are merely byproducts of advertising and commercialism, but many are actually inherent to our species, residing deep in our evolutionary psyche. For example, we have a primal need for the world around us to have an aesthetic quality.[51] We need artistic design that inspires us and products and services we appreciate and respect (as Apple founder Steve Jobs understood all too well). In principle, there is nothing profane about product consumption in such contexts. It becomes a problem when the desires lead to hyper-consumption and obscene levels of excess and waste.

We now have a consumer and entertainment society on steroids, with overflowing landfills and plasticized oceans. We have gone from mass production to mass customization to mass participation, under the imperative of satisfying more desires and creating "unique" identities while consuming endless products and entertainment in cities with kaleidoscopic diversity. Enthralled by the cultural kaleidoscope with us at the center of everything, who has the need for space telescopes showing us at the center of nothing?

APOLLO MARKS THE END OF AN ERA. During the evolution of production and consumption, communism and capitalism were transformed. The latter of course proved to be more effective when it came to developing technological innovations linked to activating consumer desires for individual expression within mass society.

When Henry Ford mechanized the world with mass production, the increased output resolved the key elements of scarcity in industrial society: *goods and products*. Ford's Model T was one design and came in one color. Coca-Cola came in one flavor, and Levi's blue jeans came in one color.

By the time the Apollo program arrived, industrial capitalism was highly efficient in making most products abundantly available, so they were branded and customized to satisfy consumer society's new scarcity: *desires and identities*. By the 1950s, General Motors dominated the automobile market by offering multiple vehicle designs and colors aimed at a diversity of desires and unique preferences (Ford was slow to follow such innovations). Credit cards were also introduced and fiercely marketed by Madison Avenue (as cleverly shown in the hit series *Mad Men* [2007-2015]).

Western society saw the rise of cultural and consumer tribalism, beginning with the Beats in the 1950s, the mods and hippies in the 1960s, then the punks, rappers, new wavers, and urban cowboys in the 1970s and 1980s, followed by a succession of yuppies, preppies, goths, gangstas, grungers, grrls, geeks, gamers, techies, hipsters, fashionistas, metrosexuals, lumbersexuals, and so on. In the 1960s, Coke gave birth to Sprite and Tab, and eventually Diet Coke and Coke Zero. Blue jeans came in pre-shrunk, bell bottoms, and women's styles, then stone washed, loose fit, boot cut, and skinny cut. Levi's was challenged by Lee and Wrangler before Calvin Klein, Jordache, and Guess arrived on the scene. By the 1970s, cable introduced specialized TV programming, followed in the 1990s by the explosion of the internet and the ever more tribalized and personalized social media of the 21st century — which encourage a daily existence of 24/7 entertainment.

From this perspective, Apollo 11 signaled the end of an era, at least for television, electronic media, and shared identities and universal destinies.

ATTENTION AND ENGAGEMENT. With proliferating and miniaturizing media technologies, electronic capitalism was poised to satisfy the next scarcity: *attention and engagement*. Television merged with microprocessors in the creation of the personal computer. This was followed by the internet, which connected computers around the world. The World Wide Web provided a way for computers to "communicate," which soon led to social media, linking people via cyberspace. But the internet soon became another delivery system for tribalism and cosmic narcissism in a 24/7 entertainment culture.

We were invited to explore a range of internet aggregators (Yahoo, Google, Amazon, YouTube) and *attention*-consuming social media (Facebook, Twitter, Snapchat, Instagram) accompanied by *engagement* phenomena (blogging, fan cultures, micro-celebrities, binge viewing, status updates). Consumer products complement these trends, including craft breweries, artisan coffee houses, and restaurants and supermarkets offering locally grown produce, grass-fed beef, and organic poultry. By purchasing these various items and products, we subsequently purchase the tribal identities they represent, all designed to make us feel hip and super-special.

LIVING IN THE WORLD OF *WALL-E*. Everywhere we turn in the world of media, we are told we are super-special and to buy products to confirm our specialness and centrality. Like the passengers on the space-cruise ship in *WALL-E*, we are endlessly sold these narratives via the advertising industry, whose expenditures dwarf the budgets for NASA and space exploration. Global advertising expenditures reached $590 billion in 2015, and Google grabbed 11% of that with over $67 billion while Facebook had $17 billion. This means spending on global advertising is 31 times greater than NASA's $18 billion budget, while Google's ad revenues are triple NASA's budget and Facebook's ad revenues almost equal NASA. Mobile-media advertising has also tripled NASA with $60 billion.

UNIVERSAL TRUTHS VS. TRANSIENT ENTHUSIASMS. It is possible the proliferation of tribes may signal a new cultural universality, a vibrant new model for a hybrid global civilization. Maybe the diversity and universality will converge and replicate within the cultural niches and media technologies. Then again, as surfers of tweets, status updates, and websites, we may become ever more shallow, ever less grounded, potentially more open-minded in some aspects yet close-minded about any cosmic truths beyond the electronic screens and our attention deficit disorders. While I do hope this era of diversity might be able to generate an age of benevolent universality, I can't help but be skeptical when I look at the Google News reader or peruse the user comments following any given internet article about the events of the day. As of 2017, superficiality and diversity seem to have overwhelmed depth and universality.[52]

Apollo and space exploration ultimately signify humanity's quest for universal truths. By contrast, media culture is solely invested in transient enthusiasms — products, messages, and events that are hollow and vacant of deep meaning and hence disposable, only to be replaced with new hollow and vacant products, messages, and events. We get bored quickly; nothing holds our attention for too long. Space enthusiasts are psyched about the idea of a mission to Mars, but in truth, such a voyage will have minimal impact. Apollo itself became just another transient enthusiasm, serving more as spectacle and entertainment instead of having any long-term meaning as a cosmic narrative for our species.

Given the cultural permeation of future shock, the media has depicted "the future" as terrifying and catastrophic. As a result, it's really no surprise that today's dominant long-term narratives are chock full of apocalyptic visions and extinction scenarios, as seen in the news and in television programming, documentaries, and Hollywood movies (especially recent space films).[53] No wonder people are obsessed with accumulating "friends" on Facebook; no wonder they're turning to sacred texts to seek the guidance of a deity or prophet. When we engage in the 24/7 media spectacle, we feel less lost and more central, less lonely and more powerful — more like the gods we wish we were.

Our cities and civilization may lend us a sense of personal meaning and significance, but they don't overcome cosmic nihilism or connect us to the cosmic sublime. With electric light constantly spewing photons into the sky, the closest most stargazers get to observing the planets and the Milky Way is by watching a science documentary on TV, a video on YouTube, or a Milky Way app on their smartphone. The nightly erasure of the Milky Way is enough of a reason to expand the "dark sky" policies around the world. Absent a cosmic cultural narrative, we find ourselves with no universal philosophical foundations for the beliefs and activities of the human species — on our planet or in the cosmos. As a species currently without a cosmology, we are lost in space.

12. STEPHEN HAWKING: "PHILOSOPHY IS DEAD"

A decade into the new millennium, astrophysicist Stephen Hawking and physicist/screenwriter Leonard Mlodinow state that "philosophy is dead" in their 2011 book *The Grand Design*.[54] This philosophical death is not because contemporary philosophers are not writing anything, but because they have collectively failed to keep up with developments in science and cosmology. As we have discovered new knowledge about the cosmos, we have uncovered new and greater questions. This is natural. It's how knowledge evolves and expands. The expansion of knowledge eliminates previous ignorance, but the vistas of discovery create new ignorances, new gaps in our understandings, and new voids in our philosophies and worldviews, as evidenced by the cosmic nihilism right before our eyes — from *Earthrise* to the Hubble Deep Field.

Well-known scientists like Hawking, Richard Dawkins, Neil deGrasse Tyson, Lisa Randall, and Brian Cox have written popular books explaining the human origins and/or the evolution of the universe.[55] Tyson, Hawking, and Cox recently hosted science documentary series for television and are among the "celebrity scientists" who have crossed from academia to pop culture, nightly talk shows, and elite status in the 24/7 media spectacle.[56] Certainly, it is great that scientists can be celebrities like movie stars, explain scientific concepts in sound bites for entertainment consciousness, and have millions of followers on Twitter (Tyson, Dawkins, and Cox). But it's one thing to write a popular book about science and be hip with tweets and quite another to integrate the big bang and the sublime into a meaningful space philosophy that will be embraced by the human species.

Philosophy may or may not be "dead," but one thing that seems comatose is a universal narrative for the human species as we venture into the cosmos. As best I can tell, the world's scientists, artists, and philosophers have *collectively* failed to embrace the *full* implications of Apollo and Hubble and the challenge of cosmic nihilism. They have yet to theorize space exploration or the cosmic sublime as the basis for a secular and nontheist narrative that provides the *universal meaning and hope* to inspire and unite humanity within a planetary civilization that ends war, sets aside nationalism, tames consumerism, protects the ecosystems, expands wildernesses and national parks, reduces narcissism and tribalism, abandons Creators and superstitions, and embraces its non-centrality as it ventures into the cosmos. Of course this is a monumental challenge, but we have to start somewhere, and it won't happen until artists, scientists, and philosophers inspire us to move beyond the worst features of humanity and the insane space philosophies that dominate the 21st-century space age.

13. CHALLENGES FOR PHILOSOPHY, SECULAR CULTURE, AND THE 21ST-CENTURY SPACE AGE

The triumphs of Apollo and the Hubble Space Telescope symbolize how science and cosmic media technologies are accelerating into the future while revealing a vast and ancient cosmos of which we are part of but not central to. However, the representations of space and space exploration in popular culture show we have not been able to handle the deeper meanings of Apollo, Hubble, and our non-centrality in the expanding universe. In response to future shock and cosmic nihilism, human narratives, ideologies, and identities are largely retreating into tribalism and the pre-Copernican past. As this chapter has shown, this narcissistic pretense is on display across the planet:

- The dual system of astronomy: Living in a universe of trillions of galaxies and sextillions of stars, theists claim we are cosmically important and possess a special destiny with a divine Creator, who still has yet to appear. The fundamentalists and evangelicals even believe this Creator has ordained their tribe to be rulers of the Earth, with a Terror War on a tiny planet that was created just for them.

- The dual system of technology: Our telescopes peer across the cosmos to reveal an immense universe in which we seem to have no meaning or purpose. As consolation, the 24/7 media spectacle is saturated with constant news and status updates on the human species' antics, ultimately displaying our imaginary cosmic centrality via billions of selfies.

- The dual system of existence: Civilization's electrified metropolises have erased nature and the cosmos from our consciousness, producing a kaleidoscopic carnival of daily events while divorcing us from our impact on the planet and our origins in the universe. Consumer-entertainment society sells tribal and personal identities via an endless array of products, services, logos, tattoos, movies, television programs, and mobile technologies that provide ever more pleasure and feelings of super specialness. Meanwhile, our trash and pollution become the fossil layers of the Anthropocene period — the human epoch of planetary transformation that might well be producing the sixth extinction event on planet Earth.[57]

In effect, we are living amid *a post-Apollo culture being confronted by pre-Copernican worldviews*, where the cosmic sublime and nihilism are countered by narcissism, theism, and technological tribalism. Via art, science, philosophy and the 24/7 media spectacle, cosmic enlightenment is possible. But we have to be willing to embrace the challenges of the cosmic sublime and philosophically advance into the new millennium.

So far, unfortunately, we're hell-bent on engaging in cosmic doublethink and upholding the dual systems of astronomy and technology. In terms of space futures, *Star Wars* is prevailing over *Star Trek*, *Gravity* over *The Martian*, and *Planet of the Apes* over *2001: A Space Odyssey*. Global culture is moving forward as it's moving backward, progressing while it's regressing. It's a simultaneous acceleration and reversal. We are moonwalking into the future, not Neil Armstrong style, but Michael Jackson style. No wonder the most famous "moonwalker" on Spaceship Earth is Michael, not Neil. In fact, Neil's not even close. Google it.

CHAPTER 4

THE COSMOS AND 21ST-CENTURY SPACE PHILOSOPHY

> There's a fundamental difference, if you look into the future, between a humanity that is a space-faring civilization, that's out there exploring the stars . . . compared with one where we are forever confined to Earth until some eventual extinction event.
>
> — ***Elon Musk***

1. THE NEW SPACE AGE

While the United States and the former Soviet Union led the space age in the 20th century, the new space age features several other governments and numerous capitalist firms. In addition to the United States and Russia, China has sent astronauts into orbit around Earth, India has a spacecraft orbiting Mars, the European Space Agency recently landed a probe on a comet, and the International Space Station continues to orbit our planet as a symbol of cultural enlightenment and international cooperation.

However, nations alone are no longer the only players entering space. There are many new and innovative space companies hoping to capitalize on privatized space travel. Widely celebrated as a space visionary, Elon Musk hopes to use SpaceX to colonize and terraform Mars after the atmosphere is possibly warmed up with thermonuclear bombs detonated on Mars's poles. (That's what Musk suggested to Stephen Colbert on television!) More pragmatically, Jeff Bezos's Blue Origin merely seeks to transport payloads to space stations and other future destinations. More idealistically, Richard Branson's Virgin Galactic plans to pioneer space tourism via rocket planes to serve the aesthetics of the sublime so more humans can experience the awe and wonder of viewing the Earth and stars from space. In contrast to aesthetics, there are the economics of endless consumption, as China and Shackleton Energy Corporation hope to strip-mine the moon for helium-3 and other minerals to ship back to Earth. Weapons are entering space, with the United States and China both possessing missiles capable of destroying satellites, while other space weapons are being developed to use against terrorists and "enemy" nations.

Meanwhile, long-time space pioneer NASA is hoping to send human *bodies* to Mars in the coming decades.[1] Additionally, NASA continues to extend human *consciousness* into space via the Hubble and Kepler telescopes, media technologies that are revolutionizing cosmology and our understanding of where the human species fits into a vast and ancient universe. Hollywood has rebooted *Star Trek* (2009) and *Star Wars* (2015) for the 21st century, while the space films *WALL-E* (2008), *Gravity* (2013), *Interstellar* (2014), and *The Martian* (2015) have received widespread critical and/or popular acclaim. Given these kinds of plans, the dominant narratives on Earth, and the visions of human destiny in space films, it seems that a critique of 21st-century space philosophies is not only necessary but vitally important to the future of our species. Otherwise, we're just moonwalking into the space future.

2. SPACE PHILOSOPHY

There is little reason to doubt the good intentions of today's space scientists, administrators, astronauts, cosmonauts, and taikonauts, as shown by the mission statements of their organizations and space agencies (see Table 1). Surely firms like SpaceX and Blue Origin seek to make a profit on what they view as an uplifting human cause. And space enthusiasts stuck on Earth want to see humans explore the cosmos. Many of us just want to see humans accomplish great things that blow our freaking minds — moon walks, Hubble images, great space films — things that prove we're a worthy species that can justify its existence to the cosmos and the extraterrestrial civilizations we are likely to encounter at some point.

Here's the philosophical question: Are scientific exploration and the economic exploitation of other planets going to improve the human species? After all, there were numerous scientific and technological benefits to Apollo, a mission of exploration that produced a global moment of the cosmic sublime.[2] Yet the past five decades suggest that Apollo has had minimal effect on the philosophies that still dominate human civilization.

All the journeys into space and all the essays, books, and films about space exploration reveal that there are two *ways we journey into space* and six basic *rationales* for going into space, regardless of where we go. In addition, there are six basic *meanings* and three visions of *human civilization* in space, all of which face *two existential and philosophical challenges* (see Table 2). Of course, the rationales and hopes present in space philosophies all overlap in complex ways, with profound implications. That's why the importance of space films should not be underestimated. Elon Musk and SpaceX tell us where and why we are supposedly going into space (to save the human species from extinction by terraforming Mars), but films like *Star Trek* and *Interstellar* provide 21st-century visions for questions such as *what does it mean* and *what can we hope for*? These may seem like overly abstract, philosophical questions, but we neglect them at our own peril.

3. WHERE HAVE WE GONE?

The 20th century witnessed the greatest explosion in technology that our species has ever seen — *sending human bodies* into space and to the moon while *extending human consciousness* far off the planet and deep into the cosmos. The Apollo program and technologies like the Hubble represent our most

TABLE 1 **MISSIONS OF TODAY'S SPACE AGENCIES AND COMPANIES**

NASA: "WHAT DOES NASA DO?"
NASA's vision: To reach for new heights and reveal the unknown so that what we do and learn will benefit all humankind. To do that, thousands of people have been working around the world — and off of it — for more than 50 years, trying to answer some basic questions. What's out there in space? How do we get there? What will we find? What can we learn there, or learn just by trying to get there, that will make life better here on Earth?

RUSSIAN FEDERAL SPACE AGENCY (ROSCOSMOS): "WHAT ROSCOSMOS DOES"
The Federal Space Agency is an authorized federal executive agency. The functions of the Agency include pursuance of the state policy and legal regulation, providing state services and administration of the state space assets as well as management of the international cooperation in joint space projects and programs [and] the activities of rocket and space industry entities relating to military space technologies [and] strategic missiles. The Federal Space Agency is also responsible for overall coordination of the activities at the Baikonur space port.

CHINA NATIONAL SPACE ADMINISTRATION (CNSA): "AIMS AND PRINCIPLES"
The aims of China's space activities are: to explore outer space and learn more about the cosmos and the Earth; to utilize outer space for peaceful purposes, promote mankind's civilization and social progress and benefit the whole of mankind; and to meet the growing demands of economic construction, national security, science and technology development and social progress [as well as] protect China's national interests and build up the comprehensive national strength.

EUROPEAN SPACE AGENCY (ESA): "WHAT IS ESA?"
Its mission is to shape the development of Europe's space capability and ensure that investment in space continues to deliver benefits to the citizens of Europe and the world. . . . ESA's programmes are designed to find out more about Earth, its immediate space environment [and] our Solar System and the Universe as well as . . . develop satellite-based technologies and services and . . . promote European industries.

BLUE ORIGIN: "ABOUT BLUE ORIGIN"
Blue Origin, LLC is developing technologies to enable human access to space at dramatically lower cost and increased reliability.

SPACEX: "ABOUT SPACEX"
SpaceX designs, manufactures and launches advanced rockets and spacecraft. The company was founded in 2002 to revolutionize space technology, with the ultimate goal of enabling people to live on other planets.

Note: Each statement was taken directly from each respective company's or organization's website.

mind-blowing and awe-inspiring scientific and technological achievements — nothing else comes close. The internet is a great technological achievement too, but it pales in comparison to the importance of humanity's space discoveries. Genetics and contemporary medical science are significant accomplishments as well but lack an overall existential and philosophical meaning in terms of the extension of human bodies and human consciousness into space. Space exploration represents our most important achievement precisely because it's provided *new knowledge that has revolutionized our understanding of the cosmos and our place in it.*

TABLE 2 PHILOSOPHIES FOR THE 21ST-CENTURY SPACE AGE: WHERE ARE WE GOING, WHAT DOES IT MEAN, WHAT CAN WE HOPE FOR?

WAYS WE JOURNEY INTO SPACE

1. We send human bodies into space.
   Apollo moon landings, International Space Station, space tourism, Mars colonization
2. We extend human consciousness into space.
   Since Galileo, terrestrial telescopes; since Sputnik, satellites and space probes; since Hubble, space telescopes; since Voyager, human consciousness outside the solar system

RATIONALES FOR GOING INTO SPACE

1. To exhibit power
   The "space race" between the USSR and the US during the Cold War
2. To exploit resources
   Accessing energy sources by strip-mining the moon and/or Mars
3. To extend the life span of humanity
   Propagating the human species by colonizing habitable planets, as planned for Elon Musk's "Mars" program and as depicted in Christopher Nolan's Interstellar *(2014)*
4. To explore the cosmos
   To further understand the universe and other life forms, such as via the Hubble and Kepler space telescopes
5. To evangelize our theologies and convert the extraterrestrials
   NASA's recent financial investment in theological programs and organizations
6. To experience the cosmic sublime
   Richard Branson's vision of space tourism based on the awe, wonder, and inspiration of seeing the Earth, stars, galaxies, and the universe from space

MEANINGS OF SPACE EXPLORATION

1. A great triumph of the human species; an expression of human reason and curiosity.
   Apollo 11 *and the Hubble Space Telescope*
2. A distraction and waste of money better spent on Earth
   Concerns stated by critics of space exploration
3. A way for the human species to "mirror" nature by launching spores into space for survival in the future
   Loren Eiseley's analysis of Apollo 11 *in the Cold War; the survival scenario presented in* Interstellar
4. A journey into nihilism that reveals the lack of cosmic meaning and purpose of human existence in a vast universe of which we are not central and are utterly insignificant
   Part of Norman Mailer's critique of Apollo 11
5. A journey into the future past with holy wars in space
   Star Wars *meets the Crusades meets the Terror War*
6. A new cosmology and human philosophy born of the cosmic sublime that eliminates all previous deities and narratives yet provides meaning and hope for an evolutionary species born of stardust
   Yet to be developed in any substitutive way

VISIONS AND HOPES FOR HUMAN CIVILIZATION IN SPACE

1. A space-faring civilization on a quest for knowledge and exploration, as portrayed in *Star Trek* (the 1960s TV series) and Stanley Kubrick's *2001: A Space Odyssey* (1968)
2. A spore-bearing civilization on a quest to survive self-destruction and the apocalypse by furthering the species, as portrayed in *Planet of the Apes* (1968) and *Interstellar*
3. A war-mongering civilization on a quest to protect and deploy "the Force" (or the notion of faith) throughout the galaxies, as portrayed in the *Star Wars* series and any number of films featuring space battles

EXISTENTIAL AND PHILOSOPHICAL CHALLENGES OF SPACE

1. Nihilism: The possibility that there is no universal or cosmic meaning to human existence
2. The sublime: Experiencing the majesty of a universe within which we are physically insignificant

The United States made it to the moon first with Apollo 11, but anyone capable of getting outside their nationalist and patriotic blinders knows the moon landing was a triumph of humanity itself — that's why people around the world exclaimed "We did it!" upon witnessing Neil Armstrong step onto the moon in 1969. The Hubble and other telescopes have peered across 100 billion light years of space and time to reveal a universe of staggering scale and dimension. Our ability to have acquired a deeper understanding of the overall cosmology of the universe — made possible by extending our consciousness into space via rockets, spacecraft, and telescopes — is plainly remarkable.

In terms of mere survival, one might say that our greatest overall accomplishment to date is the avoidance of nuclear annihilation during the Cold War, when there were 60,000 nuclear missiles in the world. The same rockets that sent Sputnik into orbit and Apollo to the moon could also be used to deliver nuclear weapons all over the planet — marvel and madness seem to exist side by side. While we have survived that terror, at least for now, 22,000 nuclear weapons still exist, and they're more than enough to destroy civilization. Fear of self-destruction or an extinction event is why some people believe we need to colonize other planets, as shown most recently in *Interstellar*. Whether we are sending bodies or extending consciousness into space, there are six basic reasons humans venture there to begin with: to exhibit power, to exploit resources, to extend human life, to explore the cosmos, to evangelize our theologies, and to experience the cosmic sublime. Since detailed discussions of these topics can be found in numerous books, essays, videos, and also on countless websites, what follows is a mere topical discussion to complement the larger questions of meaning and hope.

4. EXTENDING CONSCIOUSNESS INTO SPACE: ACROSS 100 BILLION LIGHT YEARS

The endless warfare and rivalries are temporarily subdued when we extend *human consciousness* into space, especially deep space. Unlike the futures portrayed in *Star Trek* and *Interstellar*, we have yet to send *human bodies* very far into space. Considering the scale of the known universe, a trip from Earth to the moon is like dipping our toes into the edge of the celestial ocean. By contrast, we have extended human consciousness deep into the cosmos. So where are we going with human consciousness? As far into the universe as possible with our telescopes, which empower the human mind to explore the cosmos and experience the cosmic sublime.

From Galileo's baseball-bat-sized telescope to the school-bus-sized Hubble, humans have long extended their gaze and their consciousness toward the starry skies above. In the 20th-century space age, humans began extending an electronic consciousness around the planet and far into the universe. In 1957, the Soviet Union launched Sputnik, the first satellite, and the United States soon followed with the Vanguard satellite. Ever since, humans have sent thousands of satellites into space that have revolutionized telecommunications, weather forecasting, the ecological and geological sciences, and warfare, espionage, and surveillance. NASA sent television cameras to the moon, which transformed how we viewed our planet in the cosmos.

Led by NASA, humans have sent numerous spacecraft to explore the planets and moons of the solar system, such as the Mars rovers (1971-) and the Voyager (1977) spacecraft, which first mapped the outer planets and then exited the solar system. There is also the Solar Dynamics Observatory (2010), which allows us to view and study the sun in great detail. The Wilkinson Microwave Anisotropy Probe (2001) mapped the geometry of the universe, enabling us to better understand the formation of galaxies, clusters of galaxies, and the overall structure and age of the observable universe. The Sloan Digital Sky Survey is presently mapping the Milky Way and billions of galaxies in 3-D.

Among space telescopes, the Kepler has revealed the likelihood of billions of planets in the Milky Way, while the Hubble has produced some of the most striking and profound images of the cosmos. And there are numerous ground-based telescopes around the world, from the McDonald Observatory in Texas to the Mauna Kea Observatories in Hawaii to the growing number of observatories in the Atacama deserts of Chile, all contributing to a staggering new cosmology for the universe and the human species.[3] These technologies and discoveries reflect the best of what is possible among the human species and its consciousness, physically situated on a tiny planet, orbiting a star in only one of the trillions of galaxies. These technologies and achievements give many people pride in the human species and hope for a more enlightened planetary civilization.

THE BIG BANG. At the beginning of the 20th century, the stars of the Milky Way still represented the entirety of the known universe because telescopes lacked the capacity to see beyond our galaxy. That changed with the Hooker Telescope in California, used by Edwin Hubble to make two landmark discoveries that forever changed our view of the universe: 1) The universe is much larger than previously assumed, with the Milky Way being just one galaxy among many; and 2) The other galaxies and clusters of galaxies are moving apart from the Milky Way and from each other in what is known as the "big bang" model of the expanding universe. In this model, the galaxies are not propelling themselves through space — rather, the voids of *space* are expanding and taking the galaxies along for the ride.

Of course, no one currently knows what existed before the big bang, what caused it, or even if there was an actual "bang." It's possible the observable universe emerged from some kind of tear in space-time as part of a larger universe that has existed forever, or that it emerged from the other side of a mega-supermassive black hole. It's also possible there are multiple universes in an endless existence that had no beginning. Since cosmologists are still trying to reconcile gravity (which operates on the macro scale) and quantum mechanics (which operates on the micro scale), we are likely to see a continuing evolution in our models of the universe, as cosmologists incorporate our current knowledge with new evidence produced by ever more powerful telescopes.

STARS AND PLANETS. Telescopes have revealed the observable universe to contain at least 2 trillion galaxies, most with at least 200 billion stars. The galaxies have organized into "local clusters" and "super clusters" that are arranged in "webs" of galaxies stretching across billions of light years. Some estimates suggest there may be 3 sextillion stars in the observable universe. (Three sextillion is 3 followed by 21 zeros — an astonishing amount.) We don't truly know how many there may *actually* be, for the estimates increase each time our telescopes get more powerful.

As 1 of 3 sextillion stars, the sun is the central force in our solar system. The sun and our solar system were conceivably born via the remnants of an exploding supernova and pulled together by gravity. (This is why the sun, planets, moons, and orbits of the solar system are circular in shape.) The sun comprises 98% of the solar system's total mass, and more than 1 million Earths can fit inside it.

Earth was likely created through an aggregation of meteors, asteroids, and comets leftover from the supernova, with gravity creating the attractive force for the collisions. As Buckminster Fuller theorized, Earth is very much like a planetary spaceship, orbiting the sun at about 60,000 miles per hour in a solar system that is spinning in circles and orbiting the center of the Milky Way at around 500,000 miles per hour. It takes about 220 million years for the solar system to complete 1 orbit of the Milky Way, a spiral galaxy that contains at least 200 billion stars, stretches 100,000 light years across, and is about 8.8 billion years old.

Like the Hubble, the Kepler telescope is revolutionizing cosmology and transforming how we understand Earth and the solar system in relation to the rest of the Milky Way. With its focus on a field of 100,000 stars in the Milky Way (or 1/400 of the night sky), the Kepler has confirmed thousands of planets outside our solar system. When NASA scientists extrapolate these totals to the remaining stars of the Milky Way, it's possible there may be 50 to 100 billion planets, with 500 million in the habitable zones of their solar systems.[4] Given that the stars all have the same basic chemical elements and the laws of physics and chemistry are universal, it is becoming ever more likely we will encounter life on other planets outside the solar system.

DARK MATTER AND DARK ENERGY. The galaxies' overall structure are shaped by gravity from the visible matter and energy of the universe — planets, stars, atoms, and so on — as well as an unseen force or component known as *dark matter*. According to the latest estimates, the visible universe comprises less than 1% of the stuff of the universe, while invisible atoms make up 4%, dark matter 25%, and dark energy 70%. If these observations are accurate, it is mind-boggling to realize that all galaxies visible from Earth's observatories represent a mere fraction of the stuff of the cosmos.[5] Space is still mostly empty, with dark energy taking up only 10^{-27} kg per cubic meter.[6] There are "supervoids" that span giant regions of space, including one that stretches across 1.8 billion light years.[7] Apparently, these supervoids correlate with the coldest regions in the cosmos. (To know that supervoids even exist is pretty super-cool — it's plain mind-blowing!)

In the trillions of galaxies, there are countless planets, moons, black holes, supernovas, globular clusters, and even possible life forms. Small dwarf galaxies orbit larger galaxies, such as the Andromeda and the Milky Way. All of the galaxies are theoretically under the force of gravity and dark matter, both of which hold them together. Although dark energy is an unseen force, its effects can be measured in the expansion of space that shoves galaxies apart. Whatever they turn out to be, dark matter and dark energy operate on grand scales in a duel that determines the fate of the universe.

AN ACCELERATING UNIVERSE. Dark energy is expanding the galaxies apart at ever-greater velocities.[8] According to Stephen Hawking, "The farther a galaxy is, the faster it is moving away."[9] Galaxies, clusters, and webs are thrust apart by voids and supervoids of empty space, some spanning millions and billions of light years. It remains to be seen if these spaces are empty or partially filled with dark matter. Scientists theorize that the edges of the universe are expanding at about 1 billion miles per hour. As the observable universe is 100 billion light years across and only 13.7 billion years old, the voids in space are expanding faster than the speed of light (6 trillion miles per year). Thus, the universe is accelerating in its expansion toward infinity or oblivion. In any event, for us as a species and for our consciousness, there is no exit from this universe or multiverse.

POSSIBLE COSMIC DESTINIES. In addition to modeling the origins of the universe, cosmologists have been modeling its long-term future. They say the universe faces three possible apocalyptic scenarios: the *big crunch*, the *big rip*, or the *big chill*.

In the big crunch, if there is sufficient dark matter to overcome dark energy, the universe will quit expanding and begin converging inward. Eventually, it could collapse into a point of infinite density, perhaps creating the singularity to effect a new big bang and new universe.

In the big rip, dark energy will rip the universe apart on all scales, from the galactic to the atomic. Billions of years in the future, dark energy will continue shoving the galaxies apart at ever-greater velocities. Billions of more years into the future, it will break apart the galaxies, stars, planets, and even all the atoms in the universe. At that time, the big rip will have torn through all points, annihilating the entire fabric of space-time.[10]

In the big chill, the galaxies beyond our local galaxy cluster will continue their acceleration unless sufficient dark matter exists to halt or reverse the expansion. As the universe "inflates," all the stars in the cosmos will disappear beyond all horizons, possibly fated to a slow death in the thermodynamic exhaustion of all their energy. Recent projections suggest typical stars in the universe will burn out in several trillion years and that white dwarf stars will exhaust themselves over 100 trillion years. Even the black holes will dissipate and leave behind a sea of photons tending toward a temperature of absolute zero.[11] According to astrophysicist Brian Cox, this process will take place across incomprehensible time scales: "When I say unimaginable periods of time, I really mean it: ten thousand trillion trillion trillion trillion trillion trillion trillion trillion years."[12]

"WE ARE STAR STUFF." Whether life on Earth emerged from a primordial mix of chemicals or was delivered by a comet, we now know our DNA was forged somewhere in the fiery furnaces of stars. This stunning discovery was made possible by telescopes and the genius collaboration of Margaret Burbridge, Geoffrey Burbridge, William Fowler, and Fred Hoyle, who published their landmark paper "Synthesis of the Elements in Stars" in 1957. The paper explains how

TABLE 3 **TEN MEANINGS OF 21ST-CENTURY COSMOLOGY**

TRIUMPH FOR OUR SPECIES

1. Our discovery of the epic universe represents *the* greatest intellectual triumph for the human species, bar none.
2. Through science and reason, we now know that humanity emerged from the "star stuff" of the universe, thus revealing the power of the universe to know itself and increase this knowledge.

THE FUTURE

3. The epic universe provides us with an endless amount to explore and countless planets to potentially visit in the near and distant future.
4. The evolution of 21st-century cosmology shows that our knowledge of the universe will always be expanding and evolving.
5. As our knowledge expands, so will our ignorance, thus posing continuing challenges for science and philosophy.

PHILOSOPHY

6. Knowledge of the epic universe has destroyed all previous narratives for human existence, suggesting instead our cosmic non-centrality and utter insignificance, further intensifying the issue of cosmic nihilism.
7. Because the universe is accelerating away from us in all directions — toward the "big crunch," "big chill," or "big rip" — it's creating celestial vanishing points that also destroy all previous narratives.
8. The epic universe presents the opportunity for artists, filmmakers, and philosophers to come up with a new space philosophy that embraces the cosmic sublime.
9. Our shared celestial origins with the universe might be the only way for us to find cosmic meaning for the human species.

HISTORY

10. If humans become extinct in the not-too-distant future, then the universe will have lost knowledge of itself, at least in this tiny portion of the Milky Way.

stars fuse hydrogen and helium to synthesize the other elements of the cosmos, including those that comprise Earth and its living systems. The process, *stellar nucleosynthesis*, is testable via the spectrographic images of starlight captured by telescopes. The raw materials in our bodies were created in stars — every atom of oxygen, carbon, hydrogen, nitrogen, calcium, phosphorus, potassium, sodium, and so on. In addition, the most common elements in our bodies — oxygen, carbon, hydrogen, and nitrogen — are among the six most common elements in the visible universe.[13]

In addition, each atom in our body is 99.9999% empty, the electrons spinning around the voids that surround the nucleus. We, all of us, are 7 billion billion billion atoms of emptiness, comprising trillions of cells organized into a dissipative system — a thermodynamic open system that exchanges matter with energy to survive. Comprised of *physical* matter and emptiness, we are destined to inhabit a universe with vast voids, yet we are conscious, self-aware, and tasked with filling our *cognitive* emptiness with meaning, purpose, and relevance.

Beneath all the remarkable differences among human beings, we possess a sublime universality. Given our shared celestial origins with the universe, it should not be surprising that all of us share 99.9% of the same DNA. Each of us is a temporary arrangement of energy and matter existing for a mere instant in the infinity of space and time on a tiny planet in a remote part of the cosmos. As SETI pioneer Jill Tarter said, "We, all of us, are what happens when a primordial mixture of hydrogen and helium evolves for so long that it begins to ask where it came from."[14] Or, as Carl Sagan famously said, "We are star stuff."

In relation to the cosmos, humanity is pretty infinitesimal, although our celestial discoveries show our minds as being rather substantial. Cosmology, cosmic media technologies, and everything we've learned about our universe are far more magnificent than any myth or gospel conveyed by an ancient text. In addition, nothing remotely resembling this cosmology or our universe appears in such texts because there is no way anyone could have *known* about any of it. *No one*. Not any alleged "prophet" or anyone else from the distant past. *The vast and ancient universe is only knowable via the space age and cosmic media technologies of the 20th and 21st centuries*. Though we are a tiny species, we can still be proud of what our minds can achieve. I am astonished by the cosmos and that our consciousness discovered it.

By extending our consciousness into space, we have revealed an immense and wondrous universe. In the 21st-century space age, we will soon be sending human bodies into space and back to the moon. Since we've already sent spacecraft to Mars, Saturn, Jupiter, and beyond, it is only a matter of time before we have the technological power to send humans to these celestial bodies — assuming we don't self-destruct, enter a complete cultural reversal, or have a surprise "status update" in the form of a sudden extinction event. Most likely, we'll eventually land people on Mars, cruise over the moons of Jupiter, and glide along the rings of Saturn.

But what will we do when we get there? Will we admire the moons and planets for their grandeur and beauty? Will we treat them with respect, or only as mere resources and locations to stage the usual carnival of human events? Will we protect the billion-year-old landscapes, or will we pillage them for profit, consumption, and entertainment? If we are visited by members of an advanced extraterrestrial civilization, will we be able to justify our existence as a wise, peaceful, and ecologically responsible species? Will the new space philosophies for astronauts and cosmonauts live up to the majesty of the new cosmology we have discovered?

5. SENDING BODIES INTO SPACE: "MILLIONS OF PEOPLE LIVING AND WORKING IN SPACE"

Jeff Bezos says Blue Origin is developing rockets for a future with "millions of people living and working in space."[15] What will these millions be doing? The dominant space philosophies suggest they will be doing what billions are presently doing on Earth: exploiting resources, exhibiting tribal and nationalist power, and evangelizing their theologies. In other words, the "millions of people" in space will be consuming, waging war, entertaining themselves, and praying to their imaginary Creators in the vast universe. Only a small fraction will actually be doing cosmic exploration and offering fragments of enlightenment, the majority of which will be ignored if it challenges the dominant philosophies. Why should our culture be any different in space in the 21st century?

In the 1960s, the exhibition of power was expressed in the hyperbolic nationalism of the "space race" to the moon, with the Soviet Union and the United States competing to be the first nations to send a human there, the victor supposedly being representative of the best socioeconomic system on planet Earth (socialist communism vs. democratic capitalism). In 1961, Yuri Gagarin of the Soviet Union was the first human to venture into space. The United States was the first to send humans to the moon, where 12 American astronauts walked during the Apollo missions (1969-1972). Of course, the most famous of the moon walks were performed by Neil Armstrong and Buzz Aldrin in the summer of 1969. Since the end of the Apollo program in 1972, space shuttles and space stations became destinations for astronauts, cosmonauts, taikonauts, and a few space tourists. Perhaps the most famous of the space stations are Skylab (1973-1979), Mir (1986-2001), and the International Space Station. As of 2017, almost 500 people from 37 countries have traveled into space.

Unfortunately, the nationalism and saber rattling have not fully subsided in the absence of the Cold War. The nationalist competition presently involves an exploitation of resources on the moon, where China and corporations from the United States have plans to retrieve an energy resource (helium-3) that could power fusion reactors on Earth. And, not surprisingly, the world's theologies are getting into the game of extraterrestrial exploitation and domination. As we've begun combining the nationalist drive for resources in space with the theological drive to convert the non-believers, we should ask the following questions:

1) SHOULD THE MOON AND MARS BE STRIP-MINED? Should we strip-mine the moon and Mars for resources to consume on Earth? Whether we send humans or robots to do the work, it will inevitably generate industrial waste. Will millions of space farers pollute the moon and Mars the way we have polluted Earth and the space around our planet with orbital debris? Additionally, if we mine the moon or Mars for minerals to be used here for energy or consumer products, parts of Mars and the moon will merely end up in the atmosphere as well as in our landfills. Just think: The marvel of space travel is literally being used to strip-mine the moon for resources that are destined for Earth's landfills.

2) SHOULD MARS BE NUKED OR TERRAFORMED? On a September 2015 episode of Stephen Colbert's *Late Show*, Elon Musk proposed detonating thermonuclear devices on the poles of Mars to accelerate the warming of the Martian atmosphere, thus enhancing the prospects of terraforming Mars to eventually colonize it.[16] Hence, it's altogether possible we might extend our capabilities for nuclear and planetary destruction to the Martian landscapes and atmosphere, especially if millions of Earthlings migrate into space.

Perhaps Musk and various space profiteers have mistakenly used *Interstellar* as an inspiration for leaving Earth and terraforming Mars. Recall that in *Interstellar*, Professor Brand apocalyptically states: "We're not meant to save the world. We're meant to leave it." Brand's statement should be seen as a warning, not a prophecy. If it comes true, then we'll have *failed as a species* in taking care of our home planet. If we are so stupid as to end up facing an extinction event because we have destroyed the ecosystems on Earth, then what gives us the cosmic right to terraform and trash Mars?

3) SHOULD MARS BE COLONIZED BY RIVAL NATIONS AND RELIGIONS? In effect, Ridley Scott's *The Martian* is a movie-length advertisement for colonizing Mars, with the United States and China leading the way. SpaceX hopes to launch supplies to Mars as soon as 2018.[17] Yet given current human behavior and the dominant narratives on Earth, are humans really ready to colonize another planet? In the coming century, rival nations on Earth might be interested in starting their own Martian colonies. Maybe all the tribes will live together peacefully. If so, it would be the first time in human history. What happens when the inevitable tribal disputes occur? Whose laws will apply to whom? What happens if rival colonies get into protracted disputes and declare war? Will the governments be democratic, socialist, libertarian, or theocratic? Should we blindly export our nationalism to another planet, or should we cooperate as a single species?

What happens if the religions get into conflicts, which has happened nonstop on Earth for at least 2,000 years? Some space analysts think "a new Martian religion" would provide the colonizers with a "sense of purpose and quell any existential dread they might feel due to the fact that they live on a planet that is entirely hostile to their very existence."[18] Of course, history has shown that theologies do indeed provide most people with purpose and meaning; however, these religions (and their meanings and commands) are usually at the heart of the endless human warfare on Earth. In fact, it is more likely humans will extend their old religions to Mars and elsewhere in hopes of colonization and conversion. (After all, a crucifix plays a key symbolic role in *The Martian*.)

4) SHOULD WE EXTEND WEAPONS AND WARFARE INTO SPACE? In summarizing his ideal cosmic trajectory, Elon Musk famously said: "It would be great to be born on Earth and to die on Mars."[19] Given the dominant space narratives, Musk might get his wish. If he doesn't, somebody else in the not-too-distant future might. *Scientific American* (perhaps the world's leading science magazine) is already anticipating the emergence of war in space.[20] Should we blindly extend our tribalist, nationalist, economic, and religious warfare into space along with all the ingenious technologies we have developed to kill each other? We can blast satellites out of the sky, propose nuking Mars (and other planets to follow), and dream up all kinds of space weaponry that are now on the drawing board of leading militaries around the world, particularly the Pentagon.[21] Can we doubt this weaponry will be provided to the warriors who want colonize other planets and convert the extraterrestrials?

5) SHOULD EXTRATERRESTRIALS BE CONVERTED TO HUMANITY'S THEOLOGIES? This question may seem rather absurd, but the possibility is already appearing on our cultural horizons, and the long-term implications are revealing and horrifying. In 2016, NASA funded a symposium with Princeton's Center for Theological Inquiry (CTI) to discuss the religious implications of the discovery of extraterrestrial life.[22] Apparently, NASA is so enthralled with "space religion" that it awarded $1 million to CTI to further study the theological meaning of extraterrestrial life.[23] Maybe NASA has to fund space theology to appease the religious leaders in Congress and megachurchgoers in Houston, home to Mission

Control and Senator Ted Cruz, the fundamentalist Texan who chairs the Senate Commerce Subcommittee on Space, Science and Competitiveness.

In 2014, NASA and the Library of Congress hosted a two-day symposium entitled "Preparing for Discovery" and invited various scientists and philosophers to explore this crucial and profound topic. Also invited were theological leaders such as Robin Lovin (Director of Research at the Center of Theological Inquiry) and Brother Guy Consolmagno (astronomer at the Vatican Observatory). Brother Consolmagno is a hipster space theologian who claims that if we can "give creative freedom to James Cameron to make movies, we can give God creative freedom to make the universe."[24] Cameron is a great filmmaker, but I never realized that producing and directing *The Terminator*, *Titanic*, and *Avatar* proves God "produced" and "directed" 2 trillion galaxies. The existence of Hollywood movies as proof of God's universe sounds like something invented at Disneyland.

According to Lee Spiegel (who covered "Preparing for Discovery" for the *Huffington Post*), Brother Consolmagno "publicly stated his belief that 'any entity — no matter how many tentacles it has — has a soul,' and he's suggested that he would be happy to baptize any ETs, as long as they requested it."[25] In a 2014 lecture at Leeds Trinity University in England, Brother Consolmagno elaborated:

> If there are planets out there that are suitable for life, if there is life on those planets, if that life is intelligent, if that life is in a free, self-aware, loving relationship with the Creator, if that life can communicate to us about their experience of the relationship . . . those are a lot of ifs. If so, then maybe we would have something to talk about with each other, [and] then we might be able to talk about baptizing extraterrestrials.[26]

Brother Consolmagno is arrogantly insinuating that extraterrestrials might traverse the cosmos to share in our religion and might need to *die for us*. That's because he believes the morality of the Bible should apply to extraterrestrials. He says angels are extraterrestrials created by God, and if we discover other extraterrestrials, we should find out if they are extraterrestrials that commit "sin" and "are in need of salvation." Brother Consolmagno says he would baptize an extraterrestrial "only if they ask," but suggests if the extraterrestrials reject "God's love," they will be in need of salvation. Using the concept of Jesus and Steven Spielberg's famous film *E.T. the Extra-Terrestrial* (1982) as examples, he says he'd need to ask himself whether he would be "willing to suffer or die for an ET" as well as whether "the ET [would be] willing to suffer and die" for him. He adds that "if the answer is yes," then the ETs and we can talk about being "common members in the Kingdom of God."[27]

What happens if the ETs are atheists, nihilists, existentialists, believe in another Creator, and/or have more powerful weapons? History has already shown how Christians and Catholics handled the discovery of previously unknown cultures that had never heard of a man named Jesus. In the name of Christianity and a loving God, the Spanish conquistadors immediately waged a genocidal war against native peoples in the successful colonization and conquest of the Americas.[28] By the 1800s, the United States military continued the slaughter of Native Americans throughout the western part of America in the name of God and Manifest Destiny, as depicted in numerous Hollywood westerns that were little more than racist propaganda justifying conquest and colonization. Though forgotten or conveniently ignored in the state's mythology, Mission Control's home state of Texas was a battleground of genocide and "ethnic cleansing" in the 19th century.[29] As with the rest of the Americas, the native peoples in Texas were slaughtered and their lands colonized by invaders with Christian theologies. Though utterly unknown in the Americas prior to 1492, Christianity and theology (in all its existing forms) colonized these continents and now dominate the cosmic narratives of Earthlings living there. As illustrated by the death wishes of Brother Consolmagno, conquest and colonization will accompany theism into space. Why should the future in space be any different than the past on Earth?

The popularity of the *Star Wars* film series as well as Cameron's *Avatar* answers that question. Both *Avatar* and *Star Wars: The Force Awakens* (2015) show us the inevitable end result when the toxic combination of narcissism, nationalism, and theology enter space: holy war among the stars. (In *Avatar*, Cameron updated the horror of genocide and colonization by relocating it on a fictitious planet called Pandora.) It is always possible, however, that the extraterrestrials will have superior weapons and be forced to annihilate the Earthling theists seeking to baptize them.

ARE THESE SPACE PHILOSOPHIES SANE? The question is not whether these space plans and proposals are viable but whether they are *remotely sane*. Really, how *can* they be? Given the self-evident lack of sanity, can there be any doubt that other forms of human madness and delusion will be extended into space too?

Hollywood has already envisioned such scenarios, not merely in space films set in the distant future (*Star Trek* and *Avatar*) or distant past (*Star Wars: The Force Awakens*) but in the 21st century. In the popular and critically acclaimed film *Gravity*, the apocalyptic destruction of the *Explorer* space shuttle and Hubble Space Telescope is caused by a chain reaction in orbital space debris that's triggered when Russia destroys one of its own defunct satellites. The plot and special effects depict a terrifying view of space exploration. Given that Russia instigated the events in the film, the Cold War is apparently alive and well in the space narratives of the 21st century. In the actual future, space explorers and space tourists face the danger of increasing amounts of space debris, including that from a Chinese satellite destroyed by China. If humans continue on this trajectory, then the following space farers will soon be born (if they have not been already):

- The first space explorers or space tourists to die from space debris caused by destroyed satellites
- The first person to perish in an industrial accident on the moon
- The first soldiers to kill another nation's soldiers in space, be it on Mars, on the moon, or at a space station
- The first soldiers, astronauts, or civilians to die in a space war

- The first space terrorists to kill astronauts or civilians in space
- The first fighters to wage a holy war (and torture other humans) in space
- The first interplanetary televangelists and fundamentalists to claim that the colonization of Mars is part their non-existent Creator's plan

If we extend our war mongering into space, we can expect various space weapons on Mars or on the moon, such as lasers, drones, and missiles. Imagine bomb-caused craters replacing the billion-year-old craters on the moon. Imagine military fortresses built in the moon craters or on the rims of Mars's beautiful canyons. That the rebooted *Star Trek* and *Star Wars* films have been helmed by the same director (J. J. Abrams) shows that the two franchises are promoting the exact same philosophy — one that celebrates war and violence in space. Hasn't this always been the ultimate existential meaning of the *Star Wars* film narrative — endless wars fought amid the infinite stars? Terrorism and religious fanaticism may seem unlikely in space, but it has already been foreshadowed in the film *Contact* (1997). Can't humans be a better species?

6. SPACE EXPLORATION: SPENDING MONEY AND MAKING MONEY

Astrophysicist Neil deGrasse Tyson theorizes that war, profit, and praise of those in positions of significant power (kings, emperors, and even deities) are our main motives for embarking on new frontiers or making monumental projects such as voyages into space possible.[30] According to Tyson, fear of war (politics) and desire for profit (economic development) are the most effective ways to get large-scale funding for space programs. By contrast, funding is much less for new discoveries that challenge the dominant narratives about human origins and human destiny. Of course, this is a largely true and well-deserved indictment of war-mongering and power-worshipping humanity.

The most common objection to funding space exploration involves the mistaken assumption that space programs waste money that could be spent better elsewhere on Earth. This was a prevalent complaint during the Apollo program of the 1960s, despite NASA's accomplishments, and it's survived into the 21st century, despite the discoveries of the Hubble and Kepler space telescopes. Frankly, it's hard to take such a claim seriously. If a budget-conscious critic were *really* serious about *saving money* that could be better spent on Earth, he or she should really be saying, "Why waste money on war?"

MONEY SPENT ON WAR. Since Apollo 11 landed on the moon in 1969, the United States has spent an estimated $22 trillion on the Pentagon and about $830 billion on NASA, or about 26 times as much on waging war than exploring space.[31] Since 1975, NASA's budget has ranged between about 0.5% and 1% of the total US government budget.[32] Insane war spending was not limited to the United States, for in the decade following the Apollo 11 moon landing, the combined military spending of the United States, Soviet Union, and their allies was $3.7 trillion (in 1979 dollars).[33] The stunning views of Earth from space and the accomplishment of humans walking on the moon meant little to the warring tribes on Earth. Absurd military spending continues in the 21st century. Since

2001, the year of Kubrick's space odyssey, the world has spent over $20 trillion on waging war, or about $2,100 per person.[34] It seems we are still living on the *Planet of the Apes*.

As is obvious, the Apollo 11 moon landing had no discernable impact on humanity's bloodlust and desire to squander resources by waging war while inflicting astonishing levels of pain, horror, death, and destruction. NATO and the Warsaw Pact kept right on building nuclear weapons and aiming them all over the planet. As for the United States, NASA's budgets are a fraction of the Pentagon's. Compare the 2015 budgets for both: NASA received about $18 billion and the Pentagon about $554 billion.[35] In other words, NASA's 2015 budget is about 3.3% of the Pentagon's budget. According to budgetary information provided by Tyson, the Pentagon received $26 billion for weaponizing space.[36] If we really wanted to *save money*, the most humane and logical thing to do would be to impose a budget cut on the warriors of the world who are wedded to tribalisms, nationalisms, and deities as a means for fueling and justifying their endless dreams of annihilating the timeless enemies — namely, the communists, the capitalists, the hedonists, the sinners, the infidels, the non-believers, and any number of "others."

NASA'S BUDGET AND APPLE'S PROFITS. To offer another comparison, consider that, for 2015, NASA's $18 billion budget was almost equal to the $20 billion Americans spent on hair care and less than one-third of the $60 billion they spent on cosmetics.[37] After all, everyone wants to look good for their selfies, many of which are taken on the 700 million iPhones sold since the Apple product was introduced.[38] In 2014 alone, iPhones contributed over $120 billion to Apple's overall $182 billion in revenue for the same year. So NASA's current budget is less than 20% of Apple's 2014 iPhone sales and *equals* Apple's $18 billion profit for the fourth quarter of the same year. That's right: *NASA's budget equals Apple's profits for three months*. Apple's profits even dwarf the total amount other leading nations spent on space exploration in 2014 — Russia ($5.6 billion), Europe ($5.5 billion), Japan ($2 billion), China ($1.3 billion), and India ($1.1 billion).[39] The space age has been replaced by the face age, at least according to the existential priorities of most people in the 21st century.

The deeper reason why many space critics oppose space exploration is *fear* — an existential anxiety that space exploration may jeopardize the validity of their own narcissistic worldviews or belief systems, especially their politics and theologies. As history has shown, new evidence and new discoveries don't do much to dissuade people from their flawed and mistaken beliefs — most still remain in denial of any new origins, destinies, or meanings (or lack of meanings) for our existence. Until the denial halts and a new space philosophy emerges, space exploration will continue to be a financial footnote to war, or a budgetary afterthought in comparison to the money spent raising armies and praising deities.

TWENTY-TRILLION-DOLLAR CHECKS. If space exploration receives any increased funding in the future, the prime objective may well be to exploit the universe's natural resources. The moon, Mars, and even meteors can potentially be mined for precious metals and minerals. In addition, Mars has water in the form of polar ice and permafrost, and comets have ice. Peter Diamandis is the founder of the International Space University (located in Strasbourg, France) and CEO of the X Prize, which is a fund dedicated to inspiring innovation that generates "radical breakthroughs for the benefit of humanity."[40] Diamandis asserts that space possesses a bounty of resources to be exploited: "There are twenty-trillion-dollar checks up there, waiting to be cashed."[41]

As space exploration has been undertaken by the private sector, fueled by dreams of space cash, it's not hard to imagine that the desire to exploit space for profit or resources will continue far into the future. Yet given the overwhelmingly destructive effects of industrialization and consumption on Earth's ecosystems, generating industrial waste on the moon or Mars is entirely possible, especially when trillions of dollars are at stake. Besides, who on Earth would be able to see any ecological damage? Most of us are clueless and unconcerned about the size or location of our own cities' landfills. So why worry about pollution on the moon?

There may be a plausible argument for mining some of the comets, meteors, or asteroids, as there are billions to choose from. But the planets and moons are more rare, unique, and worthy of study, respect, and aesthetic enjoyment. Generally speaking, mining them would be merely symbolic of human greed, vanity, and disregard for our own pollution. If we clean up our own planet and learn to live *with* nature, not *against* it, and integrate ecology with technology into a sustainable global civilization, then the right to exploit and *modestly* use resources on the moon or other planets might be valid. However, there is absolutely no celestial, scientific, economic, or political justification for humanity to wreak havoc on the landscapes of other planets, regardless of whether there are valuable minerals or life forms on such planets. (That's actually a key message of Cameron's *Avatar*.)

DISNEYLUNAR, X GAMES MOON, AND *REAL HOUSEWIVES OF MARS*. Given the lack of a new space philosophy and our compulsive need to stare at ourselves and obsess over our fucked-up personal dramas (individually and as a species), it seems absurd to envision extending our 24/7 media spectacle to the moon, Mars, and beyond. Serious money could probably be made in the entertainment and leisure sector, such as in space-based hotels and theme parks. Imagine a future where space exploration meets theme park, as depicted in Disney's *WALL-E*. Perhaps there will be "Disneylunar," a moon-based theme park where narcissistic and bloated humanoids gaze at their electronic screens while cruising above the lunar surface in their push-button hoverchairs. Maybe there will be luxury space hotels like the Fhloston Paradise in *The Fifth Element* (1997), populated by a bustling mix of Earthlings, entertainers, and extraterrestrials, all in a frenetic quest for fantasy and pleasure.

Imagine an "X Games Moon," with ESPN offering breathless commentary on the antics of youth who don't see themselves in team sports but want something fun to give them a sense of purpose and meaning.[42] So why not kick up some moon dust and snowboard down the side of a crater, ride BMX bikes across the lunar landscapes, or do "verts" and backflips off crater edges, with the blue Earth floating in the sky above? On another part of the moon, there will be throngs of frat boys zip-lining between crater rims as they guzzle beer through a straw rigged inside their spacesuits. Meanwhile on Mars, adrenaline junkies will base-jump into the canyons of Mars while live streaming to Earth via Snapchat or Facebook.

Even reality TV will have a place in space. Borrowing from *The Jersey Shore*, imagine a space-age Snooki and the Situation on the moon talking trash in a hot tub while musing about the best sexual positions in one-sixth gravity. Maybe the producers of *Ice Road Truckers* will release *Moon Base Truckers*, with macho guys manning giant moon buggies, hauling valuable minerals across the lunar surface as they crash through the rims of billion-year-old craters. Or can't you just see the challenges facing the femme fatales in *Real Housewives of Mars*, who strut in spiked heels inside a cocktail bar in the Martian biosphere, arguing about which Martian minerals make the best bling? Let's not forget the porn industry, sure to offer fare such as *Space Station Studs* and *Moon Girls Gone Wild*.

Coming up with space fads and consumerism isn't difficult. Imagine the temporary chic of "meteor jewelry" crafted from meteor materials, similar to the "moon rock" craze just after Apollo 11. After we mine the other planets, we'll sell their gems on the 24/7 "Space Shopping Network" or "QVCC" (Quality, Value, and Convenience from throughout the Cosmos). Consider space smoothies made with ice snagged from Titan's cryovolcanoes or hipster cocktails featuring artisan ice cubes garnered from Saturn's rings. The potential for interplanetary entertainment and celestial consumption will be, quite literally, astronomical.

WHAT HAPPENED WITH THE MOST RECENT VIRGIN TERRITORY COLONIZED BY HUMANS? Based on 21st-century cultural trends and the dominant space narratives, it is quite possible we will extend into space everything we've uploaded to the most recent virgin territory colonized by humans: cyberspace and the internet. Recall that cyberspace was once a completely new and open territory. Now it is readily accessible via sophisticated yet easy-to-use technologies designed by creative scientists, engineers, and corporations. We've uploaded much of what is great about humanity, such as art, science, humor, knowledge, philosophy, and the potential for overall enlightenment. But all that great stuff is dwarfed by the electronic empires of vanity, narcissism, ignorance, bigotry, and celebrity as well as endless advertising, surveillance, capitalism, nationalism, and tribal warfare. Following what has been long understood by the Pentagon and global militaries, NATO recently recognized cyberspace as "the new frontier in defense."[43]

Cyberspace and the internet were widely celebrated as utopian notions in the 1990s and the heyday of the dot-com boom, but such utopian potential has hardly been fulfilled. Since 1990, the United States has been ground zero for the emergence and spread of the internet. Yet there is little evidence that the nation is collectively smarter or wiser for it, despite the fact that potential enlightenment now exists at everyone's fingertips. Sure, the internet collapses space and time into a realm of instant global communication, thus accelerating the access and distribution of knowledge, enlightenment, and consumer goods from anywhere on Earth. As such, the internet could serve as the global media system for a planetary civilization.

But there is a flip side to the internet and our electronic screens that function like television on steroids, where everyone can live life as if it is a TV show, in which each person is the producer, director, and — most importantly — *the star*. As explained in Chapter 3, the internet and social media place everyone at the center of the universe — at the center of everything as consolation for the fact that we are the center of nothing.[44] Thus, the internet and social media are accelerating virtually all of the same old narratives while fragmenting attention spans and amplifying the 24/7 media spectacle. Marshall McLuhan's "global village" — global communication instantly, as if face-to-face in a village — has been realized, and it is dominated by the same tribes offering the same narratives that place humanity at the center of all meaning and value (theism, tribalism, nationalism, and so on). Why should uploading humans to Mars be any different?

7. THE "ANCIENT-ASTRONAUT" THEORY

As mentioned in Chapter 3, Stephen Hawking has claimed that "philosophy is dead."[45] If so, then we can see its mediated corpse in the hit television series *Ancient Aliens* (2010-), where an attempted philosophical launch has crashed and is still aflame in America on the History Channel. Hydrogen atoms deserve better than this space schlock. In *Ancient Aliens*, self-described "ancient-astronaut theorists" have hijacked Apollo and *2001* to claim the discovery of a new cosmic narrative for the 21st century. The ancient-astronaut theorists are wannabe radical archaeologists who present bogus and so-called mysterious evidence of the existence of extraterrestrials visiting Earth and assisting humans, who apparently cannot make any major discoveries without the aid of these superhero space farers who have yet to return.

The ancient-astronaut theory draws upon two valid cosmological concepts: 1) the reality of the immensity of space and time; and 2) the possibility of advanced civilizations somewhere in the cosmos. Given that the scale of the observable universe is immense and that the Kepler telescope suggests there may be billions of planets in the Milky Way, there is almost certainly life elsewhere in the cosmos, perhaps including intelligent civilizations. Given that the universe is 13.7 billion years old and it took 4 billion years for intelligent life to emerge on Earth, then it is possible the remaining 9 billion years produced civilizations that may have existed for millions or billions of years. If so, they may have developed space travel technologies that allow them to traverse the great distances with relative ease. (At least that is the "wormhole" scenario depicted in *Contact* and *Interstellar*.)

Such a possibility is one reason why *2001* offers such a compelling vision of human origins and destinies. After all, it would be an epochal moment to find a black monolith somewhere on Earth or the moon, beaming out a radio signal to an alert and curious species. Such a possibility is very attractive to me, at least in theory. As the astronaut Taylor says in *Planet of the Apes*, "Out there, there has to be something better than man. Has to be." Of course, if ancient astronauts have visited Earth, they would have possessed extremely advanced technologies and been viewed as gods, angels, and miracle makers by premodern humans. Much like the apes in *2001*, the humans would have looked upon the technologies with amazement and fear. But have any ancient astronauts *actually* visited Earth?

WHERE'S THE BLACK MONOLITH? Where's the equivalent of the black monolith in *2001* — that single artifact of *indisputable extraterrestrial design or origin*? Where is the *verifiable evidence* that ancient astronauts or extraterrestrials visited our planet to enlighten our species, perform great deeds, and guide our art, technology, and architecture? Since I think extraterrestrial life forms surely exist and it's possible some might be way more advanced and enlightened than our species, I am open to actual empirical evidence. Unfortunately, all the ancient-astronaut theorists can point toward is a few mysterious artifacts, none of which can be connected to extraterrestrial visitations.

Recall that *2001* appeared in 1968, along with *Planet of the Apes*, the Apollo 8 Genesis reading, and *Chariots of the Gods?*, the best-selling book by Eric von Daniken.[46] *Chariots of the Gods?* was soon after made into a documentary film, *Chariots of the Gods* (1970), and the book sold over 40 million copies during the decade. An updated version of the film, *Mysteries of the Gods*, was released in 1976. That version was hosted by none other than William Shatner, a.k.a. Captain Kirk, looking rather hip in a green turtleneck and black velour blazer and sporting long sideburns and a 1970s-style toupée. Without a doubt, *2001*, *Planet of the Apes*, the Apollo 8 sermon, and von Daniken's book and films were trying to account for human origins and destiny at the pinnacle of the space age.

WHERE ARE THE "CHARIOTS OF THE GODS"? In my youth, I watched reruns or VHS tapes of *2001* and *Planet of the Apes* many times, along with many other science-fiction films. I also recall viewing reruns of *Chariots of the Gods* and *Mysteries of the Gods*, which aired on the local television station. The shows are currently available on YouTube, and my recent viewings confirmed most of my original memories of them. Both films clearly tried to connect ancient astronauts to Apollo and space exploration, with the *Voyager* space probe and starship *Enterprise* appearing early in *Mysteries of the Gods*. Viewing the above films in my youth inspired me to read *Chariots of the Gods?*, readily available at the time in local bookstores. I viewed the films and read the book with rapt attention, precisely because von Daniken seemed to be providing "evidence" for a human narrative that was part of a larger celestial narrative outside the theism that prevailed in Texas, where I was born and grew up (in a largely secular household). Initially, this thesis was quite attractive and seemed to reflect an alternative model for human origins and possible destinies. It seemed like a plausible attack on the cultural and historical orthodoxy of the age, especially the pre-Copernican ideologies of the proselytizing evangelicals in my suburb.

Upon later reflection, however, I found myself questioning the logic of the book's assertions and came to realize that von Daniken's "ancient-astronaut" thesis was deeply mistaken. The book's flaws were exposed in a 1976 *Skeptical Inquirer* article as well as in a book entitled *The Space Gods Revealed* that featured a forward by none other than Carl Sagan.[47] By 1977, *Chariot of the Gods?* was debunked in a BBC-PBS production of *Nova* in an episode called "The Case of the Ancient Astronauts."[48] The episode refuted the following claims: An image of an ancient astronaut was carved on a Mayan sarcophagus, the Nazca Lines in Chile were originally an ancient-astronaut spaceport, ancient astronauts inspired various carvings on Peruvian stones, and ancient astronauts built the pyramids in Egypt and the Moai statues on Easter Island.

HUMANITY'S ALIEN ADVISORS. *Ancient Aliens* has aired for seven seasons and eighty episodes (as of this writing). In various episodes, the ancient-astronaut theorists assert that ancient visitors did the following:

- Consulted on the Mayan calendar
- Inspired Plato's Atlantis
- Made possible the Great Pyramids
- Designed ancient megaliths and temples
- Caused floods, plagues, pandemics, and assorted apocalypses
- Consulted with Leonardo da Vinci
- Advised America's Founding Fathers
- Contacted cowboys and Native Americans in the Old West
- Worked with Nikola Tesla in developing electricity
- Gave hints about relativity to Albert Einstein
- Helped design Nazi weapons
- Advised NASA on how to put humans on the moon
- Left behind clues to the "God Particle" allegedly discovered by the Large Hadron Collider at CERN

All of these assertions are among the most ludicrous and illogical interpretations of human artifacts made by the ancient-astronaut theorists, and all are wholly unproven. In many ways, the series is an attack on logic, rationality, and the nature of evidence. That *Ancient Aliens* has been on television for seven seasons suggests there are sizable audiences who are quite gullible, unable to think logically, and scientifically illiterate. Plus, there are irresponsible and intellectually bankrupt television programmers, but that is nothing new either.

In *Chariots of the Gods?* and *Ancient Aliens*, virtually all of the so-called evidence and arguments provided by the theorists are myth, superstition, hearsay, anecdotal, or involve an inference or conclusion that is fallacious, implausible, or unknowable. The "evidence" and arguments also contain inaccuracies, mistaken assumptions, unrelated facts, and false similarities. The few remaining pieces of "evidence" — which are a tiny fragment of the absurd claims — are simply mysteries yet to be solved or mysteries that will *never* be solved.

The essential epistemology of the so-called experts on *Ancient Aliens* is: "I don't know how humans did this; therefore, it must have been made possible by super-advanced ancient astronauts," or "I don't know how this event happened; therefore, it must have been caused by ancient astronauts." These are *non-sequiturs* and logical fallacies. From the fact that we may not know how something was created or how some event happened, it does not follow that it was created or caused by ancient astronauts, aliens, UFOs, Creators, or NASA's secret missions and conspiracies. This is especially true given the overwhelming lack of logical and verifiable evidence for ancient astronauts, extraterrestrial visitors, or cosmic Creators.

Virtually all the claims of extraterrestrial influence made on *Ancient Aliens* assume that human consciousness and civilization have little creativity, originality, or ability to innovate. The general idea is that, without assistance from the ancient astronauts, humans would be helpless and could never build such great structures or make profound scientific discoveries. Plus, the show assumes there is no room for chance, surprise, emergence, singularities, or any of the insights of chaos and complexity theory. In the end, the series represents an assault on rationality and scientific methods, not unlike all other paranormal movies and television shows. This has a great deal to do with why the equivalent of the black monolith has still not been discovered.

8. THE EXTRATERRESTRIAL PHILOSOPHER

Militarizing space, strip-mining the moon, nuking and terraforming Mars, extending nationalism and religion into space, reading Genesis from the moon, seeking to baptize ETs — these visions and behaviors collectively illustrate a delusional species filled with delusional tribes. Though the "ancient-astronaut" theory is nonsense, it is still useful to imagine what would happen if a philosophical and powerful extraterrestrial suddenly appeared on our planet.

Perhaps we need a visit from Klaatu and Gort, the peace-protecting extraterrestrials from *The Day the Earth Stood Still* (1951). This atomic-age and space-age classic provided a stern warning for the human species, which by the mid-20th century was on the path to developing enough nuclear weapons and rockets to potentially destroy life on Earth and eventually wreck havoc out in space, too. Klaatu was the first extraterrestrial philosopher hailing from Hollywood to offer the human species a message of peace and benevolence. Not surprisingly, Klaatu is gunned down by a soldier as soon as he steps off his flying saucer in Washington, DC. But fortunately, Klaatu has traveled with a peacekeeping robot named Gort, who quickly uses his laser to transform all the army's weapons into piles of dust.

Frankly, I would love for Klaatu, or for any real-life extraterrestrial astronauts and space voyagers, to visit Earth and land their spaceships on the lawn of the White House, at Moscow's Red Square, in Mecca, or maybe beside the Vatican, the Pentagon, the Great Pyramids, or the Great Wall of China. (Perhaps the most appropriate sites of all would be Mission Control in Houston and the Yuri Gagarin Monument in Moscow.)

Such a visit might wake us from our dream of cosmic centrality, which has caused so many nightmares on Earth and will eventually cause more in space. Perhaps the cool extraterrestrial philosopher would give humans a friendly interstellar "status update" on Facebook, followed by uploading some videos to YouTube and selfies to Instagram. Or maybe Gort's lasers would reduce our rockets to dust as well as the technologies we plan to use to strip-mine the moon and terraform Mars. Better yet, maybe an army of Gorts would obliterate every last one of our weapons in a planetary effort to establish "gun control." Can't you just see the National Rifle Association freaking out, not to mention the world's armies and terror warriors?

If these soldiers and terror warriors want to keep battling, let them do it with stones and spears, not drones, jetliners, and nuclear bombs. Keep in mind that humanity's extension of weapons and theisms into space pose an eventual threat to all extraterrestrial species. Look at what happened to Klaatu: He was immediately shot. Look at what has happened on Earth in the past, what is happening today, and — by all evidence — what will continue to happen in space. It's all war and violence. Our species is populated with war-mongering fanatics ready to kill for their Creators, tribes, and nations. That's a fact. Isn't war worship part of the reason *Star Wars: The Force Awakens* is number three on the list of top box-office films of all time, right behind James Cameron's *Titanic* (1997) and *Avatar* (the latter being the box-office champ with an apocalyptic warning about humanity's imperious desire for space colonization)?

What would enlightened extraterrestrials do if they visited our planet? Stephen Hawking thinks members of a highly advanced civilization might annihilate humanity and not think twice about it as they journeyed through the Milky Way. Or perhaps they would colonize Earth and convert it into a zoo, or eliminate humans altogether and use the planet for recreation and wilderness areas for their species. Given all the tribal wars and ecological destruction humans have wrought on Spaceship Earth, an extraterrestrial philosopher might indeed decide that we need to be utterly exterminated as a precautionary measure — thus removing the threat of the human species from the universe. We have known this verdict was plausible since 1951, when Klaatu announced that we would face extinction unless we could learn to live in peace as a planetary society:

> I am leaving soon, and you will forgive me if I speak bluntly. The universe grows smaller every day, and the threat of aggression by any group, anywhere, can no longer be tolerated. . . . We, of the other planets . . . live in peace, without arms or armies, secure in the knowledge that we are free from aggression and war — free to pursue more profitable enterprises. Now, we do not pretend to have achieved perfection. But we do have a system, and it works. I came here to give you these facts. It is no concern of ours how you run your own planet — but if you threaten to extend your violence, this Earth of yours will be reduced to a burned-out cinder. Your choice is simple: Join us and live in peace or pursue your present course and face obliteration. We shall be waiting for your answer. The decision rests with you.

With the emergence of the Cold War, Klaatu offered a warning about nuclear warfare and extending our propensity for violence into the universe. Sixty years later, the point is this: What justifies the continuation of our existence, given the ongoing terror wars, ecological destruction, and beliefs in cosmic centrality on Spaceship Earth? Can we hope to avoid being obliterated by an advanced extraterrestrial civilization? Isn't that the existential message of *Arrival* (2016)?

TABLE 4 **POSSIBLE RESPONSES TO HUMANITY FROM ADVANCED EXTRATERRESTRIAL CIVILIZATIONS: WHAT KLAATU, GORT, OR OTHERS MIGHT DO**

(with social media hashtags)

FRIENDLY

1. Use Facebook, YouTube, Twitter, and Instagram to offer greetings and upload selfies and videos (#hello)
2. Appear on the world's late night talk-show circuit to welcome us into the cosmic civilizations
3. Meet with world leaders, celebrities, and corporate titans to set up interplanetary systems of trade and transportation and foster general goodwill
4. Share their art, science, technology, and knowledge of the cosmos with humanity's universities and educational organizations, including their knowledge of wormholes and advanced transportation machines
   — *The wormholes and transportation machines are like the scenarios in* Interstellar *and* Contact.

FRIENDLY, BUT WITH A WARNING

5. Welcome us into the cosmic civilizations but give humanity a clear warning that our war, greed, pollution, tribalism, nationalism, and pre-Copernican worldviews cannot be extended off Earth (#stop)
   — *This is like Klaatu in* The Day the Earth Stood Still.

PRECAUTIONARY MEASURES: WITH EVACUATION WARNINGS

6. To protect the moon, Mars, and other celestial bodies: Destroy and reduce to dust all of humanity's technologies for strip-mining the moon or terraforming the red planet
7. To protect other life forms: Destroy and reduce to dust all of humanity's weapons, weapons manufacturers, and military sites (#guncontrol)
8. To prevent the interplanetary spread of human space spores carrying arrogant, narcissistic, cosmically central, pre-Copernican worldviews: Destroy all humanity's rockets
   — *Responses 6-8 are inspired by Gort in* The Day the Earth Stood Still.

EXPLOITATIVE MEASURES

9. To colonize Earth: Conquer humans, display us in their zoos, use us as a food source, use our bodies for breeding, and conduct experiments on us. (#invasion)
   — *This is like episodes from* The Twilight Zone *and* The X-Files, *the films* Earth vs. Flying Saucers, Invasion of the Body Snatchers, Alien, Men in Black, Oblivion, *etc.*

PREVENTATIVE MEASURES

10. To be 100% certain humanity will not extend its war, cosmic centrality, and planetary destruction to other parts of the cosmos: Eliminate the human species (#extinctionevent)
    — *This is the scenario Stephen Hawking fears.*
    — *Perhaps these are among the reasons extraterrestrials attacked in* War of the Worlds, Earth vs. the Flying Saucers, *and* Independence Day.

EARTHLINGS VS. EXTRATERRESTRIALS. For decades, Hollywood has been producing films featuring extraterrestrials who arrive and wage war upon Earthlings, as illustrated in *War of the Worlds* (1953), *This Island Earth* (1955), *Earth vs. the Flying Saucers* (1956), *Invasion of the Body Snatchers* (1956), *Independence Day* (1996), *War of the Worlds* (2005), *Battle Los Angeles* (2011), *Oblivion* (2013), and many others. Sure, some of these films are classics and have multiple cultural meanings. But aren't these films really a pop-culture cover for the fact that if any species attacked first, it would most likely be humans in the name of their imaginary Creator and political-military rulers?

Why should the future be any different than the past? If a comet or meteor were hurtling toward Earth and destined to render all human life extinct, and Klaatu could actually prevent the collision with advanced technologies, why *should* he? Klaatu could make the argument for our extinction in the name of peace or ecology — that he would be preventing a future holy war in the Milky Way or imminent environmental destruction on a planet like Mars. Payback for colonization, conquest, and ecological destruction — isn't that one of the messages of *Avatar*?

"KLAATU, BARADA, NIKTO." Hollywood has warned us about our violence and stupidity many *many* times. When will we pay attention? Unless a benevolent Klaatu arrives to enlighten the human species, there is no one to save us and our civilization, ecosystems, or philosophies — no one, no entity, and no Creator. No political leaders will save us, nor will any celebrities or celebrity politicians. The "one" is not Neo from *The Matrix* or "V" from *V for Vendetta*. The solution is not another superhero or super "man" — Batman, Superman, or Iron Man. Xena, Trinity, and Katniss are pretty cool, but they could not save our species either. Captain Kirk can't do it. Nor can General Leia.

Looking sexy in their leather skin fashions, Taylor and Nova might breed us a better species on the *Planet of the Apes*, maybe even a philosophical Ubermensch for the big bang multiverse, a future counter to Stephen Hawking's claim that "philosophy is dead." But who has time to wait 10,000 years to enjoy a space cocktail on a sleekly designed interplanetary hotel like the one in *2001* — a drink best enjoyed while gazing at the Milky Way through the bubble windows of the space-age bar and maybe conversing about super-cool voids or the meaning of the monolith?

9. A SANE 21ST-CENTURY SPACE PHILOSOPHY

We are an amazing and paradoxical species. We have the genius to extend our consciousness into the cosmos and discover a mind-blowing universe of 2 trillion galaxies and 3 sextillion stars along with untold numbers of moons, planets, supernovas, and black holes, all organized around supervoids and gigantic galaxy clusters that stretch for billions of light years. The energy of this universe is destined to last for trillions upon trillions of years — and yet we still can't we give up the cosmic narcissism!

No doubt our discovery of the vast cosmos and our non-centrality ranks as our greatest triumph and poses our most important *philosophical* challenge — we face the paradox of having discovered a sublime universe, and yet we are insignificant and our existence might be meaningless. Given such an existential dilemma, is this the best we have to offer the universe — sending our bodies into space to wage war, pollute planets, entertain our egos, and beam messages about imaginary Creators as we traverse the solar system and beyond? Seriously, is this *it*? Is this the *best* we can hope for? Are we just going to join Elon Musk and Brother Consolmagno and keep on moonwalking into the future? (Tesla is a progressive idea; however, terraforming Mars is not. Baptizing ETs is utterly deranged.)

Today's space explorers of the future should realize that strip-mining the moon or terraforming Mars is not going to change one damn thing for the better on planet Earth. I seriously doubt any new energy sources would reduce Earth's pollution. Sure, some people might make some big money. But big deal if their missions are meaningless and have no positive impact on the cosmos or on our future as a species! Absent a sane space philosophy, colonizing and terraforming Mars wouldn't change anything either — it would merely extend to Mars the human carnival of war, greed, theism, tribalism, unbridled consumerism, ecological destruction, and delusions of cosmic centrality. We'll just have millions of people in space doing what billions on Earth are doing. This view may sound cynical, but it only follows the logic of the dominant space narratives as described in this chapter and seen in numerous space films.

The 21st-century space age needs a new philosophy befitting the universe from which we emerged, the knowledge we have acquired, and the cosmic technologies we have created. Otherwise it's the same old stuff, and we're just doing it on other planets. That's why I've outlined a new philosophy for space exploration, one that embraces scientific discovery, philosophical inquiry, ecological protection for the places we visit, the aesthetics of beauty and the sublime, and global cooperation among nations, peoples, and corporations. Let's call this the Science Philosophy Ecology Aesthetic Cooperative (SPEAC) model for space exploration (summarized in Table 6). We should develop this philosophy and let it *speak for our species* in the universe!

SCIENTIFIC DISCOVERY. Obviously, the scientific exploration of the universe should continue in all areas of astronomy, cosmology, and related space sciences. The funding of space research should be doubled or tripled (or more), with the money coming from the war chests of the world's militaries. We could . . . if we really wanted it.

We should continue to extend human consciousness deep into the cosmos by funding and developing observatories, space telescopes, and robotic probes to explore moons and planets. The more we learn about other planets and moons, the better we will understand *our planet* and how to protect our ecosystems. We especially need to study Mars and Venus to ensure that we do not cause Earth to become like either of those planets — an uninhabitable desert or poisonous greenhouse. We need to increase the budget for NASA's Planetary Defense Office, which seeks to find all the Near-Earth Objects that might crash into our planet and cause an extinction event like the one that finished off the dinosaurs. The more we learn about the universe on the large scale, the sooner we might embrace our insignificance and develop new philosophies and narratives for our species, outlooks that provide hope and meaning in the vast universe.

At some point, we should send bodies into the cosmos, first by returning to the moon or venturing to Mars. What should we do when we get there? In the spirit of *Star Trek*, NASA wants to go to Mars to seek new life forms and begin colonizing the planet. From the first pages of the NASA report:

> NASA is leading our nation and our world on a journey to Mars. Like the Apollo Program, we embark on this journey for all humanity. Unlike Apollo, we will be going to stay. . . . Together with our partners, we will pioneer Mars and answer some of humanity's fundamental questions:
>
> - Was Mars home to microbial life? Is it today?
> - Could it be a safe home for humans one day?
> - What can it teach us about life elsewhere in the cosmos or how life began on Earth?
> - What can it teach us about Earth's past, present, and future?
>
> Mars is an achievable goal. We have spent more than four decades on the journey to Mars, with wildly successful robotic explorers. The first human steps have been taken through science and technology research aboard the International Space Station (ISS) and in laboratories here on Earth. We are taking the next steps by developing the Space Launch System (SLS) and the Orion crewed spacecraft, demonstrating new operations to reduce logistics, and preparing for human missions into cislunar space, such as exploring a captured asteroid. There are challenges to pioneering Mars, but we know they are solvable. We are developing the capabilities necessary to get there, land there, and live there.[49]

The rest of the 35-page report contains details about economic and technological benefits and new visions for space travel, along with numerous cool images of Martian landscapes populated with robots and astronauts. Obviously, finding life is a worthy goal, but there is nary a word about what it would *mean* or what *hope* it might provide us humans still living on Earth. Of course, NASA is a government agency seeking widespread public support and funding, but the absence of any discussion of what the discovery of life on Mars might mean for human narratives on Earth only proves many of the points made in this book.

Of course, we should support and increase the funding of NASA's projects. But if we colonize Mars with no ecological space philosophy, then we'll probably have theme parks, interplanetary televangelists, and *Real Housewives of Mars*. Or maybe the human presence on the red planet will resemble what we saw in *Total Recall* (1990), the Arnold Schwarzenegger film in which Mars is a strip-mined wasteland featuring tribal-corporate warfare, Wild West party towns, and virtual reality tourism. However, the ending of *Total Recall* celebrates the beauty and sublimity of the Martian landscapes, not the economic value of Martian minerals. Preventing the destruction and pollution of Mars and other planets and moons are why we need to embrace the development of a new space philosophy for our species.

ECOLOGY IN SPACE. The standard militarization, colonization, consumerism, resource exploitation models assume the celestial bodies are ours to consume and despoil. Space law currently treats the moon like sea law treats the oceans on Earth: No one owns them and anyone can take from them. So the oceans are overfished, polluted with chemicals, and filled with billions of tons of plastic.

What will the moon be like in 100 years? Most likely, it will be a strip-mined industrial wasteland with billion-year-old craters turned into garbage dumps, filled with trash, plastic bottles, and discarded computers and mobile phones.

Think we won't pollute the moon or Mars? We've already started with the clutter left behind at the Apollo landing sites. Look at all the space junk in orbit around our planet (see Chapter 2). Then consider our massive landfills, along with all the lakes, rivers, and oceans filling with trash, plastic, and chemicals.

The Apollo program had near-zero impact on the cultural narratives for a shared human destiny on Earth, except for the *Earthrise* photo, which was taken in December 1968 and helped reboot the ecological and environmental movements. By 1970, Earth Day was founded, and it is still celebrated every year on April 22. Given the levels of pollution, sometimes it is hard to see the impact of the environmental movement, but it has helped tame some of the worst extremes of pollution and industrial destruction. If our exploration of space helped inspire environmental protections on Earth, then why not return the celestial favor and extend our ecological knowledge into space to protect the places we explore?

In 2013, two members of the US House of Representatives — Donna Edwards (D-MD) and Eddie Bernice Johnson (D-TX) — introduced the Apollo Lunar Landing Legacy Act. *Time* described it as a bill "which would extend the protections afforded to officially designated historical parks to all six Apollo landing sites, preserving the artifacts and regulating access to prevent their destruction."[50] Additionally, the act would seek World Heritage Site status from the United Nations, especially for the Apollo 11 landing area. Protecting the Apollo sites is certainly a great idea, but we should go much further.

A group of space thinkers who are part of an organization called the Committee on Space Research advocates for the development of a network of planetary parks on Mars and elsewhere.[51] As with protecting the Apollo sites, this is a great idea. But it is thinking too small. If we are an enlightened species that has learned from its mistakes, we should protect almost all of Mars and the moon, not just a few territories and landing sites.

PROTECTING MARS AND THE MOONS AS CELESTIAL PARKS AND WILDERNESS AREAS. Following the models of the national park systems and wilderness areas in the United States, Mars and the moons of the solar system should be protected as territories we could label "celestial parks" and "celestial wilderness areas." To be clear, this recommendation is not about setting aside a few patches of "park land" on Mars and the moon while the rest of the territories are polluted, terraformed, strip-mined, and colonized by industrial workers, tourists visiting "Disney Mars," and bloated space consumers in McDonald's and Starbucks. Can't you just see the Golden Arches glowing atop a Martian mesa? How about electronic billboards lining the rim of a crater, creating a Mars Times Square? In contrast, this space philosophy is based in a need for ecological protection of the places we visit while ensuring they remain naturally beautiful and wondrous, thus tapping into the aesthetics of the natural and cosmic sublime.

This model would ensure that 99.999% of Mars and the moons are set aside for ecological protection, available only for scientific study, philosophical inquiry, art projects, and aesthetic appreciation. A fraction of 1% percent of

Mars and the moon would be set aside for human usage and habitation, such as biospheres, observatories, museums (with artifacts from the planet or moon), art galleries (with artwork based on the planet or moon), and sites for space tourism (hotels, camp sites, and hiking trails). The hotels could also be entirely orbital. The rest of the moon and Mars would remain untouched. Given that Mars has about 55 million square miles of surface area, protecting 99.999% would still leave 550 square miles for human development scattered among select spots on Mars. Since the moon has about 15 million square miles, protecting 99.999% would leave 150 square miles for human development scattered around the moon. These totals seem highly reasonable. Of course, the areas with human development must have minimal impact on the surfaces.

As we move out further in space, these same protections should be extended to all the sites we visit and explore in the solar system, like the spectacular moons of Saturn and Jupiter. This celestial park and wilderness vision furthers space exploration and the experience of the cosmic sublime — the wonderment of exploring Mars and the moon and seeing the stars from the dark skies of space. Space hotels, astronomical observatories, artistic and scientific projects, hiking and camping on the moon, a united and cooperative species venturing into space — these things excite me. Strip-mining, polluting and destroying landscapes, instigating unnecessary nationalist competition, and extending religion, war, and violence into space — these things, to be honest, terrify and disgust me. If we are truly an enlightened species, we need not plunder moons and planets *to show how great we are to ourselves*.

PARKS, WILDERNESS AREAS, AND SPACE TOURISM. The idea of protecting Mars and the moon as sites for science and aesthetics may seem naïve, impractical, or utterly deluded — until we consider that on Earth we have already created a huge tourist economy based on the aesthetics of nature and the sublime. Why can't this kind of aesthetic tourism be extended throughout the solar system instead of the Disney model? Why not embrace the experience of the sublime rather than the entertainment of simulated realities and endless consumption? If Jeff Bezos envisions "millions of people living and working in space," then why not have them organized around an interplanetary tourist and service economy?

People go to national parks and wilderness areas for a variety of reasons, but they mostly center on seeking and experiencing some combination of the following:

- Natural beauty
- Amazing experiences of enormity and immensity: forests, mountains, oceans, deserts, and canyons made possible by eons of biological, geological, and celestial evolution
- Solitude and remoteness away from civilization
- Ancient landscapes and ecosystems untouched by humans (or at least mostly untouched)

Mars and the moons of the solar system seem like perfect places for these kinds of experiences. After grasping the destructive effects of over-industrialization, we have learned to protect these kinds of spaces on Earth, seeing them as intrinsic

TABLE 5 **REASONS WHY MARS AND THE MOON SHOULD BE PROTECTED AS CELESTIAL PARKS AND WILDERNESS AREAS**

1. **Mars and the moon are objects of truth, beauty, and wonder: sites for scientific discovery and space tourism.**

   — Humans should protect 99.999% of Mars and the moon for the same reasons we protect nature and wilderness areas on Earth: beauty, science, solitude, ecological protection, and to place humans in a larger planetary and cosmic narrative.
   — Mars and the moon have been around about 4.5 billion years longer than humans; thus we have no intrinsic right to plunder, pillage, or own either celestial body.
   — We should think of Mars and the moon as "celestial museums" for art and science, as sites for aesthetic appreciation, scientific understanding, and existential solitude.
   — Humans should visit Mars and the moon: study them, admire them, explore them, camp on them, and even build hotels on them or space hotels that orbit them. But we should not pollute them. We should respect them.

2. **Mars and the moon should not be a part of human consumption.**

   — Humans should not mine Mars or the moon for energy and minerals to be used on Earth that we will just spew into the atmosphere and toss into landfills. We would thus be polluting Mars, the moon, and our own planet while literally putting Mars and the moon into our landfills.

3. **Mining Mars or the moon will not improve the human condition.**

   — Extracting resources from Mars and the moon will not make a better society or better species; it will only make some people rich, create some jobs, and produce more pollution.
   — The same goals (wealth and jobs) could be attained by tapping into the so-called battery in the sky: the sun and its 4.7-billion-year life span of solar energy.

4. **We do not want to pose a threat to celestial objects and extraterrestrial species.**

   — Pillaging and polluting Mars and the moon shows *we are a threat* to extraterrestrial species and other planets, not a worthy and enlightened cosmic civilization.

5. **As a species and civilization, we will become greater and more celestial if we refrain from polluting and ravaging other planets and moons.**

   — It's time to give up the pre-Copernican narcissism. From the moon, Earth is a borderless planet traversing the voids of space and time. From Mars, our planet is just a tiny speck of light. That we know this confirms our greatness and insignificance simultaneously. To admire and respect other planets confirms our wisdom and right to exist as a space-faring and cosmic civilization.

to life on Earth and crucial to the psychological and existential well-being of the human species. Protecting the planet, preserving other species, and nourishing the well-being of our species' consciousness are profound ideas in the establishment of national parks and wilderness areas. But the existential ground for the national park and wilderness concepts is the natural and cosmic sublime felt before the enormity of the natural world on Earth and in the Milky Way.

In 2014, there were approximately 17.5 million visitors to the national parks in the desert Southwest of the United States, led by Grand Canyon National Park (Arizona) with 4.8 million visitors, Zion National Park (Utah) with 3.5 million, and Joshua Tree National Park (California) with 1.6 million. Even the national parks in the most remote desert areas had significant numbers of visitors: Big Bend National Park (Texas) drew 314,000 visitors, and Guadalupe Mountains National Park (Texas) drew 166,000.[52] Since 17 million people visited the desert national parks, surely some tourists, hikers, and campers of the future would want to see the moon and the deserts of Mars. Given these numbers, why can't we imagine a space philosophy where we protect Mars and the moon for scientific study, ecological protection, and aesthetic admiration? Why not have space tourism — visiting celestial national parks and wilderness areas — as the key space industry? Space hotels can orbit Mars, the moon, and any other celestial object. How amazing would it be to hike on Mars or gaze at Earth from a lunar hotel?

The ecological and tourism narratives overlap with the desire for experiencing beauty and the sublime while also grasping our place in the grand scheme of events on Earth and in the cosmos. For example, the national parks and wilderness areas often reveal much about the geological or biological evolution on Earth and where humanity fits in the larger scheme of life and death. Arizona's Grand Canyon offers not only a visual experience of the natural sublime; the erosion caused by the Colorado River reveals *2 billion years* of geological evolution on Earth. In Texas's Guadalupe Mountains National Park, you can hike the Permian Extinction Trail and walk among the evidence of the *massive extinction event* that wiped out the majority of the species on Earth 250 million years ago.[53] At the same time, you can experience incredible natural beauty and pristine wilderness areas. At night, the Milky Way shines above.

In contrast to life in the electrified cities, the Grand Canyon and Guadalupe Mountains situate our species in gigantic regimes of space and time that more accurately reflect our place in the cosmos. These desert landscapes are immense, beautiful, and tap into the sublime. Once you leave the electrified metropolises and experience these landscapes, you see the true existential conditions of the human species — we exist in a thin web of life on a watery rock orbiting a flaming ball of hydrogen. And it is liberating to know that.

THE DARK-SKY MOVEMENT. During the past 125 years, we have erased the cosmos from our consciousness with our electrified cities and electronic screens. That's the nature of our "dual system of existence," where we live in a civilization divorced from the very cosmos that gave it birth (see Chapter 3). According to a recent study of light pollution, 99% of Europeans and Americans live under heavily light-polluted skies, such that 80% of Americans can't even see the Milky Way. Around the world, 80% of humans live in light-polluted skies.[54] As artificial light spreads, so will the light pollution. Given these totals and trends, it's not hard to imagine a near future in which most everyone will never see the Milky Way with their own eyes. (What would Vincent van Gogh's *Starry Night* look like today?) That's why the rise of the dark-sky movement is a major positive step toward reconnecting our species to the universe revealed by the starry skies above.

Founded in 1988, the International Dark-Sky Association (IDA) is leading the way in returning dark skies to human society now blinded by the glow of artificial lighting.[55] For three billion years, life on Earth existed within a rhythm of light and dark produced by the sun, moon, and Milky Way. Humans also evolved within the daily patterns of day and night, light and dark. Living in our electrified cities, we have removed ourselves from nature's celestial rhythms. As shown in the documentary *The City Dark* (2011), the proliferation of artificial light not only erases the night sky but wastes energy, disrupts ecosystems, and harms human health.[56] Through the IDA, many humans are collectively taking steps to protect the night sky in national parks and in smaller, more remote cities.

Protecting the night skies is like protecting the wilderness areas. In effect, the thousands of stars we see (with our naked eyes) in the Milky Way represent the nearest edge of the celestial wilderness that is the universe. Just as the *untouched* wilderness is important for the psychology and philosophy of our species, so too the *unpolluted* Milky Way is important for our cosmology and experience of the sublime. If the Milky Way and dark skies could be returned to human consciousness on a regular basis or become easily accessible in national parks and dark-sky reserves, then this might help inspire the development of planetary systems of value and a new cosmic narrative. Unlike the pre-scientific humans who could only see us at the center of the starry universe passing above (and under the control of a Creator), we would no longer be wedded to superstitions and could gaze upon the Milky Way through the eyes of contemporary astronomy and see it as our celestial home in a beautiful universe.

STAR PARTIES AND THE COSMIC SUBLIME. Directly experiencing the stars and nearby galaxies from both a scientific and aesthetic perspective is thrilling and inspiring. It's like what I have directly experienced at McDonald Observatory in the desert mountains of Texas — the dark skies filled with the radiant Milky Way have enabled me to experience the cosmic sublime and transcendent moments in which I am connected to a narrative much larger than the human-centered narratives that dominate the 24/7 media spectacle.

During my many visits to McDonald Observatory's "star parties" (where visitors are permitted to look at the stars, planets, and galaxies through very powerful telescopes), I have gazed upon the Andromeda and Whirlpool Galaxies, neighbors of the Milky Way. Andromeda is over 2 million light years from the Milky Way, while the Whirlpool Galaxy is at least 15 million light years away. Imagine seeing the tilted spiral of Andromeda, with photons from 1 trillion stars traversing the voids of the cosmos at the speed of light for 2 million years, light leaving that galaxy long before any human walked on Earth! On one particular visit, it occurred to me while I was gazing through one telescope that, after eons of space traveling, the starlight I was witnessing was passing through the telescope's lenses and into my own eyes, where photons from the Andromeda Galaxy were actually converting into bioelectrical patterns in my brain.

Andromeda's photons merged with my neurons. In that existential moment, my consciousness was reconnected with the cosmos, and a tiny fragment of the universe was directly aware of itself on a grand scale — connecting the infinite and infinitesimal. Though tiny in relation to the cosmos, I felt the exaltation and affirmation of human existence, the power of human reason to grasp what I was seeing and sensing. It is likely I have never felt more inspired and at peace in the same moment. That's the power of the cosmic sublime. Mind-blown! No Creator needed.

In my view, the more we can return the cosmos and dark skies to our existence and consciousness, the better it will be for our species, giving more people the chance to experience the sublime — on Earth or in space. Additionally, the protection of the dark skies helps challenge the "dual system of existence" that dominates our daily reality.

VIRGIN GALACTIC AND THE COSMIC SUBLIME. Might viewing Earth or the Milky Way from a spacecraft or space hotel help inspire the development of a new cosmic narrative and space philosophy for our species? Of all the space agencies and companies presently active, Richard Branson and Virgin Galactic seem most invested in finding that narrative and willing to think beyond nationalist, military, and resource-exploitation rationales. Affordable space travel is the long-term plan for Virgin Galactic, which hopes to build a space tourism company around experiencing the cosmic sublime. Virgin Galactic's flights into the space around our planet will permit citizens to experience what the astronauts experience: the wondrous views of Earth from space along with the majesty of the Milky Way. The corporation offers such a clear challenge to our dominant space philosophies that its mission is worth quoting at length:

> People all around the world have experienced a sense of awe as they look up at the night sky. We discover a limitless universe of wonder as we learn to identify the Milky Way, or to spot planets, rings, moons, and even entire galaxies. As we peer into the heavens we look back billions of years in time, and connect simultaneously with the most primal thoughts of our ancestors and the most cutting-edge science of our day. . . .
>
> Perhaps it is in our culture, perhaps it is in our DNA, or perhaps it is a bit of each of those, but we humans seem hardwired to explore. Not all of us feel it, but so many people today and in the past have felt an irresistible urge to see for themselves what lies just beyond the horizon. . . .
>
> Only through the exploration of the unknown can we continue to grow and evolve. Space is not only important for the future of transportation, commerce, and science; it's also important for the future of imagination. We still know so little about space and how our understanding of it can benefit life on our planet. What is clear is that the ability for more people to cross the final frontier of space will be key to human advancement.
>
> The astronauts have also found themselves transformed by their journeys. Many have experienced something called the Overview

> Effect as they look back at our home world. Seeing the Earth from space, they notice that most of the borders we fight over are imaginary lines, or that our atmosphere seems like an impossibly thin and fragile layer of protection for life as we know it. The experience is a profound and fundamentally personal one, but its magnitude cannot be denied.[57]

In this statement, Virgin Galactic is suggesting that the aesthetics of space exploration can alter human consciousness and trigger new narratives for human civilization. The "Overview Effect" (discussed in Chapter 1) is a term used to describe the perspective astronauts experience when viewing Earth from space. Not only do they feel amazement and a transcendent connection to the planet, but they also see that our human and cultural narratives are clearly not in harmony with our planet or our actual place in the cosmos. Some of the astronauts recount their experiences of the cosmic sublime in the elegant 20-minute documentary *The Overview Effect* (2012).[58] The human species certainly had an "Overview" moment during Apollo 8 and Apollo 11, but they then deployed cosmic doublethink to remain in denial about the meaning of what they saw on their televisions (see Chapters 1 and 3).

In my view, Branson and Virgin Galactic are heading in the right direction — at least philosophically — because they are tapping into the cosmic sublime and suggesting we confront "what lies just beyond the horizon." As suggested by Virgin Galactic's philosophy, aesthetic experience should be at the center of a space philosophy, precisely because it serves humanity's primal and existential needs for art, beauty, and wonder.[59] That's one reason the sublime is a deep and moving human experience.

When aboard a Virgin Galactic spacecraft of the future, we will experience the cosmic sublime, at least if our eyes and minds are open. In gazing out the window and seeing Earth amid the stars and celestial void, the majesty of the Milky Way will stimulate our *aesthetic* imagination, simultaneously affirming our rationality as a species and providing exaltation before the cosmos. We would feel connected to the larger narratives of the universe, yet likely sense a void in what it all means. The aesthetic experience will challenge and inspire our *philosophical* imagination, showing our previous narcissistic narratives are delusions, yet seducing our reason with the grandeur of existence and the possibility of crafting a new cosmic narrative for our species. This may seem like an overly optimistic and philosophical analysis of mere "space tourism," yet Virgin Galactic will be providing the kind of aesthetic experience that needs philosophical support and development for it to have the lasting and meaningful effect that Branson hopes to achieve.

SPACEPORT AMERICA. Located in the deserts of New Mexico, Virgin Galactic's home spaceport is a beautiful and inspiring structure for the 21st-century space age. Designed by Norman Foster, "Spaceport America" features curvilinear eco-domed structures emerging from the desert with curved walls of windows open to the enormity of the desert and skies. The overall design and elegant minimalist sculpture (at the entrance) make it seem optimistic and forward-looking, certainly worthy of launching humans into the majestic universe we have discovered and will be exploring. Spaceport America is owned and funded by the state of New Mexico, with Virgin Galactic its tenant for the next 20 years.

Seeing the futuristic spaceport amid the spectacular desert triggers a moment of the sublime because the structure and site are spectacular together. Frankly, seeing the spaceport in person made me feel great about human possibility as well as depressed about why so much of the civilized world is ugly and messed up. If we can only develop a space philosophy worthy of Spaceport America, then we might be on to something good for our species as it ventures into space.

LAND ART ON THE MOON AND MARS. Like the architecture of Spaceport America, we also need great art to accompany our journey into space. That's because the human species needs *art and science* to make sense of the cosmos that surrounds us, whether we are living on Earth, Mars, or a space station. As shown in Chapter 2, the cognitive need for art is why space films can be so powerful in providing visions of humanity exploring the universe. Great art can give us meaning and hope. To complement the scientific studies on the moon and Mars, I propose that we commission art projects on them as well — especially projects that situate us in larger cosmic narratives.

This is where "land art" enters the space narrative. Also known as "earthworks," land art refers to artwork built in or on the surface of Earth.[60] The greatest and most famous works of land art are at remote sites in the deserts of the American Southwest. Built or begun in the wake of Apollo, the following works are monumental in scale and have profound celestial meanings:

- Set on the edge of the Great Salt Lake in Utah, Robert Smithson's *Spiral Jetty* (1970) is a 1,500-foot spiral of dirt and boulders that references the Milky Way above, while salt crystals show emergence and entropy over time.
- Cut into the rim of a mesa north of Las Vegas, Michael Heizer's *Double Negative* (1970) comprises 2 empty trenches (together about 1,500 feet long) that directly pose the challenge of the philosophical void in the surrounding desert and cosmos above.
- Set in the flat emptiness of northern Utah, Nancy Holt's *Sun Tunnels* (1976) are 4 giant concrete tubes aligned with the summer and winter solstices; holes on the tops of the tunnels align with various constellations.
- Set in central New Mexico, Walter De Maria's *Lightning Field* (1977) is a rectangular grid of 400 stainless-steel rods designed to attract lightning strikes; the rods also glisten in spectral colors during sunrises and sunsets.
- Built into the edge of a spectacular mesa in northern New Mexico, Charles Ross's *Star Axis* (begun in 1973 and only now nearing completion) is a giant steel and stone sculpture designed to be a naked-eye observatory aimed at the North Star; *Star Axis* will be accurate for thousands of years.
- Set in a dormant volcano east of the Grand Canyon, James Turrell's *Roden Crater* (begun in 1979 and still in development) contains a series of his "skyspaces" and naked-eye observatories. According to Turrell: "In this stage set of geologic time, I wanted to make spaces that engage

> celestial events in light so that the spaces perform a 'music of the spheres' in light."[61]

Having visited most of these sites myself (the only exception being *Roden Crater*), I've found that they are all much more impressive when experienced *in person*. The photos of these earthworks might look great or interesting, but they are not a substitute for being there. That's because the immensity of the surrounding desert and skies functions as "negative space" and sets off the earthworks, forcing us to see them in a *larger cosmic narrative*. It's the same concept as *Earthrise*, in which the blackness is the negative space that frames Earth in the universe.

Far removed from museums and metropolises, these earthworks inherently situate us in universal narratives of space, time, and existence — in direct contrast to the 24/7 media spectacle that situates us in the momentary fragments of tweets, selfies, and status updates. Day or night, these monumental earthworks remove us from the center of the universe and stimulate the cosmic sublime. How cool would it be to experience our place in the cosmos via skyspaces in a lunar crater or a naked-eye observatory atop a Martian mesa?

COOPERATION IN SPACE. The idea of nations or firms competing to control and exploit parts the moon or Mars is a *natural* extension of the nationalism and corporate capitalism that dominates the large-scale social and economic systems on Earth. And that's the exact reason we should *not* follow the competitive model as we venture into space. Nationalist and capitalist competition will merely extend tribal rivalries and conflicts to Mars and the moon. Violence, warfare, and ecological destruction will inevitably result.

Rather than blindly continuing the competitive and nationalist power model, humans should fully develop the cooperative model suggested in *The Martian*, where China and the United States work together. Why can't China, Russia, India, Japan, the United States, and the European Space Agency all work on wide-scale collaborations while inviting the rest of the world to join and contribute where possible? Why can't international consortiums of corporations work together to make space tourism an industry enjoyed by people from *all* nations? After all, NASA and the world's scientists share scientific and cosmological discoveries via the internet and other media while films like *Interstellar* and *The Martian* are enjoyed by audiences around the world. The International Space Station should represent an early stage in our long-term cooperative endeavors in space. When will the United States, China, and Russia abandon their silly and unscientific tribal rivalries? It's not even remotely sane.

The views of Earth from space, our celestial origins, and our genetic code (we all share 99.9% of the same DNA) and our chemical composition (we're made of the most common elements of the cosmos) show we are one species sharing one planet with millions of other species. Our planet evolved a single biosphere and ecosystem over four billion years, a complexity of systems shared by all species on the planet. The biosphere is local, global, and celestial, as is human destiny and all the life forms that depend on the planet and the sun to survive. Though many humans like to claim special and sacred destinies for their tribes, the sciences of biology, anthropology, and cosmology clearly show that *no tribe* is inherently special on Spaceship Earth, as illustrated by the five previous extinction events on our planet. If the dinosaurs can be removed from the game of life, then so can the most advanced simians. With the challenges posed by climate change, nuclear terrorism, and Near-Earth Objects, we would do well to cooperate as we expand into the universe.

TABLE 6 OUTLINE FOR A 21ST-CENTURY SPACE PHILOSOPHY

The Science, Philosophy, Ecology, Aesthetics, Cooperative Model of Space Exploration (SPEAC)

1. **SCIENTIFIC DISCOVERY**
   — Our scientific exploration of the universe should continue, but with much more funding. We should send more telescopes into space, more robots to planets and moons, and humans to Mars and elsewhere in the quest to discover extraterrestrial life and ecological knowledge to prevent our planet from becoming like Mars (a planetary desert) or Venus (a runaway greenhouse).

2. **PHILOSOPHY**
   — If we claim to be an enlightened species, then we need to determine the philosophical meaning (if any) of our scientific and cosmological discoveries. Is nihilism all we can expect from the cosmic sublime?
   — As shown by Apollo's *Earthrise* and the Hubble images, there is no self-evident meaning to human existence in the universe. The only path out of post-Apollo culture is the development of a *universal narrative* to give us hope for a meaningful destiny in a cosmos in which we are not central or important.

3. **ECOLOGY**
   — Since we have no cosmic right to lay waste to other planets and moons, we should extend our ecological protections to all the planets and moons we explore. How can we not want to protect the beauty and sublimity of such celestial objects?
   — Destroying landscapes of other celestial objects shows we are a threat in the universe and invite future retribution from any advanced extraterrestrials we encounter.

4. **AESTHETICS**
   — As illustrated by the national parks and wilderness areas of the United States, many people want to experience natural beauty along with solitude and the sublime of ancient topographies, panoramic landscapes, and the Milky Way in the dark skies of remote locales.
   — Obviously, the untouched wildernesses will be available in much greater scale on other planets and moons while providing unlimited opportunities to experience the cosmic sublime amid the stars.
   — In our embrace of the sublime lies the greatest chance to counter nihilism and develop a universal human narrative.

5. **COOPERATION**
   — If we claim to be an advanced civilization, then the combination of science, philosophy, ecology and aesthetics should make us realize the inherent wisdom of cooperating as nations and peoples when venturing into space.
   — Our planetary cooperation is already celebrated by the original *Star Trek*, put into practice at the International Space Station, and supported in films such as *The Martian*. Similarly, NASA shares its discoveries with the world, and the European Space Agency represents many countries.
   — In the end, we are a single species exploring the universe from which we emerged, while the universal awe felt toward the Milky Way and the cosmos tells us we should cooperate.

Perhaps the SpaceX engineers and space policy wonks in Washington, DC, will laugh this off as naïve philosophizing. So what? It's their lack of cultural and philosophical imagination that reflects the key problem we face: extending our cosmic narcissism and imaginary centrality off the planet.

10. PHILOSOPHY IN SPACE: WHO SPEAKS FOR THE HUMAN SPECIES?

In the final episode of the classic documentary series, *Cosmos* (1980), entitled "Who Speaks for Earth?," the American scientist Carl Sagan famously posed the profound philosophical challenge:

> In our tenure of this planet, we have accumulated dangerous, evolutionary baggage — propensities for aggression and ritual, submission to leaders, hostility to outsiders, all of which puts our survival in some doubt. We have also acquired compassion for others, love for our children, a desire to learn from history and experience, and a great, soaring passionate intelligence — the clear tools for our continued survival and prosperity.
>
> Which aspects of our nature will prevail is uncertain, particularly when our visions and prospects are bound to one small part of the small planet earth. But, up and in the cosmos an inescapable perspective awaits. National boundaries are not evidenced when we view the earth from space. Fanatic ethnic or religious or national identifications are a little difficult to support when we see our planet as a fragile, blue crescent fading to become an inconspicuous point of light against the bastion and citadel of the stars.
>
> There are not yet obvious signs of extraterrestrial intelligence, and this makes us wonder whether civilizations like ours rush inevitably into self-destruction. . . .
>
> The global balance of terror pioneered by the United States and the Soviet Union holds hostage all the citizens of the earth. Each side consistently probes the limits of the other's tolerance — like the Cuban missile crisis, the testing of anti-satellite weapons, the Vietnam and Afghanistan wars. The hostile military establishments are locked in some ghastly mutual embrace, each needs the other but the balance of terror is a delicate balance with very little margin for miscalculation. And the world impoverishes itself by spending half a trillion dollars a year in preparations for war and by employing perhaps half the scientists and high technologists on the planet in military endeavors.
>
> How would we explain all this to a dispassionate, extraterrestrial observer? What account would we give of our stewardship of the planet earth?
>
> We have heard the rationales offered by the superpowers. We know who speaks for the nations; but who speaks for the human species? Who speaks for earth?

In an era when imaginary cosmic centrality and species-level narcissism — theism, consumerism, and the 24/7 spectacle — reign supreme and there is a rebirth of political tensions between the Russia and the United States, Sagan's question remains relevant for a species that now wants to extend its tribal baggage and arrogance off Earth.

Who speaks for the human species in space? Right now, it is our television programs echoing through space and the Voyager spacecraft now outside the solar system and hurtling through the Milky Way. But who speaks for the human species when we start sending our *bodies* into space — who speaks for us on the moon, on Mars, or on Jupiter's Europa? Is it:

- the military leaders and their weaponizing of space for the inevitable *Star Wars*?
- the theological leaders and their dreams of baptizing extraterrestrials in the name of an imaginary Creator who will give us eternal destinies that supposedly outlast the trillions of trillions of years of the universe?
- Elon Musk and the leading space entrepreneurs who want to terraform Mars in our own planetary image, or Jeff Bezos and his plan for extending Amazon's instant consumption into space for millions of people?
- the "space cowboys" leading Shackleton Energy Corporation in Texas, who plan to strip-mine the moon for human consumption? (Shackleton founder Dr. Bill Stone says: "Water on the moon is literally the feedstock for the next major Gold Rush in space."[62] Translation: "Saddle up pardners, let's ride herd on the moon. It will be a human stampede just like the Wild West. To protect your space canteen and helium-1 stockpile, you'll need to be fast on the draw, so bring your six guns and drone missiles. Yee haw!")

Are these the voices that will speak for the hydrogen atoms that have evolved for 13.7 billion years to produce the human species in our tiny part of the universe? Are we so puny a species that we feel the need to prove our greatness through war, theism, and ecological destruction? Are we unable to appreciate the beautiful and the sublime as having value to human consciousness and perhaps the consciousnesses of other intelligent beings we may encounter? Are we *truly* that crass and unenlightened?

ANTI-ENLIGHTENMENT IN SPACE. Let's be clear. These militarized and industrialized space visions do not represent enlightenment or human progress for the same reasons that *Star Wars* is not about progress. Just as *Star Wars* is medieval knights, princesses, and cosmic crusades set in space's past, the Pentagon and Shackleton are the warriors and industrial profiteers ready to pillage and plunder under the guise of space exploration and human enlightenment. The holy warriors and profiteers of tomorrow have arrived, and they still think it's the Crusades and Wild West. We're moonwalking into the future.

As humans having emerged and evolved on Earth, how can we claim the cosmic right to destroy the landscapes of the planets and moons of the solar system and beyond? From the fact that we can venture to Mars or the moon, it does *not* follow that we should exploit their resources for yet more consumption back on Earth. We will find no celestial meaning or increased happiness for our species in the ecological destruction of the moon and other planets. Have these space profiteers not seen what we have done to our own planet?

Given what we have done on Earth, we have no cosmic right — no intellectual right, no moral right, no inherent property right — to despoil and the destroy the landscapes of other celestial bodies. The space law that assumes these rights exist is merely a defense of economic and social utility bereft of any aesthetic, ecological, or cosmological enlightenment. Any philosophical or pragmatic defense of space war among nations is merely a disgraceful and regressive apology for the ideological status quo. Any call to evangelize extraterrestrials is a call for a space crusade. All of this shows we have yet to escape the *Planet of the Apes*. It's a madhouse!

The product of five billion years of cosmic evolution, the celestial bodies in our solar system *are what they are* — they do not need any improvement, modification, or exploitation and destruction from humans. The planets and moons are rare, singular, wondrous and deserve ecological and aesthetic protection, not industrial exploitation. Such protections permit scientific study and aesthetic appreciation that have only minimal impact on the celestial landscapes. When Apollo 8 and 11 turned the cameras on the moon, we saw an untouched world of timeless beauty produced over the eons by gravity and meteor impacts. As shown in *The Martian*, the landscapes of Mars are visually stunning, triggering the sublime in their age and scale. They are untouched territories, having *existed for billions of years longer than humans*. Similarly, the photos of the moons of Saturn and Jupiter reveal landscapes of incredible beauty and celestial history, with Europa's cracked and fissured surface reminiscent of a Jackson Pollock drip-and-splatter painting. The celestial bodies in our solar system are works of art, produced by the greatest artist of all time — the cosmos, with its paintbrushes of gravity and energy spread across the canvas of space and time. We should think of the solar system as an interplanetary art gallery and science museum, filled with celestial artworks that tell the story of our origins and cosmic neighborhood. *How the hell can we not respect that, admire that, and want to experience and protect that?*

IS ENLIGHTENMENT IN SPACE POSSIBLE? As this book has shown, humanity needs a new and enlightened philosophy for space exploration — one based in scientific discovery and philosophical inquiry along with the aesthetics of the sublime and the amazement of these majestic celestial bodies, which deserve our ecological protection as we cooperatively explore space as a single species. The SPEAC model outlined here *speaks to the celestial origins within u*s and is the sanest vision for a species that claims to be an enlightened space-faring civilization.

It *is* possible for the human species to extend enlightenment into space. After all, some of our greatest artists and thinkers have already pointed the way. For example, Gene Roddenberry showed humanity as a united species exploring space in the original *Star Trek*. Stanley Kubrick suggested an enlightened human destiny in space was possible in *2001*, while other directors like Christopher Nolan and Ridley Scott provided mostly inspiring visions of humans in space with *Interstellar* and *The Martian*, respectively. Via books and television documentaries, scientists such as Carl Sagan, Neil deGrasse Tyson, Lisa Randall, Brian Cox, and Stephen Hawking have produced mind-expanding and — for me, at least — poetic accounts of the astonishing universe revealed by science and our cosmic media technologies. Inspired by such thinkers and the SPEAC model presented here, space exploration and space tourism should embrace the cosmic sublime, the triumphs of Apollo, the aesthetics of Virgin Galactic, and the visions in *Star Trek* (unified human species exploring space), *2001* (the spaceplane, space station, lunar base, and lunar landscapes), *Interstellar* (the sublime black hole and the amazing wilderness areas on distant planets), and *The Martian* (the planetary desert and cooperation among nations). Among the space-faring firms, Virgin Galactic's aesthetic philosophy is the closest we have to *2001*.

The SPEAC model features no war, no strip-mining, no pollution, no terraforming, no Gods or Allahs, and no wannabe Klingons or Darth Vaders. Sadly, that's why it is *unlikely* the SPEAC model will speak for the human species when it sends human bodies into space. Too many people want to speak through war, theism, vanity, consumption, and industrial exploitation.

JUSTIFYING OUR EXISTENCE AND RIGHT TO EXPLORE THE COSMOS. What would we do if had to justify our existence to an extraterrestrial philosopher like Klaatu? Given our knowledge of the universe, it seems patently absurd to offer a defense in the name of nations, tribes, Creators, industrial wastelands, plasticized oceans, endless warfare, and all the pretenses to cosmic centrality. Maybe Klaatu would be impressed with YouTube, Netflix, *Dancing With the Stars*, Disneyland, the Super Bowl, and the World Cup.

Perhaps the best way to justify our existence would be by acknowledging our celestial insignificance while also referencing our greatest art and architecture, our greatest scientific discoveries, our observatories and museums, our medical treatments, and our minor ecological protection of the planet from which we evolved and which provides resources for us to live (obviously amplified by the science of agriculture). We probably should display our most stylish fashions because it might help to look good, too; after all, Klaatu was rather elegant in his shimmering minimalist spacesuit. For our fashion designers, perhaps we could enlist Hardy Amies from *2001*, Jean-Paul Gaultier from *The Fifth Element*, and, of course, Paco Rabane and Jacques Fonteray from *Barbarella* (1968).

If our civilization was obliterated by extraterrestrials, all the art, creativity, and knowledge that once appeared on our planet would not be experienced by future generations of humans (who would not exist) or any future visitors from other solar systems. These might be the best reasons *not* to have our species obliterated by a more advanced civilization. It sure wouldn't be for using a laptop to prevail over the extraterrestrials in *Independence Day*.

Of course, one might argue that we need not justify our existence to any extraterrestrial civilization, even if it is more advanced. That might be true, as long as we Earthlings remain peaceful and don't destroy other life forms, strip-mine planets, and extend our warfare and weapons in space. That's why we should let our greatest achievements speak for us if we encounter another intelligent species.

Would any space-faring extraterrestrials want to help us, warn us, destroy us, or merely communicate with us to let us know we are not alone in the universe, as shown in *Contact*? Keep in mind that such extraterrestrials would have picked up 80 or more years of humanity's television signals, which Neil deGrasse Tyson says would force the aliens to conclude that "most humans are neurotic, death hungry, dysfunctional idiots."[63] Does that mean we need to be destroyed, assisted, or left alone?

Klaatu and any other wise extraterrestrials would be fully aware of the enormity of the universe and would have experienced the cosmic sublime. Most likely, they too would have felt dwarfed by the age, size, and scale of the universe yet still traversed the galaxies with advanced science and technologies. Given that Klaatu's civilization lived in peace, perhaps they would have found celestial meaning for their existence in the vastness as well as pursue the enterprises that Klaatu says are more "profitable" than war. On the other hand, the space farers might face the same challenge as V'Ger in *Star Trek: the Motion Picture* — they could be a lonely species confronting cosmic nihilism because they have been unable to find any meaning for their existence. Thus they journey through the cosmos in search of their purpose and destiny. Maybe they would see us as fellow voyagers. If (or when) we have that encounter, who will speak for the human species?

11. WE ARE SPACE VOYAGERS

For Buckminster Fuller, the 20th-century futurist-philosopher, we are all *passengers* on Spaceship Earth — where there is no preordained flight plan, but we are all crew members and possess the cognitive power to discover the laws of nature and the cosmos in building a planetary civilization as we hurtle through the Milky Way.[64] I agree with this notion. But I also think we are more than passengers; we are *voyagers* on a journey of discovery through space and time. In my view, we're genetically and culturally primed to become a space-faring civilization. Here's why:

- Reliant on the sun and our planet's resources to exist, the human species emerged in Africa and has been migrating and traveling around the planet for thousands of years — this means the human species is at once local, global, and celestial. We have long been on voyages of discovery already.
- The Earth orbits the sun at about 60,000 miles per hour, while the solar system orbits the center of the Milky Way at around 500,000 miles per hour and takes about 220 million years to complete an orbit of the galaxy. We have long been voyagers through space and time on Spaceship Earth.

Since the Milky Way is home to 200 billion stars and is one of 2 trillion galaxies, there are endless places for humans to explore. We are space voyagers on a journey to experience awe and wonder, to see and know beauty, to protect the planet that gives us life, and to discover our meaning and destiny — it is up to us to discover what it might be. Countering or overcoming cosmic nihilism requires we abandon our pre-Copernican wishes and embrace the cosmic sublime in all its complexity (see Chapter 1).

For every cosmic void we face, there is a "wow" to counter it. That we can even know and experience the vastness and voids of the universe generates a "wow" for me. It's like when we look up at the Milky Way on a clear night, far from city lights. That's why I'm betting our existential meaning will be found in the sublime, if anywhere. And it starts with the awe-inspiring images of Earth from space, our tiny home that is a speck in the universe in the "eyes" of the Hubble but represents the starting point for theorizing a cosmic narrative for a space-faring civilization.

CELESTIAL ORIGINS AND A COSMIC NARRATIVE. As discussed in Chapter 1, Apollo, Hubble, and our discovery of the vast and ancient universe have destroyed the previous narratives used to explain the origins and destiny of the human species. Creators, nations, tribes, wars, celebrities, brands, and so on — these are all fictions and stories *we have invented* to provide our lives with value, meaning, and purpose while making us feel special, worthy, and connected to something larger than ourselves. As a species, we're in denial of our cosmic insignificance and possible meaninglessness, so we cling to these narratives as our planet hurtles through the universe. If we want to find any *cosmic-universal meaning* and a *shared destiny* in the universe, then we need

TABLE 7 **OUR CELESTIAL ORIGINS: THE EXISTENTIAL GROUNDS FOR A SPACE PHILOSOPHY FOR THE HUMAN SPECIES**

(These are the conditions revealed by our cosmic media technologies.)

1. **Hydrogen atoms evolved across 13.7 billion years to produce our galaxy, the sun, our planet, and all life on Earth.**
   Meaning: We are the product of a vast and ancient universe that permits us to exist.
2. **All humans are made of the most common elements of the cosmos (hydrogen, nitrogen, oxygen, carbon, etc.) and share 99.9% of the same DNA.**
   Meaning: We are star stuff; the universe is in us, and we are of the universe. We are members of one species sharing one planet with millions of other species.
3. **We are the only species on Earth that creates art, science, and philosophy to understand the universe and represent it to ourselves.**
   Meaning: We are self-aware stardust and one way the cosmos knows itself. Our consciousness has built an impressive body of knowledge about the universe, which shows that we are capable of being an enlightened species.
4. **We are the center of nothing amid the immensity and majesty of the cosmos.**
   Meaning: Cosmic non-centrality is our starting point as enlightened space voyagers who travel in peace, seek more knowledge and wisdom, cherish beauty and sublimity in the universe, and share our art, science, and technology with other civilizations we encounter.
5. **We embrace the cosmic nihilism and the sublime.**
   Meaning: We are a species humbled — but not terrified — by our possible cosmic meaninglessness and extinction; we simultaneously grasp the infinitesimal (us) and the infinite (the cosmos) as we search for our meaning and destiny in the awe-inspiring universe.

to grow up and embrace our *celestial origins* and *existential conditions* in the universe — as we best understand them and as revealed by our cosmic media technologies (see Table 7). On Earth, we are the one species that creates art, science, and philosophy in the effort to know and understand the surrounding universe. We are the species that knows it must confront the *nothingness* and *awesomeness* of a universe that spans 100 billion light years and will last trillions of trillions of years into the future. We are also the species that knows its origins and destiny exist in the stars.

Science shows we evolved from hydrogen atoms across 13.7 billion years and are made of the most common elements of the cosmos. It's a beautiful condition to be in. Simultaneously, we are cosmic specks and self-aware stardust, meaning that our species (and each of us) is infinitesimal and yet knows we are part of the infinite of the universe. As self-aware stardust, we are one way the cosmos knows itself, an existential fact that *might justify our right to explore and understand the universe*. By accepting our celestial origins and existential conditions — as intelligent creatures, yet insignificant and not the center of anything — we have empirical starting points for justifying our existence as sentient beings who generate knowledge of the cosmos and create art and science to represent that cosmos to us and any other civilizations we encounter in our voyages.

Of course, our celestial origins represent only starting points, not a fully developed philosophy for a unified space-faring and cosmic civilization. It's my contention that these five existential conditions provide the best grounds for a cosmic narrative for a species that is venturing into the universe yet hopes to survive and not be rendered extinct by either cosmic forces or advanced extraterrestrials who have no time for our carnival of death and destruction. Our best hope lies in embracing our celestial origins and existential conditions as we confront the nothingness and awesomeness in the cosmos. It might be our only hope.

TOWARD A COSMIC CIVILIZATION. Any sane and enlightened space philosophy necessarily *leads to a cosmic civilization that spans the planet and extends into the stars*. Advocating a planetary and cosmic civilization is not a call for monoculture or imperial globalization, but the recognition that humans have a shared destiny on this planet — as individuals and a species — and would benefit from a cosmology and culture grounded in the universe as best we understand it. We can have species universality and cultural diversity in a cosmic and planetary civilization. A cosmic civilization is not against tribes but *against a culture that is all tribal with no universal*. In fact, a culture that is *all* tribal and *not* universal will always be in conflict and is ultimately doomed.

To avoid the apocalyptic and weaponized space scenario in *Gravity*, the cosmic cultural narrative must move beyond warring tribes and the weaponization of space. To avoid the ecological doom in *WALL-E* and *Interstellar*, we must *merge cosmology, ecology and technology* into a sane and sustainable philosophy that protects the planet's ecosystems on a much greater scale, cleans up the land and oceans, minimizes waste and pollution, relies on renewable energies, and massively expands national parks, wildernesses, and dark skies. If we see ourselves as one species and part of the living systems of the planet, then it is far easier to embrace the development of planetary values to protect the ecosystems on Earth. Our species needs to embrace a shared destiny that begins by reducing the harmful effects of tribalism, theism, consumerism, and nationalism while retaining the openness that enables an evolutionary cultural diversity and the emergence of new traditions and planetary systems of value.

Perhaps my hope for enlightened humans staying in *2001*-style space hotels and camping on Mars will only partially come to pass. Along with astronauts and scientists, surely there will be artists and philosophers in space too. Sadly, it seems the industrialists, polluters, entertainers, politicians, bureaucrats, nationalists, warriors, and televangelists will be there as well. Given the dominant cultural narratives of 2017, it seems our voyages will extend into space everything we see on TV, Netflix, and the internet — along with the requisite wars among the stars, so celebrated in *Star Wars* and many other science-fiction films. If that's what we extend off our planet, then we deserve to be rendered extinct by Klaatu or other enlightened extraterrestrial philosophers and peacekeepers. Of course, a Texas-sized meteor (*Armageddon*) or rogue planet (*Melancholia*) could also give us a permanent "status update" with no more selfies.

More optimistically, perhaps the artists and philosophers will develop the artwork and worldviews for a more cosmic and unified civilization. Maybe human society will become more enlightened, benevolent, and peaceful because of our space voyages and seeing our true place in the cosmos. Time will tell. I wish I could say I was optimistic.

Until then, whether we find that celestial meaning and shared destiny is unknown — be it our flourishing (*2001*), survival (*Interstellar*), destruction (*Gravity*), outright annihilation (*Planet of the Apes*), utter meaninglessness (*Melancholia*), carnival of endless consumption (*WALL-E*), or never-ending warfare (*Star Wars*). Maybe our destiny is just to look good and get it on amid the skyscrapers and cool space stations while fighting off any extraterrestrials that interrupt our mating games and fashion shows (*Barbarella, The Fifth Element,* and *Star Trek Beyond*). We might end up no more than spasmodic smiles, but we might also evolve into successful space voyagers.

A PHILOSOPHICAL LAUNCH. In the introduction to this book, I noted that Nietzsche said "man is a rope stretched between the animal and the Superman — a rope over an abyss."[65] That's true over the long term, but I think we face more than that right now. Our technological consciousness is like the rope over the abyss of the vast cosmos we have discovered, populated with sprawling webs of galaxies and super-cold supervoids. We have peered across 100 billion light years to the edge of the visible universe and trillions of years into the future to see the fates of the universe. To me, that we know all this cosmic being and nothingness is damn cool. As Jean-Paul Sartre might say, we have no alternative but to hurl ourselves into the future, into the universe of tomorrow filled with the *cool voids* of meaninglessness — just as there is no escape from the universe, there is no exit from our freedom and fate.[66] We must leap into the aesthetic abyss of the cosmos we've discovered. Anything less is a cop out.

What's needed is a *philosophical launch directly into the dark skies of nihilism and the cosmic sublime* — smack dab, dead on, right into celestial nothingness and everything massive, beautiful, and terrifying in the universe. Let's touch the monolith, toss the bone, shoot the spore, fire the rockets, dive into Gargantua, zoom through the Star-Gate, probe deeper into the dark skies, and turn our neurons on to a new space philosophy for our species. If we don't do the philosophical launch, we'll never reach the space odyssey of *2001* because we'll still be battling on the *Planet of the Apes*.

Do we have the courage to do it? Apollo says "yes." The Hubble says "yes." *2001* and *Interstellar* say "yes." Virgin Galactic says "yes." But our dominant cultural and space narratives say "no." That's why we're moonwalking into the future.

After our philosophical launch, we might evolve into our own Ubermensch, a much more intellectually advanced human species with a new philosophy for the universe we have discovered. Or maybe not. We may end up enlightened, exterminated, or existentially meaningless, but we will have experienced the awe and wonder of the cosmos on scales that previous humans and all other Earthly animals could have never known. Even in eventual failure, it would be a cosmic gesture of which our species can be proud.

Though the universe remains indifferent to our situation, it permits us to exist, evolve, and wonder. Klaatu — if he's out there and knows of us — probably ponders about whether we should be assisted or annihilated. I often dream of drinking a margarita while looking at Earth and the stars from space, yet the space hotel from *2001* is nowhere in sight.

But with Apollo, Hubble, *Interstellar*, and *2001*, we are reminded to leap into the aesthetic abysses — into *Earthrise*, Deep Fields, Gargantua, and the Star-Gate. It's in the cosmic sublime that we'll find our meaning and destiny — as space spores, space voyagers, or spasmodic smiles on the surface of matter. That's the challenge posed by the sleek black monolith.

ACKNOWLEDGMENTS

In Chapter 4, I wrote that a sane cosmic narrative for the human species requires a combination of art, science, and philosophy. So it seemed natural that I acknowledge the artists, scientists, and philosophers that helped inspire this book. Without such great ideas, awe-inspiring discoveries, and mind-expanding works of cinematic vision, this book would not have been possible. Hence I offer my deepest appreciation to the following Earthlings.

CREATORS OF THE THREE GREATEST SPACE FILMS

2001: A SPACE ODYSSEY. Thanks to Stanley Kubrick (director) and Arthur C. Clarke (cowriter), followed by Douglas Trumball (special-effects supervisor) and the film's main actors: Keir Dullea, Gary Lockwood, William Sylvester, Douglas Rain (voice of HAL), Daniel Richter (Moon-Watcher, the ape), and the many others who brilliantly portrayed the apes. The team of cinematographers, art directors, and set designers created near-perfect exteriors and interiors for the space shuttle, space station, and *Discovery One*. Of course *2001* would not have the same aesthetic and emotional feel without the music of Richard Strauss, Johann Strauss, and Gyorgy Ligeti. The space-age fashions of Hardy Amies remain fabulous, and the designs of the space station make it a place I would definitely like to visit.

PLANET OF THE APES. Thank you to Franklin Schaffner (director) as well as Rod Serling and Michael Wilson (cowriters), followed by Charlton Heston for his great performance as Taylor. (Say whatever you want about Heston's politics later in his life — it took no small amount of creative courage to take on the role of the existentialist antihero astronaut at the height of the space age — a time when all astronauts were portrayed as flag-waving patriots with the "right stuff." Heston nailed his role perfectly.) Kim Hunter, Roddy McDowall, Jeff Burton, and Robert Gunner were excellent ape and astronaut complements to Heston. John Chambers's design of the ape faces remains one of the top makeup efforts in film history. The art direction teams did an outstanding job with the desert locations and designs for the ape village, and Jerry Goldsmith's soundtrack ranks among the very best of any science-fiction film ever.

INTERSTELLAR. Thanks to Christopher Nolan (director) and Jonathan Nolan (cowriter), followed by Matthew McConaughey, Anne Hathaway, Michael Caine, Jessica Chastain, David Gyasi, and the rest of the film's actors, all of whom gave great performances. Kip Thorne (astrophysicist), Paul Franklin (visual-effects supervisor), and the design team at Double Negative did a phenomenal job creating Gargantua, the scientifically realistic black hole that's among cinema's most compelling space images. Hans Zimmer's music makes a perfect match with the film's philosophical ideas and imagery.

Thanks to everyone who made these three artistic and philosophical masterpieces possible.

LAND ARTISTS

Monumental land art (or "earthworks") is my favorite form of art, precisely because it seeks to connect us to the planet and cosmos existing beyond the electric glow of our cities and screens. Thanks to artists Michael Heizer, Robert Smithson, Nancy Holt, Walter de Maria, Charles Ross, and James Turrell.

SCIENTISTS

Among individual scientists, my thanks first goes to Carl Sagan, whose *Cosmos* series blew my mind, as did his book *Pale Blue Dot*, which inspired me to begin thinking differently about humanity's destiny in space. Thanks to Stephen Hawking, whose many books — especially *A Brief History of Time*, *The Universe in a Nutshell*, and *The Grand Design* — make the cosmologically complex accessible to non-scientists. Thanks to Neil deGrasse Tyson for the reboot of *Cosmos* and Brian Cox for his great BBC documentaries, especially *Wonders of the Universe*. Thanks to Jill Tarter, whose work with SETI remains an inspiration by offering a sane vision of humanity's role in the cosmos. (The world needs more enlightened scientists like Tarter.) Finally, thanks to all the scientists who have made possible the discovery of the majestic universe we inhabit—it's the single greatest achievement of our species.

NASA

Thanks to everyone who has worked for (or with) NASA. Can there be any doubt that NASA remains the single-most important scientific organization in human history? NASA is easily America's greatest contribution to the human species; it has been central to space exploration and the discovery of our place in the cosmos. Apollo, Voyager, the Hubble Space Telescope — these are among humanity's most important technological achievements because they have extended our consciousness into the cosmos to reveal the awe-inspiring universe and our cosmic non-centrality.

PHILOSOPHERS

Thanks to Jean-Paul Sartre, whose *Being and Nothingness* was the existentialist masterpiece of the 20th century. Without doubt, Sartre is the philosopher who most influenced my ideas about human existence in the universe and human destiny in space exploration. Among cultural theorists, my thanks goes to Alvin Toffler and his seminal book *Future Shock,* which offers a species-wide diagnosis that gets more relevant every year. Similarly, thanks to Marshall McLuhan, the media philosopher whose books *Understanding Media, The Medium Is the Massage,* and *Through the Vanishing Point* helped me understand the effect of technology on human consciousness.

THE PRODUCERS OF THIS BOOK

My deepest thanks goes to Alissa Tallman, my long-time editor. Without Alissa's patient and thoughtful editing, this book would not have the clarity and polish it needed. Always demanding high standards, Alissa is truly a great editor! I also owe a big thanks to Jessica Knott, whose creative layout of this book made it not only easy to read but stylishly elegant in a space-age kind of way. And thanks to Haigen G. Pearson, the artist and professor who read the manuscript, designed the book's cover, and produced the trailer for the book (available on YouTube and Vimeo).

OTHERS

Thanks to the Board of Directors of the Center for Media and Destiny for supporting this book and its innovative take on space and human destiny. Thanks to Gail, my long-term partner, for her patient support as I wrote the book. Thanks to the students in my courses at Temple University who have discussed with me the topic of human destiny in space, especially Stacey Sullivan, Osei Alleyne, Genevieve Gillespie, Christina Betz, Abby Moore, and Kristen Ceriale. Thank you to Richard Branson and Virgin Galactic, whose rationale for space tourism is based within the sanest philosophy for extending humans in space. Thanks to Branson, Norman Foster (architect), and the taxpayers of New Mexico for the inspiring design and location of Spaceport America. And thank you to the staff of the McDonald Observatory for hosting the incredible "Star Parties" that blow my mind every summer.

ABOUT THE AUTHOR

ADADEMIC BIO

Barry Vacker teaches critical media studies at Temple University in Philadelphia, where he is an associate professor in the Klein College of Media and Communication. A professor for over 20 years, he earned a Ph.D. from the University of Texas at Austin. Vacker has authored numerous articles and books about the trajectories of art, media, science, culture, and human civilization on this spaceship we call Earth. You can find these works online (https://temple.academia.edu/BarryVacker) and in Amazon. His other recent book is the third edition of *Media Environments* (Cognella 2018), an innovative text anthology used in "Media and Society" courses in North America.

ARTISTIC PROJECTS

Vacker is currently working on a philosophical graphic novel called *The Last Telescopes* (2019 or 2020), which would make an awesome science-fiction film with the right director and producer. If you are a *2001* fan, you will enjoy Vacker's 50th anniversary tribute, *Specters of the Monolith* (2017), a 13-minute video available in Vimeo. You might also enjoy Vacker's *Space Times Square* (2007), a trippy 24-minute video about mediated culture—which won the 2010 international award for top "praxis" from the Media Ecology Association, a prestigious academic organization. The remastered version is available in YouTube. Search: Space Times Square (2014 version).

EXISTENTIAL STANCE

Vacker is an existentialist without the angst—a momentary self made of star stuff from a supernova in a remote part of the Milky Way. He is the center of nothing and utterly insignificant in the universe of two trillion galaxies and a zillion space films. *Specter of the Monolith* contains his philosophical perspectives on how we might begin the search for humanity's meaning and purpose in the cosmos, drawing inspiration from space films like *2001* and *Interstellar*; earthworks like *Star Axis* and *Spiral Jetty*; and thinkers like Sartre, Lyotard, Tarter, and Sagan.

ENDNOTES

INTRODUCTION: THE MONOLITH AND MOONWALKING

1. Robert Poole, *Earthrise: How Man First Saw the Earth* (New Haven: Yale University Press, 2008); Robin McKie, "The Mission That Changed Everything," *Guardian*, November 29, 2008, accessed January 5, 2015; and Craig Chalquist, "*Earthrise*: A Mythic Image for Our Time?" *The Blog* (blog), *Huffington Post*, January 24, 2014, accessed January 5, 2015.
2. Friedrich Nietzsche, *Thus Spoke Zarathustra: A Book for Everyone and No One* (New York: Penguin, 1972), 26. By citing Nietzsche, this does not mean I necessarily agree with everything or anything he wrote beyond the fact that he pronounced God to be "dead" and posed the profound question: What will evolve from humans?
3. Ibid.
4. Ibid.
5. Elizabeth Kolbert, *The Sixth Extinction: An Unnatural History* (New York: Picador, 2015); Jeremy Davies, *The Birth of the Anthropocene* (Oakland: University of California Press, 2016); and J. R. McNeill and Peter Engelke, *The Great Acceleration: The Environmental History of the Anthropocene* (Cambridge, MA: Belknap Press, 2016).
6. Here are a few recent space-oriented books: Margaret Lazarus Dean, *Leaving Orbit: Notes from the Last Days of American Spaceflight* (Minneapolis: Graywolf, 2015); Matthew D. Tribbe, *No Requiem for the Space Age: The Apollo Moon Landings and American Culture* (Oxford: Oxford University Press, 2014); Neil deGrasse Tyson, *Space Chronicles: Facing the Ultimate Frontier* (New York: W. W. Norton, 2012); and David Bell and Martin Parker, eds., *Space Travel and Culture: From Apollo to Space Tourism* (New York: Wiley-Blackwell, 2009).

CHAPTER 1: CONFRONTING NIHILISM AND THE SUBLIME

1. A notable exception: Elizabeth A. Kessler, *Picturing the Cosmos: Hubble Space Telescope Images and the Astronomical Sublime* (Minneapolis: University of Minnesota Press, 2012).
2. Tatiana Amatruda, "There Are 10 Times More Galaxies in Our Universe Than We'd Estimated," CNN, October 13, 2016, accessed October 16, 2016.
3. The counter to cosmic narcissism is not altruism and its faux nobility of "self-sacrifice," precisely because self-awareness, self-interest, self-worth, and some self-love are all necessary for any individual human happiness and human empowerment. Society needs more people with a true sense of self-worth and self-love. Narcissism represents the undeveloped self, the individual *particularity* wedded to self-absorption and an imaginary cosmic self-centrality, while altruism represents the unempowered self, the false *universality* wedded to self-sacrifice and the cosmic centrality of others. Narcissism and altruism are forms of moral delusion that empower neither the giver nor the receiver. Both create a false alternative world of *me* versus *they*, generating the need for masters to command sacrifices and slaves to make those sacrifices. As the presumed counter to narcissism, altruism is a bankrupt and guilt-ridden moral code used by theisms and tyrants to dominate believers and followers. Similarly, hedonism (self-pleasure) versus utilitarianism (the greatest good for the greatest number) also represents a false alternative, creating a *me* versus *they* and an *I* versus *the tribe* dynamic. Finally, the focus on our particular selves leads to fearing the "Other," even though "Others" are members of the same species and the product of the same DNA chain that makes humanity possible. The marginalization and fear of the Other contributes to war, exploitation, and domination, especially when attached to theology, tribalism, and nationalism. Most likely, all of these will be extended into space once we send humans to the moon, Mars, and beyond.

4. See Shane Weller, *Modernism and Nihilism* (London: Palgrave MacMillan, 2011); and Ashley Woodward, *Nihilism in Postmodernity: Lyotard, Baudrillard, Vattimo* (Aurora, CO: Davies Group, 2009).
5. Barry Vacker, *Slugging Nothing: Fighting the Future in Fight Club* (Philadelphia: Theory Vortex, 2009).
6. Philip Shaw, *The Sublime* (London: Routledge, 2006).
7. Immanuel Kant, *Critique of Practical Reason* (London: Longmans, 1909), photo reprint (1967), 260.
8. Ibid.
9. Jean-Francois Lyotard, *The Inhuman: Reflections on Time* (Palo Alto: Stanford University Press, 1992), 9.
10. Ibid., 10.
11. Ibid., 8-12; see also Stuart Sim, *Lyotard and the Inhuman* (Cambridge: Icon, 2001).
12. While I take credit for the original concept of the "cosmic sublime," my views have certainly been influenced by the following thinkers and works: Kant, *The Critique of Judgement* (Oxford: Clarendon Press, 1952), 90-130; Kessler, *Picturing the Cosmos*, 5, 11, 20-21; Shaw, *The Sublime*, 1-11, 73-89; and Roald Hoffmann and Iain Boyd Whyte, *Beyond the Finite: The Sublime in Art and Science* (Oxford: Oxford University Press, 2011).
13. Kessler, *Picturing the Cosmos*, 5.
14. Jean-Paul Sartre, *Being and Nothingness* (New York: Citadel Press, 1956), 83-105.
15. Historically, ticker-tape parades commemorated those who had accomplished something monumental and impressive or had served in a place of leadership. It wasn't just illustrious Americans who graced Lower Manhattan's "Canyon of Heroes" (the site of most ticker-tape parades, beginning with the 1886 dedication of the Statue of Liberty), but international dignitaries and politicians as well. Throughout the early to mid-20th century, ticker-tape parades marked humanity's continuing evolution toward knowledge, effective political leadership, technological and scientific progress, and global peace. However, after the 1969 parade for the Apollo 11 astronauts, the parades thinned out considerably and, with few exceptions, became more or less confined to commemorating New York sports-team successes. Today's ticker-tape parades are still more or less reserved for sports victories, such as the winners of the Super Bowl and World Cup. They take place in the city or country, respectively, of the winning team and are thus exclusive, regional events rather than worldwide celebrations of human excellence.
16. It is deeply disgraceful that NASA excluded women and African Americans from having the opportunity to become Apollo astronauts in the 1960s. But now there are numerous women and people of color among the astronauts and NASA administrators, including former astronaut Charles Bolden, who is now NASA's administrative director. If such blatant sexism and racism has been eliminated from the US space program, then why not work to eliminate other social ills from all space exploration, especially war, racism, theism, tribalism, nationalism, mindless consumption, and ecological destruction?
17. David Lachenbruch, "The Raging Controversy over TV's Role in Space Shoots," *TV Guide*, May 10-16, 1969, 6-13.
18. Of course, those in the former Soviet Union were very envious, given that the United States had won the "space race" to the moon. But the Soviet leaders, media, citizens, and cosmonauts could not deny the monumental achievement, though bittersweet for their space program. See Saswato R. Das, "The Moon Landing Through Soviet Eyes: A Q&A with Sergei Khrushchev, Son of Former Premier Nikita Khrushchev," *Scientific American*, July 16, 2009, accessed March 18, 2015; and *The Red Stuff: The True Story of the Russian Race for Space*, directed by Leo De Boer (2000; White Star).
19. "January 2, 1839: First Daguerreotype of the Moon," *APS News*, American Physical Society, vol. 22, no. 1 (January 2013), accessed November 9, 2014.
20. Erica Fahr Campbell, "The First Photograph of the Moon," *Time*, December 20, 2013, accessed November 9, 2014.

21. Robin McKie, "The Mission That Changed Everything"; and Craig Chalquist, "*Earthrise*: A Mythic Image for Our Time?"
22. "Triumphant Return from the Void," *Time*, January 10, 1969, accessed January 5, 2015.
23. "Men of the Year," *Time*, January 3, 1969, accessed January 5, 2015.
24. Buckminster Fuller, *Operating Manual for Spaceship Earth* (Baden: Lars Müller, 2008).
25. "The Apollo 8 Flight Journal, Day 4: Lunar Orbits 7, 8, and 9," NASA History website, transcription and commentary by David Woods and Frank O'Brien.
26. Robert Zimmerman, *Genesis: The Story of Apollo 8* (New York: Dell, 1998), 245.
27. Ibid., 273-78; Mark Kurlansky, *1968: The Year That Rocked the World* (New York: Random House, 2004), 382-83; and Robert Poole, *Earthrise: How Man First Saw the Earth*, 135-38.
28. "Man and Woman of the Year: The Middle Americans," *Time*, January 5, 1970, accessed January 7, 2015.
29. Matthew D. Tribbe, "On the Nihilism of WASPs: Norman Mailer in NASA-Land," chapt. 2 in *No Requiem for the Space Age*.
30. "To the Moon and Back," *Life*, special edition, August 11, 1969; see also Darren Jorgensen, "Middle America, the Moon, the Sublime and the Uncanny," in *Space Travel and Culture: From Apollo to Space Tourism*, ed. David Bell and Martin Parker, 178-89.
31. Loren Eiseley, "The Spore Bearers," chapt. 4 in *The Invisible Pyramid* (Lincoln: University of Nebraska Press, 1998), 75-82.
32. Tribbe, "Apollo and the 'Human Condition,'" chapt. 3 in *No Requiem for the Space Age*, 72, 76.
33. Ayn Rand, "Apollo and Dionysius," in *The Voice of Reason: Essays in Objectivist Thought* (New York: Meridian, 1990), 161-78.
34. Fuller, *Operating Manual for Spaceship Earth*.
35. Eiseley, "The Spore Bearers," 75-76.
36. Dain Fitzgerald, "22 Million Americans Believe the Moon Landing Was Faked," *Politix*, April 3, 2013, accessed January 6, 2015; and "Apollo 11 Hoax: One in Four People Do Not Believe in Moon Landing," *Telegraph*, July 17, 2009, accessed October 23, 2015.
37. Craig Hlavaty, "Stanley Kubrick Fake Moon-Landing Conspiracy Theory Just Won't Go Away," *Houston Chronicle*, December 15, 2015, accessed April 17, 2016.
38. NASA, "Did US Astronauts Really Land on the Moon?," press release, June 1977 (updated February 14, 2001), PDF publication, Rocket and Space Technology website, ed. Robert A. Braeunig, accessed October 23, 2015.
39. Carl Sagan, "You Are Here," chapt. 1 in *Pale Blue Dot* (New York: Ballantine, 1994), 1-7.
40. Andrew Carroll, Robert Torricelli, Doris Kearns Goodwin, eds., *In Our Own Words: Extraordinary Speeches of the American Century* (New York: Washington Square Press, 2000), 324.
41. For a detailed analysis of the Hubble technologies and images, see Kessler, *Picturing the Cosmos*.
42. The Hubble Deep Field images and a detailed description can be found on NASA's website: http://www.nasa.gov/mission_pages/hubble/main/index.html.
43. The Hubble Ultra Deep Field can be zoomed into on NASA's website: http://hubblesite.org/newscenter/archive/releases/2004/07/text.
44. Daniel Clery, "Building James Webb: The Biggest, Boldest, Riskiest Space Telescope," *Science*, February 18, 2016, accessed April 10, 2016.
45. Jeffrey Lin and P. W. Singer, "China's Answer to the Hubble Telescope," *Popular Science*, March 11, 2016, accessed April 10, 2016.

46. John F. Kennedy "moon speech," delivered on September 12, 1962 at Rice University in Houston, Texas, NASA website, accessed October 9, 2015.
47. For example: Michelle N. Shiota, Dacher Keltner, and Amanda Mossman, "The Nature of Awe: Elicitors, Appraisals, and Effects on Self-Concept," *Cognition and Emotion*, vol. 25, no. 5 (July 2007), 944-63; and Paul K. Piff, Matthew Feinberg, Pia Dietze, Daniel M. Stancato, and Dacher Keltner, "Awe, the Small Self, and Prosocial Behavior," *Journal of Personality and Social Psychology*, vol. 108, no. 6 (June 2015), 883-99.
48. Piff et al., "Awe, the Small Self, and Prosocial Behavior," 884.
49. David B. Yaden, Jonathan Iwry, Johannes C. Eichstaedt, George E. Vallant, Kelley J. Stack, Yukun Zhao, and Andrew Newberg, "The Overview Effect: Awe and Self-Transcendent Experience in Space Flight," *Psychology of Consciousness: Theory, Research, and Practice*, vol. 3, no. 1 (March 2016), 1-11.
50. Ibid., 8.
51. Ibid.
52. Brian Cox and Andrew Cohen, *Human Universe* (London: William Collins, 2014), 61.
53. Quoted in *The City Dark*, directed by Ian Cheney (2011; Brooklyn, NY: Wicked Delicate Films), DVD. See also Joanne Manaster, "The City Dark," *Psy/Vid* (blog), *Scientific American*, April 16, 2012, accessed October 6, 2015.

CHAPTER 2: SPACE FILMS AND HUMAN DESTINY

1. Norman Mailer, *Of a Fire On the Moon* (New York: Random House, 1970), 4, 425.
2. Ibid., 148-49, 431.
3. For example: Jason T. Eberl and Kevin S. Decker, eds., *Star Trek and Philosophy: The Wrath of Kant* (Chicago: Open Court, 2008); and Michele Barrett and Duncan Barrett, *Star Trek: The Human Frontier* (New York: Routledge, 2001).
4. Barrett and Barrett, *Star Trek: The Human Frontier*, 141.
5. Stephanie Zacharek, "Star Trek," *Salon*, May 8, 2009, accessed November 1, 2015.
6. Manohla Dargis, "A Franchise Goes Boldly Backward," *New York Times*, May 8, 2009, accessed November 1, 2015.
7. Barrett and Barrett, *Star Trek: The Human Frontier*, 144-45.
8. Ibid., 142-43.
9. Ibid., 150.
10. Ibid., 149-57.
11. Ross S. Kraemer, William Cassidy, and Susan L. Schwartz, *Religions of Star Trek* (Boulder, CO: Westview Press, 2003), 6, 11.
12. Anne Mackenzie Pearson, "From Thwarted Gods to Reclaimed Mystery: An Overview of the Depiction of Religion in *Star Trek*," pt. 1, chapt. 2 in *Star Trek and Sacred Ground: Explorations of Star Trek, Religion, and American Culture*, ed. Jennifer E. Porter and Darcee L. McLaren (Albany: State University Press of New York, 1999), 2, 13-32.
13. Barrett and Barrett, *Star Trek: The Human Frontier*, 137-97.
14. "NSA Director Modeled War Room after *Star Trek's Enterprise*," *PBS News Hour*, September 13, 2013, accessed October 21, 2015.
15. Glenn Greenwald, "Inside the Mind of NSA Chief Gen. Keith Alexander," *Guardian*, September 15, 2013, accessed October 21, 2015.
16. Leslie Dale Feldman, "From Twilight Zone to Forbidden Zone," pt. 5, chapt. 11 in *Planet of the Apes and Philosophy: Great Apes Think Alike*, ed. John Huss (Chicago: Open Court, 2013), 143-52.
17. Friedrich Nietzsche, *Thus Spoke Zarathustra: A Book for Everyone and No One*, 26.
18. Ibid.

19. Norva Y. S. Lo and Andrew Brennan, "The Last Man," pt. 9, chapt. 21 in *Planet of the Apes and Philosophy*, 265-77.
20. For example, see Peter Kramer, *2001: A Space Odyssey* (London: British Film institute, 2012).
21. Phil Patton, "Public Eye; 30 Years After '2001': A Furniture Odyssey," *New York Times*, February 19, 1998, accessed November 4, 2015.
22. "Last Two Howard Johnson's Restaurants Soldier On," *Fox News*, April 29, 2015, accessed November 6, 2015.
23. Matt Novak, "What Happened to 'Hilton's Hotel on the Moon'?" *BBC*, November 18, 2014, accessed November 6, 2015.
24. Scott Bukatman, "The Artificial Infinite: On Special Effects and the Sublime," sect. 1, chapt. 16 in *Post-War Cinema and Modernity: A Film Reader*, ed. John Orr and Olga Taxidou (New York: New York University Press, 2001), 208-22.
25. Jean-Paul Sartre, *No Exit and Other Plays* (New York: Vintage, 1999), 1-46.
26. Eric Norden, "Playboy Interview: Stanley Kubrick," in *Stanley Kubrick: Interviews*, ed. Gene D. Phillips (Oxford, MS: University of Mississippi Press, 2001), 47-74.
27. Ibid., 50-54.
28. Ibid., 51.
29. Brian Cox and Andrew Cohen, *Wonders of the Universe* (London: Harper Design, 2011), 52-53.
30. Ibid., 53.
31. "Frequently Asked Questions," NASA Orbital Debris Program Office (March 2012), accessed March 2, 2016.
32. Ibid.
33. Ibid.
34. In "It Begins with a Story," from "Behind the Scenes: Gravity Mission Control," DVD special features, *Gravity*, directed by Alfonso Cuarón (Esperanto Films/Heydey Films), Warner Home Video.
35. Of course, some of these events were implausible because the craft involved are at different altitudes and orbit on different trajectories. See Jeffrey Kluger, "*Gravity* Fact Check: What the Season's Big Movie Gets Wrong," *Time*, October 1, 2014, accessed March 24, 2015.
36. In "It Begins with a Story," *Gravity* DVD special features.
37. In "Splashdown," from "Behind the Scenes: Shot Breakdowns," *Gravity* DVD special features.
38. Marsha Ivins, "Astronaut: *Gravity* Gets Me Down," *Time*, October 2, 2013, accessed November 3, 2015.
39. In "Splashdown," *Gravity* DVD special features.
40. Ibid.
41. MaryAnn Johanson, "*Interstellar* Movie Review: Trading Worry for Wonder," *flickfilosopher* (blog), October 31, 2014, accessed March 20, 2016.
42. "Beyond: A Story in Five Dimensions," *Wired* (December 2014), special issue, ed. Christopher Nolan; and Kip Thorne, *The Science of Interstellar* (New York: Norton, 2014).
43. Thorne, *The Science of Interstellar*, 106.
44. Ibid., 105-11.
45. Ibid., 114.
46. See Susan Jacoby, *The Age of American Unreason* (New York: Pantheon, 2008); Chris Mooney and Sheril Kirshenbaum, *Unscientific America: How Scientific Illiteracy Threatens Our Future* (New York: Basic Books, 2009); and Kendrick Frazier, ed., *Science Under Siege: Defending Science, Exposing Pseudoscience* (Amherst, NY: Prometheus Books, 2009).

47. Tom McCarthy, "Scientists Shoot Down Ted Cruz after Attack on NASA's Earth Sciences Mission," *Guardian*, March 18, 2015, accessed March 11, 2016.
48. Thorne, *The Science of Interstellar*, 32.
49. Ibid.
50. Ibid., 33.
51. Ibid., 224-25.
52. Ibid., 57-99.
53. Ibid., 85-86.
54. Ibid., 99.
55. Ibid., 253.
56. Dennis Overbye, "Gravitational Waves Detected, Confirming Einstein's Theory," *New York Times*, February 11, 2016, accessed April 3, 2016.
57. Jonathan Nolan and Christopher Nolan, *Interstellar: The Complete Screenplay* (New York: Opus, 2014), xv.
58. Ellen Dissanayake, *Homo Aestheticus: Where Art Comes From and Why* (New York: Free Press, 1992); David Nye, *American Technological Sublime* (Cambridge, MA: MIT Press, 1994); and Arthur I. Miller, *Einstein, Picasso: The Beauty That Causes Havoc* (New York: Basic Books, 2001).
59. Johanson, "*Interstellar* Movie Review: Trading Worry for Wonder."
60. Stephen Hawking, *The Theory of Everything: The Origin and Fate of the Universe* (Beverly Hills: Phoenix Books, 2007).
61. Elizabeth Kolbert, *The Sixth Extinction: An Unnatural History.*
62. Cox and Cohen, *Human Universe*, 61.
63. Norden, "Playboy Interview: Stanley Kubrick," 47-74; and Patrick Murray and Jeanne Schuler, "Rebel Without a Cause: Stanley Kubrick and the Banality of the Good," in *The Philosophy of Stanley Kubrick*, ed. Jerold Abrams (Lexington: University Press of Kentucky, 2009), 144.
64. Jean-Francois Lyotard, *The Inhuman: Reflections on Time*, 10.

CHAPTER 3: POST-APOLLO CULTURE

1. I have made this cosmological-cultural argument about the Terror War in a variety of contexts and publications. For example: Barry Vacker, "Lone Stars, Lost Amidst the Big Bang," in Peter Granser, *Signs* (Stuttgart: Hatje Cantz, 2008), 4-11; with Genevieve Gillespie, "Yearning to Be the Center of Everything When We Are the Center of Nothing: Parallels and Reversals in Chaco, Hubble, and Facebook," *Telematics and Informatics*, vol. 30, no. 1 (February 2013), 35-46; and "Space Junk and the Second Event: The Cosmic Meaning of the Zombie Apocalypse," pt. 2, chapt. 11 in *Thinking Dead: What the Zombie Apocalypse Means*, ed. Murali Balaji (New York: Lexington Books, 2013), 159-78. This does not mean all Christians, Muslims, or other theists are intolerant or violent. But the theology and religious empires are at the heart of the Terror War ideologies, which are regressive and dangerous, regardless of a follower's gender, ethnicity, tribe, or nation-state.
2. "Michael Jackson Memorial Service: Berry Gordy Eulogy," YouTube video, 9:35, televised by MSNBC on July 7, 2009, posted by "We upload. You decide," https://www.youtube.com/watch?v=3vibRwe8iCk.
3. We can wonder what Chairman Mao and the uptight communists thought of Elvis and the self-indulgent decadence of the West, precisely as they were imposing the totalitarian Cultural Revolution (1966-1976) — killing about three million people in their efforts to purge any last vestiges of "capitalist thought" and obliterate any possible dissent or resistance.
4. Susan Doll, "Elvis: Aloha from Hawaii," *How Stuff Works*, "Entertainment" section, accessed October 3, 2015.
5. Alvin Toffler, *Future Shock* (New York: Random House, 1970), 13.

6. Ibid., 192-93.
7. Cortney S. Basham, "Hal Lindsey's *The Late, Great Planet Earth* and the Rise of Popular Premillennialism in the 1970s" (masters thesis, Western Kentucky University, August 2012), PDF publication, 4.
8. Ibid., 56.
9. Paul Boyer, interview by PBS for *Frontline*, "Apocalypticism Explained: America's Doom Industry," Apocalypse! PBS online, 1998.
10. Tribbe, *No Requiem For the Space Age*, 157-217.
11. Ibid., 117.
12. "Is God Dead?," *Time*, April 8, 1966, accessed January 6, 2015.
13. "Is God Coming Back to Life?," *Time*, December 26, 1969, accessed January 6, 2015.
14. "The Global Religious Landscape: A Report on the Size and Distribution of the World's Major Religious Groups as of 2010," Pew Research Center, Pew Forum on Religion and Public Life, PDF publication (2012).
15. Ibid.
16. Given that it was the 1970s, cocaine probably helped too. In a 1992 interview, Bowie reflected back on the making of *The Man Who Fell to Earth*, stating: "I was totally insecure with about 10 grams a day in me. I was stoned out of my mind from beginning to end." (Virginia Campbell, "Bowie at the Bijou," *Movieline*, April 1992, accessed January 16, 2016.)
17. Aaron Latham, "The Ballad of the Urban Cowboy: America's Search for True Grit," *Esquire*, September 12, 1978.
18. "The Mythology of *Star Wars*: With George Lucas and Bill Moyers," transcript, PBS, June 18, 1999, www.billmoyers.com, accessed February 14, 2016.
19. "International Cooperation," NASA website, "International Space Station" section, accessed February 15, 2015.
20. Annalee Newitz, *Scatter, Adapt, and Remember: How Humans Will Survive a Mass Extinction* (New York: Doubleday, 2013).
21. Steven Pinker and Andrew Mack, "The World Is Not Falling Apart," *Slate*, December 22, 2014, accessed November 15, 2015. This article draws heavily from: Pinker, *The Better Angels of Our Nature: Why Violence Has Declined* (New York: Penguin, 2012).
22. Michael Shermer, *The Moral Arc: How Science and Reason Lead Humanity Toward Truth, Justice, and Freedom* (New York: Henry Holt, 2015).
23. Carl Sagan, *Cosmos* (New York: Random House, 1980).
24. Scott Collins, "Neil DeGrasse Tyson's *Cosmos* Ratings Not So Stellar on Fox," *Los Angeles Times*, March 10, 2014, accessed October 9, 2015; Michael O'Connell, "TV Ratings: Fox's *Cosmos* Pulls 8.5 Million Viewers Across 10 Networks," *Hollywood Reporter*, March 10, 2014, accessed October 9, 2015; and Sara Bibel, "TV Ratings Sunday: NBA Finals Dominate, Miss USA Up, Tony Awards Steady, *Cosmos* Finale Down," TV by the Numbers, Zap2It.com, June 9, 2014, accessed October 9, 2015.
25. The episodes also aired on the National Geographic Channel, whose audiences are less than one-tenth the size of the three million who viewed the final episode on Fox.
26. Courtney Garcia, "September 11 Attacks, Katrina Top List of Memorable TV Moments," Reuters, July 11, 2012, accessed January 20, 2015.
27. For example: Jean Baudrillard, *The Spirit of Terrorism* (London: Verso, 2002); and John Gray, *Black Mass: Apocalyptic Religion and the Death of Utopia* (New York: Farrar, Straus and Giroux, 2007).
28. The Terror War is pulling secular society backward, not toward peace and tolerance but directly into sheer irrationality and inquisition. For example, the proliferation of antiscientific, antirational, and anti-Enlightenment worldviews has invariably led to the abominable tolerance of torture in the United States. According to a 2014 *Washington Post*-ABC News poll, 59% of Americans thought the CIA use of torture was justified, while only 31% were against it. (Adam Goldman and Peyton

Craighill, "New Poll Finds Majority of Americans Think Torture Was Justified after 9/11 Attacks," *Washington Post*, December 16, 2014, accessed January 3, 2015.) A 2012 *Huff Post*/YouGov survey found that 47% of Americans thought torture was either always or sometimes justified, while 41% felt it was rarely or never justified. (Emily Swanson, "Torture Poll: Most Americans Say Torture Is Justifiable at Times," *Huffington Post*, December 14, 2012, accessed January 19, 2015.) Should we be surprised that President Trump openly campaigned to expand the use of torture in the Terror War? (Nick Vesser, "Trump Amps Up His Call for Torture: 'We're Going to Have to Do Things That Are Unthinkable,'" *Huffington Post*, June 30, 2016, accessed November, 23, 2016. See also Jeremy Diamond, "Trump on Torture: 'We Have to Beat the Savages,'" CNN, March 6, 2016, accessed November 23, 2016.)

Journalist Sarah Posner probed deeper into how religion fared in the *Washington Post*-ABC News poll, reporting that a large percentage of religious Americans (mostly white) of various faiths believed the CIA torture was justified compared to 41% of non-believers. (Sarah Posner, "Christians More Supportive of Torture than Non-Religious Americans," USC Annenberg website, *Religion Dispatches* [blog], December 16, 2014, accessed January 3, 2015. See also Steve Benen, "This Week in God: 12.20.14," MSNBC website, December 20, 2014, accessed January 10, 2015.) ISIS beheads infidels, while the US tortures enemy combatants. Is this the new Moral Majority? Will someone eventually be able to "Like" beheading and waterboarding on his or her Facebook page? (Thumbs up!)

Since the horror of September 11, privacy and civil liberties have been in full-scale reversal in America as well as in many other nations. We've utterly relinquished our privacy to the NSA and to Facebook while surrendering most of our public civil liberties to Homeland Security and militarized police forces. The Bill of Rights is being repealed/reversed right before our eyes. The American media and military waged a witch-hunt against Julian Assange and Edward Snowden for leaking the government's own documents that apparently revealed lies, crimes, and unconstitutional activities. The US government tried to silence WikiLeaks through intimidation, coercion, and all sorts of hypocritical and unconstitutional tactics in blatant disregard of the First Amendment. The truth of the leaks did not matter, only the religious zeal and patriotic propaganda in defense of war crimes.

29. Gray, *Black Mass: Apocalyptic Religion and the Death of Utopia*, 209-10.
30. "Would You Baptize an Extraterrestrial?," YouTube video, 1:17:38, lecture by Brother Guy Consolmagno, Leeds Trinity University (April 25, 2014), posted by Leeds Trinity University, accessed June 10, 2016.
31. J. Gordon Melton, "The Rise of the Study of New Religions," paper presentation, Center for Studies on New Religions annual conference, Bryn Athyn, PA, 1999, accessed January 6, 2015.
32. Kevin Kelly, "Emergent Religions," *The Technium* (blog), February 28, 2011, accessed January 6, 2015.
33. Frank Newport, "In US, 46% Hold Creationist View of Human Origins," Gallup, "Politics" section, June 1, 2012, accessed January 20, 2015.
34. "Ipsos Global Advisory: Supreme Being(s), the Afterlife and Evolution," Ipsos website, April 25, 2011, accessed January 20, 2015.
35. National Science Board, "Science and Technology: Public Attitudes and Understanding," chapt. 7 in *Science and Engineering Indicators 2014*, PDF publication; Chris Mooney, "More and More Americans Think Astrology Is Science," *Mother Jones*, "Blue Marble" section, February 11, 2014, accessed October 14, 2015; and Brooks Hays, "Majority of Young Adults Think Astrology Is a Science," *United Press International*, "Science News" section, February 12, 2014, accessed October 14, 2015.
36. The concept of "cosmic doublethink" was first presented in my paper "Into the Voids and Vanishing Points: Spaceship Earth and Space-Age Media Theory," which was delivered at McLuhan's Philosophy of Media Centennial Conference (Royal Flemish Academy of Belgium for Sciences and the Arts), October 27, 2011.
37. George Orwell, *1984* (New York: Plume, 1984), 176-77.
38. Ibid., 218-19.

39. Jean-Paul Sartre, *Being and Nothingness*, 3-25. For other arguments against theism and the existence of a Creator, see George H. Smith, *Atheism: The Case Against God* (Buffalo: Prometheus Books, 1979); David Mills, *Atheist Universe: The Thinking Person's Answer to Christian Fundamentalism* (Berkeley: Ulysses Press, 2006); Victor J. Stenger, *God: The Failed Hypothesis: How Science Shows That God Does Not Exist* (Amherst: Prometheus Books, 2007); Richard Dawkins, *The God Delusion* (New York: Mariner Books, 2008); John Allen Paulos, *Irreligion: A Mathematician Explains Why the Arguments for God Just Don't Add Up* (New York: Hill & Wang, 2008); and David Ramsay Steele, *Atheism Explained: From Folly to Philosophy* (Chicago: Open Court, 2008). Smith obliterates every philosophical argument for the existence of a Creator, while Stenger and Dawkins present the contemporary-science side of atheism. The other authors take on various ideas, issues, and arguments related to contemporary theism.
40. Jean-Pierre Mohen, *Megaliths: Stones of Memory* (New York: Abrams, 1999); Anna Sofaer, *Chaco Astronomy: An Ancient American Cosmology* (Santa Fe: Ocean Tree Books, 2008); and J. McKim Malville, *A Guide to Prehistoric Astronomy in the Southwest* (Boulder: Johnson Books, 2008).
41. Vacker and Gillespie, "Yearning to Be the Center of Everything," 35-46.
42. Barry Vacker, ed., *Media Environments*, 2nd ed. (San Diego: Cognella, 2015), 330-38.
43. Jane McGonigal, "Gaming Can Make a Better World," TED Talk (February 2010), accessed April 4, 2015.
44. Marshall McLuhan, *The Medium Is the Massage* (Berkeley: Gingko Press, 1999 [1967]).
45. Marshall McLuhan and Eric McLuhan, *Laws of Media* (Toronto: University of Toronto Press, 1988).
46. Carl Honore, *In Praise of Slowness: Challenging the Cult of Speed* (New York: HarperOne, 2004).
47. Table 6 is a modification of the table first presented in Vacker and Gillespie, 37.
48. Cotton Delo, "US Adults Now Spending More Time on Digital Devices Than Watching TV," *Advertising Age*, August 1, 2013, accessed February 23, 2015.
49. Saroj Kar, "Internet of Things Will Multiply the Digital Universe Data to 44 Trillion GBs by 2020," *Cloud Times*, April 17, 2014, accessed February 23, 2015. The evolution of memory capacity has gone from megabytes (1 million) and gigabytes (1 billion) to terabytes (1 trillion), petabytes (1 quadrillion), exabytes (1 quintillion), and zettabytes (1 sextillion), eventually to be followed by yottabytes (1 septillion) and xenottabytes (1 octillion [1 followed by 27 zeros]). And that's not even the long-term limit!
50. McLuhan, *The Medium Is the Massage*; and McLuhan and Quentin Fiore, *War and Peace in the Global Village* (San Francisco: HardWired, 1997).
51. Ellen Dissanayake, *Homo Aestheticus: Where Art Comes From and Why*, and Frederick Turner, *Beauty: The Value of Values* (Charlottesville: University of Virginia Press, 1992).
52. This paragraph and the following discussion borrow from cultural insights in Gilles Lipovetsky, *Hypermodern Times* (London: Polity, 2005).
53. Barry Vacker, *The End of the World — Again: Why the Apocalypse Meme Replicates in Media, Science, and Culture* (Philadelphia: Center for Media and Destiny, 2012).
54. Stephen Hawking and Leonard Mlodinow, *The Grand Design* (New York: Bantam Books, 2011), 5.
55. Stephen Hawking, *The Theory of Everything: The Origin and Fate of the Universe* (Beverly Hills: Phoenix Books, 2007); Richard Dawkins, *The Greatest Show on Earth: The Evidence for Evolution* (New York: Free Press, 2010); Neil deGrasse Tyson and Donald Goldsmith, *Origins: Fourteen Billion Years of Cosmic Evolution* (New York: Norton, 2004); Lisa Randall, *Knocking on Heaven's Door: How Physics and Scientific Thinking Illuminate the Universe and the Modern World* (New York: Ecco, 2012); and Brian Cox and Andrew Cohen, *The Human Universe*.

56. Declan Fahy, *The New Celebrity Scientists: Out of the Lab and into the Limelight* (New York: Rowman & Littlefield, 2015).
57. Elizabeth Kolbert, *The Sixth Extinction: An Unnatural History*; and J. R. McNeill and Peter Engelke, *The Great Acceleration: An Environmental History of the Anthropocene Since 1945*.

CHAPTER 4: THE COSMOS AND 21ST-CENTURY SPACE NARRATIVES

1. *Journey to Mars: Pioneering Next Steps in Space Exploration*, NASA website (October 2015), PDF publication.
2. Neil deGrasse Tyson, *Space Chronicles: Facing the Ultimate Frontier*, 9. Most people are oblivious to how NASA's space technologies are part of their everyday lives. Numerous "spinoff" industries and products resulted from space technologies pioneered by NASA, including microelectronics, GPS technologies, global telecommunications, mobile phones, satellite TV, weather satellites, household water filters, memory-foam mattresses, shoe insoles, LASIK surgery, etc.
3. This highly simplified summary is derived from the following works: Carl Sagan, *Cosmos*; Stephen Hawking and Leonard Mlodinow, *The Grand Design*, 85-120; Hawking, *A Brief History of Time* (New York: Bantam Books, 1998), 37-54; Trinh Xuan Thuan, *The Birth of the Universe: The Big Bang and Beyond* (New York: Abrams Discoveries, 1993), 61-69; Henning Genz, *Nothingness: The Science of Empty Space*, trans. Karin Heusch (Cambridge, MA: Perseus Books, 1999), 261-69; John Gribben, *Stardust: The Cosmic Recycling of Stars, Planets, and People* (London: Penguin Group, 2000), 98-111; Charles Seife, *Alpha and Omega: The Search for the Beginning and End of the Universe* (New York: Penguin, 2003), 25-48; Brian Greene, *The Fabric of the Cosmos: Space, Time, and the Texture of Reality* (New York: Vintage, 2004), 272-303; Giles Sparrow, *Cosmos* (London: Quercus, 2006); Brian Cox and Andrew Cohen, *Wonders of the Universe*; Lisa Randall, *Higgs Discovery: The Power of Empty Space* (New York: Ecco, 2013); Cox and Cohen, *Human Universe*, 214; and the History Channel, "Beyond the Big Bang," *The Universe*, directed by Luke Ellis (Los Angeles, CA: A&E Television Networks, 2007), DVD.
4. "The Milky Way Contains at Least 100 Billion Planets According to Survey," HubbleSite NewsCenter, January 11, 2012, accessed March 29, 2015; and Ian O'Neill, "Milky Way Stuffed with 50 Billion Alien Worlds," Discovery News, February 19, 2011, accessed December 29, 2014.
5. Nancy Ellen Abrams and Joel R. Primack, *The New Universe and the Human Future: How a Shared Cosmology Could Transform the World* (New Haven: Yale University Press, 2011), 39-66.
6. Cox and Cohen, *Human Universe*, 214.
7. Istvan Szapudi, "The Emptiest Place in Space," *Scientific American*, August 2016, 28-35.
8. Dan Hooper, *Dark Cosmos: In Search of Our Universe's Missing Mass and Energy* (New York: Smithsonian Books, 2007); and Gribben, *Stardust*, 100-101.
9. Hawking, *A Brief History of Time*, 41.
10. Sparrow, *Cosmos*, 218.
11. Cox and Cohen, *Wonders of the Universe*, 234-39.
12. Ibid., 239.
13. Jacob Berkowitz, *The Stardust Revolution: The New Story of Our Origin in the Stars* (Amherst, NY: Prometheus Books, 2012). We are experiencing a third cosmic revolution. First was the Copernican revolution, where Copernicus and Galileo dislodged humans from the center of the universe in the 16th and 17th centuries. Second was the Darwinian revolution, where Charles Darwin and other scientists removed humans from a divine biological position. In a convergence of both revolutions, the "Stardust Revolution" unites the "outward" view (Copernican) with the "inward" view (Darwinian) to effect a cosmic synthesis of humanity's place in the cosmos.

14. Jill Tarter, "Join the SETI Search," TED Talk (February 2009), accessed March 2, 2015.

15. Irene Klotz, "Jeff Bezos Unveils Plans for Huge, Reusable Rocket," *Seeker*, September 12, 2016, accessed September 13, 2016.

16. Todd Leopold, "Elon Musk's New Idea: Nuke Mars," CNN, September 11, 2015, accessed September 12, 2015; and Samantha Masunaga, "What Scientists Say about Elon Musk's Idea to Nuke Mars," *Los Angeles Times*, September 10, 2015, accessed September 12, 2015.

17. Calla Cofield, "SpaceX Will Launch Private Mars Missions as Soon as 2018," *Space.com*, April 27, 2016, accessed June 12, 2016.

18. Coby McDonald, "The Biggest Obstacle to Mars Colonization May Be Obsolete Humans," *Popular Science*, June 10, 2016, accessed June 12, 2016.

19. Steven Benna, "25 Quotes That Will Take You Inside the Mind of Elon Musk," *Time*, October 29, 2015, accessed September 4, 2016.

20. Lee Billings, "War in Space May Be Closer Than Ever," *Scientific American*, August 10, 2015, accessed September 2, 2016.

21. *Pax Americana and the Weaponization of Space*, directed by Denis Delestrac (2009; Films Transit International).

22. Julie Fletcher, "Societal Implications of Astrobiology at the Center of Theological Inquiry," NASA Astrobiology Institute, February 24, 2016, accessed June 8, 2016.

23. William Storrar, "CTI Receives NASA Grant," Center of Theological Inquiry, accessed June 8, 2016; and Linda Arntzenius, "Center of Theological Inquiry: Where Scholars Take On Life's Big Questions," *Princeton Magazine*, April 2015, 66-71, accessed June 8, 2016.

24. Brother Guy Consolmagno, "Would You Baptize an Extraterrestrial?"

25. Lee Spiegel, "Will ET Be Here Soon? NASA Brings Scientists, Theologians Together to Prepare," *Huffington Post*, September 25, 2014, accessed June 8, 2016.

26. Consolmagno, "Would You Baptize an Extraterrestrial?"

27. Ibid.

28. The faithful have short-term and selective memories. There was no Christianity in the Americas until brought over by the Europeans. Consider the slaughter of the Incas perpetrated by Pizarro and the Spanish conquistadors, famously described in glowing prose by the conquistadors themselves, who gave credit and praise to God, Christianity, and their Catholic faith. (See Jared Diamond, *Guns, Germs, and Steel: The Fates of Society* [New York: Norton, 1997], 67-75.) The conquest is still in effect. Hundreds of millions of people adhere to the Christian and Catholic religions that colonized their continents and consciousnesses. The faithful fervently worship the leaders of the conquering theologies. For example, the popular Pope Francis was treated like a celebrity deity upon his visit to America in 2015, even though he had recently canonized Father Junipero Serra, the theocratic tyrant who orchestrated a regime of torture and genocide against Native Americans in California in the 1700s. (See Tony Platt, "Sainthood and Serra: It's an Insult to Native Americans," *Los Angeles Times*, January 24, 2015, accessed June 8, 2016.)

29. Gary Clayton Anderson, *The Conquest of Texas: Ethnic Cleansing in the Promised Land, 1820-1875* (Norman: University of Oklahoma Press, 2005).

30. Tyson, *Space Chronicles*, 1-18, 78-83.

31. $22 trillion is my estimate based on the Department of Defense totals (adjusted for inflation) in the charts provided in the following article: Dylan Matthews, "Defense Spending in the US in Four Charts," *Washington Post*, August 28, 2012, accessed April 13, 2015. The NASA budgets are detailed in this article: Simon Rogers, "NASA Budgets: US Spending on Space Travel Since 1958 Updated," *Guardian*, February 1, 2010, accessed October 25, 2016. After viewing various sources, these estimates are accurate for their purpose, which is to illustrate the wide disparity between US spending for war and space exploration. NASA receives about 3% to 4% as much as the Pentagon on an annual basis. For more budgetary comparisons, see Tyson, *Space Chronicles*, 331-42.

32. Rogers, "NASA Budgets."
33. Edward Hay, "NATO Outspends Warsaw," *Bulletin of the Atomic Scientists*, vol. 37, no. 6 (June 1981), 9.
34. "SIPRI NATO Milex Data: 1949-2013," Stockholm International Peace Research Institute website, accessed April 11, 2015. See also Sam Perlo-Freeman, Olawale Ismail, and Carina Solmirano, "Military Expenditure," *Stockholm International Peace Research Institute Yearbook 2010* (Solna: Stockholm International Peace Research Institute, 2010) 10-11; and Perlo-Freeman and Solmirano, "Trends in World Military Expenditure: 2013," SIPRI Fact Sheet (April 2014), Stockholm International Peace Research Institute website, accessed April 11, 2015.
35. Stephen Clark, "NASA Gets Budget Hike in Spending Bill Passed by Congress," *Spaceflight Now*, December 14, 2014, accessed December 27, 2014; and John T. Bennett, "Congress Inserts $554 Billion for DoD in 'Cromnibus' Spending Bill," *Defense News*, December 11, 2014, accessed December 27, 2014.
36. Tyson, *Space Chronicles*, 337, appendix F.
37. Clark, "NASA Gets Budget Hike in Spending Bill Passed by Congress"; and Bennett, "Congress Inserts $554 Billion for DoD in 'Cromnibus' Spending Bill."
38. Don Reisinger and Shara Tibken, "Apple by the Numbers: 700 Million iPhones, 25 Million Apple TVs Sold," CNET, US edition, March 9, 2015, accessed September 11, 2015.
39. Karen Masters, "How Much Money Is Spent on Space Exploration," *Ask an Astronomer*, June 22, 2015, accessed December 28, 2015.
40. "Who We Are," X Prize website, accessed October 18, 2015.
41. Daniel Honan, "The First Trillionaires Will Make Their Fortunes in Space," BigThink, 2011, accessed March 26, 2015.
42. I don't blame them. Skateboarding and snowboarding are more exciting than hanging out at the mall or playing *World of Warcraft* for 60 hours a week. Playing the X Games sports surely beats bowing before a testosterone-laden athletic coach yelling at you for not "manning up" or "stepping up" for your school!
43. Julian E. Barnes, "NATO Recognizes Cyberspace as New Frontier in Defense," *Wall Street Journal*, June 14, 2016, accessed June 18, 2016.
44. Vacker and Gillespie, "Yearning to Be the Center of Everything," 35-46; and Vacker, ed., *Media Environments*, 330-38.
45. Hawking and Mlodinow, *The Grand Design*, 5.
46. Eric von Daniken, *Chariots of the Gods?* (New York: G. P. Putnam, 1969).
47. John T. Omohundro, "Von Daniken's Chariots: A Primer in the Art of Cooked Science," *Skeptical Inquirer*, vol. 1.1 (Winter 1976), accessed April 5, 2015; and Ronald Story, *The Space Gods Revealed: A Close Look at the Theories of Erich von Daniken* (New York: Harper & Row, 1976).
48. "The Case of the Ancient Astronauts," *Nova*, BBC Horizon/PBS, 1977.
49. *Journey to Mars*, NASA website, 1.
50. Jeffrey Kluger, "National Parks on the Moon? It's an Excellent Idea," *Time*, July 20, 2013, accessed March 29, 2015.
51. Leonard David, "'Planetary Parks' Could Protect Space Wilderness," *Space.com* (January 17, 2013), accessed March 29, 2015.
52. "America's Natural Wonderlands: The 50 Most Visited National Parks," *USA Today*, August 20, 2015, accessed November 25, 2015.
53. Having recently hiked the Permian Extinction Trail, I can say that the distant skies are not crystal blue, for they are hazy with pollution caused by various emissions from coal-fired plants located in Mexico, Texas, Arizona, and New Mexico. You can also see the haze and pollution in Big Bend National Park, which is 200 miles south and even more remote. Climate change and global warming may not produce the extinction of the human species, but the Permian Extinction Trail shows that life is not assured on our planet or in the universe. The human species would do well to embrace that message.

54. Michelle Z. Donahue, "80 Percent of Americans Can't See the Milky Way Anymore," *National Geographic*, June 10, 2016, accessed September 2, 2016; and Bahar Gholipour, "Most of Us Can't See the Milky Way Anymore. That Comes with a Price," *Huffington Post*, June 10, 2016, accessed September 2, 2016.
55. For more information, see: www.darksky.org.
56. *The City Dark*, directed by Ian Cheney.
57. "Why We Go," Virgin Galactic website, accessed October 11, 2015.
58. The documentary is available in Vimeo and on the website for the Overview Institute: www.overviewinstitute.org.
59. Ellen Dissanayake, *Homo Aestheticus: Where Art Comes From and Why*; and Frederick Turner, *Beauty: The Value of Values*.
60. See John Beardsley, *Earthworks and Beyond* (London: Abbeville Press, 2006); Jeffrey Kastner, ed., *Land and Environmental Art* (London: Phaidon, 2010); and Philipp Kaiser and Miwon Kwon, eds., *Ends of the Earth: Land Art to 1974* (Los Angeles: Museum of Contemporary Art, 2012).
61. "Celestial Events," Roden Crater website, accessed October 12, 2016.
62. "Founders," in the "About" section, Shackleton Energy website, accessed October 12, 2016.
63. Neil deGrasse Tyson, "Our Radio Bubble," *Death by Black Hole: And Other Cosmic Quandaries* (New York: Norton, 2007), 238-45.
64. Buckminster Fuller, *Operating Manual for Spaceship Earth*, 57-63.
65. Friedrich Nietzsche, *Thus Spake Zarathustra: A Book for Everyone and No One*, 26.
66. Jean-Paul Sartre, *Being and Nothingness*, 100-105.

INDEX

KEY TOPICS AND CONCEPTS

PEOPLE AND CHARACTERS

SPACE FILMS

CPSIA information can be obtained
at www.ICGtesting.com
Printed in the USA
BVOW06s0031030917
493819BV00006B/68/P